THE MOON OVER THE OAK

The Lycanthrope Protection Agency
Book 4

CJ Ravenna

Editing by Carta's Editorial Services

Copy and line edit by Jennifer Smith

Proofreading by Lori Parks

Beta reading by Rare Bird Beta Reading

Cover designed by Danielle Doolittle | DoElle Designs | www.doelledesigns.com

The story, all names, characters, and incidents portrayed in this production are fictitious. No identification with actual persons (living or deceased), places, buildings, and products is intended or should be inferred.

This book contains sexually explicit materials only suitable for mature readers.

First edition 2023

CONTENT WARNINGS

- Graphic depictions of violence and gore

- A side character suffering from a disease similar to Alzheimer's

- Death of a parent and a family member's funeral (on-page)

- Parental neglect

- Discussions of anxiety and on-page anxiety attacks

Please read at your own discretion.

Chapter 1

DOES THAT MEAN WE'RE MATES?

RYAN KELLY WAS TWELVE when his mother got sick.

It was May and in just two weeks, the last day of school would arrive, and summer break would begin. For regular kids, summer break was already a blast since at long last, classes were over. For werewolf kids, it meant he could let the wolf out.

Finally, his family could leave the city behind, and Ryan could already feel the sand beneath his paws, the sun hot and dense in his fur. He hoped his mom and dad would let him shift in public at the beach. How awesome would that be?

He rode his bike home from school. Since the quiet side streets from the school to his house were blissfully empty, he rode fast, zigzagging as he pleased without having to worry about hitting anyone, and the bike handles were slick with sweat when he arrived home. Ivy crawled thick and green over the face of the apartment like a bushy beard.

The stairs creaked as he jumped up them two by two, and he was panting by the time he reached his apartment door. He practically danced inside, the music from his earbuds blocking out all other sounds, and threw his backpack on the floor.

See you in a few months, schoolwork!

The apartment was empty. Curious, he popped out an earbud, listening. All seemed quiet. Where were his parents? Closing his eyes, he concentrated on the pack bonds that connected him to his parents. The bonds were still and settled, and their scents were fresh. They were probably in the bedroom.

Figuring they could discuss summer plans when they were ready, he stopped in the kitchen for some water. A sudden wave of fear crashed over him, radiating from his father's bond. At the same time, his mother's bond burned with fury that made Ryan choke on his water. It felt like acid in his chest.

Something was terribly wrong. He ripped out his earbuds. "Mom? Dad?"

The bedroom door slammed behind him, scaring him so badly he dropped the glass into the sink. He whirled around, fangs bared, and realized it was his father. "Dad! Jeez, you scared the crap out of me!"

His father didn't admonish him for cursing. He was breathless, pale white, and wide-eyed. His father charged, grabbing Ryan's arm so tightly he yelped. "Go! We have to get out, quickly!"

Ryan tried to tug himself free. "What? Why, what happened?"

What he said next chilled Ryan's blood. "It's your mother. Something's wrong!"

He dug his heels in, tried to turn around. "She's fine! What are you talking about?" She'd walked him to school this morning, smiling as she always did.

"Ryan, don't! Come here!"

Ryan broke free and ran for his mom's room, the blood roaring in his ears. His father was joking. This wasn't right. His mother was fine. She was always fine.

The door to the bedroom crashed open before he'd even reached it, and a wolf stumbled into the living room, tattered clothes dangling from dense fur. It was his mother's wolf, pure white and beautiful. But something was wrong. His mother liked to set a good example by never shifting inside the house. She'd scold him if he so much as tried.

"Mom?" His voice shook.

Then the coppery smell of blood hit his nose, turning his stomach inside out. The wolf turned toward him, revealing her blood-soaked snout. His father had smelled like blood. Had she *bitten* him?

A growl vibrated in the wolf's throat. His mother's eyes flared brightly. They were yellow, the pupils so dilated they were pinpoints. Feral. His mother was *feral*.

"Mom?" he croaked. "Mom, what's wrong with you?"

She leaped toward him in a blur of white fur and Ryan's instincts screamed *run* and *danger!* Ryan's father grabbed his wrist and this time he didn't resist. They ran from the apartment, and his dad kicked the door shut behind them. The wolf hurled herself at the door, claws scrabbling. Throaty, savage barks made Ryan whimper with dread. His father's hand trembled on his shoulder. "Let's go downstairs. Quick."

His throat ached and his eyes blurred with tears as he followed his father downstairs. In the lobby, his father's big arms went around him, holding Ryan tight, and Ryan let go of his emotions and sobbed wretchedly, confused and frightened.

"I know, Ry, I know." His father shook violently, his voice weak with terror. "Are you hurt? Did she hurt you?"

"No," Ryan croaked. "What h-happened to Mom?"

"I don't know. I'll call the LPA. Maybe they can help her."

The Lycanthrope Protection Agency dedicated themselves to serving NYC's werewolf population. If anyone could help his mom, it was the LPA.

Ryan stumbled to the windowsill and collapsed, coughing and feeling ready to throw up. His glasses had fallen off, and it blurred his vision even more with the tears in his eyes.

Once his father was off the phone, he sat with Ryan and hugged him tight until a big pickup truck pulled up outside, the agency's logo painted on the doors. Ryan ran outside and waved. "Over here! Hurry!"

The doors slammed and Ryan gasped, recognizing the man striding toward him. With his long mane of brown hair, piercing silver eyes, and a full, well-kept beard, he couldn't be mistaken for anyone else. It was Benjamin Stroud, the leader of the agency in NYC. "Wow," he gasped. Ben helped their kind. He was a hero. "I-it's very nice to meet you, sir!" He tipped his head back and exposed his throat. His dad had always told him it was the respectful thing to do when meeting someone important—if they were a wolf. Humans would think it was weird.

"Hey, big guy." Ben knelt down at Ryan's level. "Like the glasses." He was big and bulky, but when he smiled, Ryan felt safe and secure. Suddenly, breathing was easier. "Don't know many werewolves with glasses."

His cheeks heated from the compliment. "Th-thanks! The doctors said it's rare for werewolves to need glasses. But I do." He shrugged. "It's the way I am, I guess." Some kids at school made fun of him, but he tried to ignore them, like his parents said.

Ben chuckled. "Well, it suits you. Don't be embarrassed. Everyone's different."

"Please don't hurt my mom. Okay?" Tears stung his eyes, and he wiped them away.

Ben squeezed his shoulder. "I won't hurt your mom. I promise. I'll calm her down and then she'll come to the agency for treatment."

Ryan gulped and nodded. "Okay. Can... can you make her feel better?"

Ben dipped his head. "I'll do everything I can."

Ryan and his father waited for what seemed like forever while Ben went upstairs. Then he returned and Ryan's mother was with him, naked and wrapped in a quilt. Her eyes were unfocused and when he called out to her, she didn't react. She shook violently, as if she were freezing. Ryan wanted to go to her, but his father held on tight. "Mom!"

That time, she heard him. She looked at him, her blue eyes cloudy. There was no recognition in her eyes.

As if she didn't know him at all.

"When can we see her?" Ryan asked. They'd been at the agency's clinic forever. The people who had been in the waiting room when they'd arrived had gone home, with new faces taking their place. He hated hospitals, hated the smell of blood and sickness and tile cleaner. He hated seeing people in pain.

"I don't know," his father answered. He hadn't touched the coffee in his hand in a long time. It was probably cold now.

"What if she's really sick, and they can't help her?" Ryan squeezed his fists together, suddenly struggling to breathe.

"She'll be okay, Ry. Sometimes werewolves go feral. They can help her."

Ryan didn't understand. All werewolves needed something or someone important to remind them of their humanity. From what he'd read, werewolves only went feral when they didn't have a mate or a pack. Intense trauma and stress could also trigger a wolf to go feral. "But she has us, and nothing really bad happened that made her lose control, right? How could she go feral?"

"I don't know, Ryan." His father's voice was sharp, and Ryan flinched from his anger. A thousand what-ifs stampeded through his mind until the doubts made him feel sick. What if she never got better? What if she forgot about him and his dad?

"Mr. Kelly?" The nurse smiled at them. "Follow me." They followed her into a quiet office. "Doctor Radzikowski will be with you in a minute." Ryan's father sat down with a heavy sigh as Ryan walked around the room, staring blankly at posters of the human body and wolf anatomy. One chart asked, Have You Gotten *Your* Mad Dog Shot? Ryan asked if he had.

"Yeah, Ry. When you were a pup," his dad answered, his eyes closed. "Everyone gets that shot when they're pups."

"Good." The symptoms sounded bad. Aggression, forgetfulness, difficulty shifting back to human form. But it wasn't what his mom had. So, what was wrong with her? A fresh wave of terror clenched his stomach.

The door opened and a tall doctor with a cool mustache strode in. "You're Kaitlyn's pack? Nice to meet you." He shook both their hands and took a seat. "She's sleeping now. We gave her a sedative for the nerves. She won't be awake until tomorrow morning."

"What's wrong with her?" Ryan asked. Suddenly, he was scared to know.

"We're still running tests. I won't have a clear diagnosis until tomorrow afternoon at the earliest. Has she ever gone feral before?"

"Never," Ryan's dad answered. "She was human before I turned her, but she's always had mastery over her shifts." Pride warmed his voice.

Ryan swallowed hard. "Can you fix her?"

The doctor typed away at his keyboard. "I'll do everything I can. The minute I have the test results, I'll call you."

Ryan cried himself to sleep that night, terrified that his mother would never be the same. But the doctors could help her, he told himself again and again. Whatever was wrong, they could help her.

Ben let them stay overnight at the agency. First thing in the morning, Ryan beat his father in a race to his mother's room. She smiled at him from the bed. She had bags under her eyes, and she was clearly exhausted, but there was an awareness in her gaze that hadn't been there yesterday. "Hey, baby." Ryan threw himself into her arms and she held him and his father tight.

"I don't remember what happened," she explained. "I remember you were talking about summer vacation." She held his father's hand tightly. "Then everything's a blur. I woke up here and the both of you were gone. The doctor said I went feral."

"You did." Ryan's father smiled in the way he did when he was trying to look brave. "I thought you were going to take a bite out of my butt." Ryan laughed despite the clump of worry in his stomach. His mother smiled and kissed his father's cheek. For a moment, it was easy to think that everything would be okay.

The doctor walked in, and everything wasn't okay. He had his hands clasped, his head low, and a frighteningly sad air about him as if someone had died.

The doctor said, "Mrs. Kelly, you have Lyell's syndrome."

A glance at the confusion on his parents' faces confirmed they'd never heard of this disease before.

"It's a very rare neurological condition that affects werewolves. There are maybe ten shifters in the world with this condition."

His mother said, "So what does that mean? Is there a cure?"

The doctor said the one thing Ryan had been terrified to hear. "No, Mrs. Kelly. There are steps we can take to stabilize your condition, but treatments have been mostly unsuccessful…"

The doctor's voice faded away. Ryan couldn't hear anything but a roaring in his ears. His legs felt numb; his fingers tingled. He caught snatches of words. "Difficulty returning to human form. Aggression. There are antianxiety medications we can try to keep you from shifting, but there is no cure. I'm sorry, Mrs. Kelly, but eventually you will lose your memories permanently."

No cure. His mother could never be cured. She was going to get worse and worse. She would forget him. His father. His grandma. Everyone.

"But you're a doctor." His voice came from far away. At his sides, fingers curled and his eyes burned. "Help her. You're a doctor. It's your job!"

"Ryan. Hey, baby, calm down." He shook off his mother's grasping hands.

"You're a doctor!" he roared, as if that would make it all better. "Help her! You have to!"

His parents' voices couldn't reach him. He shook away their comforting touches, so furious he could scarcely breathe. This was wrong, all of it! His mother wasn't supposed to be sick; she'd been fine yesterday and now suddenly she would never get better? All because she had some disease only ten people in the entire world had?

"This is bullshit!"

"Ryan!"

He kicked over the chair and ran from the room.

THE AGENCY RELEASED RYAN'S mother from their care after giving her meds to take.

His mom tried to smile, tried to pretend things were normal. She even insisted they all go for a walk in Central Park since it was a nice day. Central Park had the most elm trees in the city, maybe even in the country. He'd always thought that was cool, but today he kind of wished the whole park would burn down.

The shade of the elm trees cooled his back as he wandered away from his parents. They'd stopped to get hot dogs and water from a cart, but Ryan wasn't hungry. He wanted to be alone where he didn't have to see his dad's frowns and his mom's fake smiles.

He climbed over a fence and walked among the elms until he came upon something... different. An oak tree grew among the elms. That was weird. The tree bore deep scars in the bark, as if people had tried to cut it down. Why was there an oak here? It looked stupid. Everything was stupid. Stupid doctors who couldn't help his mom. Stupid Mom and Dad trying to act like everything was normal when it wasn't. Nothing would ever be normal again.

His anger came rushing back. His claws came out and he lunged, tearing into the bark of the oak tree. Tears prickled his eyes, and his throat closed. He swung wildly and when his arms were too tired, he kicked at the tree until his toes hurt.

There is no cure.

Sobs tore at his throat. He could no longer stand up and he dropped to the ground, the tree hard against his back. His glasses tumbled off his nose and into the grass, their absence turning his vision into a blur of colors. His mother had a disease that could never be cured. Of all the families in the world, why his? Why his mom? It wasn't fair. He cried until his throat ached, not caring who heard.

"Aww, man! What did you do to my favorite tree?"

"Who cares about your stupid tree?" he shouted, scrubbing tears from his eyes. He yanked his glasses on and a boy came into view, tall and Black with short, curly hair. The boy wore fancy pants with a plain white shirt and tie. Ryan would have laughed, except the boy made the outfit look cool and sophisticated. Like he was older than he was, though he must be around Ryan's age or a little older since he was taller.

"I care," the boy said defiantly. "But fine. You look pretty bummed out, so I won't kick your butt."

Ryan snorted. Like fancy pants here could fight.

The boy walked around him and frowned at the marks on the tree. "Man. You did a number on this thing. And now it smells like you. I couldn't even mark it with my claws. Heck, no one can. See? People tried to cut it down but they couldn't. It's strong."

Ryan looked up, seeing the boy in a new light. "You're a werewolf?"

The boy nodded. "Couldn't you smell me?"

Ryan sniffed. His nose was totally blocked up.

"Here." The boy handed him a tissue.

Ryan blew his nose. He felt stupid. This kid must think he was lame.

"Thanks." He pocketed the tissue. "I'm Ryan Kelly. Don't make fun of my last name: it's Irish."

"I'm Zachariah DeShawn. But everyone calls me Zach. It's too fancy."

Ryan stood to give an introductory sniff. He smelled like clean clothes and coconut deodorant, but oddly enough, nothing else. Every wolf had a scent unique to them, but Zach's was completely undetectable, as if he was somehow hiding his scent from Ryan.

"What?" Zach looked uncomfortable.

"How do you *do* that?"

"Do what?"

Ryan sniffed harder until his nose stung. "Hide your scent like that!" It was so weird. "What gives?"

Frowning, Zach sniffed his arm. "I have a smell."

"Uh, no you don't. Whatever. I'll just pretend you smell like the beach. That's my favorite smell."

"I hate the beach."

Ryan gaped. "What do you mean, you hate the beach?"

"Because of all the sand. It gets everywhere."

"The beach is the best part about summer!"

Zach folded his arms and said matter-of-factly, "No, baseball's the best part about summer."

Ryan gasped. "I love baseball!"

Zach grinned. "Me too!"

Laughing, Zach dropped into the grass and opened his book bag.

"Ryan?" Ryan gasped. His parents had come looking for him. Ducking down, he clapped a hand over the boy's mouth. His lips were soft and warm. Ryan wasn't sure why he noticed that. The voices of his parents faded away, and Ryan exhaled. For a moment, he'd forgotten about his mother's diagnosis.

"Phew. My parents almost found me."

The boy smacked Ryan's hand away. "Those were your parents? Why were you hiding from them?"

"I don't want to go home. Not yet." Ryan swallowed, blinking back a fresh onslaught of grief.

Zach sighed. "Yeah. Me too."

Ryan glanced at him. "Why? Your mom has some super, super rare disease, too?"

Brown eyes widened. "No! It's complicated, all right?"

"Yeah. I get that. Life sucks." Ryan scowled, tearing up some grass. "Sorry about your tree."

Zach shrugged. "It's cool."

Ryan frowned. "Me, or the tree?"

Zach pressed a hand to the bark. "This tree's one of my favorites. It's different from the other elm trees."

Grinning, Ryan said, "It's an oak."

Zach quirked a brow. "No. They only plant elm trees here. Did they plant an oak by mistake?"

"It totally is an oak! See the trunk and the shape of the branches? And the smell too." Ryan sniffed deeply and sighed at the sweet smell of the leaves. He'd always loved trees. His feet had carried him here, and now he knew why. He always felt calmer surrounded by trees. The way the wind whispered through their branches made them sound as if they were talking to him in soft, gentle voices.

"Safe. You are safe. You're never alone. You are ours, prince of the forest, and you will always be safe…"

"Uh, dude?" The boy was squinting at him as if he were nutso. "You okay? You spaced out."

Remembering, Ryan said, "But yeah, it's an oak."

"You know a lot about trees."

"Trees are awesome. They keep me cool in the summer, and they smell great. My grandma is a botanist. She taught me a ton about trees. Like how some wolves and trees have this relationship, and we're connected or something. She's kinda weird. Like a hippie or something." She'd smiled at him, all secretive when she'd told him that, as if it meant something bigger than what she was saying. "Anyway, sorry I scratched up your tree, bro."

"It's our tree now."

Ryan grinned. "Really?"

"Yeah. We can share it. It's our pack territory now."

Ryan gasped. He had a pack that wasn't his immediate family! This was officially the best day ever, even if it was also the worst. "Okay, let's make this official!" He popped one of his claws, then carved R+Z into the trunk of the tree. Zach arched a brow. "Isn't that what boyfriends and girlfriends do?"

"Nuh uh!" Was it? "Just so you know, I'm the alpha of our pack."

"No. Alphas aren't a thing unless you're on the Council. That's just outdated wolf research." Zach scoffed. "Besides I'm older, so I should be the leader of the pack."

"You don't know that." Ryan stood up, looming over the boy. "Maybe I'm just short."

"Well, I'm more mature."

"Hey!"

The boy laughed, his smile brightening his face. "Fine. We can both be leaders."

Ryan blinked. "Can two boys lead a pack together?"

Zach shrugged. "Sure. We can do whatever we want if it's for the good of the pack."

His face warmed. Usually, it was a man and a woman who led a pack—and they were often mates. "So, does that mean we're mates now?"

"No! You're so weird! Besides, two boys can't be mates." Zach frowned and pulled up some grass. He smelled sad all of a sudden.

Ryan stuck out his chest. "Says who? I'll do whatever I want!"

"It's just different. That's what my dad says."

Birds twittered and the wind whispered through the emerald leaves. Pearls of sunlight dotted the ground, glimmering between the branches. They chatted for a bit. Zach was fifteen. That was awesome; big kids could do tons of cool stuff. His favorite subject was lycanthrope history, just like Ryan's. He loved all kinds of sports. Every nugget of knowledge about Zach just made him cooler and cooler to Ryan.

"I'm totally telling my parents my mate is a boy."

Zach sputtered. "We're not—come on, dude!" He laughed, softening his exasperation.

Ryan's phone rang in the grass. His parents were looking for him. "I guess I should go." It sucked. He was feeling so happy, and he knew he wouldn't feel that way if he went home. And he didn't want to say goodbye to his new friend. "Hey! Can I have your number? That way we can meet up and defend our territory."

Zach grinned. "Sure." They exchanged numbers. "I'll see you around, Ryan."

Ryan's face warmed all over. This guy was so cool! "Yeah. You too," he said lamely.

When he got home, his parents chastised him for worrying them, but Ryan didn't care. "I met this guy named Zach! He's so cool. Hey, Mom, Dad, can two boys be leaders of a pack?"

His parents laughed, but it was true—Zach had turned the worst day of Ryan's life into one of the best.

Chapter 2

What Makes Us Awesome

Zach was fifteen when he lost control for the first time.

"We are DeShawns," his father, Josiah DeShawn, told him once, a wreath of cigarette smoke around his head. "The legacy of our pack spans centuries. Even humans know to respect our name. The only way to rise above the humans is to be one step ahead, Zachariah. They think we're animals; we'll show them just how wrong they are." He coughed, and Zach could practically hear the cancer healing itself in his lungs. He wished his dad would quit. "Never lose control. Never shift in public. Be better than they think you are."

But he couldn't help it. All he could hear was the principal's voice repeating "C-minus." His grades were dropping. He was failing school. His parents would be so disappointed when they realized their A-plus son was an idiot. A failure. They'd promised him that if he did well in school this semester, they would take him to San Francisco. He'd wanted to go to San Fran for forever. Now, they'd tell him he couldn't go.

If he failed school, how would he go to college? If he couldn't go to college, how could he hope to earn his place in the family business? If he couldn't work in the family business, what else could he do with his life? His family legacy of business was all he knew.

He couldn't breathe and his heart felt ready to explode in his chest. His parents would be so mad. They'd spent so much on his education, dedicated so much time and effort to shape him into their prodigy heir.

And he was failing them. His claws popped out and fangs stabbed his lower lip.

Oh no. Not now, not now!

But his stress had reached its limit. His wolf was howling, hurling itself against the bonds of his restraints. Zach couldn't fight the call. His clothes ripped and strained, his sense of smell and hearing threatening to overwhelm him. As fur grew thick on his face, Zach bolted from the office and ran. He tore past the blurry shapes of his classmates, their heartbeats slamming against his eardrums, their shrill voices sending a spike of panic through him. A hot summer wind blasted him as he crashed through the doors, the pavement burning his hands as he dropped to all fours.

No. Contain it. I'm in control. I'm in control!

Zach wouldn't lose control. It was bad enough his very future was spiraling out of his grasp. He wouldn't lose control of himself too.

How would they feel if they heard I'd shifted in public like a freaking animal? Control it!

He ran until the shade of the elm trees sheltered him. Cool grass tickled the soles of his bare feet and he collapsed behind his and Ryan's tree, huddling in on himself. He was still human, but his clothes had ripped in places while he'd struggled against the shift. He was supposed to meet Ryan at their tree in a few minutes and he looked like a disaster.

If his parents found out he'd almost shifted, they'd be so disappointed in him. Only feral werewolves lost control of themselves. He screwed his eyes shut, fighting back sobs.

"Hey, Zach! Whoa, did you shift? Awesome, I've wanted to see your wolf for forever!"

Zach rounded on Ryan, panting hard. "No, it isn't awesome! There's something wrong with me!"

Ryan squatted, his elbows on his knees. "Dude, just calm down."

"I can't!" Zach's claws pierced the soil, tearing up grass. He panted, unable to take in a deep breath. "I'm a savage animal. A monster. I—"

Ryan frowned at him. "Says who?"

"My... my parents said only ferals lose control of themselves. I'm a monster, Ryan." Tears burned his eyes.

He struggled to catch his breath. A hand, slick with sweat, grasped his. Ryan said, "My mom loses control a lot these days. She didn't use to. She's not feral. I almost lost control once but you helped me keep it together. And I'm not feral, am I?"

Zach shook his head. His breathing slowed, and his heart settled. Somehow, holding on to Ryan's hand helped anchor him. Ryan's heartbeat pulsed in his fingertips. Zach closed his eyes tight and focused on the steady rhythm of Ryan's heart. The shaking stopped and breathing was easier. "You're a little crazy."

Ryan said, "Being normal is boring." He sat in the grass beside him, one hand still in Zach's.

Leaning on the oak tree, Zach sucked in deep breaths. The racing of his heart was slowing to a canter.

"So, like, do you ever turn into a wolf? Ever?"

Zach shook his head, wiping sweat from his brow. "No. My parents don't approve."

Ryan's mouth slipped open. "That's so lame! We're werewolves!"

"But we still have our humanity," Zach said, remembering his dad's words. "It's... it's what separates us from animals. We're not animals, so we should be better than that."

"We *are* animals! It's what makes us awesome!"

Zach didn't see what was so awesome about being a werewolf. It was just a constant reminder of the normal life he would never have. Sure, he'd love to shed his human skin and run through nature as an animal of the wilderness, but it was wrong to give in to the beast. "*I* have to be in control of myself, not my inner wolf."

Ryan scoffed. "Lame."

Zach hadn't expected him to get it.

"Dude, you've gotta shift sometime. It's good for you. I'd go crazy if I didn't transform. Not shifting, it's like, I don't know, holding in a fart or something."

Zach doubled over with a snort of laughter. "What?"

"The more you hold it in, the worse it feels." Ryan spoke with such certainty, Zach almost believed him... if he weren't talking about farts. "As long as you don't shift around humans, who cares? Hey! Your last class was today, right? So that means you should come up to my family's beach house for the week!"

The thought delighted Zach, but he quashed it down. He needed to spend more time making up for his bad grades. "I can't. I need to study. I'm flunking all my classes."

Ryan rolled his eyes. "Fine. We can study—a little."

"More like a lot." Zach pulled his knees to his chest.

"Wait, so why are you failing?"

"I'm stressed, okay?" Zach dropped his head back against the tree. "My parents want me to have perfect grades so they can send me to the perfect college, and I can earn a perfect degree and inherit their business." He felt stupid for complaining. Poor Zachariah, the spoiled rich boy with his future all planned out for him by his attentive parents.

Ryan got up and left. Zach supposed he'd chased him off, until Ryan returned clutching two ice creams he'd purchased from a cart up the pathway. "Which one you want? You look like a strawberry kind of guy."

Smiling, Zach accepted the strawberry dessert, removing the plastic wrap. He shivered as he took a bite, enjoying the blast of cold. Ryan licked his vanilla cone, biting off the covering of chocolate. "Do you wanna take over their business?"

Honestly, Zach didn't know. The business was all he knew. They had groomed him to inherit since the day he was born. What else could he do with his life? He shrugged. "I guess. Why, what do you want to do?"

"Anything I want." He smiled, his face upturned toward the sky. The sunlight sparkled in his green eyes, caught in his mop of wavy brown curls, and glinted off his glasses. He was a cute kid, Zach thought, his chest tightening with affection. "I wanna be a writer. Write bestselling books about werewolf history like my dad." He envied Ryan then, envied how fearless and free he was. He made pursuing his dreams sound easy.

Maybe there was something else out there for him. Zach chased away the thought. If he threw his family's hard work back in their faces, they'd be disappointed and angry.

"Hey, Zach! Come to the beach house with us, okay? It'll be awesome, and at night, no one cares if you shift or not. Come on, please!"

Zach could already see his parents' disapproving faces and hear their lectures, but saying no to Ryan was hard, so he didn't. "I want to go, Ry, but my parents and I already have plans."

"Oh." Ryan pouted. "Okay..."

ZACH'S STOMACH WRITHED AS he approached his apartment building. The doorman held the door for him with a pleasant smile Zach struggled to return. Cool air conditioning blasted him, and he sighed his relief. The setting sun gleamed on marble-tiled floors, and red velvet carpet whispered beneath his ruined sneakers. He stepped into the elevator and watched the floor numbers rise, his heart racing fast. He was going to be in big trouble. A DeShawn wolf didn't lose control. DeShawns were never anything but the best. They had to be.

They were waiting for him in the living room. Floor-to-ceiling windows wrapped around the room and offered breathtaking views of Central Park. His mother, Rebecca, sat with one leg folded over her knee, her glossy hair long and straight. She smelled of her signature Chanel perfume. Ruby lips smiled at the sight of him, but the smile was strained. She was displeased.

His father leaned on the bar, a glass of whiskey in his hand. The sun gleamed on his bald head, and he wore a short-sleeved T-shirt that showed off the tattoos from his youthful wild days. He always covered them up outside the house. His father hadn't always been the pristine head of DeShawn Land Development. Zach took some satisfaction in knowing his dad wasn't perfect. So then why couldn't his father have more tolerance for Zach's rare mistakes?

"Hi, Mom, Dad." His voice cracked and he tried to smile.

"Sit down, Zach," his father said, smiling stiffly.

Stomach churning, Zach sat at the end of the sectional sofa. His father sat beside his mother and looked to her, and she took that as her cue to begin the lecture. "Zach, we heard some troubling news from your principal today. He said your grades are slipping."

Zach curled his fingers in his lap. "Yeah—yes. They are."

"I don't understand, Zach. Haven't you been studying hard? You're always such a hard worker."

"I don't know why," he said through gritted teeth, feeling cornered.

"Zach, sit up straight and be honest with us," she snapped.

Zach swallowed, struggling to gather his thoughts as the whirlpool of emotion inside him threatened to overflow. He blinked hard, trying to keep himself together. "I just don't... I can't do this." His voice broke and he clenched his jaw hard. "It's too much. I can't."

"What's too much?"

"It's like everything's just piling up. I couldn't breathe during the last exam. I started forgetting everything and... and..." His claws pierced the fabric of his shorts and the pain jolted him from his panic. What was happening to him?

His father stood and grabbed Zach's shoulders so hard, he yelped. "Control yourself, boy!" His father snarled, and he shook Zach roughly. "You control your beast, not the other way around. Do you understand me?"

Zach's fangs lengthened, his gasps turning to snarls. He didn't want to control it anymore. He was sick of being the perfect student, the prodigy son, the perfect shifter. It was too much.

"Zachariah," his father said, "I didn't get to where I am now because I gave up when things were difficult. The only way you'll learn to be a proper shifter is if you overcome the challenges you face, not crumble under them."

"Maybe I don't want to be a proper shifter!" Zach jumped to his feet, shaking so badly he could hardly stand. "Maybe I just want to be a normal kid, Dad!"

"You aren't. You're a DeShawn, and you need to act like it."

"What about what I want, Dad? You and Mom never asked me if I wanted to take on all those classes, or work in your business, or... or find a mate. None of the other kids in my school want to get mated to the first girl their parents introduce them to!"

"We only want what's best for you," his mother said. "You are very lucky, Zachariah. Very few shifters have the privileges you do, the opportunities. There are others out there who have it much worse than you."

Guilt gnawed at him. "I... I know." But didn't his feelings still matter, even if someone out there had it worse? Whenever she said that, it made him feel like a jerk for being anything less than grateful.

She lit up a cigarette. "You cannot squander our hard work by shifting at school."

His father's eyes blazed. "You shifted?"

His mother sighed. "I was going to tell you, Jo. Settle down."

Zach winced away from his father's furious glare. "A-almost! I almost shifted!" he corrected. "But I didn't. I ran before it could get too bad, I swear!"

His father's full lips thinned, and he gave his head a frustrated shake. "I told you. I told you to control yourself."

Zach panted, heart stuck in his throat when his father's hands curled into fists. "I know. I'm sorry, but I couldn't. I was so stressed and angry and—"

His mother put her hand on his father's arm. "Jo, that's enough. He made a mistake. He won't do it again. Right?" She shot him a pointed look.

"I won't. I swear." He didn't know if he could keep his word, though.

His father pointed around his mother at him. "We're going to work on this. I'll hire a tutor over the summer to help you with your grades."

Biting his lip, Zach was almost afraid to ask. He had to know. "What about California?"

His father curled his lip. "That trip was going to be a reward for your good behavior. I'll cancel our plans."

Tears sprang to Zach's eyes. "Dad, come on. Please. I promise I'll do better."

"Your consequences have actions, Zachariah. Next time you act out, remember that."

Zach slumped over the counter, digging his fingers into his short curls. He struggled to hold in his sobs because men didn't cry, but Goddess, he wanted to break apart.

"Okay, that's enough shouting, the both of you," his mother declared. "Zach, work on your grades. If you do well next semester, we can go somewhere fun. Okay?"

He couldn't speak and just hid his face in his arm so they wouldn't see him crying. He didn't even care about the trip. Not really. All he'd wanted was to spend the summer with his parents. To talk to them about something other than his responsibilities. To act like a normal family. For his father and mother to be proud of him just for *once*.

Lurching from his seat, Zach ran to his room and called Ryan.

"Hey, Zach! Were your plans cancelled? Can you come to the beach house?" Ryan meant it as a joke but Zach burst into tears. Through his tears, he told Ryan everything.

"But they promised you could go to Cali! What the heck, dude?"

"I know." Zach blew his nose into a tissue. "They always do this. They promise me something and if I mess up, they change their minds."

"But you didn't mess up! Right? Your dad said you'd get in trouble if you shift, but you didn't shift completely."

Sniffling, Zach hugged his knees to his chest. "He doesn't care."

A growl rumbled through the phone. "That's so fucking lame."

"You shouldn't curse. You're too young."

"Come to the beach house!"

"I can't!" Zach snapped. Hadn't he been listening? "My parents won't let me."

"Then sneak out and come meet me at my house!"

Zach thought he'd misheard. "You... are you serious?"

"Yes! Just lie and say your mom and dad let you come."

"So, let your parents kidnap me?"

Ryan groaned. "It's not kidnapping if you agree to it!"

A snort escaped him. "You're crazy." But hanging out with Ryan would sure beat being stuck at home with his moody parents.

He exhaled. "Okay. I'll do it."

"Yes!" He could practically see Ryan jumping up and down.

"Do I need to bring anything?"

"Uh, a healthy attitude for sun and fun? Oh! A swimsuit, scuba gear, sunscreen, and some sick shades."

Zach made a checklist and went over it in his head at dinner. The family cook made roast chicken with vegetables, and after dinner Zach headed for his room. "Zach." His father motioned him onto the balcony. "Come here a second."

Oh boy. Had he somehow heard Zach making plans to run off with Ryan and his family? Heart pounding, Zach shuffled onto the balcony. The heat of the day had simmered to a cool wind. The distant sound of traffic from far below barely reached his ears. "I'm sorry, Dad. I promise I'll do better."

His father waved a big hand. "I'm always on your back. I know. I just want to make sure you're successful, Zach. I wasn't exactly a model citizen when I was your age, but you're already doing better than I was."

Zach couldn't picture his father getting in trouble. "You made mistakes?"

His father's laughter rumbled out. "Oh yes. I was quite the rebel in my youth." He ran a hand over the tattoos on his skin. "My dad beat my ass when he found out I got inked. Now they're a reminder of my foolishness and so I strive to be better than I was. I don't want you making my mistakes."

"Tattoos aren't really my thing, Dad."

"I shifted a lot when I was your age. Whenever I thought my dad wouldn't find out. He did, of course. Tanned my hide for it. He said, 'Joe, humans already got enough reason to look down on us. Don't give them more. Be better than anyone says you are.' That's what you'll be, Zach." He tipped Zach's chin up with a big finger. "Don't let me down."

"Got it, Dad." He smiled until his father returned indoors, then looked at the view, suddenly feeling small and insignificant though he stood over the city like an emperor in his palace. What if this life wasn't for him? Was there room for him to grow outside the cookie-cutter model his parents had constructed around him?

Chapter 3

LIKE TRYING ON SHOES

WHEN ZACH'S PARENTS CALLED him during the drive to Long Beach Island and demanded to know where he'd gone, Ryan covered Zach's mouth and hissed, "Don't tell them!"

"Don't tell who what?" Ryan's mom looked wearily into the back seat.

"Where in the hell are you?" His father boomed, voice surely audible through the speaker.

Zach caved. As Ryan's parents got the gist of what was happening, they pulled over. Zach's parents were furious he'd gone behind their back, and Ryan's parents weren't happy they'd taken Zach away without his parents' consent. Ultimately, however, Zach's dad caved and allowed Zach to spend the week with Ryan. They got a long lecture about being truthful during the drive, and Zach had never been so embarrassed.

The drive to Long Beach Island where Ryan's family beach house awaited them didn't take long. The heated mood mellowed during the trip and everyone relaxed as best they could. As Zach's flip-flops slapped over the smooth stones in the driveway, it was hard not to feel excited. Ryan took off his shoes and walked barefoot on the rocks, Zach laughing at the faces he made. "Try it! It's like a massage!"

Zach humored him and removed his shoes, limping from one rock to another until he stumbled through the front door as Ryan's mom and dad laughed at them. It hurt but his feet did feel oddly relaxed. The beach house was big with a bedroom upstairs and three extra bedrooms on the ground floor. "Which one is your room?" Zach asked, lugging his bag over to Ryan.

"That one," Ryan said, pointing to the one in the middle. Zach dragged his bag into the room next to Ryan's.

"We'll be neighbors," he said, laughing at the way Ryan's face reddened.

"Y-yeah, cool. Okay! Last one to the beach is a loser wolf!" Ryan hurled his suitcase into his room and threw off his clothes, revealing his swimming trunks. Zach snorted.

"You've been wearing those the whole time?"

"Beat you there, sucker!" Ryan pelted out of the door in a blur. Zach could smell the ocean from here and had no intention of delaying, following the tornado that was Ryan over hot pavement past quaint beach houses in vibrant tropical colors. The sun blazed in a cloudless sky and squeezed beads of sweat from his forehead.

"Hey, Ry, wait up! Your mom'll kill me if you get hit by a car." He quickened his stride to catch up to the younger boy as they neared a busy road. It seemed cars were supposed to yield but not all did, Zach noticed with worry. Ryan practically vibrated with excitement beside him, his big eyes darting around to check for an opening.

He instinctively grabbed onto Ryan's hand as a car whizzed by, blowing Ryan's wavy brown hair around his face. "Okay, go!" He and Ryan tore across the street and the pavement gave way to sand.

The beach sprawled in all directions, hot gusts of wind blowing sand into Zach's face. The ocean seemed endless, reaching toward the horizon. Zach realized he'd forgotten to apply sunscreen. "Ry, we should put on—" But Ryan was already chasing the waves, laughing as they lapped at his feet.

Ryan's mom and dad, Kaitlyn and Declan, arrived, bringing umbrellas and towels. Declan wrangled his son back for sunscreen while Kaitlyn set up some lounge chairs. Zach helped, opening a chair up and dropping it in the sand. She smiled. "Thanks, hon."

They spent the day chasing waves and getting sand in places Zach would rather not have it. Kaitlyn read for most of the day while Declan joined

Zach and Ryan in the water. Zach's stomach growled but he tried to ignore it. He should have eaten before he left the house and worried he'd annoy the Kellys if he asked. His parents usually got frustrated if he didn't keep track of his own needs.

Declan said, "Boys, it's almost lunchtime. Take a break and get food. Here." He handed them both some money.

Zach's face warmed. "I-it's okay, Mr. Kelly. I can buy my own food."

"Nonsense. My treat. Whatever you boys like."

"As long as it's not tubs of ice cream!" Kaitlyn called.

Zach was too flustered to refuse, even though he probably should. The Kellys were different from his parents, that was for sure.

Ryan led the way from the beach, and they walked along the road that went to Ryan's house. Cars occasionally sped past but the road was quiet and mostly empty. They followed it to a small stretch of town. "So, what do you feel like?" Ryan asked. "There's a sandwich shop, and the ice cream parlor is awesome."

Zach frowned. "Your mom said—"

Ryan waved a hand. "She won't know."

Nerves tingled in Zach's stomach. "Are you sure we won't get in trouble?" His parents didn't approve of sweets.

"Jeez, dude, chill. My mom couldn't yell at a ladybug."

Ryan's parents seemed pretty cool, so Zach tried to ignore his worries. Besides, he really wanted ice cream too. "This town is so cute." He was glad Ryan had invited him. "I like it here."

Ryan bounded ahead, holding the door for Zach. He chatted up the teen behind the register, who knew his exact order: lemon poppyseed, two scoops, with sugar cookie pieces and loads of sprinkles. Surprised by the variety of flavors, Zach took his time. Ryan said, "The poppyseed is the best." So Zach ordered the same thing Ryan had, minus all the sprinkles and cookies.

They found a bench to sit on and ate, melty ice cream running down their fingers.

Zach hummed happily, trying to go slow and savor each bite. "So good."

"Told you!"

"Can't remember the last time I had ice cream."

Ryan gaped at him. "Seriously? Dude, do your parents let you have any fun?"

Zach licked his lips, chasing the taste of lemon poppyseed. "We went to see a Broadway show."

"Cool! When?"

Zach couldn't remember. "I passed a test, so they took me out to celebrate." He smiled. "It was nice. We hardly ever do stuff like that unless I do well in school."

Ryan blinked at him, stupefied. "That's the saddest thing I've ever heard."

Zach squirmed on the bench. "It's not sad. My parents say I have to work hard and earn things."

Ryan made a face. "That's dumb. That settles it. I'm gonna teach you how to have fun!"

Zach snorted. "I know how to have fun, Ryan."

His friend grinned, big and bright. "Wait till tonight. The beach is always almost empty. We can go there and shift."

Zach frowned, remembering his father's admonishments. "We shouldn't. We'll get in trouble."

Ryan scoffed. "That's right! The crabs will tell on us to the cops, and we'll get arrested!" He rolled his eyes. "Come on, Zach, it'll be fun."

Zach wanted to see the beach at night but wasn't sure he'd shift. "Okay… but if you get caught, I'm leaving your ass—I mean, butt." He'd never cursed before he and Ryan had started hanging out the past two weeks. His parents would say Ryan was a bad influence but Zach decided he didn't care. Ryan was his friend, and that was that.

Ryan's eyes danced with mischief. "Okay, but I'll kick your ass for abandoning me."

They returned to the beach house, stopping to hose off their shoes and sandy feet. "You guys find food?" Declan called.

"Uh, yeah," Zach said, hoping there wasn't any ice cream on his face.

"Well," Kaitlyn said, peering up from her book. "I hope you boys have room for dinner. Or did all that ice cream fill you up?"

"How'd you know?" Ryan squawked, dismayed.

"You have sprinkles on your face, Ry." Kaitlyn smiled as she turned the page of her book.

Zach winced. Craaap. "I-I'm so sorry, Mrs. Kelly!"

She cocked her head. "For?"

"I'm older, so I should have been more responsible. We can go back out and—"

But she only laughed, a bright, tinkling sound. "Ice cream for lunch once in a blue moon won't kill anyone, Zach."

He relaxed, relieved she wasn't mad.

She stood and touched his shoulder on her way past him. "You're a good influence on my son. I can tell already."

Despite a stomachache, the day went by blissfully. The two of them spent the rest of the day on the couch watching reruns of their favorite TV show, *Ruffy the Werewolf Slayer*. They joined Ryan's dad for dinner, eating burgers he'd grilled in the backyard. Ryan's mom didn't join them. "She's not feeling well," Declan explained.

Zach frowned. That was odd. She'd seemed fine earlier this evening. "Oh. I hope she feels better."

"She will." Declan patted his son's shoulder as if to reassure him.

Ryan had stopped eating and was oddly quiet for the rest of dinner, only humming or nodding in response to things. After dinner Zach tried to help with the dishes, but Declan insisted he get ready for bed. Zach brushed his teeth and washed his face. He scowled at his reflection; his acne seemed like it was here to stay no matter what products he used. As he exited the bathroom, he heard voices over the clink and rattle of dishes.

"Do we have to go home?" Zach hardly recognized Ryan's voice, it was so small and worried.

"No, pup. She's been on the meds for two weeks. The doc says she's doing well on them. She'll be fine."

"For now."

"The doctor said that if the medicine worked, she could travel. How about we take his word for it?"

"But what if…"

"Ry. She'll be fine. Okay? You can talk to her in the morning."

Feeling uncomfortable, Zach slipped into his bedroom. What was wrong with Ryan's mother? Hadn't Ryan mentioned something about an illness the first time they'd met? The door rattled behind him and Ryan walked in, his head down low and his lips set in a pout. He jumped at the sight of Zach and grinned. "Wanna head out now?" His smile seemed heavy, but he was trying. Zach was still apprehensive about going to the beach at night, but he wanted to cheer Ryan up.

"Yeah. Let's go."

He let Ryan lead the way to the beach as they shone flashlights around the path. The stars winked at them, more visible here than they were in the city. The moon was bright and full, the perfect night for shifting. Excitement swelled inside him. It was hard to resist the urge to howl.

The moonlight shimmered on the sand and scattered into fat gems on the surface of the churning waves. Watching the waves break on the shore, an eager yip distracted Zach. He turned, grinning at the sight of a white wolf with mottled black patches. The wolf lunged into a play bow, rear end high in the air and tail wagging.

Zach looked up and down the beach. It really seemed deserted. But if they got caught—

The white-and-black wolf tugged at Zach's sleeve, his big sandy paws clawing at his shirt. Zach grinned. "I don't know. Maybe I'll just stand watch." Disappointment clenched in his gut. His wolf was not happy.

Ryan barked loudly, jumping up and down and spinning in circles. Zach laughed at him, his heart slamming against his chest. His wolf was close to the surface, growling in his throat. "Okay. Okay. But just for a while." Ryan howled in delight as Zach peeled off his shirt and kicked off his shorts. Hair was already growing on his arms, his fangs lengthening and his nose elongating into a snout. He dropped to all fours and the change came over him.

Ryan! Pack! Play? Play! his wolf cried, jubilant.

He bounded toward Ryan's wolf and they collided, tumbling over in the sand. Ryan ran and Zach gave chase, spewing a sandstorm behind him. They ran until Zach's tongue lolled from his mouth, his ribs expanding frantically. Finally, he pinned Ryan beneath him, growling playfully as Ryan licked at his ears and face. His wolf felt so safe while he cuddled with Ryan. Exhausted, he lost the strength to stay in wolf form.

"Uh? Zach? You're crushin' me."

Zach's eyes snapped open. He lay sprawled on top of Ryan. Heat sprang to his face. "I'm sorry!" He scrambled off his friend and sat in the sand beside him. His heart raced, and his stomach fluttered like he'd swallowed a butterfly.

"Awkward," Ryan sang, shaking sand out of his mop of hair. "Crap! I lost my glasses."

"Chill. We'll find them." Zach tousled his hair, sending sand flying. "They're probably with our clothes."

Ryan's eyes went wide, all the blood rushing to his face. "Uh... your wolf is really cool."

Zach's mouth twitched. "Really? What does he look like?"

"You've never seen yourself before?" Ryan gaped at him. "You have mostly brown fur with some gray and white. That's so weird you don't know what you look like. My dad says shifting is important."

"Really?"

Ryan bobbed his head. "Like, our instincts will be dulled if we don't shift. Dad said he almost didn't know my mom was his mate because he resisted shifting. It took him forever to find her special scent." He wrinkled his nose, sniffing.

Zach hadn't known that. "I don't shift a lot. My parents are pretty strict."

Ryan nudged Zach. "Don't worry. I won't tell. It was fun, though, right?"

He laughed, curling his toes in the sand. "Yeah. Yeah, it was." He couldn't remember the last time he'd had so much fun. They dressed, Ryan found his glasses, and they walked back together in the dark. Then Ryan's flashlight went out. "Walk next to me." Zach reached out until he'd clasped Ryan's hand, and Ryan jumped as if Zach had shocked him.

"O-okay..."

They held hands the entire walk back. Zach's hand tingled with every step and he smiled, happier than he'd been in a long time.

THAT WEEK WITH ZACH was the best of Ryan's life. Every day, they ate together and played on the beach. Some nights they shifted and ran as wolves, others they curled up on the couch and watched TV until Ryan fell asleep. His mom took an embarrassing picture of Ryan asleep with his head on Zach's shoulder.

Things felt normal again. His mom was happy like she'd always been, though she was tired often. The medications prevented her from shifting. It was easy to believe she would get better, that one day she might not even need the medication anymore. The doctor was wrong. Sometimes doctors were. She would get well again.

Ryan watched her and his dad dance on the patio to old Bee Gees songs. The sun set behind them and caught in his mother's hazel hair. She was laughing, smiling in a way that made it impossible not to smile with her. Zach cheered, clapping for them, and his mom and dad bowed. Grinning widely, his father was flushed and breathing hard.

"We danced to that song at our wedding reception. I'm surprised I still remember it."

"You guys got married?" Zach asked.

"I know, it's uncommon for werewolves," his mother explained. "I was human once. I wanted a big reception. One big ceremony before I left my human life behind. Declan turned me after we were married. What about your parents, uh..." Her face wrinkled in confusion, her scent souring with embarrassment. "Sorry. I'm forgetting. What's your name?"

Something cold dropped into Ryan's stomach. He stopped breathing, suddenly feeling sick. He glanced at his father and saw that he'd stopped smiling, his expression unreadable.

Zach reintroduced himself without missing a beat. "They're both werewolves. Super traditional too. They want me to carry on the pack legacy."

The conversation carried on normally, but Ryan had stopped listening. Did that momentary forgetfulness mean something? She'd been doing so well. Why did this have to happen?

"Ry?"

Ryan jumped at the sound of Zach's voice. "Tired. I'm gonna go to sleep." He left without another word and went to his room. The ceiling fan whirred as he stumbled in and turned off the lamp by his bed. With the room darkened, he crawled into bed and lay in the dark.

He'd thought the medicine was working. She hadn't gone feral at all, and she hadn't forgotten anyone until now. She was supposed to be better. Otherwise, what was the point of taking the meds? What was the point of doctors if they didn't know what they were even doing?

He gnashed his teeth, scrubbing furiously at the tears in his eyes. He didn't realize he'd fallen asleep until he woke the next day, smelling coffee. The house was quiet, and his father sat at the table in his T-shirt and briefs. He smiled. "Hey, kiddo."

"How's Mom feeling?" Ryan asked.

"We'll see how she feels today. She probably just blanked, Ry. It happens sometimes."

"What if she doesn't feel better? What if she gets worse?"

His father sighed, closing his eyes. "Then we'll cut the vacation short and return to the city. We'll talk to the doctor again, see if she needs a change in medication."

Ryan scratched at the wood of the table. "But she'll get better, right? Once she gets the right medicine?"

His father gripped his shoulder, his touch as warm as the bond that glowed between them. "It's like trying on shoes, bud. Sometimes you have to keep trying until you find the right fit. She'll get there. And even if she doesn't, Ry, we'll love her anyway. Right?"

Ryan blinked hard. He nodded.

Behind him, the door closed. Ryan scented his mom and turned. She stood frozen in the living room, her face pale white, her eyes huge.

"Wh-who are you?" Backing away into the doorframe, she looked from his father to Ryan. She looked at him like he was a stranger, and losing her recognition punched a hole into his heart.

"Mom." Ryan's voice was barely a whisper. She'd forgotten him again. Tears burned his eyes. He couldn't imagine a world where his own mother didn't remember him. "M-mom, it's me. It's Ryan. I'm your son."

He tried to go to her, to make her remember, but his father grabbed his shoulder. He gasped in pain.

"Ry, go outside. Now." He stood slowly, as if he were approaching a frightened deer. "Kait, it's me. It's your mate. Don't you recognize my scent?"

"Stay away from me!" Her scream left Ryan shaking. She lunged for a lamp. "I'll call the police! Get out!"

"Kait, listen to me. I'm not going to hurt—" She hurled the lamp. Ryan flew off his feet, hoisted into his father's arms. His father shielded Ryan from the lamp and grunted in pain. The lamp lay in pieces, glass cracking under his father's feet, his blood dripping onto the floor.

"D-Dad!"

His mother had hurt his father. She'd made him bleed again.

"Go, now!" His father shoved Ryan toward the sliding doors. Ryan's hands shook so badly he could barely unlatch it.

A door slammed and Zach raced into the living room. Shock left him frozen as Ryan's mom whirled toward him and screamed in terror. "Help! Someone, help me!" She ran, crashing through the door and out into the yard. Ryan's father shot after her.

Ryan tore after her too, terrified that his mother would get lost and they'd never see her again. "Mom! Come back!"

"Zach!" his father roared. "Take him and go! Both of you!"

"No! Mom!" Ryan tried to run to her, but his feet left the ground again as Zach lifted him into his arms and ran. He screamed, struggling to free himself because if he didn't, he would never see his mother again. Then all he could do was sob, clinging to Zach as they ran. The waves roared; gulls cried in lonesome voices. The sand burned his feet as Zach set him down and Ryan turned, trying to run back. "Mom!"

"No, Ry! You can't help her!"

Ryan whirled around, Zach's tall dark shape a blur through his tears. He struck, slamming his fists into any part of Zach's solid body he could reach. "Let me go! I need to go back! I need to help her!"

"You can't!" Big dark hands clasped his face. There was a growl in Zach's voice and his eyes glowed like ferry lights across the ocean. Ryan's breathless pants turned to shuddery sobs.

"I have to help her. I *have to.*"

"You can't," Zach repeated. His hands trembled on Ryan's face, but his touch was like an anchor while the world around him went on spinning. "Just be strong. Okay? That way, you can be there for her when she needs you."

"I can't do anything. I'm useless. I'm stupid. Otherwise, she'd remember me." All he wanted to do now was hit himself.

"No way. Hey, listen. It isn't your fault, Ry."

"Yes, it is!" He tore free of Zach's touch and suddenly felt cold and lost at sea. "If I was better, she wouldn't forget." Werewolves went feral when there wasn't anyone to remind them of their humanity. If he weren't so stupid and useless, his mother would love him more. He would be her humanity.

"She loves your dad, doesn't she?"

"Yeah, but—"

"So, she loves you, Ry. This isn't your fault. Or your dad's. It's the way she is."

Ryan trembled, hardly able to see through his tears or speak through the ache in his throat. "I thought she was getting better."

"Oh, Ry." The sadness in Zach's voice undid Ryan. Big warm arms went around him, and he stumbled into Zach's chest. When Zach lifted him, Ryan's legs wrapped around Zach's waist as the bigger boy carried him away from the chatter of beachgoers and noisy stereos.

Something wet dripped on his hair, and he realized Zach was crying with him. Zach's shirt was wet with snot and tears by the time Ryan was calm enough to speak. "I wanted to tell you. Just... I thought I didn't have to. I thought she was better."

"It's okay." Zach's hand glided up and down his back. "That kinda stuff is hard to talk about."

Ryan sniffed, his nose stuffy. "I'm so lame. Men aren't supposed to cry."

Zach said, "I guess I'm not a man yet then."

"Do you think we're a bunch of freaks?" Ryan was suddenly so frightened he couldn't breathe. He didn't have many friends. He was the chatty know-it-all kid who always had an answer to the teacher's question. The other kids whispered about him behind his back and laughed when they raised their hands with him, twitching in their seats. So he didn't want to lose Zach—the thought made him want to cry again.

Zach laughed, the sound deep and throaty, and Ryan's face warmed. "You're the biggest freak I know."

Laughing, Ryan wriggled out of Zach's arms. "Shut up."

Zach smiled. His eyes and nose were red, but he looked… some kind of way Ryan hadn't seen before, but it made his heart race fast and left him at a loss for words. "I'm joking, man. You're… you're my best friend."

And at his words, warmth bloomed in Ryan's heart. A thread that whispered *pack, friend, Zach,* thrummed within his chest. Zach touched his own chest as if he could feel the thread connecting them. Maybe he could. Ryan wanted to know for sure.

He smiled and through the golden bond connecting them, he whispered, *"Hey, Zach. Hi. You're my best friend too."*

Zach gasped softly, tears bright in his eyes. *"I… I know, Ry."*

Ryan scoffed and said aloud, "Wow. Modest."

"Shut up." Laughing, Zach sat in the sand. Through their new pack bond, he said, *"I've never had a pack before. Not with anyone outside my family. I'm glad it's with you."*

His voice filled Ryan's mind with warmth and light. "If anyone else wants to be in our pack, they have to like *Ruffy the Werewolf Slayer.* We need a passcode!"

"For what?" Zach asked, grinning in his confusion.

"For our BFF club, dummy! The Zach and Ryan Club."

"Okay…" Zach twirled a curl around his finger. "How about numbers?"

Ryan snorted. "Lame. You'll get hacked if you just use numbers. It should be a phrase. Something we both know."

Zach poked his tongue out while he thought, which made Ryan laugh. "I got it! The moon over the oak. That's the password."

"Oh, an oak! Like our tree. Cool idea!"

Ryan's phone rang. When his father spoke, he was breathless but calm. "She's settled down. You can come back to the house."

Ryan swallowed hard. "What are we going to do?"

"Once your mother's got her bearings, I'll talk to her about whether she'd be more comfortable here or back in the city. We need to schedule more doctor appointments, and that'll be easier if we're in the city."

"Okay." He hung up and sighed. "Come on," he said to Zach. "Mom's calmer now. We can go back."

They walked slowly, neither excited to return to the house. "She'll be okay, Ry." Zach's hand settled on Ryan's shoulder.

"I hope so."

Zach didn't move his hand away until they arrived home.

CHAPTER 4

BOY STUFF

LIFE IN THE KELLY pack had its ups and downs over the next year, but life went on. Ryan's mother went to doctor after doctor. The good news was the disease didn't appear to be progressing; her episodes never lasted longer than a few hours to a day at most, so she wasn't getting worse but she wasn't her normal self either.

There were good days when she seemed like the same cheerful mom she'd always been. Then one day she forgot his thirteenth birthday, and Ryan tried to smile and act like he didn't care, but it hurt him. She knew. She made up for it with a trip to the movie theater and bought him as much candy as he wanted from the concession stand. When she asked if he'd liked the show, he smiled and nodded. Truth was, he hadn't been able to focus on it at all.

His parents fought more than they used to. Ryan wasn't supposed to know, but he heard them arguing at night. His mother would call his father overbearing and said she felt suffocated by him. His father yelled at her for leaving the house alone or when she took forever to return his calls, but his mother wanted her independence. On those nights Ryan would pull his pillow over his ears and try to sleep, his tears dampening his sheets. He wondered if they still loved each other and worried they'd break up.

One afternoon, they went to celebrate his grandmother's birthday. It was a good day. Ryan's mom wasn't forgetful, and his dad laughed and smiled. The drive upstate was full of lighthearted chatter and fun music.

Nothing raised Ryan's spirits more than when he ran into his grandma's backyard, the smell of basil and fresh ripe tomatoes wafting through the air.

"Gran!" He ran into Grandma Rose's warm embrace. The sun shone through her white, translucent hair.

She squeezed him tight. "There's my bonnie wee lad," she said in her deep Irish accent. "Declan, come and give your ma a kiss! Kait, you too!"

Ryan laughed when his father, blushing, hugged his gran.

"Come with me, lad," Gran said, taking his hand. "What would you like to plant today?"

Ryan had thought very long and hard about this. "Blueberries! No, strawberries!"

She laughed. "Let's do both."

They planted the berries while his parents sipped fresh lemonade. Ryan insisted on not wearing gloves, loving the smell and feel of the soil.

"You love nature, don't you, lad? Your da tells me you spend time among the trees in the park," Gran said.

"Yeah." Ryan shoveled dirt over the planted seeds. "I love trees. Sometimes, I feel like they're talking to me."

His mother and father exchanged glances. Not like they thought he was weird but almost like they were... worried? Ryan wasn't sure.

Gran only smiled, big and bright. "Oh, they are. Listen to them closely. They will guide you."

Ryan didn't understand but brushed his confusion away. He went inside to wash his hands so he could enjoy his gran's cucumber and cream cheese sandwiches, the best summer snack ever. He passed by the open window and peered into the yard. His gran sat beside his mom and dad in the lawn chairs. They spoke quietly.

"—do anything to help," Gran said, taking his mother's hand. "I know the risks, and I have made my peace with it."

His mother shook her head. "No, Rosemary. I can't ask that of you."

"I could help you—"

"No." His mother's voice was choked. "Please."

"Thank you, Ma." His father took Gran's hand. "It's kind of you to offer."

Ryan didn't ask what they'd talked about. Their words were not meant for him and he felt guilty for overhearing. A week later, his gran texted him a picture of the berries, fully ripe. When he asked how her crops always grew so fast, she'd never say. Ryan liked to think it was magic.

And then there was Zach. Even on his worst days, a text from Zach would bring a smile to his face. He always looked forward to after school when they could meet. Some days however, Ryan didn't see Zach at all. Not for a week at the longest. Zach didn't answer his calls, and Ryan stayed up at night worrying he'd done something wrong.

Eventually, Zach would pick up the phone and Ryan would nearly cry with relief.

All Zach would say was, "A teacher told my parents I wasn't concentrating in class. My parents grounded me."

Zach wasn't himself for a while after that. He was withdrawn. More cautious.

Ryan wondered if he was too young to hate people, because he did *not* like Zach's parents.

Zach went away for the summer that year and Ryan's family went back to the beach. Without him there, the beach house wasn't the same and it brought back memories of when they'd run through the sand together as wolves. They texted every night and called whenever they could. Zach was in Africa visiting distant relatives, and he sent pictures of Cape Town, a coastal town surrounded by rugged mountains and water. He said they had beautiful beaches and that he thought of Ryan whenever he ran as a wolf at night. Ryan wished he could go. He wished he could be there with Zach.

He missed him. A single text got his heart racing and hearing Zach's voice brought a smile to his face, always. Summer would be over soon. In no time they would see each other.

One night, Ryan's cell phone rang. Zach's name flashed across the screen. Rubbing his eyes, he checked the time. It was midnight here in the States, but he remembered that Cape Town was six hours ahead. It was weird that Zach was calling him late, though.

Swiping, he answered. "Zach?" His voice sounded like a car wreck.

Shaky breathing answered him. "Ryan."

Something was wrong. He'd never heard Zach's voice so high-pitched before. He sounded terrified.

"I-is everything okay?" Ryan's heart started beating fast.

"My p-parents locked me in my room." Zach's voice shook so badly, Ryan almost didn't understand him. "Th-they want me to do something, and I t-told them I didn't want to, so they locked me up and—and I can't breathe. They won't open the door. I'm so fucking scared."

Ryan knew right then and there that he wasn't too young to hate anyone. Because he hated Zach's parents. He hated them so much. "Why can't you breathe?" he asked, voice shaking.

"I don't know," Zach gasped. "Chest's too tight. My h-heart won't stop racing."

What did he do? What could he say? He wished he was there with Zach so he could help him.

"Um..." The phone shook in his hands. "So, something hilarious happened at school before summer break."

"I don't c-care about school!" Zach snapped, panting into the speaker.

"Just listen!" If he could distract Zach, maybe he'd calm down. Goddess, Ryan hoped he wouldn't die. "So, in class Ian was using the word 'gay' as an insult. You know, 'that's so gay, you guys.' So I told him there's nothing wrong with being gay and that he should use a different insult. He said okay and asked what he should say instead. I didn't really know, so I just said dickhead. So..." Ryan snorted just remembering what happened next.

"So the teacher came in and Ian was like, 'Hey, Mr. Dickhead!' And he had to clean the boy's bathroom!"

Ryan laughed just remembering.

"You're such a jerk," Zach said, but he was laughing.

"Hey, it's not my fault he insulted the teacher!"

Ryan had to hide his face in his pillow so he didn't wake his parents up from laughing. To his relief, Zach laughed, too. And then, he cried. He cried in great wrenching gasps that made Ryan want to cry with him.

They talked for an hour. Well, Zach did. Ryan didn't know what to say, so he just listened as Zach told him between sobs that he wished his parents loved him, that all he seemed to do was disappoint them, how frustrated he was that he was never a good enough son, a good enough wolf.

But he was. He was all of those things. Everything.

Ryan just wished he knew how to put it all into words.

It was always bittersweet to leave the beach and return to school. His classmates had grown and had new experiences to talk about. The boys in his class talked about the girls they met over the summer. "Jess actually let me touch her boob!" one boy exclaimed. His friends guffawed, as if that were the coolest thing ever.

"Did she have a bra on?"

"Yeah, so?"

"That doesn't count!"

"Yeah, it does!"

Ryan was barely listening, occupied with his salami sandwich, until one boy tapped him on the shoulder. "Hey, Ry, have you touched a girl before?"

"No." Ryan didn't notice girls. They were nice. He didn't want to touch a girl's boob, though. That sounded gross.

"Who are you always texting then?" another asked, trying to peek at his phone. Ryan shoved it in his pocket. The boys jeered.

"He's totally got a girlfriend."

"No, I don't." Ryan's ears were blazing.

"You should ask Hannah out. She's hot."

Ryan just nodded. He wasn't sure what to say. What was wrong with not having a girlfriend? Did he need one? Should he want one? Girls were all right. Some of them were pretty, but he never wanted to touch one or kiss one.

But he did dream about kissing boys. And he liked it.

"Hey, Ryan. Hi." Zach's warm voice ignited their bond and filled the parts of Ryan that had been empty all summer without him.

Ryan's wolf sang through the golden bond they'd forged a year ago. He didn't have to look for Zach. The street was full of people, but their eyes met like it was the easiest thing in the world. Zach's eyes were a deep brown but, in the sun, they were honey orange. When Zach smiled, Ryan couldn't breathe. Suddenly, he was terrified, like a deer frozen by rustling in the underbrush.

Zach was even taller than last summer, his skin a deeper bronze from all the time under the African sun.

"Hey!" Zach bounded to him and opened his arms.

Ryan lurched away from him. His heart galloped, something like fireworks bursting in his stomach. Zach frowned and Ryan couldn't explain what he'd done or why. "Yeah." His voice cracked and his whole face burned hot. "Hey, Zach. Hi." What was wrong with him? He felt such a burst of panic when he tried to look Zach in the eyes.

"You good? You didn't text last night."

Zach noticed? Had he stayed up waiting for Ryan to text him? Had he missed Ryan as much as Ryan had missed him all summer long?

Ryan's lips moved but no sound came out. What should he say? He'd never been so speechless before. "Yeah. I'm fine. Uh... let's go. I'm starved."

A curious smile tugged at Zach's wide mouth. He looked different—in a good way. His hair was longer and braided. He had nice, soft-looking lips and a bright smile that lit up his whole face. Did Zach like girls? Had he met one while in Africa?

"Sounds good, man. Where to?"

"What?"

Zach barked out a laugh. A rush of excitement swept through Ryan's stomach, like when he scored a goal during soccer practice. "Food? Duh, man! Where do you wanna eat?"

"Oh. Uh... I don't know. Anywhere."

"I'm dying for a burger. Hey, hang on!" Ryan jumped when Zach grabbed his arms. "You got taller, didn't you!"

Ryan's lips flapped uselessly. He couldn't think when Zach was touching him. "Yeah. People grow. It's a thing." He wriggled out from Zach's grip, his face hot.

"Damn, man. You'll be as tall as I am soon!" A big warm hand settled on his hair and ruffled. His fingertips tickled over Ryan's scalp, weaving through his hair and making Ryan's breath catch. Zach's touch made his skin tingle and filled his body with heat. It felt good. Really good.

"I missed you, Ry. You should come to Cape Town sometime. Get a taste of that African culture." He pulled Ryan close, and Ryan leaned into his chest, listening to his heartbeat and breathing in the smell of salt and sand. Zach's hand slid over his back and that was when Ryan felt it, a surge of heat past his hips. The front of his shorts felt unbearably tight suddenly and—

Oh, craaap.

It wasn't the first time he'd gotten an erection. It happened sometimes when he woke up or if he had a sexy dream... usually about kissing boys he found attractive. He'd had The Talk at school and at home. He knew what his penis was capable of, thank you very much. But why did he get one when Zach touched him? Zach would think he was a freak! He shoved Zach away.

"Whoa! What gives!"

"Sorry! Just, uh, feeling sick! Gotta go puke!" All he could think of was to get as far away from Zach as possible before he saw. He turned tail and ran for his life.

When he got home, he slammed the door so hard, it made his mother jump. "Honey! Don't slam the door. The neighbors will throw a fit!"

"'Kay, Mom, whatever." He ducked past her and ran for the bedroom.

"Hold it, Ry, what is going on? You stormed in like a wild animal. Aren't you supposed to be meeting Zach?"

Ryan didn't know what to say, so he shrugged.

She surveyed him as if he'd grown a third head. "Did something happen?"

Ryan's phone rang. It was Zach. He shut it off. "No. Not really." He inched toward the bedroom door, desperate to just be by himself.

"Ryan, what's wrong? Are you and Zach having trouble? You were so excited to see him."

"I am." Ryan's jaw tightened, and he glared at the floor, trying to burn holes through it. "Can we not talk about this?"

She threw up her hands. "Okay, okay."

Instead, his father came to talk to him in his room. Trying to ignore him, Ryan turned the music up louder. His father popped out one of his earbuds and smiled. "Hey. How was school?"

"School's school." Ryan tried to focus on his book.

His father nodded. "That's the truth of it." He sat on Ryan's bed, and Ryan hoped he wouldn't say anything. "You smell pretty distressed, Ry. Do you wanna talk about it?"

"I can't!" Ryan threw down his book. "It's too embarrassing."

His father raised his brows. "I know a thing or two about embarrassment. I ever tell you about the time I shifted around this girl I liked? She told the whole school I was wearing banana-patterned underwear."

Ryan snorted. His dad *would* wear weird, patterned underwear.

"So, what's the problem? School stuff?" He smiled openly and nudged Ryan. "Girl stuff?" Ryan buried his face in his book. "Boy stuff?" At that, he almost threw the book across the room in his surprise.

"Dad, what the heck?" His face burned hot. His father laughed and clapped him on the knee.

"Zach. Isn't it? Mom told me you left him hanging. You were looking forward to seeing him all summer. What's up? You can tell me. We've all been there. First crushes are terrifying."

Ryan held the book so close to his face, the words blurred and his head started hurting. "He... hugged me. I felt weird."

"Good weird?"

Ryan shrugged, too embarrassed to say. "Guess so. I couldn't talk to him. I had all this stuff I wanted to say but... my heart started racing and I couldn't think." His father smiled. "It's not funny. He probably thinks I hate him." Ryan swallowed, suddenly feeling sick. "It's weird. All the boys at my school are into girls."

"Not all of them, I guarantee. It's just harder for guys to admit they like other guys. Are there any girls in class that you like?"

"I don't know." He blinked hard, suddenly wanting to cry.

"Hey. It's fine, Ry. Look at me." His father lowered his book, but Ryan was still reluctant to look at him. "Boys or girls or both, it's fine. Your mother and I love you. Okay?"

Ryan nodded and smiled. "I know."

His father ruffled his hair and Ryan picked up his book, feeling much better than before. Stopping in the door, his father said, "Call Zach, bud. He's a good guy."

"Okay." Ryan wasn't ready. He had to figure out what to say. "What should I tell him?"

"Ry, crushes come and go, but friendship is constant. If Zach doesn't feel the same way, it might make things awkward."

"You mean he'll... hate me?"

His father chuckled. "No! I'm sure he won't."

"How will I know if he... you know?" Ryan was sure his whole face was red. "L-likes me back?"

"You'll know," his father promised. He turned for the door then reconsidered. "Hey. What's Zach smell like?"

"You mean, is he my m-mate or something?" The word came out high and squeaky. Ryan coughed to clear his throat. "He smells... like nothing."

His father cocked his head. "Huh?"

"It's really weird. Like, his scent is not there at all. Is scent really important anyway?"

"It can be." Scooting back on the bed, his father leaned his back against the wall. "Your mother smells like pine trees. My father took me hiking when I was a boy—one of my favorite smells in the world. It's how we wolves know that we're going to be together forever."

So... if Zach didn't have a scent did that mean they wouldn't be friends someday? Tears stung his eyes, but his wolf snarled in defiance, bringing a growl to Ryan's throat. So, he decided.

"I don't care what Zach smells like!" Zach was cool, funny, nice, and kind of... cute? Maybe? He crossed his arms. "I don't need some dumb scent to tell me we're gonna be together forever. My wolf knows it, so there!" Anyone who said otherwise was a liar.

His father laughed softly. "Then there you have it. Hold on to him, Ry. Don't let him go."

"I won't, Dad." He didn't know if they'd be friends or something more but one thing was clear: he would never let Zach DeShawn go.

CHAPTER 5

DON'T FORGET ABOUT ME

THE HOT SUMMER SUN warmed Ryan's face as he sat beneath his and Zach's tree. His stomach twisted and he worried he'd throw up if he tried talking to Zach. Or worse yet, get an awkward boner like yesterday. Good thing he'd worn oversized pants. Growling, he hit himself on the forehead. Goddess, why was he so lame?

He still didn't know what to say. His mom always said he was honest, and he liked to speak his mind and didn't like keeping secrets. Maybe he would tell Zach he liked him. Or not. Ryan shredded some grass in annoyance.

"Hey."

Ryan froze. What did he say? What did he do?

The grass rustled. Zach sat beside him, his warmth seeping into Ryan's clothes.

He's right next to me. Right next to me! What do I do?

"Hey, so... about yesterday, we're cool. You don't have to say anything. I was pretty nervous too. You know, we hadn't seen one another in a while. I didn't really know what to say." Their hands sprawled inches apart in the grass and Zach's fingers curled, fisting blades of grass.

"I-I felt sick," Ryan stammered, unable to look Zach in the eyes. "Th-that's why I ran off."

"Feeling better?"

No. I feel like vomiting. Ryan forced himself to nod.

"That's good. How was your summer?"

He didn't have to look to know Zach was looking at him. He could feel those chocolate-brown eyes on him, igniting his skin, making every pore tingle and tying his stomach into knots he had no hopes of untangling.

"It was okay." He wished he'd enjoyed it more but being at the beach house had just reminded him of their summer together, reminded him that Zach wasn't there.

"Mine was too. I missed hanging out with you."

Ryan's heart jumped. In his surprise, he looked at Zach for the first time. Sitting so close, Ryan noticed he had facial hair growing on his upper lip and around his jaw and he was wearing a smile that made Ryan's heart flutter.

"Yeah. Same." Ryan looked away quickly and remembered to breathe. "What did you do in Cape Town?"

Zach shrugged, smiling fondly. "Went boating a lot. Cooked fish for dinner most nights."

"I thought you said you were coming back early."

"I did," Zach admitted, not meeting Ryan's gaze. "I've actually been back for a week now. I just... I couldn't come and see you."

Ryan flinched. "Why?"

"I met a girl."

Ryan felt as if someone had hit him in the stomach. Zach's smile fell away, and he didn't look very happy about it. "She's the daughter of my mother's friend. Her name's Trisha. My parents want me to spend more time with her. So, that's where I've been. With her."

"That's awkward." Summoning his voice was harder than usual.

"Yeah. I mean, she's nice and all. Pretty. I don't know. Our parents force us to hang out and it's just weird. We don't have a lot in common. I didn't even want to date her. My parents got pissed off and made me."

A growl rumbled in Ryan's throat. "So, stop hanging out with her. You don't always have to do what your parents say."

"Yeah, I do. I'm the heir to their business. It's what I was born to do. Sometimes, Ry, listening to your parents is important." There was a bite to his words.

"Not if they tried to run my life." Ryan hated this, and he hated Zach's parents, and he hated Trisha for stealing Zach from him.

"They're not trying to— Look. You don't get it, okay? It's not that easy." Zach looked away, scowling, and Ryan hung his head. This wasn't what he'd wanted. He bumped his head against Zach's chest, nuzzling just under his chin. It was a wolfish gesture, but one he knew Zach would get.

A laugh rumbled in Zach's throat, and his arm went around Ryan's shoulders. "It's okay. We're cool."

"Stop seeing Trisha."

Zach snorted. "I can't."

"Do you like her?"

Zach's chest heaved when he sighed. "She's okay. Hey, maybe you two can meet. That way I can see her and you too."

Ryan shot him a glare. "I'm not your side piece."

Zach doubled over. "What? How do you even know what that is?"

He didn't know how he knew half the stuff he did, but he got the feeling he was too young to know most of it.

They spent the rest of the day together, walking around the park and chatting about their summer break. Ryan wanted to stay out later but Zach insisted he get him home before curfew. After saying goodbye, Ryan climbed the stairs to his apartment. He hadn't told Zach how he felt, but that was fine. He'd still had fun.

His parents were sitting in the living room as if they'd been talking about something, and they stopped suddenly when he walked in. His father smiled but it looked strange. They smelled strange, nervous and sad. Ryan dropped his bag by the door. "What is it?"

His mother patted the couch. "Come sit down, hon."

His stomach churning, Ryan sat down next to her.

"Ry," his father began, wetting his lips. "Your mother and I have been thinking. You know Mom's never getting well, right?" Ryan nodded, squeezing his fingers in his lap. "The medication's helping. But…"

His mother touched Ryan's knee. "Ryan, I feel better than I did before, but I don't like forgetting you or Dad. You know how we said we'd take this in stride. Well, that's not working anymore. So, there's a clinic with some of the best doctors in the world. They work with people like me, like our family. They have coaches who could help us."

Ryan thought this was good news. "So why do you both smell sad?"

His father sighed. "The clinic is in California."

Ryan's heart dropped. "But that's all the way across the country."

"Yes." His mother took his hand. "It is. It would be such a big change for all of us. We wouldn't be in the same state as Grandma. You'd have to go to a new school. That's why I thought I should go alone. I'd be gone for a few months at a time, but I'd stay in touch. Every day." Her eyes watered and her lips trembled. "It wouldn't be forever."

Ryan shook his head, blinking hard. "No." He didn't want to be away from his mother. But he didn't want to leave New York.

Zach. Would they still be friends? Would he ever see him again?

"Ry, are you sure? You'd be in a new school. A new place. You'd be far away from your friends."

"I don't know," he croaked. "I wish you weren't sick."

"I do too." She tried to hug him, but he wriggled away. Running to his room, he locked the door. He stayed up most of the night in tears but in the morning, he'd decided even if it made him ache inside. He wanted their family to stay together, so he and his father would accompany his mother to California.

His mother wanted to have a big meetup before they left, so she invited their friends and family to the beach house. They were going to sell the house, and Ryan wondered who else would live there. No other family would love it like he did. It was his house; it smelled like him, like his pack. He wondered what the new owners would do to his room, what they would change about the house, and the thought made him sad enough to cry.

"This is the start of a new adventure, laddie!" his grandma Rose told him.

"A stupid, scary adventure."

She smiled, raising the pouches around her cheeks. "Aye, all adventures are scary at first. We don't know where the road will take us when we step out into the unknown. But we meet new people and have new experiences along the way. Like The Fool."

Ryan sighed. His grandma was really into tarot cards. He used to think her premonitions were silly, but now he couldn't help wanting to know what the uncertain future held. "Can you tell me my future?"

She grinned toothily, her teeth bright and white despite her age. Drawing a deck of cards from her shawl, she shuffled and her eyes lit up. "Now, this is interesting." She laid out three cards before him. "The Fool. Wheel of Fortune. The Tower. Curious. Now, The Fool symbolizes a journey into the unknown. You have challenges to face and lessons to learn. The challenges are ever present, but what matters is the expedition. The now." She held out The Wheel of Fortune card. "This is exciting! You have a truly great destiny awaiting you." Ryan smiled, liking the sound of that.

"What is it?"

"That's up to you to find out. Now, The Tower, when upright, signifies sudden change and revelations, an awakening. Chaos." A shadow darkened her face.

Ryan frowned. "That doesn't sound good."

"Don't fret, my boy." Her hand was soft and leathery when she took his arm, but it trembled. "Good can come from chaos. From chaos comes creation. In times of strife, we must turn to those we love and support one another through trying times. But this great destiny we spoke of too... it may be the salvation to the chaos ahead. How fascinating..."

"Mom?" His father stood nearby. He wore a strange expression on his face. "What are you doing?"

"The boy wished to know his future."

"He's too young, Mother." His father's voice was sharp. He gave her a look, as if he were speaking without saying a word, probably through the bond connecting him to Gran.

"I hope I didn't worry you, lad." His grandma looked worried.

Ryan shook his head. "Nah. This was really cool. Grandma says I have a great destiny!"

His father frowned, his nostrils flaring. Ryan quickly shut up. "Come have something to eat, Ry." His father ushered him away from his grandma before he could argue.

He dumped a handful of chips on his plate. "Dad, what gives? We were just having fun."

"You're too young. Why do you need to know about fortunes and magic? Gran should allow you to be a boy. While you still can." His father clenched his jaw and tried to smile. "Sorry. I didn't mean to lose my temper. Don't worry about it, Ry. Okay?" He patted Ryan's shoulder.

The door opened behind his father, and the sight of Zach made Ryan sad and happy in equal measure. Until a girl walked in behind him, tall, brunette, and plain-faced. She put her arm through his and laughed at something he said, and Ryan's wolf howled a song of fury and despair in his heart.

Zach would forget about him. He had a girlfriend. Soon they would be miles apart and their friendship would fade. Ryan turned away before Zach could meet his eyes, pain twisting in his chest like a knife. He ran out the back door and scaled the fence, then ran through the trees. The beast howled and thrashed inside him, extending his claws and sharpening his fangs. He was breathless when he reached the beach. Waves crashed and gulls cried. His wolf calmed and Ryan slumped in the sand, drawing his knees to his chest. He closed his eyes tight, but the girl and Zach were burned into his memory. Tears stung his eyes.

"Ry?"

His breath caught. Zach stood behind him, his chest rising and falling, his braids long and loose around his shoulders.

"Ry, come on. This is our last day together. Don't ignore me."

His words struck Ryan in the heart. He swallowed around the ache in his throat, wiping away tears with his arm. "You'll stay in touch, right? 'Cause I will. I'll call every day, so you better answer."

"I will. Ry, I will." Zach knelt in the sand, uncomfortably close. Ryan couldn't hide anything from him. He felt as bare as if he'd just come out of his shift. "Why wouldn't I?"

Anger made him clench his teeth. "'Cause you have her."

"Trisha?" Zach laughed. "Ry, we're just friends."

"Dude, come on. She's into you. Can't you tell?"

Zach's eyes widened. "No way. And even if she was, you and I are friends, Ry. That's not gonna change just 'cause I have a... friend who's a girl."

Rolling his eyes, Ryan sniffed. "You're pretty thickheaded about stuff, Zach."

Zach sighed. "Like what?"

Ryan's chest tightened and suddenly he was too scared to speak. "Everything," he said unhelpfully. His voice quavered. He hoped Zach didn't hear it.

"And you're annoying." Zach smiled, and Ryan wanted to kiss him. Instead, he picked up a stone and hurled it into the water. It sucked. It totally sucked. He wouldn't see Zach forever, and he couldn't even kiss him goodbye. The stone bounced off the surface and skipped over the waves before disappearing.

"That was pretty cool. Let me try." Zach tossed a rock in, and it sank. He pouted and Ryan laughed.

"Like this." His fingertips brushed Zach's arm, angling his wrist.

Zach's stone bounced over the waves, and he grinned triumphantly. For a time, they said nothing, even though Ryan felt he had a lifetime's worth of things to say. He didn't know how to say any of it, though. The sun hung lower in the sky and Ryan wished it would stay there forever. That the day didn't have to end. That he and Zach could stay together.

"Promise you'll call."

"I will."

"Promise you won't..." Tears burned Ryan's eyes. He balled his hands into fists, trying to be strong. "That you won't forget about me."

Zach's eyes glistened and his throat clicked when he swallowed.

The waves crashed over their feet and pulled away from the shore. Ryan threw his arms around Zach's waist, burying his face in his chest. With a catch in his breath, Zach hoisted him up and Ryan clung to him. Zach held him tight, his tears damp on Ryan's shoulder. "I won't forget you, Ry. I promise."

The sun silhouetted them before it disappeared beyond the ocean.

CHAPTER 6

THIS IS FOR YOU, LITTLE DUDE

FIFTEEN YEARS LATER

SO MUCH HAD CHANGED in Ryan's twenty-eight years. Ryan's family had returned to NYC after three years in Cali. His mother had received all the help she could, and they'd left Cali with coping strategies from her coach. She had her good days and her bad days, but their family took it all in stride. Ryan had trained at The Lycanthrope Academy with Zach and for four years, they'd studied to become agents dedicated to serving NYC's shifter community.

Zach had struck out from his family to join the Lycanthrope Protection Agency after meeting Gabe Reyes, who he'd crushed hard on all through Academy training. It wasn't until a few years after graduation that Zach finally worked up the nerve to tell Gabe how he felt. That hadn't been a good day for Ryan. Even though Gabe was a nice guy, he'd clearly had priorities in his life and Zach hadn't been one of them.

They'd dated for three months. Since they were all agents at the LPA, Ryan had to see them at work every day, being sappy, and it had killed him inside. After Gabe found his mate, they'd broken up. That had been a rough time for Zach, but it had been over three years now, and Zach was finally over Gabe, to Ryan's relief.

Ever since he was a boy, Ryan and his wolf had known who Zach was to him. Zach was his mate, even if he didn't have a special scent to tell him, Ryan didn't need it. Life had proven time after time they were meant to

56

be. Lovers and friends had come and gone. They'd faced dangers, romantic rivals, and loss, but though the universe had tried, nothing could kill his wolf's song for Zach. They were fated mates, and nothing could shake Ryan's belief in that. All he had to do was prove it to Zach and at long last, he had his chance. Zach was single now. So was Ryan. It was time for them to have a shot at happiness.

He had no idea if Zach shared his feelings but he was tired of seeing Zach get hurt by the wrong guys. If Zach could date jerk after jerk, then Ryan figured he at least stood a small chance.

Dread sat heavy on his chest when he woke, fear and uncertainty facing off against excitement and hope in a tango to the death. Today was the day he was finally going to confront the love of his life and tell him how he truly felt. For so long, the timing hadn't been on their side, but what better time than now?

So Ryan reached for his glasses and gave them a polish. Turning on his ABBA playlist, he danced his way out of bed to "Lay All Your Love on Me." He sang and danced his way through the empty house to the bathroom, where he showered speedily. He fried up some duck bacon and scrambled some eggs and did the crossword, which he got right as always. Today, though, focusing was hard. He hoped that wasn't a sign of bad luck.

Checking the clock, he realized he had to be at work soon. On his way out the door, he stopped to stare at a framed photo of himself and Zach. The photo had been taken the summer they'd met. They were on the beach building sandcastles. Ryan wore big dopey glasses, his hair a wavy bowl cut. Zach was tall and skinny, his cheeks pimply. Young Ryan had eyes only for Zach, oblivious to his parents taking the photo. Older Ryan smiled. "Today's for you, little dude with the world's biggest crush."

By the time he arrived at the LPA, Ryan had already gone over his plan several times, but his nagging doubts insisted it wasn't good enough. Maybe he could ask the pack for advice. He knew they'd love to tease him about it. Behind him, a motor rumbled. The gates opened and Isabella Reyes's purple car drove onto the grounds. She hopped out, smiling triumphantly with her brother, Gabe. They laughed, giving one another a high five.

"Hey, hey, no high fives for me?" Ryan wanted in on their excitement. Humoring him, Gabe slapped him a high five. "What's all the celebrating for?"

"You know the shifter twins we found?" Izzie asked as they walked to the estate. Ryan vaguely recalled seeing two young children wandering around the building. "We finally located their parents."

"She did," Gabe said, nudging his sister. "I just accompanied her to the reunion to share in all her warm fuzzies."

Gabe's mate Max waved his prosthetic arm as they approached the stairs leading into the estate. Several other staff members leaned out the windows to share their applause and cheers. Izzie flushed and Gabe made her bow. Max hurried down the steps and jumped into Gabe's embrace. They shared a slow kiss before Gabe's arm went around Max's waist and guided him inside. Trying to ignore the sting of jealousy, Ryan reminded himself that if all went well tonight, that might be him and Zach. The thought made his stomach tingle.

"Hey, what about me? Don't I get a kiss too?" Ryan asked, grinning when Max flushed as red as his hair.

"As long as you don't mind if Gabe bites you," Max said.

"Has Ben got anything on the agenda for you, Ry?" Gabe asked.

Ryan shook his head. "Nah. I'll probably just hang out in the archives all day." He could spend forever in the library, where the shelves of books and scrolls reached up to the ceiling. The LPA had the biggest archive of werewolf history in the country, second only to the Council. "Hey, anyone seen Zach?"

Izzie sighed dreamily. "Zachariah!"

Ryan growled. Oh boy...

Gabe made kissy noises. "Tonight's the big night!"

"Guys, cut it out," Max said, and Ryan hugged him away from Gabe's side.

"At least someone will protect me from your ruthless teasing." He cuddled into Max's neck, grinning when he felt the younger man flush warm with embarrassment.

"Ry, let go. I need to go check on Luna and Tommy." Max squirmed, pawing at him. "No, Gabe, go relax. I'll get them." Ry wanted to see the pups, so he followed Max away from the others and up the staircase.

Max led him to a playroom within the estate where the children of working parents could pass the time until the end of their parents' shift. Happy howls greeted them as pups swarmed the gate, some big, others small. "Dad!" Luna waved, smiling brightly. She ran over, carrying a fully shifted wolf pup. "Look how cute he is! He's my favorite. Can we keep him?"

Max's eyes widened. "Uh... sweetie, I think that's someone else's pup."

Luna pouted and shook her head, her bushy curls flying around her face. "No, he's mine."

Someone snorted behind them. Thomas, Luna's older brother and Max and Gabe's adopted son, said, "Luna, put him down. It's time for lunch." He helped lift her over the gate and grinned at Max. "Hey, Pops. Still working?"

Max stretched his arms over his head. "Yup. Just a few more hours and we can head home. What have you been up to?"

"Just doing some chores around the agency." Tommy ruffled Luna's hair. "I hope Ben will let me join someday."

"Can we have pizza for dinner?" Luna asked, giving him puppy eyes.

"Sure thing," Max said.

Tommy walked off, hand in hand with his sister.

Ryan chuckled and sat inside the playroom. The pups swarmed him, sniffing, yipping, and climbing all over him. "How do you say no to that cutie pie?"

Max blew out a breath and sat beside him, his back to the gate. "It's difficult. She really wants a kitten. I don't know how to tell her cats are afraid of werewolves."

Ryan petted a pup's soft head. "I don't envy you your problems, man."

"You're really gonna tell Zach?" Max rubbed a pup's tummy.

Ryan exhaled and winced as a puppy nipped his hand. "Ow! Yeah. Unless I lose my nerve. Or my lunch." His stomach gurgled.

Max tipped his head back to watch the ceiling fan. "I was so nervous when Gabe confessed his feelings to me. I was scared he'd choose Zach over me. Can't imagine how you were feeling."

"Hey, I was rooting for you guys," Ryan admitted.

"Now, we're all rooting for you two. I know Gabe and Izzie tease you, but we're all really excited."

Ryan shrugged. He knew. "I guess that means you guys think we have a chance."

"Yeah!" Max exclaimed, as if Ryan were dumb. "You'd be way better for him than any of the other jerks he's gone out with."

"Sure, but do you think he likes me?"

Max smiled. "Only one way to find out. How are you gonna tell him?"

"First, we'll go out to dinner at Hudson Yards, at the top of The Edge. You know, the observation deck. We'll have the most amazing views of the city." His wallet would hate him for that, but it was all for love. Zach was worth it.

Max's mouth slipped open. "Okay, okay, Mr. Fancy Pants, I see you."

Ryan flushed, pleased with himself. "Then I'm gonna take him to a game at Madison Square Garden. A walk in Bryant Park afterward..."

"Sure."

"Once we've found a nice place to sit, I'll tell him how I feel and ask him out again."

Max sighed dreamily. "That sounds great."

"Yeah, I think so too. I hope he'll feel the same..." About the date, about Ryan.

"Even if he doesn't, at least you'll know. But I think he will." Max's stomach growled.

Ryan chuckled. "Give me the pup. You can go eat."

Max handed over the soft, fluffy pup, said goodbye, and left. Ryan sighed, running his hands through her dense fur. "You sure have it easy, don't you? Lots of love from a big pack, free food. You've got the life, and you don't even know."

She blinked up at him, hearing but not quite understanding.

"Someday you'll be dating boys, or girls. Don't jump into it. Love is... scary. Especially when it's the real deal and you've found your fated mate. Not some silly crush. What if he doesn't feel the same, huh? I think it would kill me. I've loved him since... since before I even knew what love meant. And sure, being his friend is great. I'd rather be in his life as friends than not, you know? But that... that'll be a real hard pill to swallow."

The puppy started gnawing on his hand.

"Right. No more grown-up talk. Go on and play. Knock yourself out." He let her run and frolic with the other wolves.

When he looked up, Ben loomed over him. Ryan jumped. Ben was always an intimidating sight, even to those who knew him, with his bushy beard and ever-present scowl. "Hey, buddy. Nice to see you too."

Ben rumbled a wordless response. "Gettin' therapy from kids?"

Ryan shrugged. "I guess so. You heard?"

"Every word."

Ryan smiled a tight-lipped smile. "Cool." And because things weren't awkward enough, Ryan said, "So... you got anyone special you wanna tell us about, big guy?"

"Nope," Ben answered, his heartbeat never wavering. The set of his jaw got tighter and his brows furrowed even more. Asking Ben about his love life always seemed to evoke a scowling response, as if it were a closely guarded secret. Ryan patted Ben's boot.

"Okay. Thanks for sharing. So, boss, since I've been a fantastic employee lately, how about letting me off a bit early with Zach?" He grinned his biggest grin.

Ben sighed. "Just this once."

Ryan gave him a thumbs-up. "You're the best, Alpha Stroud."

The older wolf just grunted.

Ryan figured he'd worn out his welcome. He'd really stepped on Ben's toes when he'd asked about his love life. He hadn't seen Ben date anyone in all the years he'd known him. Seriously, when was the last time the guy had even—

Ryan quickly cut that thought off because he really didn't care about Ben's sex life. He patted Ben's shoulder as he swept past.

"Ry," Ben said.

He looked back. "Yeah?"

Ben offered a smile. "Have fun tonight. And if you back out of telling Zach how you feel, I'll never let you hear the end of it. Got it? You... deserve to be happy. All right?"

Now didn't that just make Ryan feel warm and fuzzy?

"Thanks, Ben."

"Good luck."

Ryan exhaled. "Thanks." He couldn't help thinking he would need it.

Chapter 7

It Felt Like a Date

It surprised Zach when Ben came to him in one of the exam rooms. He'd just finished a Humanity Restorative Treatment with a patient. She still refused to shift to a human, but she was making good strides.

"What's up, Ben?" Zach asked, locking the wolf back in her cage.

Ben shrugged. "It's been quiet around here today. You and Ry can leave early if you want."

Zach was surprised. "You sure?" He wouldn't complain. Today had been slow but it was always a good thing when fewer werewolves needed help.

Motioning to the door, Ben said, "Go ahead."

"Thanks, man." Zach couldn't believe he had the rest of the evening off. The first thing he'd do when he got home was pull on some loose-fitting sweats and watch the upcoming game, maybe eat some pizza pockets... He wished he could see the game in person, but he'd never liked to take time off work for personal pleasures.

"Have fun tonight," Ben said, giving him an oddly excited smile.

Zach cocked his head. "Hey. What's with you?"

Ben cleared his throat. "Don't know what you mean."

Feeling confused, Zach pointed at him. "Something's up with you. Do you know something I don't? Wait. Why are you letting Ryan and me leave together?"

Coughing, Ben said, "So, we haven't really sat down and talked man-to-man for a while. How's your father?"

Zach's smile fell off his face and Ben winced. "Sorry. Shouldn't have asked."

A few years back, Zach's father had fallen ill and never recovered. Ever since, he'd been on a slow decline toward the end of his life. Shuffling his feet, Zach said, "He's... he's hanging in there, you know? He's lived way past the doctor's expectations, but I'll be amazed if he makes it through to the end of this summer. I've hardly seen him since he got sick. He's shut out pretty much everyone except Mom."

Ben grimaced. "I'm real sorry to hear that."

Zach shrugged, finding it hard to look at him. "I've made my peace with it." It was more or less the truth. He didn't want to think too hard on it unless he had to.

Closing the distance, Ben squeezed Zach's shoulder. "You'll always have a home here, Zach. A family. No matter what happens, okay?"

Dismayed by the sting of tears, Zach blinked fast. "Yeah. Yeah, man. I know. Thanks." He gave Ben's forearm a squeeze.

Ben's mustache twitched when he smiled. "Go on. Get outta here. See you tomorrow."

With the cracks in his heart soothed, Zach left Ben's side with a smile on his face and hurried out the door, heading for his locker. Ryan was in the changing room just off the gym, grabbing his belongings from his own locker. "Hey," Zach said, entering his lock combo and swinging open the door.

Ryan's eyes went wide. "Yo."

Zach snorted. "Yo, yo, yo, my dude. My broseph, my main man, my bestie, my dawg."

Doubling over with a laugh, Ryan said, "So fucking lame."

Zach laughed along, grabbing his backpack. "Watching the game tonight?"

Ryan was taking an awfully long time getting his stuff. "You bet. Go, Timberwolves!"

He howled, grinning as he slammed the locker door. "Man, I wish I could see the game. It sucks that the first time I actually get off early, the tickets are all sold out."

"Actually…" Ryan stood. He had that look on his face, like he was trying not to smile and failing, and his hands were behind his back. "I asked Ben to let us off early."

"Why?" Zach asked, pleasantly surprised.

Ryan held up two tickets as a grin broke across his face. "'Cause you work harder than anyone else, except maybe Ben. And you deserve a break."

Zach's jaw dropped. No way. No way… "Are those—" He snatched the tickets out of Ryan's hand. Two tickets to the Timberwolves tonight, front row seats. Zach laughed, unable to believe it. "Holy crap, Ry! I love you, man!"

The sweetest, dopiest smile burst across Ryan's face and he looked away, scuffing the ground with his toe. The rush of affection Zach felt wrapped tight around his heart, and he tugged Ryan close without another word. Zach held him there against his chest, tight and close, the bond between them bright and warm as summer sunshine. It felt right, having him so close.

"Thank you." Zach squeezed the back of Ryan's neck.

"You're welcome." Ryan sounded as if he had Zach's T-shirt in his mouth. The tips of his ears were red. He patted Zach's chest as he stepped out of his arms, his face the color of a tomato.

"Let's do this," Ryan said, as if he didn't know his face looked ready to melt. "I got us reservations at this amazing restaurant, so we'll head there first and catch the game right after."

Zach was stunned—Ryan had put so much thought into tonight. "Who are you and what have you done with Ryan Kelly? Where're we eating?"

Ryan shrugged. "It's a surprise, but it's also in Manhattan and the reservation is in an hour and a half, so we gotta go. Like, now!"

They bolted from the changing room, laughing as the staff watched them like they were a couple of rowdy kids. They raced each other out the door, the summer sunshine beating down on their backs as their feet pounded the pavement. Zach beat him to his car. "Beat you."

Ryan huffed, his hair windswept and his glasses slipping off his nose. "By five seconds. Wow!"

Zach tousled his hair. It was soft and slightly damp between his fingers. Ryan batted his hand away and warmth bloomed in his chest. Touching Ryan, being touched by him—it felt natural and warm.

They left the agency behind and drove among island greenery. After a lighthearted argument over whose playlist to choose from, they settled on Queen and drove to Freddie Mercury's voice, singing along to what they knew.

"Hey, can you crank the AC up? It is *hot* out there." With a sigh, Ryan wiped sweat from his brow, grasping the hem of his striped shirt and flapping it to cool off his chest. The shirt rose, giving Zach a glimpse of Ryan's soft stomach and his happy trail disappearing beneath the waistline of his chinos. His skin was lightly tanned from time in the summer sun and dotted with freckles.

"S-sure." Zach looked away, his stomach fluttering from the sensations that peachy, freckled skin stirred. He could still remember the exact moment he'd realized how deep his feelings for Ryan really went.

Two years after Ryan moved away, Zach visited him in Cali. Ryan met Zach at the airport with his dad in the car. He leaned out the window, freckled and suntanned, his wavy brown hair windswept. Had Ryan always been handsome? He'd been skinny and awkward as a kid. Now he had a jawline Zach could cut himself on. A bit of scruff that caught the sunlight. Long lashes that framed green, green eyes. The bond between them surged with joy and excitement and made Zach's heart skip. At Ryan's wave, Zach bounded to the car and climbed into the back seat with him. Ryan wrestled him into a hug, clapping him on the back. "Have a good flight?"

"Yeah. Hardly any turbulence."

They drove to Ryan's house. Declan asked Zach questions, and Ryan talked his ear off about everything under the sun. He had grown some more, Zach realized as they left the car. His head was level with Zach's chest, and he was long-legged and skinny with a square jaw and a face that was neither boy nor man. They stopped at the house long enough to say hello to Ryan's mom. "How are you feeling, Mrs. K?" Zach asked.

"Well, thank you." She smiled radiantly. "And I remembered you! Did you notice?"

"I did!" Ryan tugged at his arm.

"Come on! Let's hit the beach!" Ryan had the ocean in his backyard. A road beyond the house led to a boardwalk that opened to the beach.

"Your mom looks great."

"Hey, just 'cause you and your girlfriend broke up doesn't mean you should date the first woman that shows interest." Zach shoved him but Ryan just smiled and it was tender and hopeful. "Yeah. She's... she's doing great. We all know she'll never be cured. Her episodes are spread far apart, but we know things will eventually get worse." The smile trembled on his face. "But the doctors have given us coping strategies. Things to do and say if she forgets us, techniques to help strengthen her memory. She still... She has days where she forgets Dad. Me." He cleared his throat. "But it's okay."

Zach's heart hurt for him because he knew it wasn't okay. He knew that every time Ryan's mom had an episode, it cut him down, because he would call Zach and break apart over the phone. Confide to him how useless he felt. How he wished she'd never gotten sick. Zach bumped their shoulders together. "I'm happy she's doing better, Ry."

Ryan laughed breathlessly. His hand, warm and sweaty, nudged Zach's. "I know."

"Man. You got tall." Zach could hardly believe it. It seemed like yesterday Ryan had been a short twelve-year-old, clambering all up on him like a hyper koala.

Ryan grinned, his tongue poking out between his teeth. "I know! Finally! I'll be taller than you, just watch!"

(Spoiler alert, Zach thought to his past self, that never happened.)

The sand, almost painfully hot, warmed Zach's feet. Surging toward the shore, the ocean beckoned to him. His wolf whined, longing to come out and play in the water. Ryan nudged him. "We'll shift later. I know you're probably itching to transform." Zach was—it was hard to resist. "After moonrise," Ryan promised with a wink.

Setting his surfboard in the sand, Ryan went in search of a place to change into his wet suit. The board looked new. He'd outgrown his other one, the one with their names carved into it.

Ryan returned, dressed for surfing. Whoa. Zach's stomach did some odd, fluttery thing.

He'd been working out; the wet suit hugged the outline of his chest, elegantly defined with muscle, and stretched across his abs, revealing the curves of his buttocks and the swell of his—

Zach tore his eyes away, swallowing hard. Ryan was a guy... he was Ryan. By the goddess, he was about to get a boner over his best friend.

"You good?" Ryan's touch felt like a jolt of lightning. His hand was warm, his touch tingling against Zach's skin.

He fumbled for words. "Y-yeah. Let's hit the water."

Ryan ran ahead, his board under his arm, and Zach watched him go, the sunlight turning his hair a reddish brown color. Hey, he could think his friend was attractive; he just wasn't allowed to get turned on by him. Zach was eighteen and Ryan fifteen—it wasn't cool. But Ryan was attractive. He was long and thin like a noodle, but he was growing into his looks the way a tree grew into its leaves. He had a nice face and a nice body. It was just one guy admiring how fit a fellow dude was.

Ryan was off-limits.

He'd buried his feelings for Ryan a long time ago. The timing had been all wrong and even when Ryan had eventually moved back to NYC, Zach had been head over heels in love with Gabe. But a lot had changed since then. They were both adults now. Zach had embraced his sexuality and stopped dating the women his parents had kept forcing on him. They'd lived in the same state for years now. And best of all, Zach was no longer in love with Gabe, and his heart was available for the taking. If there was anyone he should be able to trust with his heart, it would have to be his best friend. And yet... and yet Zach held back like he always had with his feelings.

Closing his eyes, he inhaled Ryan's scent. He always smelled good, but his scent had never spoken to Zach's wolf. Then again, no one's had, no matter how much he'd liked them.

He suspected his dulled instincts had everything to do with his up-bringing. He hadn't been allowed to shift like other kids his age. Even though he did a lot of shifting nowadays, his wolf's instincts were still stifled compared to wolves like Gabe and Max, who'd known who their mate was with just a whiff of their scent. In his case, he thought there were three options: he would never find his mate, he had already and just couldn't tell, or his mate was still out there somewhere and would pop up at the worst possible time. He wasn't sure which possibility was the worst, so how could he put Ryan through all that uncertainty? It wasn't right, and Zach's heart couldn't take any more failed relationships.

And yet, Zach felt so good around Ryan he couldn't help but wonder why it even mattered if Ryan was his mate or not. If they got together, maybe what they had would be enough. But thinking about this was dangerous. Ryan didn't see him that way. They'd known each other for years. Surely if Ryan felt something for him, he'd have said something, right? They were friends, and only friends. It was something he'd long since accepted, and he'd learned to keep the fantasies in check—for the most part.

The sunset was staining the sky with orange when they parked the car and walked the streets of Manhattan. Zach asked where they were going but Ryan remained tight-lipped as he led the way up Tenth Avenue. The Hudson Yards, a cluster of elegant high-rise buildings, towered over them. Most of the buildings were offices, but some boasted elegant malls filled with prestigious clothing lines and accessories. Zach recognized The Edge right away, a sky deck atop one building. Supposedly, it was the highest outdoor sky deck in the western hemisphere.

"I've been wanting to go to The Edge since it opened," Zach admitted.

"Where do you think we're having dinner?"

Zach arched a brow. "Where?" Ryan grinned and pointed up with a whistle, toward the observatory deck. "No way. *There?*" Zach craned his neck to gaze up at the triangular deck. "Ryan Kelly, are you for real?"

He laughed, sounding pleased with Zach's reaction. "Yeah, they have a restaurant and champagne bar on the Edge."

"A champagne—wait a minute." Something was different. This whole evening was different. Zach tried to think if there were any special occasions coming up, but Ryan's birthday had been a month ago and so had Zach's. They were born in the same month, in the same week, three years apart. "Ry, what's this all about?"

Ryan checked the time. "Yikes! We should go get our tickets so we can eat and make the game."

"Tickets?" Zach followed him. Their shoes squeaked over marble-tiled floors and Zach looked up at the rows of balconies and crisscrossing escalators spiraling above them. He wanted to take in all the glitzy stores, but Ryan motioned wildly at him. Chuckling at his unusual uptight attitude, Zach followed him toward the elevator. They bought tickets from a kiosk and Zach insisted on paying for them, practically elbowing Ryan out of the way. The guy had splurged on reservations at what was likely to be an insanely pricey restaurant and a game. He had to even the score a little.

Why exactly had Ryan made such a grand gesture? They went out to games, movies, or to dinner at a few of their favorite diners or fast-food joints but never anywhere so fancy by themselves. If they went out to a fancy restaurant, it was usually a pack occasion like a birthday and they invited everyone.

This... this felt different, but Zach couldn't explain how.

They presented the tickets to the ticket taker and got in line to board the elevator, passing several information displays about the Hudson Yards that Zach wanted to read but he knew any more stops would likely give Ryan an aneurysm. The elevator ascended to the top and Zach gasped as they stepped out into the interior of the observation deck. Outside, crowds gathered to admire the stunning views closely, but the floor-to-ceiling windows that wrapped around the room offered amazing views of their own.

They had ten minutes until their table would be ready, or so the host said. Zach wanted to explore the deck outside. Ryan swallowed beside him, looking out the window. "We're so high up…"

Zach nudged him. "Do you feel okay?" He'd forgotten Ryan was scared of heights.

Ryan blinked, wide-eyed. "Yeah. Sure. Oh shit. Did the building just sway in the wind?" He looked ready to bolt.

"You can stay here if you want," Zach said.

"No." Ryan balled his hands into fists, his jaw set in determination. "I'm good. I got this. Maybe." Before Zach could argue, Ryan stepped outside with him. The cool summer wind tickled Zach's skin. A tall wall of glass bordered the deck, allowing Zach to see for miles.

"Whoa!" Zach hurried to the glass wall, astounded by the views. He could see Manhattan in all directions, from the Empire State Building to Central Park to the Hudson River and the horizon beyond. Bridge lights blinked in the mist far away, though Zach couldn't tell which bridges they were. He walked toward Central Park, standing with his chest to the glass. "I could see Gabe and Max's place if I looked hard enough…"

"Really? Cool." Ryan sounded faint. He tugged at Zach's shirt, pulling him away from the edge as if he thought Zach would fall through the glass and be lost forever.

Zach smiled at his concern and humored him, taking a few steps back. "Want to go inside?"

"Yeah," Ryan said and made a dash for the doors. After taking a few pictures, Zach followed him to the restaurant.

"You okay?" Zach asked, hoping Ryan wasn't too freaked out. The scent of unease from him grew less pungent as they took their seats inside the restaurant.

"I think so, I—oh man, I'm totally getting their steak!" Ryan buried his nose in the menu.

Zach chuckled. He was all right.

True to his word, Ryan ordered the steak and Zach ordered a salmon dish. They both had champagne and drank it while admiring the views of the city just beyond their window. Zach sighed. "Not every day you get to see the city like this."

"I know, right?" Ryan seemed to feel better now and looked out the window in awe rather than fear. "Hey." He raised his champagne flute. "To tonight. To us."

His face warming, Zach smiled. "To us." They clinked their glasses together.

Suddenly, there was a lump in his throat as he sipped his champagne.

The waiter arrived with their food. Zach took a bite of salmon, which was cooked to flaky perfection and seasoned just right. He squeezed some lemon over it. Blinking, Zach gazed across the table at Ryan, struggling to figure out what he'd done to deserve an amazing dinner in a beautiful place with his best friend. "Ry," he began, but he was speechless.

"Hm?" Ryan arched his brows, his expression open and welcoming. "What's wrong?" He reached out and touched Zach's hand across the table. They touched often. It was just the way they were with each other.

But tonight the touch of Ryan's hand made sparks ignite in his stomach. It surprised Zach when he could hardly hold Ryan's eyes for long at all without feeling his stomach flop around like a fish out of water.

And he realized then what tonight was. Why it was different.

It felt like a date. With Ryan, with his friend he'd known longer than anyone else. Ryan probably didn't mean for it to feel that way, and Zach realized he was likely overthinking things since it had been so long since he'd been in a relationship. But damn it, Zach *wished* more than anything that this was a date.

"Zach?" Ryan gazed at him, his tongue running over his lower lip.

Zach smiled. "I'm great. Everything's perfect." Because it was. There was nowhere else he'd rather be tonight than with Ryan.

AFTER DINNER, THEY ARRIVED just in time to find their seats at the game. Their team won, and Ryan and Zach walked along the streets, full of team spirit at the win. Zach yawned and stretched his back. Tonight had been a blast, but it was getting late. He turned to Ryan but lost his voice when Ryan looked away, swallowing hard. Nervous anticipation spiked his scent, and Zach's own heart tripped along with his friend's.

Ryan said, "Hey, how about we walk over to Bryant Park?" Ryan's heart was loud, his eyes wide. Zach could tell he really wanted Zach to say yes, but he also smelled like fear, which confused Zach greatly.

Since Zach wasn't ready for the night to end, he said, "Sure." His voice was hoarse from yelling at the asshole referee and cheering for the team. He and Ryan set out for the park, which was seven blocks from the Garden. Ryan said little and kept his head down as they walked, his brows furrowed.

The park was quiet and dark, with only the gentle light of a few streetlamps. The noise of traffic became less oppressive as they walked farther into the park. Zach breathed in and smelled green leaves and freshly mowed grass.

"Check it out," Ryan remarked, not sounding too interested. On the lawn, people had gathered for an outdoor showing of Stephen King's *Carrie.*

Zach grinned. "Sick. I forgot Bryant Park holds outdoor movies in the summer. I haven't seen *Carrie* in forever."

Ryan chuckled. "Do you wanna watch?" He didn't sound like he wanted to.

With a shrug, Zach asked, "Do you?"

Ryan jerked his head farther into the park. "No. Can we walk a bit?"

"Sure." Zach didn't understand why he seemed so stiff and nervous, but he followed his friend deeper into the park until the noise of the movie had faded to distant buzzing.

Ryan stopped, looking around and exhaling shakily.

"Wanna sit?" Zach motioned to a couple of metal chairs and tables nearby.

"Yeah, this spot's okay." It was quiet. They sat and Ryan whipped out his phone and scrolled through it, the screen's light making his glasses glow white. Zach reclined with a comfortable sigh, his eyes closing fast in exhaustion. His skin prickled. Opening his eyes, he saw Ryan looking away fast. Zach's mouth twitched and he nudged Ryan's foot under the table, coaxing a tiny smile out of him.

"How are you?" Ryan suddenly blurted.

"Good. Great. Tonight was fun."

Ryan nodded, exhaling as he drummed his fingers on the table. "Good. That's... good."

"It is." Zach grinned.

Ryan glowered at him, biting back a smile. "Oh, fuck you."

Zach cackled and kicked Ryan's foot.

Silence. A firefly glowed as it drifted between them. Ryan said, "You seemed really down for a while after that Will guy dumped you."

His breath hitched at the mention of Will. Thinking about him still hurt. Zach thought back to Will, as he often had in the few months after their breakup. He'd really liked Will. He was the first guy Zach had been serious about since Gabe and yet it hadn't worked out.

Boyfriends had come and gone, but Ryan was steadfast. Their friendship had been built to last from the day they'd met, no matter what hardships came between them. Ryan himself was still single, to Zach's knowledge. He'd been dating some guy a few months back, but they'd broken up. Ryan deserved better.

Ryan was a bit of an acquired taste, showing his true self the minute he met someone and never trying to be someone he wasn't. That didn't gel with certain people, but Zach had only come to appreciate that about him more and more as they grew older. He just hoped Ryan would find someone who could appreciate all of him. Someone like... Zach, maybe? He forced the thought away, his cheeks heating.

"Screw him," Zach said.

"Screw him," Ryan agreed with venom.

Shrugging his shoulders, Zach willed the hurt to roll away. "I don't get it, you know? There's gotta be something I'm doing wrong."

"What do you mean?" Ryan was stiff, his muscles coiling as if ready to spring to his friend's defense.

Zach brushed a leaf off the table. "Werewolves don't date. We just... know who our mate is the minute we smell them. We don't have to shop around until we find the one we fit with. Does that make sense?"

"There's nothing wrong with you, Zach." Ryan's eyes narrowed, his lips thinning. "Gabe took forever to realize Max was his mate, remember? Max almost freaking died before Gabe was willing to admit it."

"He knew right away, just denied it to himself." Zach sighed, wishing he could believe that there wasn't anything wrong with him. "I don't know, man. I avoided shifting so much as a kid. It really messed with my instincts."

"That's not true." Ryan was breathing hard, his heart so loud in Zach's ears.

"Maybe it is," Zach snapped, though not at Ryan. He was angry at himself for his utter blindness when it came to finding a mate. He always chose wrong. "Think about it. Gabe, Will, all the others before them—"

"Uh, most of the 'others' were girls your parents wanted to pair you up with. Remember?"

"Still." Zach rolled his head back to stare at the trees. "I make terrible choices."

"Maybe you're not looking hard enough. Maybe your mate is closer than you think?" Ryan's phone rang. He ignored it.

"Will was my fault. I never should have dated him."

"He didn't know he'd find his mate. For all he knew, you were endgame. Some wolves know right away. Others don't, like you said, especially if they suppress their instincts like you did all those years ago."

"Do you think..." Zach bit his lip. "What happens if a wolf never finds his mate? Or if he gets rejected by them? Is he just destined to be alone forever?"

Ryan twiddled his fingers, his eyes widening. "I... don't know. My dad always believed that once you find your mate, that's it; you're destined to be together forever. It was a sure thing for him, anyway. But look at Ben. He had a mate, and he left him. No one else has measured up since. Maybe some folks only get one shot because for them, a mate's rejection just hurts too much. I think it depends on the wolf, honestly. How they handle that rejection, if they can keep their heart open for another person to come along."

Zach's stomach clenched. "So, I'm beyond hope?"

Sadness pinched Ryan's face. "I don't think so." Their eyes met. Ryan stared him down until Zach looked away, feeling warm inside and out. Ryan's phone rang again. With a savage snarl, he shut it off. "No, come on! You just gotta keep looking." Ryan looked away, wetting his lips. He exhaled shakily. "I, uh—"

"I'm—" Zach laughed and cut himself off. "Sorry, go ahead."

Shaking his head, Ryan said, "Nah, that's okay."

"I'm tired of it! The heartbreak, the stress. I'm tired of guys. You know, maybe this whole dating thing isn't for me. I don't seem to be any good at it."

And besides, the only person he'd ever truly wanted was the one person he couldn't have.

"You're way too hard on yourself, you know that?" Ryan's fingers drummed furiously on the table. After a moment Zach took his hand

and Ryan went still. Zach's breath hitched, unable to focus on anything except the warmth of Ryan's hand beneath his fingers. When had his hand stopped listening to his brain? All he'd wanted was to ease whatever was making Ryan's scent so sharp with anxiety.

"Sorry." Zach's mouth had gone dry, and his heart was banging against his rib cage. Then Ryan looked up, his wavy locks of chestnut hair swaying over his forehead. His emerald eyes were wide, and Zach felt as if he were drowning when their gazes met. His fingers twitched, and he suddenly wanted to sweep Ryan's hair away from his eyes. What the hell was wrong with him? Like Ryan would ever let him. He didn't see Zach that way.

"Whoa. I'm really sorry. Don't know why I'm so touchy-feely tonight." Zach should pull away. He really should. The seconds were ticking by, and they were well into awkward territory by now.

But Ryan's hand fit so perfectly in his, and the white of Ryan's skin contrasted with Zach's brown complexion perfectly. His hand was bigger than Ryan's, and he felt a stupidly protective urge to cover Ryan's hand in both of his to keep him safe.

When Zach tried to pull his hand away, Ryan tightened his grasp around his fingers. "Zach, wait." As Ryan sat there clutching his hand, the nervousness that had hung over him was long gone. He sat up straighter, his eyes narrowed in sudden determination. The fire in his eyes burned over Zach's skin and left him breathless. Squeezing his hand tight, Ryan said, "Look, there's... something that's been on my mind for a while."

Zach nodded but found it hard to focus while Ryan was holding his hand—Ryan's was so warm and held his with such care.

"So..." Ryan wet his lips. "Can I ask you something?"

"Sure. Anything. Hit me."

Ryan exhaled, eyes wide. "Okay... so, theoretically, right? If you have this friend, and you sort of... like them. You know. You think they're attractive, and awesome, and just great. Would you maybe tell them you're into them, or would that sort of ruin everything?"

That was an unexpected question, but one Zach had ruminated on for years. He gave it some thought. "I don't know. I mean, it's a risk, sure, but would it be worth it, do you think?"

Ryan smiled. "Yeah. He's totally worth it."

Zach's heart dropped into his stomach. What? There was a 'he'? Shit. This wasn't theoretical at all. Ryan liked someone.

Ryan was staring at him, wide-eyed and confused.

He realized whatever the hell just happened with his stomach must have shown on his face. "Uh..." Shit, what did he say? "You like someone? That's... nice." His voice came out cracked and he cleared his throat. What was with him? "You haven't dated anyone since that one guy Ben hired a few months back."

"Tim? Oh man. Don't start. That guy couldn't remember the date the Werewolf Rights Amendment was signed. I told Ben he's gotta let me do the screening next time. Serves me right for dating a coworker..." Ryan laughed and shook his head.

Zach barely suppressed a growl. He hated the thought of Ryan with anyone.

Come on, come on. You can't go there. He's your friend! He likes someone else! You missed your chance years ago.

"Ow." Ryan tugged his hand free and Zach realized he'd been crushing it. "Uh, anyway, this guy..." Ryan shook out his hand. "He's really great. He's loyal, he's always there when I need him. I can tell him anything, you know?"

Zach bit his lip. Who the hell *was* this guy? He thought back to all the new agents who'd joined in the past few months. Ryan barely spoke to any of them. Maybe he'd met the guy on a dating app? Swallowing his jealousy and choking on it, Zach nodded along, trying to ignore the ugly sensation crawling across his skin. This guy sounded great. Ryan was lucky. He deserved happiness, and someone who saw his worth—and Zach hated that guy, though he hadn't even met him yet.

"That's really great, Ry." The metal table screeched as Zach's claws suddenly popped out.

Ryan squeezed his hands together on the table. He smelled nervous but Zach didn't get why, unless he'd sensed Zach was being an unsupportive bastard. He put on his best listening face as Ryan went on. "I'm just not sure he feels the same way, that's all. I'm pretty sure he thinks it would be a bad idea if we did anything. 'Cause we're friends and all."

Zach snorted. "Ry, the guy's crazy not to love you, okay?"

His best friend blinked. "Yeah?"

"Hell yeah!" Zach slapped the table. "You're funny, smart as hell, loyal to the core. Anyone would be lucky to have you."

Ryan's eyes widened. "Really?"

"Yeah." Zach tried to smile. "He sounds like a stand-up guy. You should just tell him, see where it goes." He had to force the words out and sounded like he was choking. "Why haven't I met him?"

Laughing, Ryan gazed at Zach with such tender disbelief it made Zach's stomach flutter. His humor faded. "You're... you're serious right now?"

No. Zach hated this guy, whoever he was. Hated that Ryan looked so tender and sweet when he talked about him. "Yeah. Introduce us."

Why did it feel like someone had punched him in the stomach?

He was such an awful friend. Ryan had found the one. Probably even his mate. And instead of being happy for him, Zach realized he was seconds away from crying.

"Zach?" Ryan was staring at him, face pinched in concern. "What's wrong?"

He couldn't speak. He hated himself for noticing the shape of Ryan's lips and realizing he'd never know what they tasted like. How soft they were. And he was burning up inside with jealousy but to his horror, he wasn't jealous of Ryan's happiness. No. He was jealous of Ryan's friend. Ryan's friend who'd get to kiss his lips and touch his soft, wavy hair.

"Hey." Ryan touched his hand and Zach jumped. "You're growling, man."

He covered his mouth. Oh fuck. He was the worst friend in the world.

"I…" He had to get out of there. "I'm happy for you, Ry. Really. Just…" How did he explain himself? Panic choked him. He had to lock it all up and throw away the key, the way he'd always done.

"I gotta go. There's something I…" At a loss for words, Zach lurched out of his chair.

"Zach. Zach, wait!" A hand seized his wrist and yanked him around. Zach stumbled and caught himself, gripping Ryan's shoulders tightly.

"Is this…" Ryan's brows furrowed and, fuck, Zach knew that look. It was the look he had when he'd pieced something together. "Are you jealous, Zach?"

"No."

Yes. Yes. Yes.

Zach could hardly breathe.

"Of what?" Ryan asked.

Wetting his lips, Zach said, "Look, it's nothing. I'm happy for you. I—"

Ryan's eyes widened, and he looked at Zach in a way he never had before. Like he was seeing the sun for the first time. He laughed softly, and the sound did something to Zach's stomach. "Zach, I love you, man. But shut up, okay? Just for a second?"

Zach shut his stupid mouth, speechless when Ryan touched his face. Zach's knees wobbled and his eyelids fluttered. Ryan had *never* touched him like this before, like he was fragile and precious above all else. He wanted more. So much more. For such a long time, he'd convinced himself he could never have this. That he shouldn't. Goddess, he was so tired of denying himself the truth.

For a moment, they were suspended, inches apart. Ryan came no closer, his eyes heavy-lidded and dark, and Zach's stomach did a somersault. Then Ryan wet his lips, his heart thudding hard in Zach's ears, and he moved in.

Zach knew he ought to pull away. These were dangerous waters. Ryan's mouth looked so soft, though, and Zach didn't *want* to push him away.

But he should. This could ruin their friendship... or he could finally have everything he ever wanted.

Curling his fingers in Ryan's shirt, Zach closed his eyes and parted his lips.

Ryan pressed his mouth against Zach's in a dizzying kiss. The way his small body fit so perfectly against Zach's... His warm, soft mouth contrasting with the rough scratch of his stubble... The gentle touch of his fingers through Zach's curls... Even the awkward bump of his glasses against Zach's nose felt so right. Ryan felt right. This. Them. Together. Zach never wanted to let him go. Why hadn't they done this sooner? What had Zach been afraid of? The perfection of the moment stole all his doubts and fears.

Zach lowered his head a few more inches, leaning into Ryan's kiss, needing more of his warmth, of his taste, of the giddy sense of total rightness fluttering like butterflies in his stomach. He ran his tongue over Ryan's lower lip, soft and springy. Ryan curled his fingers in Zach's green cotton tee and uttered the single sexiest little moan Zach had ever heard. Fuck, he'd never known Ryan could make such a noise. At this rate, he'd be hard as iron, and wouldn't that be one hell of an awkward conversation?

Lips tingling, Zach moved away to catch his breath. Ryan's cheeks were dusted pink, his lips, soft, were a delectable ruby red, his green eyes heavy-lidded and dark as the deepest ocean. Zach had to hold himself back from diving right back in for more, desire blooming hot in the pit of his stomach.

"You just... we just..." Zach's brain was fried and he struggled to put two and two together.

Ryan grinned. "Holy crap."

"Whoa," Zach whispered. "You just—I just..."

Ryan chuckled. "Yeah. We did." That sound hadn't always made Zach's balls tingle and ache, had it? His brain wasn't functioning enough to cast his mind back and remember. "Is that a bad thing?"

Zach opened his mouth, but the words were all jumbled up. His world had just somersaulted onto its head.

"Shit." The dreamy look vanished from Ryan's face. "I freaked you out, didn't I? Fuck, I shouldn't have just lunged in like that. Sorry!"

Zach reached for him, but Ryan darted out of his grasp. "Ry, wait!"

"I should go. Uh... bye!" Ryan turned tail and ran, leaving Zach frozen under the weight of the revelation that had come crashing down on him.

He raised a hand, running his finger over his mouth. His lips still tingled from Ryan's kiss, and the taste of him lingered. His cheek burned from where Ryan's stubble had rasped his skin. "Holy shit."

Well, their friendship was totally fucked.

RYAN RAN UNTIL HE was breathless and sweat was pouring down his forehead. What had he done? He'd just ruined their friendship. Or had he? Zach hadn't exactly pushed him away. Actually, he was sure Zach had slipped him some tongue. The cheeky bastard.

He stopped to catch his breath, his hands braced on his knees. The shock faded, and he managed a grin. He'd done it. After all these years, Zach knew how he felt. Or at least that he could get it up for Zach. He hadn't exactly gone and confessed to all the years he'd spent pining over Zach like a fool. Zach didn't need to know about that embarrassing shit.

His phone rang. He'd put it on silent mode and had three missed calls from his mom. Cradling the phone to his ear, Ryan answered. "Hey, Ma. I'm in the middle of—" Panicking, truth be told.

She sniffled. "I know, your date. I'm so sorry, honey, but this is urgent."

"What's wrong?" Ryan's heart sank. She sounded close to tears.

"It's Grandma, Ry. She's going."

Ryan was silent a moment, stunned. "Oh no. Ma, I'm so sorry I didn't answer. I was with Zach and—how much time does she have left?"

"We don't know. It could be minutes. Hours. But she wants to see you, before…"

"Yeah. Yeah, okay." Ryan blinked away the burning in his eyes. "Is Dad there? You're not by yourself?"

"No. He's with her now."

Ryan exhaled. "I'll be there real soon. Okay? Love you." Ryan hung up, the streets blurring through his tears. He looked up at the indigo sky. "Damn it, Gran. You sure picked one hell of a night to go, didn't you?"

CHAPTER 8

THE KELLY SECRET

RYAN RAN FROM THE subway, breathless and sweaty as he lurched past the doorman and into the lobby of his parents' apartment. He took the elevator to the thirteenth floor and raised a hand to knock when his mother answered the door. "We felt you coming," she said, and the bond between them was heavy with sorrow. Ryan tugged her close and squeezed tight.

"I'm so sorry. How's Dad?"

She shook her head. "He's coping. Just trying to be there and make her as comfortable as possible before... Come in, come in."

His mother and father lived in a three-bedroom apartment in Queens. Family photos of the Kelly pack covered the walls, from his parents' mating ceremony to Grandma Rose on his dad's side and nasty Grandma Helen on his mother's side. There were also photos of Ryan and Zach on the beach and with the LPA pack in stupid poses.

He traced the frame of a picture of him and Grandma Rose in her garden in upstate New York. She'd loved that garden, but after her fall last month, his father had insisted she move in with them so they could look after her.

Ryan remembered spending hours with her in her garden, smelling all her amazing flowers and fruits and herbs, even helping her plant some blueberries one summer. Under her care, they had always grown so quickly. His mother made a sad but happy sigh. "She loved those plants."

He blinked fast, unprepared for the finality of the end of his grandmother's life. "She had this way with those plants. I remember planting with her and just a week later, they'd grown. Like magic." He swallowed. "She's like magic."

"I know, hon." She squeezed his arm and Ryan looked down at his toes, trying to hold himself together.

"She's awake." Ryan's father poked his head out of the bedroom door. He looked exhausted. "She wants to talk to you, Ry." There was a tightness in his voice.

Ryan nodded, unsure what to say. This was his dad's mom, after all. He'd never seen his father this sad before, not even when Ryan's mom got sick. "Okay." He approached the door, trying to steel himself. "What do I do? What do I say?"

"Anything you want." His father held the door for him. "Just..." He suddenly gripped Ryan's arm. "She's going to tell you things, Ry. It's going to be a lot to take in. I held this off for as long as I could, but..."

"Dad, what are you talking about?"

His father shook his head. "You'll see." He heaved a reluctant sigh, as if he didn't want Ryan to talk to Rose at all. "Just know that your mother and I are here if you have questions."

"I know what dying is, Dad. I'm not a kid anymore." Beyond confused, Ryan squeezed past and into the bedroom. His grandma lay in bed, her breath a rattling sound in her chest. The smell of decay filled the room and made Ryan's insides churn. Though a human wouldn't have been able to smell it, Ryan did. He could smell her organs failing, and he heard the slow, tired thump of a dying heart. He sat at her bedside and took her cold, frail hand.

"Ryan..." she wheezed without opening her eyes. Her wrinkled mouth smiled.

"Hey, Gran. I'm here." He blinked hard against the burn in his eyes. "How are you feeling?" It was a stupid question, but he couldn't help it. "Are you in pain?"

"Oh, I'm in no pain, sweet lad," she crooned, her voice warm and Irish. "In fact, I'd rather like to close my eyes and take a nap."

Ryan nodded slowly, surprised. He'd always thought of dying as painful, but she seemed comfortable, oddly at peace for a woman who would no longer be a part of this world soon. In a way, it was comforting.

"Your da told me you had a date, lad." She coughed around a trembling smile, her eyes tired as she looked at him.

"Yeah," Ryan said. There was still some clarity in her eyes, a light, though faint. He wondered how long it would last.

"Did you tell that Zachariah boy how you feel yet?"

Ryan's face warmed. "I did, actually. I'm pretty sure he feels the same way."

"Lad!" she said, smiling feebly. "I'm so thrilled for you. I always feared you'd die a wee virgin and alone and unhappy."

Ryan became flustered. "I'm not a virgin—wait, what does that have to do with anything?" Had he really just told his dying grandma he'd had sex? What the hell was wrong with him?

She laughed, and the windows rattled. Ryan jumped, startled to see the vines along the windows grow thicker than ever before until they almost obscured the view. Had the vines outside just freaked out? He glanced back at the windows but couldn't see through the dense vines growing there. "Did you see that?"

Her laughter turned into a hacking cough. Ryan panicked, ready to run and get his parents, but Rose recovered, panting. "Oh? That? It's simply Mother Nature tellin' me to hurry before it's too late."

Ryan was confused. "What do you mean?"

She smiled, and her teeth were as white and strong as always despite her old age. She looked to the dying roses at her bedside—and they grew, the wilting petals flourishing with life anew. Ryan lurched to his feet and rubbed his eyes. "I'm sorry, what? Did you see that? Tell me you saw that."

She chuckled hoarsely. "I didn't just see it, laddie. I was the cause of it."

On her dresser a mossy plant grew out of control, its greenery spilling over the pot, its roots creeping down to the knobs on the drawers. Ryan's knees went weak.

"Sit down. I'm not done speakin' to you." She was smiling serenely when he looked back.

"Gran... what is this? What are you?"

And she said, "I'm a druid, lad. One of the last in all the world."

There was a buzzing in Ryan's ears. "Huh. Okay. A druid. The people who were hunted to extinction and burned at the stake. No way."

She laughed. "Sit down. I have a story to tell you, one you might not believe. But it's your history, lad, and you deserve to know."

"My history?" Ryan croaked. "But how come I'm only learning about it now?"

Oh shit. His father had known! Ryan glared at the door. His father had known exactly what his grandmother wanted to tell him on her deathbed. "My dad knows. How long has he known?"

"Since he was a lad!" she said, as if he were silly. "Before you were born, I thought your da would be the one to inherit my magic. But the gene skipped his generation. The moment you were born, I sensed it in you. The magic, lying dormant. All you need now is the spark to ignite it."

Ryan's head was spinning. "But magic has been nothing but trouble historically. Atticus, the King of the Druids, abused magic. Used it to bend wolves and humans to his will."

"Tell me, what do ye know of him?"

"I know a lot," Ryan said. He'd studied magical and paranormal history religiously in school. "So, the goddess created the druids to serve and protect werewolves when they left her hunting grounds and came to earth. But Atticus was a tyrant. He was supposed to serve the wolves like the others, but he convinced a ton of druids that magic made them superior to humans and shifters. He and his supporters went on a rampage, burning and conquering territory all over Europe. So humans were all like, 'Fuck magic, it's evil, burn all the witches,' and burned any druid—or perceived druid—at the stake. I mean, I don't blame them for fearing the druids that sided with Atticus but seriously, not all the druids supported Atticus. They didn't deserve to be lumped in with him. Werewolves were all, 'Hey, humans, we know you don't like us, but how about we help you hunt the people who served and protected us and in exchange, you let us live?' and turned on the druids and helped humans commit mass genocide. Kind of a dick move, honestly, but if they hadn't, wolves would have been lumped in with druids and hunted to extinction. So humans and werewolves fought against the druids, and Atticus's reign of terror ended. The end. Right?" Had he missed anything?

Rose said, "Close, lad, but you don't know your own ancestors' role in that history."

Ryan swallowed, both awed and terrified.

"The Kelly Coven served the wolves in those ancient days, as did all druids. It was our duty to use our magic, bestowed on us by the goddess herself, to help her packs navigate this strange new world they'd found themselves in. We were there when Atticus, strongest of all druids, declared he would not bow to wolves or humans. Atticus's actions doomed our kind, and because of his arrogance and lust for power, they hunted us to extinction." Anger made her frail voice wobble.

"But not all of us," Ryan said, gazing at the old druid before him.

She smiled. "Some werewolves refused to hunt us. They remembered how things were meant to be, druid and werewolf side by side, united. So they helped our ancestors escape and for centuries we hid our magic and told the story of Atticus's blatant abuse of power to keep generation after generation wise."

Too restless to sit still, Ryan stood and paced. "Wait, so are there more like you?"

She shook her head sadly. "No, I am afraid I am the last of my kind. The backlash against druids made our ancestors wary of ever using magic again. So generation after generation, they suppressed the magic in our veins until it risked fading entirely. Then, during my generation, my father taught me differently. That magic is a gift, a blessing to serve Mother Nature alone."

Ryan remembered the garden she'd tended, how beautiful and lush it had been. He understood her so much more now, her passion for botany and the environment, all the times she'd dragged him to volunteer to help clean up parks and plant new trees. She truly had used her magic for the benefit of nature and her family. "I believe you," Ryan said. "But is your magic the same magic Atticus used?"

She nodded grimly. "Magic is a tool, lad, and Atticus used his magic for evil. It's what led to his downfall. We all have a choice. A choice to help this world, or a choice to worsen it. I trust you, Ryan, with my heart and soul. And I know you will not use our family's blessing for evil."

Ryan's heart tripped over itself. "What? Wait, what do you mean? You're going to make me a druid?" He stumbled to sit down as the world spun around him. "Gran, I wouldn't even trust myself with that kind of power! What if I snapped and went all Sauron or something?"

She laughed. "I do not know who that is, but I trust you implicitly. You will treat it well, Ryan. You'll use it to aid your pack, as your ancestors did before you."

He could use magic to help his pack? "How?"

She shrugged. "Any way you imagine. You can use it to restore a feral wolf's humanity, to heal wounds, to strengthen the bonds of a pack."

"Did you use it to help Mom?" Ryan asked.

Her face fell. "I offered. Many, many times. But your ma would not hear of it. I was not in good health when your ma got sick. Using so much of my magic could have meant my death. It's not what your ma wished." His grandmother coughed hard, gasping for air, and Ryan took her hand, terrified she would die right before his eyes. "Lad, my time is running out. Will you accept this gift I offer?"

To Ryan's horror, a part of him wanted to say yes, but he didn't know a thing about magic, and he was scared he couldn't handle it. "I... I don't know, Gran." At the same time, the thought of letting such an astonishing piece of his family history die with his grandma felt like a crime. "This is a hell of a lot for you to just put on me, you know?" He laughed hollowly.

"I know, lad. But..." Her lip quivered and she glanced at the door concealing his parents. "Your ma cannot fight this disease for long. Use my magic to heal her the way I couldn't."

Was it possible he could help his mother? "H-how?" he croaked. "I don't know how. You've got to teach me, Gran."

"You will learn. My grimoire will guide you. It's my biggest regret that I will not be there to see you become the druid I know you can be." She extended a veined and wrinkled hand. "Take my hand, lad."

Heart pounding, Ryan took Rose's hand and she chanted in Gaelic. The windows rattled and cracked. Ryan shouted in alarm as vines burst in through the windows and crawled across the carpet. They wrapped themselves around Ryan's ankles and coiled around Rose's wrist. The ceiling shook as cracks formed in the plaster, vines protruding and bursting with green leaves.

Ryan's neck burned. He clutched the skin there and found it was hot to the touch, as if it were being poked and prodded by white-hot needles. His grandmother's voice rose, still chanting in guttural Gaelic as everything shook and the plants overtook the room.

Then Rose slumped onto the bed. Her body was withered like an old tree. "Find my grimoire, lad," she whispered. "Become the druid you were meant to be. You must be ready."

"I... I will. I'll try."

She struggled to keep her eyes open. "Ryan... we are out of time, lad. T-there is a great danger coming... Have seen it in my dreams. My grimoire. Read it. Do what I could not. Find the last sacred grove and destroy it..."

"A sacred what?" Ryan removed his hand from his neck, expecting blood. There was ink instead. The old tattoo of the Celtic triquetra symbol on his grandmother's neck had faded, and Ryan didn't have to see his reflection to know where the tattoo had migrated to. The room spun, and every breath was short and shaky in Ryan's lungs. "Gran? What happens now?"

She didn't speak. Her eyes were glazed over and sunken, her skin wrinkled. Her heartbeat had fallen silent.

"Gran?" He dropped to his knees and clutched her hand. "No. No, you can't leave now. I need you to tell me what to do! Who's gonna stop me from lighting shit on fire?"

Grandma Rose, last of the druids, was dead, and all that remained of her was the magic she'd gifted to Ryan. Magic he'd spontaneously and recklessly accepted. Ryan slumped, panic knotting up his chest. "What am I gonna do?"

His father said, "I can teach you." He stood in the doorway with tears in his eyes, Kaitlyn's arm around his waist. "Your grandmother trained me to succeed her before we realized I couldn't inherit her magic."

Ryan exhaled roughly. "Why didn't anyone tell me?"

His father closed his eyes tight. "Ryan, I'm sorry. I was scared for you. The world is a hard enough place for werewolves. Humans hated magic so much, they burned any perceived druids at the stake. I was scared that if you accepted her gift, you'd be in danger. When I realized what good Rose's magic could do, I realized that my fear was probably what had held Kait back from the treatment she needed. I wish you two could have spoken earlier but the timing was never right. Your gran had books and tomes of spells. She kept a grimoire…" He sighed, a frustrated sound. "I'll gather her books together and teach you what she taught me. You won't be alone, Ry."

"I know that," Ryan whispered. Because the plants were telling him the same thing.

They had voices, little whispers he'd never been able to hear clearly before, tugging at his mind.

The ivy said, *I'm here. I'm here. I'm here.*

The wind whispered through the vines outside the window. It said, *Me too. I'm here. I'm here.*

And as the trees danced in the wind that swept their branches, their scents sweet and green, they all said, *You're not alone. You will never be alone. Call on us. We will always answer.*

They all said, *We've been waiting for you. We love you. Our king. You are home.*

And Ryan wasn't afraid anymore.

THE NEXT DAY AT lunch, Zach gathered with the pack in the cafeteria. A familiar scent brought back memories of soft hair between his fingers and warm lips brushing against his. Twisting to look over his shoulder, Zach saw Ryan standing behind him. He was... wearing a scarf. In the middle of summer.

Zach's mouth tingled at the memory of what had happened between them the previous night. The sight of Ryan made him want to run and hide while simultaneously wanting to throw himself into Ryan's arms and finish that kiss they'd shared. Damn it.

This is why romance ruins everything, Zach thought, wanting to smack himself. But he couldn't do either of those things. Ryan's grandma was dead. Zach had to be a good friend and be there for him, amazing kisses and heart-fluttering revelations about his best friend be damned. Now wasn't the time or place to talk about what happened between them anyway.

He smacked a smile on his face. "Ryan! Hey!" He bounded to his best friend's side. Ryan didn't smell like grief or sadness, but he looked off as he waved limply and smiled heavily.

"Hey."

Zach didn't know what to say. He hadn't known Ryan's grandma, but she and Ryan had been close. "I'm really sorry, Ry. Look, if you need anything, we're all here for you."

He nodded. "Thanks, Zach. I just... Thanks." His voice cracked. "You're, uh... You're the greatest. You know?" Ryan's heart sang loudly in Zach's ears.

And that was when every single light in the cafeteria exploded. People screamed as glass rained down upon them and Gabe yelped, yanking a shard of glass out of his hand.

"Are you okay?" Max grabbed a napkin and pressed it to the cut.

"Yeah, just hurts," Gabe said, sucking on the wound.

Max tugged on his arm. "Come on. Let's stop by the clinic and someone can bandage that."

Ryan lurched back, his face going deathly pale. "S-shit. You okay, Gabe? I didn't... I didn't mean..." He shut his mouth and didn't finish whatever he'd been about to say.

"Holy shit!" Zach said, grateful for the windows that let light in. "A fuse must have blown somewhere or something."

"I'm really fine!" Gabe insisted.

Ryan's eyes were huge. "Gabe, get up right now!" He marched over and wrangled Gabe to his feet.

"It's just a cut!" Gabe said, but Ryan stormed past, using his grip on Gabe's arm to pull him along.

Ben jogged into the cafeteria as Ryan hurtled past him with Gabe, nearly knocking him over.

"What in the hell?" Ben exclaimed, stupefied at the sight of glass all over the floor. "Everyone, watch your step! Zach, alert the cleaning crew!"

Zach's phone buzzed as he jogged out of the dining hall. Once he'd sent a cleaning crew to the dining hall, he checked his messages. There was one from his mother. Zach's heart skipped a beat. His mother hardly ever texted and his father was even more distant. Something heavy sank into his stomach and he knew before he opened the message that whatever it was, it was bad.

Mom: The doctors have done all they can. Your father's going off of treatment. We've both agreed this is for the best. Call me.

Zach lowered the phone, feeling as if all the air was lodged in his chest. A year ago his father had been diagnosed with lung cancer. His father, like his mother, had always been an avid smoker, and he'd believed that his supernatural healing would protect his lungs. He'd ignored his doctor's warnings that abusing his supernatural healing would use up more energy than was wise. Just like the doctor had told him, he'd overexerted himself and left his body vulnerable, and the cancer had taken over swiftly.

The doctors had told him he would be lucky to last a year. Zach had tried to reach out to him. He and his father had never had the easiest relationship. Zach was a disappointment to his father—he knew this. But this was his father, and Zach loved him, even if his father didn't love him back. Instead of using what little time they'd had left to bond, his father had shut out most people except his mother. Zach hated him for it, but he understood why. His father detested weakness. He wouldn't want anyone to watch him decline.

Josiah DeShawn's time had run out. And now, his father was dying.

His mother wanted him to call her. What was he supposed to say? His relationship with his father had been strained ever since Zach had told them he'd wanted to join the LPA rather than follow the path they'd laid out for him. His father had barely spoken a sentence to him in the years since. What was there to talk about?

Zach didn't have fond memories of his dad. Most days, he'd been in his office or at work. Zach knew the faces of his many nannies better than his own father's. He hadn't done fatherly things like shift together and bond as a pack like most werewolf families did. No, if anything, he'd made Zach suppress his wolf to the point where his natural instincts had been impaired.

Zach had so much to say to him, but none of it was kind or sympathetic. He turned off his phone and spent the rest of the day in the kennels, feeling unanchored in a stormy sea as his thoughts warred with each other.

He's my dad. I should want to say goodbye, shouldn't I? Then again, I guess that says loads about our relationship if I'm even debating this with myself...

Zach didn't want to burden the pack with his problems, so he kept to himself. He stayed in his bungalow the rest of the day, alone with his thoughts as the sun set and the skies darkened. Unable to sleep, he tossed and turned long into the night.

How much time did his father have? Surely not long now that he was off his treatments. The illness would consume him, and he would die. The thought made Zach's stomach churn. He wished the decision were easy. He wished he didn't have any hesitation about running to his father's bedside to be with him in his final days. But their relationship wasn't that simple, and he hated his father for it. Hated himself a little too, because if he'd just been the role-model son his father had wanted, their relationship might be better.

His heart raced, making sleep impossible. His wolf panted and paced beneath his skin, wanting out, and Zach craved the simplicity of an animal's mind. Kicking off the blankets, he did away with his pajama pants and shirt. He was half-changed before he ran out the door, dropping to all fours as his hands became paws. The wind ruffled his fur and moonlight invigorated him as he ran. The cool summer wind and the smells of the beach swept all his worries away.

His paws led him to a familiar yellow bungalow. The lights were off within. He pawed at the door, barking when no one answered. Reaching up a huge paw, he twisted the knob just enough so it opened.

He padded through the cool dark, his toenails clicking on the wood floor. Up the spiral stairs, a hallway led to a bedroom and bathroom. The bedroom was quiet and smelled of the soothing scent Zach's anxious mind craved most.

Maybe if his father hadn't been so strict, Zach could tell if Ryan just had a nice smell or if he smelled nice because he was Zach's mate. Yet another thing to be annoyed at the old man for.

He sprang onto the bed, jostling the shape buried beneath the blankets. Zach nosed the shape, his tail wagging.

"Zach. What the… Hey, bud." Ryan smiled sleepily at him. "What's going on?"

Lying down beside him, Zach bumped into Ryan's hip. He laid his head on Ryan's chest, his tail wagging when Ryan put an arm around him and cuddled up against him, his face nuzzling into Zach's fur. "Whatever's going on, tell me in the morning. Okay?"

Zach whined in response and licked his ear. Ryan giggled, curling his fingers in Zach's fur. They fell asleep cuddled close, and Zach's racing mind was finally at ease.

Chapter 9

WE'RE GOOD, OKAY?

In the morning Ryan made them both steak and egg sandwiches for breakfast. Ryan had his bread on the side as usual and ate while Zach filled him in on the situation with his father.

"Damn. That's rough, Zach. That's why you came crawling in last night. I wish you'd just told me so you didn't stress over it."

Zach sighed and took a sip of the bitter coffee. "I didn't want to burden you. Your gran just died." But no, his stupid wolf had decided he wanted to go straight to Ryan, Zach's plan to keep it to himself be damned. Did his wolf's urge to be with Ryan mean something? Was it the hint Zach needed that they were meant to be together? He wished he knew for sure.

"Sorry for waking you up last night. I hope I didn't disturb you."

"It's fine, Zach. Don't worry about it." Ryan nudged his foot under the table. "Talk about bad timing, huh? My gran dies, your dad's dying…"

Zach squeezed his hand without thinking. "It's just another thing we can go through together."

Ryan's cheeks flushed. "Yeah." His hand twitched beneath Zach's. He thought about pulling away but banished the thought when Ryan squeezed his hand tight. For a moment neither of them said anything. Right. They weren't talking about that kiss. The timing was completely off, but Zach still remembered the warmth of Ryan's small body against his, the scratch of his stubble against Zach's mouth, the ticklish sensation of his fingertips on the back of Zach's neck…

Ryan cleared his throat. The air between them smelled like a brothel. Zach pulled away and chugged his orange juice as Ryan crammed a piece of burnt toast in his mouth, his brows furrowing thoughtfully as he chewed. He knew Ryan had to have dozens of opinions on the situation but was likely holding back.

"Spill it, Ry."

Ryan swallowed so fast he almost choked. "Let's get the obvious outta the way. You don't owe your parents anything, Zach. If you want to see your father, then you should go. But if you don't, it's only understandable. I mean, your pops treated you like shit all your life. Don't let your mom try to guilt-trip you into seeing him just because he's family. He sure as hell never treated you like family. But if you're losing sleep over this, you've gotta talk to him. Get it all off your chest."

"You think so?"

"Yeah! He's dying, Zach. You two have years of this toxic tension that's been building and building. If you don't say it now, then after he's dead, it'll haunt you. This is your last chance to unload it!"

A sigh spilled from Zach's lips. Ryan was right, damn it. "When did you become a psychiatrist?"

Ryan winked. "Part-time psychiatrist, full-time friend. Gonna talk to him?"

"I should." Part of Zach feared their last conversation might be as disappointing and hurtful as all their other encounters.

"Want me to come with you? Not inside, obviously. But I could drive you there? Meet you afterward? Whatever works."

Zach would like that, but he didn't want Ryan to see him all sad and depressed. "No, I can do this on my own."

Ryan tossed a piece of steak in his mouth. "You're always looking out for us, Zach. If you need company, I'm there."

He didn't want to put any burdens on the pack right now but being able to confide in Ryan kept him sane. Around his best friend, he could show his doubts, and he never felt weaker for it.

"Just stay at the estate, okay? I can face my dad." Exhaling out his nerves, Zach turned on his phone for the first time since yesterday. His mother hadn't tried to reach him again. He typed out a quick message, telling her he wanted to meet. Her reply came quickly.

Mom: Come to the penthouse. Any time is fine.

Straight to the point, cold and clinical. That was his mother.

"Let me know how it goes," Ryan said, accompanying him to the door.

"Okay." He sighed, trying to smile.

"Zach, no matter what happens, at least you made an effort to connect with him." Ryan's warm hand on his arm soothed Zach's nerves.

Color bloomed in Zach's peripheral vision: roses, their vines ascending the walls of the house. "Whoa. Beautiful roses, man."

Ryan squinted at him. "I don't have—" He turned and panic spiked his scent. "Roses! Yeah, I totally planted those in honor of my grandma. You know, 'cause her name was Rose."

Zach smiled, a bit perturbed by Ryan's panicked scent. "That's nice. They're pretty."

Ryan laughed, the sound manic and a bit unsettling.

"Are you okay?" Zach asked.

"Nope, you're not allowed to worry about me. Focus on yourself right now, okay?" Ryan walked Zach back to his cottage to get his car, his hands on Zach's shoulders pushing him forward. "Call me if you need to. I'll answer. You won't regret being able to say goodbye, trust me."

Zach repeated those words over and over during his long trip to the city. Even if his father's dying words were all about what a disappointment his son had turned out to be, at least he would've tried.

Looking back, his father had every right to be angry. What Zach had done was the closest thing to a betrayal there was in his father's eyes.

AFTER HE AND GABE Reyes became friends, Zach had spent countless dinners at the Reyes family home. He'd gotten to meet Gabe's human mother, Veronica, and his adorable young sister, Izzie. One night they'd invited over a guest Zach hadn't met before. He was broad-shouldered and tall, with a neatly shaven head and a bushy beard. He smelled like a wolf but looked more like a bear from the untamed North. The earth seemed to tremble with each step he took, and his shoulders rippled like he was a wolf on the hunt. It was Ben Stroud; Zach would know him anywhere.

Gabe threw his arms around the older man, and to Zach's amazement, Ben's gruff features softened and he wrestled with Gabe, a big hand tousling his hair.

Gabe said, "Zach! This is Ben Stroud, the leader of the LPA."

"I—I know. Wow. It's so cool to meet you, Mr. Stroud!"

"Quit it, kid, I'm ugly when I blush." Ben was handsome. For an old man. "Gabe's told me all about you, Zach." Zach was stupidly pleased to hear it. Ben allowed Zach to scent him. He smelled like woodsy cologne, beard oil, and the bitter ash of cigarettes. They settled in for an amazing dinner, courtesy of Veronica. Afterward Gabe carried Izzie to bed and Veronica said goodnight, and Ben made good on his offer to drive Zach home, finally giving them a moment to talk. Gabe adored Ben and had chatted with him all evening.

"Climb in," Ben offered, opening the door of his pickup truck. "Where ya live?"

"Thanks. I'm living on campus at NYU." The truck bumped over the signature cobblestones of the Village and the buzz of traffic soon swept the quiet away as they drove to Zach's on-campus NYU apartment. "How'd you and Gabe meet?"

"I've known Gabe's family for ages. They were practically my own family after I moved from Ohio to the big city. I was scared, but the shifters of NYC needed the agency's help. I'll never regret making the move. It gives me purpose, knowing I've made even the smallest difference in a wolf's life. Gabe's been going through a rough patch, so I suggested he study at the Lycanthrope Academy so he could join the agency."

It moved Zach that Ben was trying to make the world a better place. Someone had to. "My dad," Zach began. "He's told me all his life the only way for humans to respect us is for us to be at the top."

"Your pa's a smart man."

"But that's just watching out for our own hides. That's not the same as helping people who need it." Zach balled his hands into fists and realized he was shaking. A fire burned in the pit of his stomach. He was close to something, closer than he'd ever been in his life.

"True." Ben grunted, his silver eyes illuminated by the headlights of passing cars.

Zach looked out the window, breathing hard. He didn't want to become just another rich, privileged werewolf at the top of the food chain while others below him lived on the scraps of human society. He wanted to help people, like Gabe and Ben.

"If you wanna join, the door's always open." Ben's knowing eyes saw right through him.

"I-I don't know," Zach stammered, but it was a lie. He knew. Finally, he knew what he wanted to do with his life.

Ben hummed, smiling beneath his beard. "Well, if you decide, let me know."

"Have you guys heard of the LPA?" Zach asked his parents at dinner the next night.

His father hummed in interest. "Of course. I've met with Ben Stroud occasionally. He's a remarkable man from an excellent family."

He hesitated, his steak turning to a lump in the pit of his stomach. "I want to join them."

His mother stopped eating. His father's eyes widened.

Zach pushed the words out. "I appreciate everything you've done for me. But I want to make a difference. I want to help werewolves who've been hurt by human prejudice." The outrage in their faces nearly scared the words away from him, but he held on fast to his resolve. "I've decided to change schools." Zach's voice shook, but he didn't back down. "I'm going to enroll in the Lycanthrope Academy and study to become an agent of the LPA." He shivered, awaiting their response.

His mother's eyes shone with outraged tears. "How could you? Do you have any idea how hard we've worked to get you to where you are now? How could you just throw it all away?"

"M-mom," Zach began, his heart breaking to see her so upset.

She threw down her napkin and stormed into the next room, slamming the door behind her.

His father was quiet for a long time. "Let me make something clear." His father's voice rumbled like thunder. "If this is what you want, then you'll pay for your own college tuition. With your own money. Not the money we've set aside for you. We will not support you in this decision."

Zach had expected as much, and he'd prepared for that. He'd started working as a busboy in an Italian restaurant shortly after he'd started school. He'd take on more shifts, save every paycheck from his job, and keep himself on a tight budget. "I know. I can do this on my own."

Slumping down, his father shook his head.

Zach tried and failed to avoid feeling guilty. He'd let them down. He knew it.

"Zach, we have worked all our lives to raise you to take over this business." His dad's voice shook with hurt and anger.

"I know, and I let you because I thought that's what I wanted too. But I don't, and I'm not going to apologize for it."

His father abruptly left the table, dropped his plate in the sink, and nearly bumped into Zach's mother as she emerged from the bedroom.

With her hands in fists at her sides, his mother said, "You've disappointed us."

"I know." Zach's throat ached and for a moment, he wanted to take it all back. He didn't let himself. "But this is what I want. You and Dad always talk about being the best, being strong. And that's worked for our pack. But other werewolves don't have it as easy, and I want to help."

His father instructed the maid to clear the table. "This fantasy of yours won't put food on your table, Zachariah. When you're cold and hungry, just remember that your mother and I were willing to give you everything you ever needed. And you chose not to accept our help." He stormed from the room.

Zach stood on shaking knees and paced to the balcony. He exhaled, feeling faint. Then he smiled so hard it hurt. For the first time in years, he felt as if he truly held the city in the palm of his hand.

It felt surreal as he parked outside the luxury high-rise he'd grown up in. He hadn't returned to this building in years. All his life, he'd felt so stifled living under his parents' roof, confined by the mold of the boy his parents wanted him to be: straight, the heir to a land development empire, and dating the perfect pure-blooded girl of their choosing.

He'd never come out to them, knowing exactly how they'd react. They didn't deserve to see that side of him. Meeting so many other gay shifters within the LPA had made him feel so much more comfortable in his own skin when his own flesh and blood family hadn't accepted him. He didn't recognize himself as the boy who'd once called this stone-cold palace his home. Would his parents recognize him?

With trembling knees, Zach eased himself from the car. The doormen didn't recognize him, and their scents weren't familiar. The staff must have changed several times over in the years he'd been gone. Stopping at the front desk, he said, "Zach DeShawn. I'm here to see my mother in penthouse seven."

The doorman called the elevator for him and Zach rode it up, watching the floor numbers tick by. Taking in a deep breath, he squeezed his hands together in his pockets as his nerves climbed higher. The elevator dinged and the doors slid open to a private vestibule.

Zach removed his shoes like he'd done as a boy coming home from a hard day at school with a mountain of homework in his backpack. Wetting his lips, he rang the doorbell and waited. The lock clicked, the door gliding open to reveal his mother, who was clad in silk pajamas. Her hair hung long and unkempt to her shoulders, and her face was free of makeup. Her eyes were heavy and red-rimmed, and Zach's heart broke for her.

Opening his arms to her was easier than he'd expected, and he was surprised when she fell into his embrace and cried. All his life, she'd been the Ice Queen, stoic and distant, but now she was finally being open and vulnerable with him.

"I'm so happy you came." Pulling away, she dabbed at her eyes. She caressed his cheek, and Zach was so surprised he almost flinched away from her. She smiled at him in a way she never had before. "I didn't want to go through this on my own anymore."

Guilt walloped him in the chest. "I'm sorry." He cleared the lump from his throat. "I wish I'd come sooner, but I'm here now." As sad as this day was, perhaps their grief would bring them together. Even if his dad was gone, Zach hoped he could have a fresh start with his mom.

The apartment was the same as he remembered, with a glass-wrapped living room with a panoramic view of the city and a sprawling open floor plan. The vastness of his parents' home made him feel like he was being swallowed. Wouldn't his mother be lonely in such an enormous apartment after his dad died?

"Are you hungry? We have leftovers," his mother offered.

Zach's stomach gurgled sickeningly at the thought of food. "No. I'm good." He glanced around for his father's room just past the living room. He wondered what his dad looked like and realized he was afraid to find out if he'd deteriorated. Suddenly, he was too nervous to see his dad. "Maybe just some tea?"

"Sure. I've got your favorite." His mother carried two cups of peppermint tea to the table.

Zach thanked her, blowing away some steam for a cautious sip. It was too hot to drink, so he warmed his fingers on the mug. His mother had her tea iced as usual.

"He'll be happy you're here." His mother smiled weakly at him.

Zach doubted it but humored her. "You think so?"

She nodded. "He has regrets, Zachariah. About many things. He can't tell you this, but I know he's wanted to see you for a while now. It would make him happy that you're here."

"Can he still speak?"

She shook her head. "He's too weak," she explained, blinking fast. The words settled heavily in Zach's stomach. He would never hear his father's voice again, never hear from his own lips whether he was proud of who Zach had become.

"He's sleeping. It's all he's done for days now. The doctor tells me he can still hear and process information. I've been reading to him. I wish he would tell me if he's interested in the books or not." She sighed, her hands folded in her lap. "He's going, Zach."

He swallowed and looked away, unsettled by how the words pierced his heart.

"Would you like to see him?"

Zach's breath caught. "Can I?" He cleared his throat when his voice trembled. With a nod she led him to the bedroom. Zach didn't recognize his father. His dad had always seemed like a giant when Zach was a kid. Now he couldn't breathe without the ventilator keeping him alive. His body was small and frail, the outline skeletal beneath the sheets. His skin was ashen, stretched too tight over the bones of his face. Every breath came slowly, with such a long pause in between that Zach worried he'd breathed his last.

"I'll leave you alone." His mother quietly closed the door behind her.

The heart monitor beeped, and his father's slow, rattling breath occasionally filled the quiet. Zach sat at his father's bedside, his eyes wandering from the dying man to the picture on the bedside table of his father and mother. His father wore his hair long, smiling vibrantly and in a way Zach had rarely seen, with his strong arms around his soon-to-be mate.

Zach took his father's cold hand and squeezed gently. "It's me, Dad. Zach. I came to say goodbye." The words sounded hollow, their meaning not having sunk in yet. If he'd just been a better son...

"No. Sorry, Dad. You're not gonna make me feel guilty for making my own path in life. I know you disagreed with my choices. I know I disappointed you. But I'm not sorry. I'm proud of who the LPA made me. I'm proud that I'm gay, even if my love life has left something to be desired. And I'm proud of my choices, I just wish they hadn't driven us apart. If only you could see the person I became and love me for it."

His words dwindled, his father's hand growing steadily colder. He thought he saw his eyelids move, his mouth twitch beneath the oxygen mask. But it was wishful thinking, nothing more.

Zach leaned over to kiss a gaunt cheek. "I love you, Dad." He swallowed, gritting his teeth against the sudden, gutting pain. His father had always scolded him when he cried. He wouldn't disappoint his father this last time. "I know you love me too. We're good. Okay? You can go now. I'll look after Mom. I promise."

Sucking in a gulp of air through a tightening throat, Zach released his father's frail hand. He closed the door behind him. His mother sat at the table, dabbing at her eyes. The sight of her tears made Zach struggle to hold in his own. He would be strong for her, he swore to himself as he sat beside her and held her hand. Silently he put an arm around her shoulder and drew her close but as her tears dampened his shoulder, holding himself together was the hardest thing Zach had ever done.

Sometime later, his mother played some of his father's favorite records. Bach's classic pieces filled the silence while they heated leftover seafood jambalaya and drank their way through a bottle of pinot noir.

His mother speared a shrimp on her fork. "As horrible as it sounds, a part of me will be glad he's gone. Seeing him suffer, caring for him, especially on my own... it's been very hard on me."

Zach averted his gaze. He wondered if she meant to make him feel so guilty. "I'm sorry, Mom. I did offer to help."

"Oh, I know. He wouldn't hear of it. Drove his own nurses to quit one after the other. He only trusted me with his care until he got too weak to fight with the doctors anymore. He liked control in all aspects of his life. That's why he was so surprised by you."

Zach snorted, spooning some jambalaya into his mouth. He took his time chewing, savoring the spices and mingled flavors. "Disappointed, you mean."

She sighed. "Maybe at first, yes. He was so excited for you to inherit the business and carry on his legacy. It's what he did for his father. He never had a choice to do otherwise. It was decided from his birth who he would be and what he would do. What you did was foolish and selfish. But I think in his own way, he envied you."

Zach almost choked on a piece of shrimp.

She wrinkled her nose. "I won't say I understand your choices, but he was proud of you. I just know it. Whenever we heard news about the LPA, his eyes would get that twinkle in them."

Looking into his bowl, Zach blinked fast. He hoped she was right.

His mother swirled her spoon through her food. "It will be hard managing the business with him gone. He was my partner in all things." Tears sparkled in her eyes.

Zach squeezed her hand. "You can do this, Mom."

"I don't know how I'll ever complete his final project without him." She sniffed.

He frowned. "What final project?"

Stubbornly wiping away her tears, she stood. "How about I show you?"

Zach followed her to his father's office. His mother spread a blueprint over his father's mahogany desk. The plans were for a luxurious resort. It had to be his father's most ambitious project yet.

"It would have been such a beautiful location." His mother sighed. "But I don't know if I want to do it without him."

The thought of his mother trying to hold the business together alone didn't sit well with him. He wished there were some way he could help. The business was his family's legacy, the culmination of his parents' lifework.

"You should," he said. "Dad was excited about it, right? It was what he wanted. It's only right."

"I suppose you're right." She gripped his hand, a gleam in her eyes. "How about you and I team up and finish his final project?"

"Mom, I..." The part of him that had always longed to please his parents itched to say yes. "I haven't been involved in the business for years. I'm not sure I'm the right choice."

"But this is your chance, Zachariah. Your chance to make him proud, to do right by him. Isn't that what you wanted? It would have made him very happy."

What about what makes me *happy? You and Dad never cared about that,* he thought.

Zach gnawed on his lower lip, conflicted. He had responsibilities at the agency. People were depending on him. "I'll think about it, Mom."

They said their goodbyes at the door, and his mother gave him a container of jambalaya. "Make sure to freeze it when you get home."

"I will." He pulled her close, kissing her cheek. "Love you, Mom. I'll come and see you and Dad again tomorrow."

She squeezed him tight. "I love you too, Zach."

During the drive back to his apartment, Zach mulled over his mother's offer. For so long, he'd been nothing but a disappointment to his parents. He would never regret walking away from them to do what he wanted, but he hated that they'd grown apart. This was his chance to have a fresh start with his mother. The question was, was this a chance he wanted to take? Or would his mother just disappoint him?

It was past one in the morning when he arrived at his apartment. The door was unlocked and a white timber wolf with streaks of black on his snout and the tips of his ears lay on his couch, his shaggy head on his big paws. Zach grinned, astonished. "Ry?" He kept a spare key under the mat, so Ryan must have helped himself to it.

The wolf's big ears flicked, his green eyes glowing. Ryan's tail wagged and he loped to Zach's side, sniffing at the bag of jambalaya. Zach threw it in the freezer, set his phone on the coffee table, and collapsed on the sofa too exhausted to make the trip to his room.

Leaping onto the couch, Ryan took up all the available room as he draped himself atop Zach's body. Crushed pleasantly in the cushions, Zach decided he might as well sleep here. "Can't believe you waited up for me. Did you get any work done for Ben, at least?" Ryan squeaked out a yawn but Zach didn't know how to interpret that.

His phone lit up with a message, and he realized there were several more and a missed call, all muted during his long drive. Stretching his fingertips toward the phone, Zach tugged it off the coffee table. The messages were from his mom and had been sent an hour ago, shortly after he'd left their apartment.

Mom: Call me.

He knew what was coming before he placed the call, but her tearful voice still shattered him. "He's gone, Zach. Right after you left. I think he was holding on for you. So he could say goodbye."

Zach couldn't speak.

"He loved you, Zach. Remember that."

He blinked as his eyes burned. "Yeah. I know." His throat ached, feeling so tight he could hardly grunt out the words. "I'll call you. Okay? In the morning."

Men didn't cry, his father had told him. Zach was a DeShawn and a strong wolf, and strong wolves didn't weep. He'd only really been heartbroken twice in his adult life. Once, when Gabe had broken his heart and told him they'd never have a future together. The second time, it had been the man who'd raised him, who'd loved him in the only way he'd been taught.

The force of his grief left him doubled over, tearing him apart from the inside out. A cold nose bumped his cheek and whiskers tickled his skin. Zach latched onto the wolf, clinging to him as his walls came down around him, sweeping him out into rocky waters. Suddenly, the wolf's fur fell away and warm arms held him tight. Ryan ran his hand up and down Zach's back, holding the nape of his neck tightly as if to keep Zach together.

"I got you. Hey, I got you." They swayed like a ship in a storm, and Zach nestled into the warmth and security of Ryan's body.

"I should have been a better son." The words poured out of him before he could stop them. "Sh-should have told him how much I appreciated him."

"He knew," Ryan murmured. "Your dad loved you. Just in his own way. He held on for so long 'cause he wanted to see you one more time. That's how much he loved you."

The storm died slowly, leaving exhaustion in its wake. Outside, roses had overtaken the window, blooming red and bright. It was beautiful and calming. Zach closed his eyes and slipped into sleep with his head on Ryan's shoulder.

ZACH WOKE THE NEXT day with a headache, his chest heavy with grief—and a wolf sprawled on top of him. He smelled vanilla, cinnamon, and nutmeg. Peering over the wolf on his chest, he spotted plates of French toast on the table. Affection welled in his chest, overflowing until he didn't know what to do with it. He slid his fingers into the wolf's dense fur and held him tight. "Thanks, Ry."

The realization floored him. Ryan had waited up for him last night. He'd known Zach's heart was breaking even as Zach had wrestled with his grief. While Zach had stayed strong for his mother and had held himself together when all he'd wanted was to break apart, he didn't have to be that way with

Ryan. He wasn't used to people taking care of him. When he'd been afraid to burden the pack with his problems, Ryan had been there for him.

"What would I do without you, Ryan Kelly?" he murmured.

Though grief fogged his mind, there was a sense of clarity there too. He knew what he wanted to do, even if the thought left him with an ache in his chest.

Ryan had the day off, so Zach let him sleep in. He left a sticky note by Ryan's plate, thanking him for the food. After debating with himself, he scribbled a heart on the note and ran out before he could second-guess himself.

Despite his grief, Ryan's kindness warmed his heart during the commute to HQ. The agency bustled with activity as werewolves, in both human and animal form, crowded the pool in the estate's backyard, and howls echoed from the woods as wolves hunted in packs. Not that there was much to hunt except seagulls on this island.

Zach followed Ben's scent to the wraparound porch. Coffee steamed in the mug between his big hands and a plate of eggs and bacon was propped up on his knee.

"I heard," Ben said, turning to face him as Zach came up behind him. "Josiah DeShawn left behind one hell of a legacy. You included."

Zach smiled, though it was heavy. "Thanks." He blinked hard and quickly sat, not wanting to reflect too much on his loss again.

"Losing a parent is hard, but it's harder when the relationship was like yours and your dad's. Saying goodbye must have been hard."

With a nod, Zach said, "I'm glad I did it."

Ben's hand fell heavy on Zach's arm. "Take time off if you need it. As much as you need. The place won't burn down without you."

Zach wet his lips, suddenly at a loss for words. "Actually, I want to take time off. But I'm not sure when I'll be coming back."

Ben swirled his fingers, motioning for Zach to spill it.

His heart pounding, Zach exhaled. "My father told me that being a werewolf meant never showing weakness. It meant being strong when I didn't think I had anything to give. Never letting anyone see me at my worst."

Ben regarded him, a shadow of a smile beneath his bushy beard.

"But you taught me to be a leader, and that being part of a pack means looking after those who can't help themselves. Putting others' needs before your own. Relying on others when things get too hard to bear. It means being family. You, the LPA—you were my family when my own turned me away for the choices I made. But my mom needs me, Ben." He looked into his eyes, hoping he hadn't hurt him. Ben smiled, and it was the saddest thing Zach had ever seen.

"Don't tell me you're leaving me now." Ben held on tighter to his arm.

Zach laughed, shaking his head. "No. Not forever, anyway. My mom wants help with Dad's final project, and I want to stay nearby to help her." Zach's stomach clenched. He hoped Ben understood, though his own heart was breaking at the thought of being away from the pack.

Ben ran a hand over his beard. "Zach... I know you're grieving and you want to do the right thing. But make sure this is something you really want to do, and not because you feel obligated."

Shaking his head, Zach said, "I want to do this. I know I have obligations here, but she's my family too. And... I disappointed my father for years. And now he's gone, and I don't want to turn my back on my mother too."

Ben's big hand settled at the nape of Zach's neck. "Enough. I get it. I'm proud of you, Zach." His eyes twinkled. "Just stay in touch. Got it? Anytime you're ready, the door's open."

Zach bumped their foreheads together. "I will."

"Just..." Ben hesitated, running a hand over the smooth skin of his scalp. "Just don't let her get her claws in you or make you feel like you're not enough. You are more than enough."

Struck speechless, Zach swallowed.

Ben grinned suddenly. "Just hope you like going-away parties. 'Cause you're getting one."

Zach's eyes widened. "Wait, what—"

CHAPTER 10

A GAMBLE OF HEARTS

"Surprise!" Ryan cried, the pack's echoing cheer nearly drowning him out.

Zach jumped as a champagne cork flew past his face. Ryan and the pack had decorated Zach's bungalow with balloons and streamers. On the table were plates of burgers, a big bowl of salad, and Izzie's famous tres leches cake.

He smiled at the happiness plain on Zach's face, but the twinge of sadness in his chest couldn't be ignored. He hated that Zach was taking time off from the agency, even if it was only temporary.

Zach bounded through the door and greeted the pack one by one, hugging Izzie and Gabe, high-fiving Eddie, and waving at Vicenzo, who sat on the sofa away from everyone.

It was nice to be around the pack and see them in such a cheerful mood. Ryan had been hoping to have them all in one place so he could confess about his magical abilities, but he could tell now wasn't the right time. Today he wanted to celebrate Zach.

His best friend motioned him over. All Ryan really wanted to do was to crawl into his bedroom and be alone, but he went to Zach and buried himself in his arms. He held on tight, unprepared for the wave of hurt that broke over him, bringing tears to his eyes.

"Hey." Zach tilted his chin up, the molten brown of his eyes full of tender sadness. "I'm coming back. I promise."

Ryan forced a smile on his face. "I know. Come on, like you could stay away!" He wriggled out of Zach's arms, feeling overwhelmed. As he turned toward the kitchen, he caught Izzie's knowing gaze and she smiled sympathetically. Ryan looked away and went to pour himself a beer, the first of many.

"Chin up, kid. It ain't forever," Ben said, snatching up a bottle of stout.

Ryan took a gulp to help swallow down his selfish feelings. "I know," he said through gritted teeth. That didn't mean he couldn't be bummed out about it. He turned around and found Max and Gabe giving him that same sad look. "Everyone cut it out! This isn't a fuckin' funeral!"

Gabe hugged Ryan's head to his chest. "Come on. Bring it in. There we go. He'll be back before you know it, man." Ryan started choking as Gabe's arm dug into his windpipe. He reached out to Max for help. "His mamacita will drive him cray-cray and he'll come home to your sweet embrace."

Ryan tried to curse him out and failed.

"Gabe, you're suffocating him." Max tugged Gabe's arm away and Ryan sucked in a greedy gulp of air.

Gabe gasped. "So sorry!"

"Maybe work on *your* sweet embrace, huh?" Ryan said, rubbing his neck.

Max looked over at Zach, who was chatting with Vicenzo and Eddie. "He's always been here. Always. Not seeing him around the estate just won't feel right." Gabe put an arm around his mate's shoulders.

Ben cleared his throat pointedly. "I know I'm not nearly as pretty as Zach but come on, what am I? Chopped liver?"

Max flushed bright red and stammered, "N-no! Not at all, I just meant—"

Ben rolled his eyes and slapped Max on the back. "Cool it, kid, I'm just screwing with you."

Tearing his eyes away from Zach, Ryan felt his heart racing as a rush of feeling swept over him. He didn't know when he'd next see Zach. Perhaps if he just told Zach how he felt, he would want to stay? Ryan scowled. There he was, being selfish. This was about what Zach wanted. He found a spot on the sofa to drink his beer, hardly in a celebratory mood.

Vicenzo dropped beside him, a beer in his hand. He was scowling as usual and Ryan smirked at him. "Guessing you don't like parties."

"Hate 'em." Vicenzo grunted, taking a swig of beer. Honestly, was there anything Vicenzo didn't hate? Ryan sometimes wondered why he was even part of the LPA at all.

"So, you just came for the free beer and food, right? Not that I'm judging or anything," Ryan assured him.

"Zach's a good guy. Only fair to see him off."

Ryan drank to that, his eyes seeking Zach's tall form. He had the feeling Vicenzo Salvatore was a terrible person to ask for advice, but what the heck, he'd try anything once. "Hypothetically speaking, right? Say if someone had feelings for someone who was going away. Should they confess to this person so they'd maybe return the feelings and decide to stay? Or should they not be a selfish crapsack and let them be happy? Thoughts?"

Vicenzo scoffed. "Subtle."

Ryan glared at him. "'Bout what, exactly?"

"If you were any more into him, you'd be screwing him on the kitchen counter."

Ryan's beer went down the wrong way and he thumped himself on the chest. Face warm, he glared daggers at Vicenzo.

"Don't bother," Vicenzo grumbled, his blue eyes frigid as glaciers. "If he hasn't caught on by now, he doesn't feel the same. Time to stop living in your teen-bop drama. Find some sexy thing on a dating app and forget all this true love crap."

Ryan winced. "Ouch." He dropped his head on Vicenzo's shoulder. "So jaded. Let me guess, you got your heart broken by the love of your life—*Eddie,* if we're being specific—and now you've given up love forever? Talk about cliché." He patted Vicenzo's solid chest and earned a growl. "I'll send you the bill for my therapeutic services in the mail."

"You're fired."

Sometime between his second and sixth beer, Izzie took Vicenzo's place on the sofa.

"Someone's having a good time!" Izzie waved one of his empty cups in his face.

"Zach may suck at choosing boyfriends, but he's always got the best beer." Ryan hiccupped, splashing more beer in his cup. His eyes sought the man himself and found him talking to Eddie, who'd found a quiet corner away from Gabe's and Ben's raucous laughter. Zach's gaze strayed and Ryan's stomach did flip-flops as their eyes met. Quickly looking away, he wondered if that kiss was still on Zach's mind. He knew *he* hadn't stopped thinking about it. Just looking at Zach, all he could remember was the hardness of his body, his warmth, the way Zach's tongue rubbed Ryan's lower lip...

Izzie wore a knowing smile. She leaned her head on the couch, tucking ebony hair behind her ear. "He's been looking at you all evening. I think he wants some time with you alone."

Ryan tried to ignore the fluttery feeling her words inspired. Across the room, Zach met his gaze again. He stood by the spiral stairs and cocked his head in invitation before ascending the steps. Ryan's mouth ran a little dry. "Yeah. He wants to speak to me. Alone."

Izzie squeaked and grabbed his arm. "Go for it, Ryan! This is your time to confess!"

He hadn't told Izzie or the others about their kiss. Word spread fast in the pack and unless Zach was ready to talk about it, Ryan didn't want drama. But now was the time to talk, finally, about what had transpired between them. He had to know if Zach felt the same, if they could finally be more than friends. "I'm going for it, Izzie. Wish me luck!" he yelled to the room, then stampeded up the stairs. The door to the rooftop deck was open, allowing the ocean breeze to curl in. Up the stairs, Zach leaned on the railing. The setting sun burned the sky orange and plump pink clouds smeared the horizon. It was like a sign from the universe: this was his time.

Ryan cleared his throat and leaned on the railing, hoping to come across less nervous than he felt. "Hey. You wanted to see me?"

Zach laughed softly. "You're mad at me, aren't you?"

"No. I mean… maybe a little."

Sighing, Zach said, "I knew it. You haven't spoken to me at all. Come on." He slapped Ryan on the back. "Spit it out."

"I'm just worried, that's all. Your parents were always dicks to you. If you go back, your mom's gonna try to lure you back into the business. Then she'll fix you up with snobs again!"

"She can try. That doesn't mean I'll let her. You don't have to worry about me, you know."

Ryan bumped their shoulders together. "Maybe I enjoy worrying. About you, I mean." He made himself meet Zach's gaze. "Look, just promise me you'll come back. The LPA needs you. Ben's old. He'll have a freaking aneurysm trying to keep those morons downstairs in check."

He gripped Zach's shirt and realized his hand was shaking.

"I'll miss you, you idiot. So much. So you better call every day, and we'd better see each other at least once a week. Or I'm moving into that fancy penthouse of yours and you will never get rid of me."

Zach's lips trembled when he smiled. He leaned in close, giving Ryan's heart palpitations. Ryan closed his eyes, his breath hitching when Zach's lips brushed his forehead and long gentle fingers carded through his hair. The ivy curled over Ryan's hand, and he shook it off before Zach could notice. "I'll miss you too," Zach whispered before the wind carried the words away. "When I think about it too much, I don't want to leave at all."

"You should," Ryan murmured, hating himself for it. He clutched onto Zach's wrists, feeling the race of Zach's pulse beneath his fingers. "It's the right thing to do. I'll be here when you get back."

"Thanks, Ry." Their eyes met and in the moment of quiet between them, the wind howled, answering the song in Ryan's heart. As if Zach's wolf were calling out to him, urging him to answer. "For being there for me last night. For breakfast this morning. For… everything? I know that sounds lame but—"

"It doesn't." Ryan couldn't look away from Zach's lips. The wind swept over the deck, urging him into the warmth of Zach's body. "You know I'd do anything for you, Zach."

Zach's Adam's apple bobbed and he blinked, eyes glistening.

"What?" Ryan asked, alarmed to see him so emotional.

Shaking his head, Zach worried at his lower lip. "No one's ever said anything like that to me before, Ry." He ran his fingertips over Ryan's jawline, his thumb caressing his cheek. Unable to help it, Ryan sighed. Zach's gaze lowered to his mouth, and a butterfly flapped its wings in Ryan's stomach. The orange sunset glowed on Zach's tawny skin, turned his black curls into a deep auburn halo.

Ryan shrugged, trying to pretend his insides weren't dancing a waltz. "I said it because you deserve it."

At last, he couldn't resist standing up on his toes and finally kissing Zach the way he'd wanted to for days now. Zach put his arms around Ryan's waist and drew him close, and Ryan leaned into Zach's chest, blanketed in the warmth of his body. He couldn't resist nipping Zach's plump lower lip and running his hand over Zach's short curls.

He moaned against Ryan's mouth and the sound had Ryan's cock twitching against the front of his pants. Zach's big warm hands rubbed up his back, squeezing his shoulders, then glided back down to squeeze his hips. Tugging, Zach brought their pelvises flush. Holy hell, Zach's cock was like iron against him. Ryan whimpered, unable to believe Zach actually wanted him—that this was real, and he could have Zach in his arms.

Zach pulled away suddenly, and Ryan caught his breath against Zach's chest.

"Are we making a big mistake?" Zach's breathy voice made Ryan dizzy.

He rocked his hips and Zach shuddered as their erections rubbed together. "These guys don't seem to think so. I think we should listen to them."

Zach bit his lip, his brow furrowed in concern. "Ry... I've been thinking about this for days."

Ryan swallowed hard. "Yeah?" He palmed the tent in Zach's jeans.

A shudder racked Zach's body. "Just... hold on a moment."

Anxiety squeezed Ryan's insides when Zach pulled away from him. Taking in a slow breath, Zach said, "Have I ever told you that I can't smell my fated mate?"

A block of ice fell into Ryan's stomach. "N-no. I... I didn't know that." It certainly explained Zach's trouble with relationships, and why Ryan had never scented Zach, too. Not that Zach's lack of scent had been enough to dissuade him. Life had proven they were destined for each other, and Ryan was content with that. But from the fear that soured Zach's scent, Zach clearly wasn't at peace with uncertainty.

Blowing out a breath, Zach leaned on the railing. "It has a lot to do with how I was raised, I think. Because I resisted shifting. So I don't know if I've already met my mate and I just can't tell, or if he's still out there somewhere and that's why none of my relationships have worked out."

Ryan's wolf howled in fury and despair at the thought. Finally, he understood why Zach didn't have a scent, because of how deeply Zach had been forced to suppress his wolf. His wolf couldn't sing to Ryan's like Ryan's sang for him.

"I've thought I've found the one only to lose them. I can't offer you anything more than just a night together. And you're not someone I'd want for just one night, Ry. So, unless you're okay with that, then maybe we shouldn't do this."

A lump rose in Ryan's throat, and he had to look away. Zach didn't know what they were to each other. Logically, the smart thing to do was to call this off and avoid any risks to Ryan's heart. And yet, Ryan's wolf had known who Zach was to him the day they met. Special scent be damned, *Ryan* and his wolf knew because life had proven time and again they were meant to be. For Ryan, that was enough. But it wasn't enough for Zach.

Ryan was an optimist, but Zach was practical. After all the heartbreaks he'd endured, he wanted proof, and Ryan couldn't fault him for that.

By being with Zach, Ryan was gambling with his heart. The only question was whether this was a risk he was willing to take—and damn it, he and his wolf had made that decision when he was a kid.

"Fuck. Ryan, what if we both end up getting hurt?"

He hated that Zach couldn't see his own worth. "You can't mess this up. There's nothing you can do to scare me off." He grasped Zach's hand and led it past his hips, letting Zach feel just how much he truly meant that. "I want you, Zach. Want you so badly." Nothing between them could ever be a mistake. They were meant to be together and if Zach didn't realize that now, Ryan had faith he would.

Zach's eyes widened. "What if I just disappoint you?"

Growling, he took Zach's chin in his hand. "Hey. You won't disappoint me. You can't. Zach, nothing about you could ever be a disappointment."

Zach's eyes, heavy-lidded and dark with desire, strayed from Ryan's face. "Ry, if I lost you—"

Ryan took Zach's face in his hands. "You won't. Not ever." Goddess, he loved this man, but Ryan couldn't just unload years of love on Zach by confessing, not when Zach was so anxious. It would freak him out. That confession would have to wait until Zach was ready to hear it, but that didn't mean they needed to remain in limbo.

"Look... How about we just try it. Okay?"

Throat bobbing as he swallowed, Zach gazed at Ryan's lips but the two of them were like the opposite ends of a magnet while Zach warred with himself. "Give sex a try? Ry, sex isn't like a shoe. You can't try it on and return it if you decide you don't like it. It changes things."

"We both want this so let's just give it a go and if it makes things weird..." Ryan stopped, having trouble getting the words out. If Zach decided they were better as friends, it would kill him. Would he really be okay with being just friends again after finally having his fantasies come true? He didn't know, but unless they tried, he'd never be certain. "If things get weird, we can go back to the way things were. I promise." It was risky, but he trusted that they were meant to be. Tonight could only change things for the better. He just had to get his wary mate to see that.

Zach sighed. "It's not that simple."

"But what if it works for us?" Ryan blurted, gripping Zach's hands. "What if this leads to something incredible! Zach, we're already so good as friends. We would be amazing together. Isn't that worth the risk?"

"I wish I had your confidence." Zach worried his lower lip, and Ryan wrestled the urge to stop him before he broke the skin. "Can your wolf scent mine, is that why you're so sure?" Tentative hope lit up Zach's eyes.

Ryan had to work hard to say the words he knew would disappoint him. "No, Zach. Maybe it's because you suppressed your wolf, but I can't scent you."

Zach's shoulders slumped. "Oh." His voice trembled.

Ryan could groan at the thought of being so close to having Zach, only to lose him to self-doubt. Who knew when they'd have time to see each other after tonight?

"Listen to me." Ryan took his hands and squeezed. "You and me, we're built to last. I don't need a scent to tell me that so if you can't trust yourself, then trust me."

"I want to, Ry." Worry creased Zach's brow. "But that's what I thought when Gabe and I—"

A blast of sound came from downstairs as the pack started playing "Hungry Like the Wolf." Because of course they chose that song. Ryan groaned and Zach slumped against his shoulder.

"The pack." Zach sighed. "They threw this party for me. I can't just ditch them so we can run off and... uh..." He tried to wriggle away.

Ryan tugged Zach back toward him. "Yes, you can ditch them so we can run off and uh. Send them a card or something."

Zach frowned and moved away. "I can't do that."

"Yes, you can!" Ryan hit his head against Zach's seriously hard chest. At this point he was so desperate for Zach he thought he'd sever all ties with their pack if it meant he and Zach could have an evening alone doing all the things Ryan had fantasized about doing to his best friend for years.

"Fine! Ugh, why do you have to be such a nice guy all the time?" Ryan grumbled. Zach deserved to spend time with the pack too. Those assholes. "But I'm not sticking around to watch Izzie and Vicenzo do tequila shots. If you've decided, come and meet me at my place, okay?" It was more than a question. He was laying his heart in Zach's hands. He wanted Zach in his bed, but he didn't want doubt there with them. Either Zach would see him tonight and they could settle years of unspoken feelings, on his part at least, or Zach could leave him alone to nurse a broken heart. Whatever happened, he wanted it to be Zach's choice.

Unable to look him in the eyes and wait for a response, Ryan forced himself to turn away, hoping Zach didn't notice the way his knees trembled.

CHAPTER 11

CROSSING THE LINE

Zach couldn't wait for the party to end. He felt guilty for feeling that way after his friends had gone to such an effort for him. But he also couldn't lie to himself; he'd been thinking about that kiss he and Ryan had shared in Bryant Park for days, though he knew he shouldn't. Sex and friendship didn't mix. It was a tempting offer; he and Ryan were so close already and so far, just kissing him had been explosive, not at all awkward like things should have been. When they finally did more than kiss, he could only imagine how good it could be...

Zach winced, wanting to hit himself. He was really considering this, really willing to put their friendship on the line. But what if Ryan was right, and tonight lead to something so much more than just sex?

"Who pissed in your margarita?" Gabe asked, plopping down on the sofa beside him. The music nearly drowned out Gabe's teasing. Over in a corner, Izzie and Eddie, both drunk off their asses, were singing along to ABBA. Vicenzo looked like he was in the seventh layer of hell. At the breakfast bar, Ben and Max were laughing as Eddie's voice cracked hilariously on the chorus.

Zach downed the last sip. It really wasn't that bad, though Izzie had overdone it on the citrus. "Let me ask you something." He needed advice before he jumped into bed with his best friend. Someone to talk him down. Even tipsy, Gabe tended to be more thoughtful than Izzie, who after a few drinks thought robbing a bank was a great idea.

"Shoot," Gabe said, facing him pretzel-legged.

Zach exhaled. "There's this guy."

"Uh-huh." Gabe licked at the chili pepper salt rim on his glass.

"He and I have been friends for a while. Now I think I'm actually into him, and tonight we're supposed to meet and…"

Gabe grinned. "Ryan."

Zach choked on the lime wedge and coughed like he was trying to hack up a lung. It took Ben performing the Heimlich maneuver and nearly cracking Zach's rib cage to dislodge the murderous fruit and send it slapping wetly against the window.

Zach rubbed his throat, gasping.

"The hell'd you swallow the lime for?" Vicenzo glared at him.

"I didn't mean to!" Zach rolled his eyes.

Izzie rubbed his shoulders. "My drinks are that good, huh? Time for another!" She whizzed off to the kitchen.

The pack dispersed and Gabe rubbed his fingers against his eyes. "Sorry, man. Didn't mean to almost kill you."

Zach coughed, his eyes still watering.

Gabe bobbed his brows. "I'm right, huh? That's why he left, isn't it?"

Slumping against the couch, Zach said, "I'm not saying anything."

"Don't have to. His scent is all over you." Gabe slapped his back. "You dog. I'm happy for you. For both of you."

Zach made a face. Gabe was encouraging this craziness? "I'm sorry. Maybe I oughta go talk to your sister. She's got more sense than you tonight."

Gabe looked wounded and tugged Zach back into his seat when he tried to rise. "Hey, come on. Zach, this is great. You and Ry, it just makes sense."

"It does?"

"Are you kidding? You two would be amazing together. I'd totally give this a chance."

Shaking his head, Zach said, "I'm bad at love, Gabe. Look at what happened to us. Look at all my relationships."

Gabe waved a hand. "Yeah, we were a mistake. A sexy mistake."

Zach chuckled. "That's true."

A few years after graduation, Zach and Gabe had hooked up. It was a mistake, though for Zach it had been a dream come true. Gabe had been dealing with a lot of grief and trauma, lost in the pain of his past, and he'd put up a wall between them after their first night together. To cheer Zach up, Ryan had invited him on a trip to London. He'd called it American Werewolves in London, because of course Ryan had named their trip.

While there, Zach had gone to visit a seer Gabe had raved about, claiming she was the real deal. She'd shown Zach a vision that had changed everything. A vision of him and Gabe in a beautiful house upstate. A little girl in a pink cowboy hat had run into Zach's arms, and the bonds of pack and family and love had surged in Zach's heart. She loved him. He was her pack. Her family. Gabe had smiled at them, and all the darkness in him was gone.

Zach had known that he would wait forever for that future, for that family.

But it hadn't been at all like he'd thought.

The hope of their eventual union had kept Gabe and Zach coming back to each other for three months. No matter how far apart they strayed, no matter who else filled the spaces between, they collided time and again. Gabe had tried to be the man Zach deserved, and Zach had wanted to be the one to see him through his darkness into the light.

But all that hope had ended the day Gabe met Maxwell Gallagher. Their connection had been... instantaneous. The moment Gabe had shown the frightened red wolf his scars, scars they both shared, Zach had realized that, through the wounds of their past, they had a connection he and Gabe would never have.

Max simply understood Gabe, and Gabe understood Max. He didn't have to hold him and kiss him to make Gabe's pain go away. He hadn't struggled to breach the barrier Gabe had erected around his heart. When

Gabe had put his arms around the red wolf, he'd let Max in to see the parts of himself Zach would never see.

Zach had finally understood. It wasn't Gabe who couldn't give Zach what he needed—it was Zach who couldn't give that to *Gabe*.

It had destroyed Zach for a long time. But Gabe was happy, finally happy. Max's love had rescued him from the darkness of his past. And Zach was happy for him, and since Max was important to Gabe's happiness, he'd vowed to be a friend to Max and to protect him from harm.

Gabe and Max's mating ceremony had reopened old wounds Zach thought had finally closed. He'd forced himself to smile, told himself to be happy for them, but he hadn't been able to deny that seeing Max beneath that wooden arch in front of Gabe, where Zach had once envisioned himself, had broken his heart anew.

Once he'd gotten home, he'd showered, trying to scrub away the ache in his heart. He'd stopped when he'd seen himself in the mirror through the shower door, noticing his long, braided hair for what felt like the first time. He'd been growing his hair out since their academy days, when he'd been young, stupid, and madly in love. When he'd believed that the power of love could save a boy lost in darkness, even if that boy was incapable of returning his feelings. It was time to grow up and move on.

He'd turned on the razor and brought it to his scalp, cutting away the memory of the naïve, lovesick boy he'd been. When he was done, he'd run his hand over the short, curly hair on his head. He hadn't recognized the freer, light-spirited man staring back at him from the mirror.

In time, he hoped to be happier, and he was. But he still wasn't whole, not really.

"I was an idiot," Zach said.

"No." Gabe squeezed his shoulder. "No, you weren't. You wanted a family. You wanted love. That just makes you human, and it makes me an asshole for stringing you along like I did."

"You thought you'd return my feelings."

Gabe sighed. "I don't know what I thought. I was lost." Squeezing Zach's knee, he held his gaze. "I'm sorry that I hurt you. I don't know if I ever apologized for that. But I am sorry, Zach."

He waved a hand. "I know." He'd stopped being angry and hurt a long time ago. "I still do want a future like the one I saw," Zach admitted. "I would love a family like you and Max have." The little girl from the seer's vision had turned out to be Gabe and Max's adopted daughter, Luna. Even if Zach wasn't her father, he was still happy to be Uncle Zach.

Gabe chuckled. "I mean, you can borrow the kids sometime if you want."

Zach smiled.

"Zach, you and Ry are different. This isn't a you and me situation." Gabe grabbed his shoulder. "You guys... you're meant to be."

Trying to fight back his smile, Zach said, "You really think so?"

Gabe frowned. "What's there to doubt? What's his scent like?"

"I, uh..." Zach winced, heat flaming in his cheeks. "So, he's never actually had a scent that speaks to my wolf. I mean, he smells amazing, but not like Max does to you. No one I've been with has spoken to me."

Gabe blinked several times, processing. "Oh. Right. Because you didn't shift a lot when you were a kid. That makes sense."

Zach sighed. "So how am I supposed to know if he's... you know? It. The One. Or if it'll blow up in my face?"

Gabe considered, rubbing the neat scruff on his jaw. "Scent is important. My wolf knew Max was it for me the moment I smelled him, even if it took me a while to act on it. But Zach, from an outsider's perspective... you guys are endgame. I mean, think about it! You respect and support each other, you're kind to each other, and you've got each other's backs when shit gets rough. And how many times have you parted ways only to find your way back to each other? If that doesn't scream 'fated,' then I don't know what else does." Gabe shook him lightly. "Zach, what if tonight leads to something more, huh? What if you don't make any mistakes? What if you lose out on the best thing that could happen to you 'cause you were too scared and let self-doubt ruin everything?"

Anxiety warred with Zach's longing. There were many reasons not to do this. He'd thought of all of them. They were friends. He couldn't scent his fated mate. What if Zach got hurt, or Ryan? But unless he was willing to take that risk, he might lose out on something beautiful with Ryan. As scared as he was, he wanted to take a chance and see if they could have a shot at being more than friends. What-ifs tried to intrude on his decision, but he slammed the door on them. He took his courage in his hands and lurched to his feet. "Thanks, Gabe."

Gabe slapped the small of his back. "Hell yeah, go have awesome sex for me." He blanched. "And I just pictured you and Ry together... My mind didn't need that."

Grinning, Zach went around and thanked the pack for the party and told them he was heading out. The way they sniffed him, Zach thought they suspected where he was going. Izzie shouted, "Give Ryan a kiss for me!" and the pack laughed him out the door. Face burning, Zach caught his breath and managed a laugh.

Still, his knees were like jelly, and his stomach felt like a washing machine. He started hyperventilating and had to stop and breathe in a deep lungful of salty sea air. Ryan's bungalow was just up the street, the lights glowing golden in the night. Zach exhaled, hoping that though he felt like a moth to Ryan's flame, he wouldn't get burned tonight. That neither of them would.

Zach's heart slammed against his ribs as he raised a hand to knock. Gathering his courage, he pounded on the door a few times and waited, running his hand through his hair even though it was too short and tightly curled to get messy. He checked himself in the window's reflection. Hoping his breath didn't taste too sour from the drinking, he fumbled in his pocket for a mint.

Who was he kidding? Ryan wasn't some stranger he had to impress. They'd been sweaty around each other more than once after a few basketball games during the summer. He was sure they'd farted around each other before and laughed about it like immature kids...

Ryan didn't answer the door and Zach paced up and down. Had Ryan changed his mind? Oh, he hoped not. He wanted this. Wanted Ryan so badly. Now that tonight might be off the table, he was realizing just how badly he wanted this, nerves and all. He whipped out his phone and pondered what to say.

Zach: Hey. I'm outside.

He exhaled a few butterflies out of his stomach and jumped at Ryan's reply.

Ryan: At the beach.

Ryan's scent drifted to him on the breeze. If he had a mate's special scent, what would he smell like? He'd pondered that so many times. Zach walked around the house and through the palm trees in the backyard and Ryan's scent got stronger, mingling with the scent of the ocean and the sand. Taking in a deep breath, Zach urged himself not to panic.

Here goes...

The moon was nearly full and hung round and bright over the rippling ocean waves. Like a lighthouse, the moon's light traveled across the water and pooled silver on the sand. Ryan, silhouetted by the moon's light, faced the water. The ocean breeze whipped his hair back and sent grains of sand drifting over his bare feet. As Ryan turned toward Zach, his open shirt billowed around him. A frown left his mouth thin, and there was a crease between his brows. "Hey." He smiled, and the tension slid from his face.

"Hey," Zach said in return, nerves bubbling in his stomach.

"Thought you wouldn't show," Ryan confessed. Zach was relieved he wasn't the only one nervous about tonight.

Zach tucked his shaky hands deep into his pockets and bowed his head to keep the sand out of his eyes. Or to avoid his heart having palpitations the longer he looked into Ryan's eyes. Tension hung between them, heavy and awkward.

"I want to give us a shot." Zach cleared the gravel from his throat.

Hope brightened Ryan's eyes. "Really?"

Heart racing, Zach balled his fists and nodded. "Yeah. Let's do this."

Ryan said, "So, should I take my dick out first, or you?"

Zach snapped his head up to look at him, saw the teasing tip of Ryan's tongue poking out, and doubled over laughing. "You first, definitely. Mine takes a little while to take all the way out, if you know what I—hey!" He leaped back, shielding his eyes when Ryan kicked sand up at him.

"You're so full of it," Ryan said, grinning as he advanced, kicking more waves of sand at him.

Running around him, Zach shouted over his shoulder, "Not as full as you're gonna be!"

Ryan tackled him and tried to pile drive him into the sand. "Hey, why me?"

"Everyone knows shorties are the bottom!" Zach flailed but Ryan was damn scrappy for his size. Ryan clambered onto Zach's back and flattened him into the sand, and Zach screamed as sand flew all over his hair and clothes. "I let you do that."

"Yeah, right!"

Squirming and bucking, Zach rolled himself onto his back. They caught their breath and Zach sobered when their noses bumped together and Ryan's breathless laughter warmed his mouth. He had little dimples when he smiled, and Zach wanted to kiss each of the cute little things. Instead he was frozen in place, unsure how to make the first move that would thrust their friendship into a whole new light. Or ruin it completely.

"Zach." The sound of his name on Ryan's lips made him shiver. Ryan had said his name so many times before, but tonight Zach felt as if he were hearing it for the very first time, his whole life given new meaning. No one said his name like Ryan did. "If you've changed your mind, that's fine. I know what we're doing is nuts." Zach bit his lip to keep from laughing and Ryan rolled his eyes. "No pun intended." Zach snorted, which made Ryan giggle.

Such a sweet sound had Zach lunging forward, claiming Ryan's mouth with his. He allowed himself to kiss each dimple, groaning his approval when Ryan tongued and sucked his lower lip. Zach pulled back, his lips tingling. He raised a hand and brushed sand from Ryan's hair, twirling his finger around a wavy lock, and Ryan tilted his head into Zach's touch. "More," Ryan murmured, his voice low and raspy. Zach had never heard a sexier sound. "I won't bite."

Swallowing his nerves and apprehension, Zach glided his hand down Ryan's shoulder and the slope of his back, stopping just below the waistband of his shorts. Ryan was breathing hard, his eyes heavy-lidded when he leaned in. Closing his eyes, Zach met Ryan's mouth halfway. He couldn't stop now, not if a freaking meteor fell out of the sky next to them.

Ryan parted his lips, moaning shamelessly when Zach thrust his tongue past them. A shiver ran down his spine when Ryan tangled his fingers in his hair, the points of Ryan's fangs nipping his lips. He couldn't keep his hands idle any longer, curling his fingers around Ryan's hair and running his palm over the plump curves of Ryan's ass, grabbing and squeezing tight. Being able to touch Ryan like this, without worrying about overstepping the boundaries of their friendship, was freeing. He'd wanted this for so long, and he hadn't even realized it—hadn't *allowed* himself to want Ryan like this, not until tonight.

Ryan grunted his approval and thrust his hips against Zach's waist. He moaned when the length of Ryan's hard shaft glided over his hip bone. Bucking his hips in kind, Zach growled when his aching cock received the friction he desired.

"Fuck, you're so hard," Ryan panted.

"So are you, Captain Obvious," he shot back, rocking his hips against Ryan's erection.

Ryan whined and retaliated, grinding into Zach's pelvis. His head spun as all the blood drained to his dick. Fuck, he could come from this alone, grinding like a couple of horny, inexperienced teens.

"Zach. Zach, fuck, wait."

Panting, Zach squinted up at Ryan, disappointed when he scrambled off of him. "What is it?"

Ryan ran a hand through his tousled hair, his lips flushed and oh so tempting. "Let's take this back to my place."

Smiling, Zach accepted Ryan's hand, pushing off from the sand and to his feet. "Romantic."

Ryan flushed. "I've got sand in places I really don't wanna have it."

Zach laughed, all his worries forgotten, and grabbed Ryan's hand as the sand turned to asphalt and they walked the dark road back to Ryan's bungalow.

CHAPTER 12

ARMS AND LEGS AND FEET

RYAN COULD HAVE SCREAMED.

It was happening.

It was happening! He clamped his mouth shut to silence his squeal and settled instead for dancing a jig beside Zach while Zach fumbled with the key to Ryan's beach house.

"You have no shame." Zach laughed, turning the key in the lock. Ryan lurched in first and Zach had barely crossed the threshold when Ryan crowded him against the door. Pushing his mouth against Zach's, Ryan enjoyed the pleased grunt that came from Zach's lips. He thought he could kiss Zach's mouth a thousand times and never get bored with it. He ran his hands through Zach's curls, then down the back of Zach's neck, finally cupping his face. When Ryan tongued Zach's lower lip, Zach moaned softly. He felt light-headed when Zach parted his lips and their tongues tangled.

Being a pure-blooded werewolf, Ryan couldn't get drunk, though that sure as hell didn't stop him from trying. But he *could* get drunk off of Zach's scent—ocean waves and sun-drenched sand, so rich and warm he felt as if he stood right at the ocean's edge—and lose himself in Zach's taste, sweeter and more intoxicating than any beer or wine could ever hope to be.

"Wow," Zach rumbled, his fingers running along the crease of Ryan's ass. "There really is sand everywhere."

Ryan shoved his hand down the back of Zach's shorts. "Same here." Zach shivered when Ryan nudged his fingers between Zach's cheeks, and he enjoyed the way Zach clenched his gluteus muscles in response. "We better shower, huh? Or I could just use my tongue to make sure every inch of you is nice and clean."

Zach snorted. "When did you become such a perv?"

Ryan brought his lips to the spot between Zach's neck and shoulder and nipped hard. When he got the guy from his wildest teenage dreams in his bed, that was when. Instead of saying that, he shrugged and said, "Maybe I've always been a perv and you just didn't notice?"

Zach shrugged, angling his neck so Ryan could suck a hickey into his skin. It faded quickly, though. "Good thing I'm a perv too." Ryan shrieked when Zach lunged, flipping him over his shoulder.

"Hey! Put me down! This is discrimination against short people!" Ryan hammered his fist into Zach's back, laughing too hard to give Zach any genuine grief over being manhandled like a sack of potatoes instead of, say, a person. Laughing maniacally, Zach carried Ryan up the stairs to the bathroom, where he set Ryan on his feet on the cool tile.

Ryan pounced, determined to get even, and grabbed Zach's cock through the fabric of his shorts. Zach doubled over with a grunt into Ryan's shoulder and thrust his hips into Ryan's touch. "I'm pissed," Ryan panted, hoping Zach didn't see how big he was smiling. "You're gonna suffer for this, Zach DeShawn."

Zach bit his lip, his head thrown back against the ocean-themed wallpaper. "If this is suffering, spank my ass and call me a masochist."

Ryan grinned and did just that, enjoying the dull slap of his palm against Zach's clothed flesh. Desperately, Ryan crushed his mouth to Zach's, swallowing the moan he'd earned. He fumbled with Zach's buttons. "Who wears a button-up in the middle of summer? What are you, some CEO or something?" Ryan freed the shirt's last button and shoved the damn thing off Zach's shoulders.

Latching onto Zach's nipple with his mouth, he sucked hard and pinched the other nipple, and Zach's chuckle turned into a breathless grunt. Zach whined, running his big, warm hand down Ryan's back and fastening his fingers into the hem of Ryan's shirt. Ryan flailed out of his shirt and lunged back in to kiss Zach.

Something exploded nearby. Zach shouted in alarm and covered Ryan with his body. Ryan didn't know whether he should be terrified they were about to die or swoon that Zach's first instinct had been to protect him. Peering around Zach, his heart sank. A potted plant had fallen off a shelf, and ceramic shards and dirt had scattered over the tiles. The plant's roots had grown so long, they'd ruptured the pot.

"What happened?" Zach asked. "How'd that fall down?"

Craaap on a stiiiick.

"Shit! The water. It takes a while to warm up." Ryan threw himself at the bathtub and yanked on the faucet, turning up the heat. The jets of water spattering the tile were freezing cold. "Uh. You just sit right there and look sexy. I'll have this cleaned up in a jiffy."

"Jiffy?" Zach muttered.

Ryan ignored him, carefully picking up the shards and tossing them in the garbage can. He grabbed the overgrown plant and carried it outside, hurling it across the backyard. Shit. He wasn't ready to unload his family's secret onto Zach. But if he got worked up, how would he control his magic? "Fuck!"

Getting an idea, he tore around the house, throwing all the potted plants outside and for extra measure, removing every single light bulb in the house, minus those in the bathroom. When he returned to the bathroom, he was panting and sweaty.

Zach cocked a brow. "Okay?" He was sitting on the edge of the tub looking like a damn snack.

"Oh, I'm perfect." Ryan pulled Zach to his feet and put his hands on his hard chest, squeezing his plush pectorals. Zach wasn't rippling, bulging muscle, but he wasn't boyish by any means. For years he'd admired Zach's lean, muscular body, and now he could finally put his hands right where he wanted them. He pressed his lips to Zach's chest, nipping and biting his pecs and circling a dark brown nipple with his tongue, then giving it a flick. Zach's chest rose and fell fast, his long, thin fingers curling in Ryan's hair and squeezing.

Spreading his fingers, Ryan glided his hands down Zach's stomach, memorizing the curve of his hips, which he grabbed and squeezed. The buckle on Zach's belt popped open under Ryan's fingers, and his shorts cascaded to the floor, raining sand onto the tile. He worked his hands around, cupping and squeezing Zach's round buttocks through his boxers. He had the most perfect ass...

Slipping his fingers under the waistband of Zach's briefs, he stopped to peel down his underwear. Zach's cock sprang free, long and thick. Ryan let himself look the way he'd always wanted to every time he'd seen Zach naked after a shift, dark-haired and wild-eyed, his fangs still sharp and dangerous. Mesmerized, Ryan traced the little vein that twined over Zach's flat abdomen and dipped his fingers in the perfect V-line that pointed to the patch of dark pubic hair between his thighs. Zach watched him, his eyes heavy-lidded and his lower lip between his teeth.

"Looking okay down there?" Zach asked, his voice tinged with nervousness.

Ryan bristled. Had any of the jerks Zach had been with made him feel bad about his body? Oh, if he ever got his hands on them—

Standing up on his toes, he smacked a kiss on Zach's mouth. Ryan took him in his hand, relishing the hardness of him, the silky smoothness of his foreskin, and Zach's breath hitched. "I wanna come all over your abs."

Zach chuckled and hid his face in Ryan's shoulder. "Fuckin' hell, Ry. Totally shameless." He leaned into the kiss Ryan pressed to his mouth. "Let me look at you too."

Ryan held his breath, his skin tingling when Zach's hungry eyes roamed his body from his head to his toes. Zach ran his hand down Ryan's chest, then through the hair that led the way down to his shorts. Leaning in, Zach kissed his mouth, tonguing his lower lip and coaxing a groan from Ryan's throat. "You're fine as hell, boy."

Laughing, Ryan felt his shoulders loosening a little. "Shut up." He hauled Zach back to him, their lips colliding and noses bumping. He tugged Zach toward the shower.

"Uh, Ry? You're still dressed."

Ryan jumped as water coursed down the back of his shorts. "Crap!" He kicked off his shorts and threw them at the wall with a wet splat.

Zach grabbed his wrists. There was a gleam in his dark eyes. "Let me."

His knees wobbled. Fuck. He'd do anything Zach asked.

Zach hooked his fingers in Ryan's boxers and tugged them down. The silk caught on his rigid shaft, and Zach helped them the rest of the way down, then let them flutter into a silken pool around Ryan's ankles. Zach wet his lips and gave the head of Ryan's cock a squeeze. Seeing stars, Ryan steadied himself on Zach's arms as Zach reached around to explore, feeling and kneading Ryan's buttocks with both hands.

Ryan took a step back, leading Zach beneath the spray with him. Water rained over their naked bodies. Countless droplets ran in rivers down Zach's chest and dripped from the tip of his nose, drenching his dark pubes and dribbling off the length of his dick. Ryan dropped to his knees without a second thought, grasping Zach's wet hips and steering his back up against the tiles.

The tile was hard beneath Ryan's knees but kneeling before Zach, his cock straining toward him, Ryan felt as if he knelt before a shrine of worship. And in the shrine of Zach DeShawn, the only worshipping was done not with prayer but with his hands and his lips.

Zach gasped when Ryan kissed the tip of his cock. "Mmm. You look good on your knees."

Ryan licked the water coursing down Zach's abdomen, then licked the length of Zach's cock and swallowed him to the root.

With a groan Zach latched onto Ryan's hair, the muscles in his abs clenching as Ryan swallowed him down. "Oh fuck. Baby, that's so good."

Ryan's cock twitched at the nickname. He'd love more than anything for Zach to call him that, and no one else. Maybe Zach called everyone he went to bed with "baby." Ryan wrapped his lips tight around Zach's cock and glided up and down, swirling his tongue around Zach's silky cockhead.

Zach whined and Ryan pulled back and let Zach thrust in and out of his mouth in slow, shallow motions. Feeling between Zach's thighs, Ryan cupped his heavy balls. Zach groaned his disappointment when Ryan pulled off, his brows puckered and his lip clasped tight between his teeth. Zach's eyes glowed amber, his fangs protruding below his lip. Ryan's dick gave a heady throb, the knowledge that he'd brought Zach's inner wolf so close to the surface a huge turn-on.

Tonguing Zach's balls, Ryan drew one into his mouth. Zach's voice bounced off the tiles and his claws pricked Ryan's scalp as he clutched Ryan like he was a lifeboat and Zach would be adrift without him.

"Fuck, Ry, I'm close, I'm—" Zach grunted when Ryan pinched the spot just beneath his cockhead hard, effectively keeping him from coming yet. "What the hell?"

Ryan grinned but had the good grace to feel guilty when Zach pouted at him.

"Where'd you learn that cruel trick?"

Ryan kissed the tip of his cock, earning a sigh from Zach. "Lots of practice."

"With who?" Zach asked. "And did they curse your name and all your descendants?"

Placing an open-mouthed kiss to Zach's hip bone, Ryan said, "Did it to myself so I could stay awake all night thinking about you until I was damn well ready to finish."

Zach gaped at him. Ryan was sure if his complexion had been fairer, there'd be a big blush staining his cheeks. Judging by Zach's speechlessness and the way his dick twitched in Ryan's hand, he was forgiven.

"You... you can't just say shit like that." Zach couldn't even look him in the eyes.

"Fine. I'll put my mouth to better use." Ryan fisted Zach's length and let his meaty cock breach his lips. Cursing, Zach rocked his hips in time to the pumps of Ryan's fingers around his shaft. Zach panted, his body shuddering with each stroke. He fisted Ryan's hair and fucked into his mouth. His balls were heavy under Ryan's hand, his cock like iron in his mouth. Since he could tell Zach was close, he pulled off so he didn't choke and panted, "Come in my mouth. Want you to. Go ahead, babe. Spill all down my throat."

Zach cried out Ryan's name when he finally found release, spurting thick and hot in his mouth. Ryan's cock throbbed, aching for a release of his own, and he swore he nearly came the moment that first spurt of Zach's cum hit his tongue. Swallowing what he could, he licked Zach clean from the base of his shaft to the tip.

"Goddess," Zach panted, squinting at Ryan through dazed, heavy-lidded eyes. "Ry. Fuck. That was... Holy shit."

Ryan chuckled, over the moon at Zach's reaction. "Guess I'm not as rusty as I thought." He patted Zach's hip.

Zach's brow crinkled. "Hell no. When's the last time you were with someone?"

Ryan cast his mind back, then gave up and stood, wiping water out of his eyes. "Don't remember."

Zach knocked his head back against the tiles. "For real? And you just went to town on me! You must be ready to bust." Frowning at him, Zach ran a big brown hand down Ryan's chest. He stopped to pinch and squeeze Ryan's nipples, sending little jolts of pleasure through him. Ryan hissed, the sensation intoxicating. Zach dragged his lips over Ryan's cheek, his voice deep and low in Ryan's ear and tingling down in his aching balls as he said, "Let me show you my appreciation."

Ryan jumped when Zach plunked a towel over his head, shut off the water, and steered them both from the shower, rubbing the towel against Ryan's wet hair as they went. He followed Zach blindly, trusting his best friend not to let him walk into anything. Maybe it was a bit stupid, but his desire had taken the wheel over his common sense. Zach kept a firm grip on Ryan's shoulders, and he didn't betray his blind trust.

Ryan scented the subtle odor of the Febreze air freshener he used in his bedroom. Zach removed the towel, revealing Ryan's bed with its sea-blue sheets, the balcony doors open wide to let the ocean breeze in. The night air tickled over Ryan's damp skin and, without a care who might be walking around in the dark this late at night, he strode out onto the balcony.

"Into exhibitionism?" Zach chuckled, his big hand warm on the small of Ryan's back.

Ryan shrugged, turning around to curl against Zach's muscular chest. "I don't care who sees." How could anything else matter when he had the man he'd longed for all these years naked right next to him? Zach bumped their shoulders together, his mouth settling hot and soft against Ryan's bare skin. The warmth of Zach's hand cocooned Ryan's cock, his long, thin fingers squeezing and stroking. Ryan arched back and closed his eyes, biting his lip to stifle himself, and Zach chuckled. "I haven't even gotten started yet. Chill."

He cracked open an eye. "Think I'm playing it up?"

Zach shrugged. "Maybe."

Ryan rolled his eyes to the sky, first in exasperation, then in pleasure when Zach swiped his thumb over Ryan's slit. "Truth is, Zach, you're fucking hot as hell. Just your hands on me is driving me crazy."

Zach's breath warmed his ear, his tongue tracing the shape of Ryan's earlobe before his teeth closed around it. The prick of his fangs was like an electric shock. "Oh yeah? Tell me where you want me, Ry."

His face flushed but not from embarrassment. He was thrilled, and moved, by how much Zach wanted to please him. "Just this is fine. The two of us, out here."

Nodding, Zach's face was serious. "I just want to make sure you get what you need. That I don't... I don't know, mess this up somehow?"

Ryan kissed him before he could overthink things. "Zach. You're here now, with me. That's already more than enough."

"Ry. Tell me what you need so I can give it to you."

A shiver ran down his spine. "Okay, so... no guy I've been with has, uh... rimmed me before." Heat flamed his cheeks but he refused to look away from Zach's wide eyes. "If that's not something you're into, that's totally fine. We can always do something—"

"Stop talking and turn around, sweetheart."

Holy fuck. Those words had no right being as hot as they were. Gulping, Ryan turned around.

With a low, dark chuckle, Zach pressed his body against Ryan's back. His arm went around Ryan's shoulders and drew him close, his chest to Ryan's back. Slowly, his hand descended Ryan's back, leaving goose bumps in its wake. Those talented hands cupped Ryan's left buttock, then the right, squeezing until Ryan gasped. With his chin on Ryan's shoulder, Zach kissed the corner of his mouth. It was innocent enough, but then his big hand slid between Ryan's cheeks, his long fingers brushing tantalizingly over his hole. Ryan jolted, his breath hitching in his throat.

Zach chuckled, dark and sweet like molasses, and raised his fingers to Ryan's mouth. "Suck?" he requested. Ryan did, enjoying the little shiver his lips coaxed from Zach. Zach's sharp fangs nipped Ryan's ear while his fingers spread Ryan's cheeks, the tip of his finger caressing his puckered entrance. "Hold on to the railing, sweetheart."

A whimper pulled from Ryan's throat. His cock ached, and he clasped the railing so hard he thought it might splinter. Ivy grew, thick and green along the railing, but Zach didn't seem to notice. Ryan popped out his claws and cut the ivy away before Zach could see it. His stupid magic was not ruining things tonight.

Craning his neck, he met Zach's mouth in a kiss that was full of stroking tongues and sharp fangs. Ryan moaned into Zach's mouth when the tip of Zach's finger pressed inside him. Fuck. How many times had he fantasized about having those long, thick fingers in him? The fantasy was nothing compared to this. "More," Ryan whispered, hoarse and breathless. "Give me more, Zach. Fuck. I can take it. Please."

"Okay. I got you, babe. Just let me get the lube, okay? I don't wanna hurt you."

Ryan panted, "Top dresser drawer on the right."

Zach departed briefly and when he returned, he nestled against Ryan's back. Then there was a chuckle. "Half-empty. Someone's been busy." A cap popped behind Ryan and cool, slick fingers entered him. He exhaled, the sensation intoxicating. Zach pushed in deeper and Ryan's knees shook. He opened his legs wider, biting his lip and wriggling his ass in encouragement.

When Zach curled his finger and caressed his prostate, Ryan saw stars. "Yes! Fuck, yes! That's it!" Ryan threw back his head with a hoarse sound, rocking his hips back on Zach's finger. It was so good, but it wasn't enough. He wanted Zach to stuff him full of his cock, spreading him wide and filling him to the brim.

Zach closed his fingers around Ryan's cock, and Ryan leaned back into him. He dropped his head back onto Zach's shoulder, growling when Zach leaned down and kissed his neck and shoulders. Zach's big warm hand stroked him faster. Zach added a second finger and worked Ryan open. Ryan reached around and clasped the back of Zach's head, tugging on his hair. "Fuck, Zach. Oh my Goddess. So good, babe, that's so fucking good."

Zach panted into Ryan's ear and worked in a third finger. Ryan groaned at the burn, but the pain was eclipsed by Zach ramming his prostate. Ryan's balls tingled, aching and heavy, and the tingles spread to his hands and feet. "Zach... Shit, babe, I'm gonna come." Craving release, Ryan bucked into Zach's fist, faster and faster, until he was teetering on the cusp of a mind-shattering orgasm. He panted Zach's name and arched back into his sturdy body.

Then Zach pulled away from him, and Ryan gasped for air, suspended on the brink of release. "Zach... Come on. Please. Please. *Please*." He'd never begged for it before, but with Zach, his pride was second to his need.

Zach knelt behind him, laughing softly. "I got you. Gonna make you feel real good, baby. Okay?"

Clutching the railing, Ryan looked over his shoulder. Zach knelt, his face level with Ryan's ass. Zach clasped his ass cheeks and squeezed, pushing them together, then opening them wide. "Fuck. Ry, your hole's so damn sexy."

Ryan bit his lip to stifle his whine and arched back to better present himself. He'd never felt so bare before another person and yet so unafraid. He would give Zach everything he had and knew Zach would never make him regret it.

Capturing his lower lip between his teeth, Zach watched as he slowly inserted his finger again. Ryan groaned and gave him a show, rolling his hips back and taking him in deeper. "Fuck. See how hungry I am for you, Zach? The way I swallow you up like that..."

"Ry, stop. You're gonna get me hard again," Zach panted in response, watching reverently as he inserted another finger, stretching Ryan wider. He curled them, and Ryan threw back his head and cried out to the night sky. He was so close, his legs were quaking, his cock leaking pearly droplets of cum onto the balcony deck.

"Zach!" He groaned, needing something more, anything.

Then Zach's fingers were around him, and Zach's tongue was inside him, hot and wet and so perfect Ryan could weep. He slapped the railing, dislodging a few tangled vines. "Fuck, yes! Eat my hole, Zach. Eat it, make a fucking mess of me."

And Zach did, licking into him until he was sopping wet. All the while, Zach jacked him so hard and fast, Ryan lost the ability to string words together as he teetered on the edge. He shouted wordlessly, hurtling over the edge of a release that surged up from the tips of his toes and left his balls tingling. Panting Zach's name, Ryan pumped his hips in time to every stroke of his fist. Zach was panting in his ear now, his cock hard against Ryan's back.

Ryan reached blindly, but Zach pressed him down onto the railing. Looking over his shoulder, Ryan blinked through eyes that stung from sweat and possibly tears. Zach's face pinched in desperation, his eyes closed and his lip between his teeth, and he jerked himself fast, coming with a hoarse cry. The thick, wet stripes of his release painted Ryan's hole and amazingly, another spurt of cum shot from Ryan's balls. Just knowing Zach had gotten so worked up pleasuring him could have made Ryan hard all over again if he hadn't just expelled every drop of semen from his body.

Stumbling, Zach slumped against him, and he turned, unable to resist any longer, and fell into Zach's arms. Zach clutched Ryan to him, his chest rising and falling quickly beneath Ryan's head.

"You're amazing," Zach whispered.

Ryan kissed him, licking the sweat that dappled his upper lip. *I love you so fucking much*, was what Ryan wanted to say. Instead, he buried his face in Zach's shoulder. "Says the guy who made me come so hard I nearly blacked out."

Zach barked out a laugh and the next thing Ryan knew, he was off his feet and in Zach's arms. Then the softness of the mattress cushioned him, squeaking under their combined weight as Zach crashed into bed beside Ryan. The glow of the moon bathed Zach's tawny skin, which was dewy with sweat and glowing with post-sex satisfaction. Ryan rolled onto his side and reached out across the space between their pillows. He took Zach's hand, smiling when Zach looped their fingers together.

Yawning, Ryan squeezed his hand. "Is it gonna get weird if you stay the night?"

Zach closed his eyes, nuzzling into his pillow. "Weirder than me eating your ass? Not really."

Ryan's heart sang. He hadn't wanted them to part ways, and he was glad Zach felt the same. "Then stay. It's late." And he wanted to fall asleep in Zach's arms.

"Okay," Zach replied, stretching languidly. Ryan gazed at him. He'd never noticed how long his lashes were. "Do we talk now?" Zach asked, stifling a yawn.

Ryan grinned and hugged his pillow to him. "Do you usually?"

Zach shrugged. "Sometimes, if I have the energy." He nudged his cold foot against Ryan's.

Wincing, Ryan said, "How the hell are your toes still cold after that?"

Zach smiled, eyes heavy-lidded and content. "I have weird toes."

Ryan laughed into his pillow. There was a lot he wanted to say, most of it too personal on top of what they'd just done. How he didn't think he could bear to have anyone else in his bed after this. How the thought of anyone else with Zach felt like a stab wound to his chest. That tonight he was happier than he'd ever been in his life. Okay, maybe that one he could get away with.

"Zach?"

He opened his eyes and gazed at Ryan like he'd hung the moon in the sky. "Hmm?"

Ryan rubbed his foot against Zach's cold one. "I'm so fucking happy."

A grin bloomed across Zach's face. "Me too."

Unable to resist, Ryan leaned over and kissed his mouth, soft and sweet. "Night, Zach."

Zach clasped the back of Ryan's head and held him close, letting their lips linger just a few seconds longer. Ryan counted to three Mississippi before their lips parted. "Night, Ry," Zach murmured. He wanted to curl up in Zach's arms and never leave, but they weren't together. They weren't boyfriends... not yet, anyway. He would wait for Zach until he was ready. He just hoped Zach didn't keep him waiting too long.

Ryan rolled over onto his side of the bed and gave Zach one more smile before he turned off the lamp and blanketed the room in darkness.

In the night, they crossed the line dividing their sides of the bed. Ryan pretended to have simply rolled a little too close, his arm over Zach's shoulder. Zach was a cuddly sleeper even in human form, so he shifted close, and his arms went around Ryan's shoulders. Not moving, Ryan feigned sleep, afraid to move and break the spell.

His eyes grew too heavy to stay open, and he fell asleep in Zach's arms the way he'd always dreamed he would. Only it was better, because it was the real thing.

Zach opened his eyes to Ryan's sleeping face on the pillow beside him as he snored, his mouth agape and drooling onto the pillow. Stifling a laugh, Zach felt his chest overflowing with tenderness. He reached out and brushed Ryan's hair from his face. Huh, that was odd. Ryan had a tattoo on his neck, a strange symbol. Zach wondered when he'd gotten that done and why. Ryan had never liked tattoos before.

Yawning, Ryan hugged his pillow tight, and Zach's heart damn near melted.

What had he been worried about? He could have hit himself for waiting so many years to cross the line from being friends to something more.

Last night had been the best night of his life. The memory of what they had done still curled Zach's toes and woke his cock up with a vengeance. Like a drug, his body still craved Ryan. More than that, he was... happy. So stupidly happy. Lying next to Ryan without touching him was physically painful when all he wanted was to bundle himself up in Ryan's arms and find the scent of himself that still clung to Ryan's skin.

Maybe it was remembering the way Ryan had gathered him into his arms and held him while he wept, then made him breakfast the next day. Taken care of him when Zach couldn't. Zach could take care of himself, of course, had done it for years, but Ryan had told him without words that he didn't have to. Told him to just be himself and let Ryan worry about everything else.

Maybe it was looking into Ryan's eyes and seeing how badly he wanted Zach to stay, and yet he'd told him to be with his family. Realizing in that moment how truly selfless he was, Zach had been swept away by him. From the day they'd met, Ryan had been there for him.

Goddess. He loved Ryan Kelly. Wasn't that enough? He'd never know if Ryan was his fated mate, but maybe that didn't matter. Just loving him, being loved by him, would be more than enough.

He could wake Ryan up now with a kiss and tell him he'd made his choice. Ryan was his choice.

But was Zach *Ryan's* choice?

And at that moment, a memory surfaced from years ago. A memory that had once pained him deeply and even now still hooked into his chest with a vengeance.

The moment Gabe walked into Zach's apartment, his scent sour with nerves, Zach tried to pretend he didn't know what was coming. But he did. He wasn't stupid. He knew Gabe had been pulling away from him since he met Max. It hurt, but Max needed someone like Gabe for support. Zach wouldn't forgive himself if he came between them, no matter his own feelings.

They sat down at Zach's table. His stomach churned, and his heart wouldn't settle.

He thought to himself, Please, *and,* Don't. Don't let this be what I think it is. Let me be wrong. Just... please.

Gabe looked him in the eyes. "Zach, I'm in love with Max."

His confession pulled the air from Zach's lungs. Cracks formed in his heart. Okay. Okay. He knew this. It was obvious Gabe felt something for Max. Everyone knew. But Zach was the idiot who'd refused to accept it.

Gabe exhaled. "It's more than that. He's my mate. Zach, I thought I would return your feelings. I did. I wanted to try. I—"

"How do you know?" Zach's voice shook, and he hated himself for falling apart like this. For being so stupid *to think Gabe was his mate when he couldn't even fucking smell his special scent. For believing some stupid seer.*

"What?"

"That he's your mate. How do you know?"

Gabe looked down at the table as if searching for words scratched into the wood. "I didn't, not for a long time. I knew I wanted to protect him, and that he had this amazing scent. The minute I met him, I wanted to keep him safe, make sure no one ever hurt him again. I think that should have been my first clue..."

Gabe had known Max was his mate because his wolf *had known. Because of Max's scent. Because Gabe had instincts that had been stamped out of Zach ever since he was a kid. Zach's heart shattered in his chest, and he was sure he would be alone forever.*

An iron band snapped around his chest and squeezed until Zach couldn't manage a full gulp of air. Afraid he'd wake Ryan, Zach pulled himself from the warmth of Ryan's bed, but the scent of him still clung to his skin. Ryan had burrowed under Zach's skin down to his bones and was there to stay. The bathroom door snicked shut behind him, and Zach let his trembling knees bring him down to the floor. Cradling his head between his knees, he took in as deep a breath as he could manage, counted, then blew it out.

To his horror, tears slipped down his cheeks, and he dashed them away. Last night had been a mistake. They were moving too fast. Zach had been so overjoyed to have Ryan in his arms that he'd stopped thinking rationally. Ryan could break his heart the same way Gabe had done, and Zach could easily do the same to Ryan. What they needed was to take a step back, let things cool off, and decide if the risks outweighed the rewards of being together. Ryan acted with his heart in all things, but Zach had to be the one with his head on. No matter how much it hurt Zach to walk away.

When he opened the door and saw Ryan sitting up in bed, Zach's heart sank.

Hair bedraggled and glasses askew, Ryan bolted from bed and hurried to Zach's side. "What happened? Were you crying?"

"I, uh..." A lump formed, hard as an egg in Zach's throat. "I just think we need to take a step back. Cool things off." He'd probably be more convincing if he didn't sound like he'd burst into tears if Ryan didn't hold him close and refuse to let him leave.

Instead, Ryan stayed quiet while Zach stumbled past and picked up his clothes.

"It was fun, you know?" Zach's voice cracked, and he wiped frantically at his eyes while pulling up his pants with one hand. "It was great. I just don't think we thought through the pros and cons."

He pulled on his shoes, grabbed his shirt. Wiping his nose on the back of his hand, he made for the door.

He wished Ryan would yell at him. Call him out as the cowardly prick-head he was. Criticize him for being so back and forth, accuse Zach of using him. But what Ryan said next was worse than any outburst.

Ryan said, "Come sit down, baby. Talk to me."

His words halted Zach in place, froze his breath, and stopped his aching heart.

"Please?"

Zach's heart broke to pieces. He was such a piece of shit, and he didn't deserve Ryan's tender words and warm understanding. A sob escaped him before he could stop it. Arms went around his shoulders, and Ryan rubbed up and down his chest. Murmuring reassurances between soft kisses against Zach's shoulders, Ryan tugged Zach back to the bed. Boneless, Zach collapsed onto the mattress.

"It's okay, sweetheart. You're okay." Ryan parted his legs so Zach could sit between them and wrapped his body around Zach's like a blanket.

"S-sorry," Zach croaked, wiping frantically at his streaming eyes.

Shushing him, Ryan kissed the back of his neck. "Sorry for making you stay. I wasn't letting you leave while you were so upset." A shivery exhale escaped him. "Do you regret last night? Did I push you too hard for this? I'm so sorry."

"No, no!" A laugh escaped Zach, watery and broken. "Last night was amazing, I just... I'm so stupid. I don't know what's wrong with me,"

"Hey." A growl edged Ryan's words. He grabbed Zach's chin and tipped his head back just enough to meet Zach's gaze. "You are not stupid. You're smart and gorgeous and fucking amazing."

Zach snorted. Right. Sure. Ryan was way too good for some insecure nervous wreck like him. "I enjoyed last night. But I'm still..." The lump in his throat ached. Ryan would be so disappointed. "I'm still so doubtful. About everything. I don't know how to trust that this will last, how to stop waiting for something awful to happen that will tear us apart."

Squeezing him tighter, Ryan peppered kisses over Zach's shoulder. "You're scared. I get it. But if you don't trust your instincts, then trust mine."

"You said last night you can't scent me. There's no way of knowing this will work out."

Leaning back, Ryan pulled them both down to the bed and held Zach's head to his chest. "I know we will, Zach. So when it's too hard to trust yourself, then trust me."

Zach wanted to more than anything. Ryan had never betrayed his trust.

Brushing his fingers over Zach's hair, Ryan murmured, "But if this is too fast, we can step back and cool things off until you're ready to give us a chance."

Zach wanted to retreat into his shell, to hide behind the walls he'd built and protect his heart. But he knew if he said yes, Ryan would be disappointed, even if he didn't show it. He'd already disappointed his father; he wouldn't disappoint Ryan, too. "Ryan, I..."

"I can wait, baby," Ryan spoke with such honesty it made Zach's eyes sting. "I've waited a long time for you. What's a little longer?"

His words gave Zach's heart a lurch. What did that mean? Just how long had Ryan liked him this way? Craning his neck, he looked up at Ryan and found him wide-eyed like he'd said something he shouldn't have. "What do you mean?"

A smile wiped away the nerves on Ryan's face. "If I told you, you really would run out of here. So let's table that for when you're ready. For now, just let me know if you really want to step things back. And whatever you say, it sure as hell better not be because you're afraid of disappointing me."

Zach chuckled, running his fingers up and down Ryan's arm where it draped over his stomach. He worried he was crushing Ryan beneath him, but Ryan was sturdier than he looked for being smaller than Zach. Hell, he was stronger than Zach would ever be.

"I think... I need time to think this over when my head is clearer. But I'll see you and the pack on Wednesday for Pack Night. We can talk then. I promise."

Lacing their fingers together, Ryan squeezed tight. "Sounds good."

They lay together in the brightening room, arms and legs and feet tangled together, and breathed in the quiet of the early morning.

Zach never wanted to leave Ryan's arms.

CHAPTER 13

NO MORE DATES TO PACK NIGHT

IT HAD BEEN HALF a day since Ryan and Zach slept together.

His best friend had consumed Ryan's thoughts, and it took every ounce of self-control he had not to pick up the phone and call him to make sure he was doing all right working with his mom—and that he wasn't making himself sick with worry over their relationship.

They'd see each other tomorrow night. Hopefully, Zach would be in a better mood and feeling more optimistic about their relationship. They'd talk, and a new chapter of their relationship would begin. Even if Zach was doubtful, Ryan could be optimistic enough for both of them. He believed in their bond, in his unshakeable feelings for Zach that told him they were meant to be no matter what. It hurt his heart that Zach couldn't trust in them, but he had faith that in time, Zach would see their relationship for what it was.

They were fated for each other. All Zach had to do was take that leap and know Ryan would jump right along with him, hand in hand.

And yet, he had to consider the alternative, as well. If Zach wanted to go back to being friends, would Ryan be able to do that?

It would kill him, but truth was, he'd have Zach any way he could, but he'd never want another man in his bed or in his heart. Not after having Zach in every way he'd dreamed of only to lose him. Tears nipped his eyes

152

at the thought, but he wiped them away. They'd find their way back to each other, and Ryan would wait as long as it took.

The door to the study flew open, and his father walked in. "Ry, I don't see you practicing."

Ryan shook himself out of his Zach-induced daze and picked up one of his gran's tomes. He had to get this magic stuff under control, but it was hard. His eyes ached from going over pages of incantations, all written in freaking Gaelic, all day. Gran had taught him some basic Gaelic when he was a kid, but he was rusty, so he kept a Gaelic dictionary propped on one knee and his gran's grimoire on the other.

His parents' home upstate was the perfect place to practice—secluded, and nestled among nature. Ryan was starting to think he had been too spontaneous when he'd accepted his gran's magic. Maybe he couldn't do this...

His dad sighed. "Gran's funeral is Thursday."

Ryan's mood deflated. "You have everything sorted?"

"Yup. The venue, the guests."

Humming, he flipped through the pages of his gran's grimoire. "I'm inviting my pack. I... I'll tell them about my magic. Do you think that's a good idea?"

"I think that's a smart idea."

Ryan paused to read a page of his gran's grimoire. It was a cross between a diary and a spell book, where his gran had chronicled her magical growth and accomplishments. On one page, she'd sketched a precious object given to her by her mother, and it had an accompanying journal entry.

I finally found a way to control my magic today!

"Dad!" Ryan called, excitement shooting through him.

"What is it?" His dad knelt on the carpet beside him.

"Look! Gran figured out how to control her magic."

Gran had written, *Every druid must have a way to focus their magic. To control it. The same way werewolves need someone to anchor their humanity to, a druid needs an anchor for their magic. It can be anything, anyone. For me, it was my mother's ring. The memory of her—*

The rest of the entry was illegible from age, but Ryan had gleaned enough from it. "So, this is it! I just need a... a something! An important object."

"Or a person," his dad added thoughtfully.

Ryan racked his mind for meaningful objects he possessed. He'd think more on it later but this was good. He was a step closer to controlling his magic. To helping his mother. "Dad." He gripped his dad's hand, blinking hard through a surge of emotion. "Dad, I could help her soon." She'd never forget him again. She could be *cured.* His wildest, most impossible hope since childhood was close to becoming a reality.

His father's lips trembled when he smiled. "I know, but we have to be patient. *Careful.*" He squeezed Ryan's shoulder. "You must have your magic under control before you try to help her."

"I know." Ryan wouldn't risk hurting his mother, no matter how impatient he was to cure her illness.

He turned a few more pages in the grimoire and paused. The final entry was dated the day before she'd died.

His gran had written, *I saw him in my dreams. He is not gone. Somehow, he lives on and soon he will return. I thought the sacred groves had all been destroyed. I was wrong. Only a druid can stop him for good. Ryan... he must be ready. She-Wolf, please forgive me for the burden I must place upon him.*

His dad blinked hard and ran his finger over the words. "If we'd just had more time with her, we might know what she meant."

A chill ran down Ryan's spine. "It feels important." Hadn't his gran tried to say something to him before she died? To give him some kind of warning?

"What's this?" his dad asked. He plucked a folded scrap of yellowed paper from the grimoire. When his dad unfurled it, Ryan realized it was a map of the world. Gran had sketched trees in specific spots. And not just any trees—oak trees. Ryan would always recognize the shape of the tree because it reminded him of Zach.

"A map of trees?" his dad asked, his brow furrowing.

"Yeah. Looks like it." There were dozens of trees drawn on the map, and many of the trees were in Europe. Dublin, London, Berlin, Rome, and New York were among the locations. Oddly, almost all the trees had been crossed out. His gran had sketched three oak trees in NYC. Two she'd scratched out like the others on the map. The other one she'd left unmarked and drawn a question mark next to it. So out of all these oaks, only one hadn't been crossed off.

"Why trees?" Ryan asked. "I know oak trees are symbolic to druids."

His father scratched his chin. "Well, druids would conduct their rituals in sacred oak groves. There are many of these groves all over Europe. When Atticus and his druids went to war, these ritual sites began popping up all over the world. So it looks like this map is a list of ritual sites. I don't know why they interested her, considering these sites were destroyed after Atticus's defeat."

Ryan got an idea. "Is there any way to know the exact locations of these ritual sites?"

"We could contact the Council. They're bound to have records. But what does this matter, Ryan? We need to focus on your magic."

He couldn't explain why this was important, but it was. Ryan swallowed hard. His gran had sensed impending danger linked to these oaks, danger only *he*, the last druid, could stop.

Well, wasn't that just peachy?

RYAN GOT BACK TO his apartment late that night. Once in his room, he gathered some of his favorite things and set them on his bed. Among them was a gold-dipped maple leaf Zach had bought him that one time they'd all gone to Vermont and a football signed by his favorite quarterback on the Timberwolves. Okay, he wasn't sure a football could be his focus considering how big it was, but he really liked it, so he had to include it.

He placed his hands on the items, waiting to feel something. Anything. He wished his gran were still alive so he could ask her how she'd known her mother's ring was her focus. Had her magic reacted in some way? Was there an incantation he was supposed to recite? By the She-Wolf, he was the worst druid to ever exist.

Sighing, he dropped onto the mattress, holding the football to his chest. He tossed it into a corner of the room, then took his phone out of his pocket. Ryan realized he hadn't told Zach where they were meeting tomorrow. Usually, they piled into Gabe and Max's home upstate. This week they'd decided to meet in Prospect Park, but they'd discussed that in person at the agency and Zach hadn't been there.

Scrolling through his long list of messages—Zach had always cringed when he saw how many texts Ryan forgot to delete, some going back years—he found Zach in his contact list and shot him a text.

Ryan: FYI, we're doing pack night at Prospect Park around 8pm. Hope you come.

His phone rang. Not buzzed. *Rang.*

Holy shit.

He lunged for his phone and paused. It wasn't Zach's name on his screen but oh, he recognized that name. Heart sinking, he checked his messages and cursed. He'd texted the wrong person. The last person he'd ever wanted to text again.

"Fuck my life," he muttered. He had to answer. He'd dug this grave by stupidly not deleting his old messages, so now he had to lie in it. "Hello?" he squeaked.

"Well, well, well. Ryan Kelly. I knew you couldn't stay away. They always come back to Jackie."

Once upon a time, when Ryan had been in a Zach-induced depression, he'd downloaded Howlr, a gay werewolf dating app. He'd swiped mindlessly, not sending any messages or trying to match with anyone, just looking at pictures of sexy guys in their underwear. None of them had done it for him. They hadn't been Zach. But one guy had looked a lot like Zach—tall and Black, muscular and sporting a buzz cut. His name was Jack. No wonder Ryan had seen his name in his contacts and misread it as Zach. Jack's profile had invited sexy guys to message him, enticing them with the classic combo of an eggplant and a peach emoji.

Ryan had swiped, and they'd matched. Jack had messaged to meet up, and they'd had sex. It had been by far the worst sex Ryan had ever had. Jack had begged Ryan to go out with him, but Ryan hadn't been interested in a relationship with him. Not then and not now.

"Tell me," Jack said, "to what do I owe the pleasure after... how many months has it been?"

"Not long enough," Ryan muttered. The last time he'd seen Jack, they'd hooked up and Ryan had dragged him to Max's graduation dinner. He hadn't wanted to, but he'd been running late to the dinner and hadn't had the guts to tell Jack to piss off.

"What was that, sweet thing? Oh, you're just dying to see me again? I am flattered! Ryan? You still there?"

Ryan gritted his teeth. "Yes, Jack."

"What's wrong, sweet cheeks? You sound awfully annoyed. Is someone bothering you? Does Jackie need to bring the pain?"

"You'd have to punch yourself, but—" Ryan cleared his throat. "Look, just forget about that text I sent you, okay? It was a... a moment of weakness. Sorry to bother you."

"I don't think I *can* forget about it, sweet thing. Just admit it. I was the best you ever had and you can't live without me."

Seething, Ryan said through clenched teeth, "Zach—I mean *Jack!*—I didn't mean to text you!"

There was a moment of stunned, hurt silence. "Oh." Jack's voice trembled.

Fuck.

"I guess I just... I thought you'd realized we had a good thing going. That you'd changed your m-mind and decided to give us another chance. Of course nobody wants to spend time with me. My mama always told me I was too much for people."

Oh shit. He sounded like he was about to cry.

Well, now Ryan felt like the biggest asshole in all the five boroughs.

"Okay," he blurted out. "Fine! You can come."

Jack gasped. "Oh yay! You've made my entire night! I've never been to a... what did you call it? A pack night! I know, I'll bring my homemade cheese Danishes! Those are always a hit. See you, boo!"

Jack hung up, and Ryan collapsed into his pillows and fell asleep, feeling like he'd made a big mistake but too tired and heartbroken to care.

"WE'LL COME TO YOUR grandma's funeral, for sure." Gabe sighed and threw a stick into the roaring fire. "Sorry, man. I still miss my grandmother sometimes."

Ryan heaved his shoulders, absently turning his stick so his marshmallow didn't burn. "She was ninety-eight years old. That's amazing, huh?"

Vicenzo stood farther away from the pack like he usually did, but he met Ryan's gaze. "Sucks, man. Some of my favorite memories are with my grandparents. How are you feeling?"

"Okay, I guess. Thanks, Vico." As okay as one could be after discovering his family had hidden their legacy of magic from him, and he had to use said magic to stop some vague threat his gran had thought was coming.

"Hey, Ben," Ryan said, remembering his idea. "Could you ask the Council to dig up any books on druids?"

Ben chewed his marshmallow. "Any specific topics?"

"I'm looking for the location of sacred groves. Ritual sites created by the druids."

"I'll ask, sure."

Izzie squinted at him. "What's with the sudden interest in druids?"

Crap. Ryan wasn't ready yet. "Max!" he snapped. "Your marshmallow's burning."

Max gasped and withdrew his charcoal marshmallow from the fire, and Tommy laughed at him.

Ben handed a s'more to Luna, who was sitting on Tommy's lap. "Careful, it's hot."

"Thanks, Uncle Ben!" Luna smiled brightly.

Ben patted Ryan's knee. "We'll be at the funeral."

"Thanks." Ryan chowed down on his own s'more. He could still feel their sad, worried eyes and it made him want to hide under a rock.

"Ladies and gentlemen!" boomed a voice.

Ryan groaned. "Crap on a stick..."

Max's mouth fell open. "Oh, hell no."

Sighing, Ben said, "Seriously, Ryan?"

Striding toward them was Jack. "The whole gang's here! Good to see y'all again!" He pointed at Gabe. "Wait. Stop! I remember you... Greg? Greg. It's great to see you again!"

Gabe opened his mouth, then shut it. "Yup. Greg. That's me." He glared at Ryan.

"Bam! Knew I was right!" Jack let out a laugh that sounded like a goose being strangled.

"Oh my Goddess," Izzie muttered.

Luna wrinkled her nose. "Not the annoying man again." Max admonished her with a look.

"So, like, can we start having fun? I thought this pack night stuff was supposed to be fun!" Jack must have been oblivious to the glares of the pack, or he just didn't care.

"What's your name again?" Izzie asked, smiling coolly. "Jack? Zach?"

Ryan glowered at her. Jack was nothing like Zach. Okay, maybe he looked like him, but that was where the similarities ended entirely.

Jack grinned. "It's Jack, Elizabeth."

"Isabella."

Jack shrugged, snorting. "Whatever, am I right? Same difference."

Gabe grimaced. "When did Jack, sorry, *Zach*," he said with a pointed look at Ryan, "say he was getting here?"

Glaring back, Ryan checked his messages. "Said he was on his way about fifteen minutes ago." His stomach churned. Would Zach be angry at him for bringing an old fling?

"Hey, how about a Run-N-Howl?" Ben said, rising with a stretch. "Zach can catch up."

"Finally!" Jack boomed like an impatient child, and Eddie jumped and dropped his marshmallow in the fire.

The pack spread out, undressing to prepare for the shift. Ryan caught Jack checking out Gabe and waggling his brows crudely. Already shifted to his red wolf, Max snapped at Jack's ankles as he passed. Eddie couldn't shift thanks to his silver collar, but he kept pace with the wolves.

Jack shifted to a wolf and bounded up to Ryan. Before Ryan could stop him, Jack bumped up against him and circled him, rubbing the length of his body over Ryan's waist. "Hey, cut it out!" Ryan snapped, shooing him away.

Beside Ryan, Ben groaned, running his big fingers over the silver fuzz on his broad chest. "This pack has more drama than a damn soap opera."

Ryan sighed his agreement. Aside from Jack, tonight was a perfect night for a run in the woods. The sky was clear and full of stars and the rain made the forest smell fresh and green. Ryan closed his eyes, listening and feeling the ground beneath his sneakers. The wind whispered through the trees in voices only he could hear. Beneath his feet, the roots stirred and worms tunneled deep. It was surreal, being able to feel nature like this, but he liked it.

The forest was still and quiet until Max let loose a warbling howl in the distance. He recognized Gabe's throaty howl when he returned his mate's song. Eddie howled, and though it was human, it was a good howl. Izzie's,

Vicenzo's, and Ben's howls joined the chorus and Luna and Tommy added theirs too.

Then Jack's off-key, goofy howl interrupted the harmony of the pack's song. Ryan cringed. Then another voice joined the chorus, raising the hairs on Ryan's arms. He turned, smiling at the sight of an enormous wolf, moonlight glimmering in his mottled brown fur. "Hey, Zach." He'd come after all.

Tail wagging, Zach came toward him, then froze when he spotted Jack at Ryan's side.

Zach's ears flattened back, and his growl rumbled through the air.

Jack showed his fangs in retaliation.

Ryan gaped in astonishment at Zach. "Zach. Hey. Wait a moment!"

Zach's ears were back, fangs bared and glistening. Jack answered with a growl, and the wolves prepared to strike.

ZACH COULDN'T SAY WHAT had come over him. He'd left all his nervous anticipation behind when he'd shifted from wolf to man, the thrill of pack and the hunt chasing away the worry about seeing Ryan again. Despite his anxiety, he'd been overjoyed at the sight of Ryan until he took a whiff of his scent and smelled another male wolf. And not just any male wolf—the fling he'd brought to Max's graduation dinner.

The rage came over him then, as intoxicating as the blood of freshly caught prey. Zach hadn't liked Jack then, and he sure didn't like him now that he had rubbed himself all over Ryan. As if Ryan were his property. Zach had been gone a day, and Ryan brought his *one-night stand* to pack night.

Slow down. Maybe it's a misunderstanding. Maybe Jack just showed up. Stay calm, come on...

The wolf's possessive rage overwhelmed his rational mind and for the first time since he was a kid, his control was slipping out of his reach. The wolf wanted to tear into Jack for daring to erase Zach's scent from Ryan's skin.

Ben shoved himself between Zach and Jack. Fur and muscle shifted and receded, and Ben stood between them as a man. "Back off," he growled through a mouthful of fangs. Jack flinched. "You show your teeth at our pack member again, and you're outta here. Got it, Jack?"

Jack shifted to a man, his arms folded over his muscular chest. "He showed his teeth first! I'm Ryan's date. That doesn't count for something around here?"

All the anger was walloped out of Zach. He stopped growling, lost the ability to do anything except stare in silent astonishment. Jack hadn't just shown up then. Ryan had invited him as his date. He'd been so adamant about waiting for Zach. Unless... unless he'd just been saying what Zach wanted to hear. Doubts bubbled to the surface and threatened to boil over into rage he longed to direct at Jack for touching what was his.

Ryan wasn't his boyfriend, and from the way Zach had run off on him, Zach couldn't blame Ryan for wanting someone who liked him back with the confidence Zach didn't have. Someone who wasn't insecure, or doubtful. Someone whose heart wasn't too damaged to love Ryan the way he deserved.

Fuck. *Had* he moved on?

Ben replied, "Ry, control your date. Zach... cool it."

Zach sneezed, his fur bristling. *You cool it,* he wanted to say. Ben shot them a weary look, then morphed into a wolf and bounded after the others. Jack shifted and ran ahead, throwing an uneasy glance at Zach.

Ryan cleared his throat. "Hey... Didn't think you'd show up."

Whining apologetically at the sour scent of Ryan's guilt, Zach bumped his head into Ryan's stomach. Ryan shouldn't be feeling guilty because Zach had blown up at his stupid date.

Too sheepish to face Ryan man-to-man, he settled on communicating as a wolf, but he didn't have the guts to do it via telepathy. He bumped his nose under Ryan's fingers and licked them. Zach leaned his body into

Ryan's, making him stumble, and Ryan raised both hands. "Okay, okay! I know you've had a tough time lately. Guess I should have warned everyone I was bringing someone, but I knew they'd give me shit for it." Ryan peeled his shirt over his head and draped it on a tree branch. Moonlight glimmered on Ryan's pale thighs as his boxers and jeans pooled around his ankles.

In seconds, Ryan's white-and-black wolf had disappeared among the trees. Zach pushed his human thoughts to the side and tried to enjoy the shift. Instead, all he could notice was when Jack pounced on Ryan and nipped his ears. When Ryan and Jack tussled, snapping and growling. When they stopped to rest and Jack licked Ryan's ear, smelling of desire. Ryan didn't return any of Jack's romantic gestures, which relieved Zach beyond measure. Instead, Jack drooled all over Ryan like he was a piece of meat.

Leave him alone, Zach thought, growling. *He's not interested.*

But Jack was, and maybe that was what Ryan needed. Jack was showing interest in Ryan by playing with him and sitting close to him. Unlike Zach, who had slept with him and bailed on him the next morning like an asshole. He couldn't blame Ryan for wanting to be around someone who desired him.

What if Zach had pushed Ryan away for good? Pushed him right into Jack's arms. Maybe they'd reconnected because Ryan had realized Jack was his mate. Zach barely swallowed the pained whine that rose to his throat. If he'd lost Ryan for good, he would never forgive himself for letting his own doubts push them apart. He had to talk to Ryan and figure out where they stood.

Zach shifted to a man and turned away from the others.

The black wolf that was Gabe morphed into human form. "Not leaving already, are you?"

Zach tried to smile. "It's supposed to rain in an hour. Maybe we should all head over to Wolf's Eye before we get caught in the storm." Wolf's Eye was a shifter bar beyond the park, and they usually grabbed drinks there after a run. Though the Slaughtered Lamb was their preferred haunt of choice, Wolf's Eye was the closest. He and Ryan could have the talk they desperately needed there.

Gabe stood, dusting grass off his bare legs. "I'll buy you a round, my friend. For your dad."

Zach managed a smile. "Thanks."

"Did someone say a round?" Jack ran over, his pants halfway up his thighs. "Is this place any good?"

"No—" Gabe began.

Zach said, "It's all right. They have specials on the night of the full moon." He hated himself as soon as he spoke. Maybe he was taking his duties as Ryan's supportive friend who *wasn't* insanely jealous too far.

Gabe elbowed him. "Why would you do that?" he hissed.

"Cool. Let's go!" Jack pumped his fist in the air.

Jack left the park with them and chatted up a storm to Ryan, who looked more annoyed than intrigued. Every so often, Zach would catch Ryan's eye. There was something unreadable in their depths, and Ryan wasn't known for being unknowable. Shit. Zach knew Ryan must be angry at him for being so rude to Jack earlier.

They arrived at the bar. Usually late on Wednesday nights, the bar would be quiet, but this was a werewolf bar on the full moon. Partially shifted werewolves packed the tables, their fangs and claws glinting as they sipped beer and wine or chowed down on the bar's famous pulled pork sandwich. Max stayed long enough to wave goodbye, then took Luna and Tommy home. The pack split up with Eddie and Ben at the bar, Gabe, Vicenzo, and Izzie at a table, and Zach sat opposite Ryan and Jack. The bartender brought them pitchers of Blue Moon, and when Jack fed Ryan an onion ring, Zach took a very hearty gulp. Ryan looked like he'd just swallowed a poison dart frog.

Fuck it. How could he call himself a good friend if he didn't rescue Ryan from this crummy date? Zach slammed down his beer. "Ry, you know that thing we have to do tomorrow?"

Ryan squinted at him. "Huh?"

"The thing we have to get up really early for."

Ryan's eyes widened. "Oh, yeah! That thing!"

Jack looked from one to the other. "What thing?"

Without answering, Zach threw some money on the table to cover their beers plus tip. "Sorry, man. We've gotta run. Early morning."

Jack shrugged and poured himself another beer from the very full pitcher. "Hey, more beer for me."

Ryan grabbed his sweatshirt from the back of the chair, and Zach beat him to the door. Sheets of rain cascaded from the sky, and thunder rumbled and drowned out the howling wind. Ryan threw his sweatshirt over his head and Zach ran to open the door to his car. A fork of lightning split the sky and Ryan shrieked in fright, hurling himself into the passenger seat. Leaping in, Zach turned on the windshield wipers and pushed wet curls back from his forehead, grinning in astonishment at the downpour soaking the streets.

"Jack's gonna curse your family line for making him walk home in this," Zach said, surprised he actually felt bad.

Ryan toweled his hair off with his sweatshirt. "Ugh. I'll live. Thanks for getting me outta there."

Zach started the engine. "Where to?"

His face flushing, Ryan said, "I don't want you driving all the way to the Bronx in this. Could I crash on your couch?"

Zach's throat went dry. He would've welcomed Ryan back into his bed if he'd asked, but he hadn't. Damn it, Zach was so confused about where they stood. "Sure, Ry." Zach drove them toward his apartment near Central Park, his stomach churning the closer they got. They stopped at a light on a stretch of empty road and rain pattered around them, filling the quiet.

Zach exhaled, needing to know what was going on between them. "Sorry for being a jerk to Jack."

Ryan turned to him across the armrest, his stare long and piercing. "What got into you tonight? You're never ready to pick fights like that."

Squeezing the wheel, Zach searched for answers. "I don't know. A lot on my plate, I guess."

Ryan nodded but he was frowning. "Yeah, 'course. Your dad…"

Zach stepped on the gas, exhaling with the thrum of the engine. It would have been easy to leave it there, but no, he couldn't let his dad's death serve as an excuse. "That's not it, Ry." He had to be honest, even if he felt like he was digging himself a grave. In his peripheral vision, he saw Ryan turn toward him, but Zach found it easier to avoid his gaze. He cleared his throat, his hands tightening on the wheel. "I smelled him all over you, and it… it bothered me, all right? Like he thought you were his mate or something. You deserve better than that."

Zach eased off the gas as the light turned yellow, then flashed to red. He waited, suspended in limbo.

Ryan cleared his throat. "So, uh… Whatever you're thinking that thing with Jack was, I promise it was just a mistake. I texted him instead of you and then he guilt-tripped me into inviting him."

An enormous weight lifted from Zach's chest. *That* was why Jack was there. Not because Ryan had changed his mind about waiting for Zach, or because Zach had disappointed him by saying he needed more time. "O-oh." Coughing, he cleared his throat, hoping Ryan didn't notice the tremor in his voice. He couldn't believe how strongly his doubts had crept up on him. He'd genuinely believed Ryan had been ready to move on with someone else but now, he felt so stupid for second-guessing Ryan's devotion to him.

Ryan sighed softly. "Baby. You really thought I'd moved on. Didn't you?"

Squeezing the wheel, Zach laughed around the lump in his throat. "Kinda, yeah. It's stupid, I know." He couldn't meet Ryan's eyes. Ryan would be so hurt knowing Zach had doubted him like that. "Logically, of course you hadn't. You wouldn't do that without telling me. But…" He raised his hands and dropped them to his sides hopelessly. "I thought I'd lost you for a second there."

Ryan laughed, incredulous but warm with affection. Zach's heart soared to hear it. "As if! That guy's got nothing on you."

Zach shrugged. "I don't know. He's hot. Confident. Fun-loving."

"He's not you, Zach."

The breath caught in Zach's throat.

Wetting his lips, he turned the wheel to the left. "I'm, uh… I'm glad you aren't dating him."

His skin prickled under Ryan's heated gaze. "Got pretty jealous back there, didn't you?"

"I guess." Zach's cheeks warmed.

"I've never seen your wolf so pissed before. And in my defense, too. Swoon!"

He laughed. "Shush."

"I liked it." When Ryan stroked Zach's thigh, the heat of his touch went straight to Zach's cock. "Liked seeing you get all riled up for me. All pissed and possessive. Knowing I made you lose your cool like that. Fuck, baby, it was hot."

Fully hard now, Zach squeezed the wheel. "We haven't talked yet. About what we want from this. Us."

"Pull over," Ryan commanded.

Zach's heart skipped, and he did as Ryan asked. He parked the car and in the quiet, the windshield wipers beat in time to Zach's heart.

"Do you wanna see other people?" Ryan asked, a growly undercurrent in his voice like thunder on the horizon.

Zach shook his head, unsure if Ryan could see. "No," he croaked.

"Do you want me to?"

Growling in response, Zach could not stop himself as his wolf flared to the surface. "Wanted to rip his hands off so he couldn't touch you again. I wasn't fully decided, not until I saw him with you and I thought you'd chosen him."

"Tell me what you want, baby."

Zach swallowed hard, need burning under his skin. "You. Only you. For however long we last. A week, a month. Forever. I want to be your first thought when you wake up, and the last thing on your mind at night. I want to be the one you turn to when you're sad or lonely. The only one you want in your bed. I want to be everything to you."

"You are, Zach." Ryan squeezed his thigh. "You always have been."

But none of that would happen if Zach didn't take the risk. So, he pushed past his fear and doubts and said, "I want to date you, Ry. I—I know I'm a mess and I'm not half the guy you deserve, but I want to be. If you let me."

A sigh fell from Ryan's lips, quiet but devastating, full of decades of wanting. "Never thought I'd hear you say that." The salty scent of tears and the sound of Ryan's fluttering heart made Zach's heart skip.

Ryan's seat belt clicked and next thing Zach knew, his lap was full of Ryan, and Ryan's mouth was crushed against his. Zach's hands flew from the wheel and grabbed onto Ryan's back, crushing his best friend to him.

"I'm so happy, baby," Ryan panted as he tugged Zach's lower lip into his mouth. "So," he growled as he trailed scorching kisses down Zach's jawline to his neck. "Fucking happy," he said with a moan when Zach grabbed handfuls of his ass and squeezed hard enough to bruise. Ryan kissed and sucked the spot between Zach's neck and shoulder, and for one crazy moment, Zach wanted to order Ryan to bite down, to claim him so thoroughly there could never be a doubt they belonged only to each other.

Tugging on Ryan's hair, Zach yanked their lips back together to stop himself from acting on that, and Ryan's glasses tumbled off and thumped onto Zach's chest. Without breaking their kiss, Zach plucked them off his chest and tucked them onto the dashboard so they didn't get lost, and then his hand was in Ryan's pants, stroking and squeezing. Ryan whimpered, breaking their kiss and panting. He rocked his hips, begging for more, and Zach wanted to take care of him and ensure his every desire was thoroughly met. "I got you, babe. I'll give you what you need." Ryan's cock was like iron in his fist, damp and leaking, and Zach swiped his thumb over the head.

"Fuck, Zach," Ryan panted. "Keep that up, and I'll shoot in my underwear."

"I'll buy you another pair." Zach fumbled one-handed for the seat belt buckle and they floundered into the back seat. Sprawling out on the seats, Ryan wriggled out of his jeans and boxers. The head of his cock was an angry red color, dribbling glistening precum. Zach went to kneel between Ryan's legs and cracked his head against the ceiling. "Ouch!"

Ryan covered his mouth, but his eyes danced with amusement. "You okay?"

"I'm too damn tall for this," Zach grumbled.

Ryan folded his arms. "'I'm Zach! I'm too tall, boo-hoo!' Cry me a river, man."

Chuckling, Zach knelt on the floor instead, the top of his head just brushing the ceiling. He couldn't remember laughing with anyone during sex. Zach leaned down and parted his lips around the head of Ryan's dick, licking his slit. Ryan bucked beneath him, grabbing onto Zach's hand and cutting off his circulation. "So good, baby. That's so fucking good."

Zach pressed his thumb into Ryan's heavy balls, swirling his finger in a tight circle and relishing the groan he earned. Ryan laid his feet flat on the seat, pushing himself up into Zach's mouth, and Zach pulled back just enough so Ryan could fuck into him at his own pace. Bobbing his head in time to the rise and fall of Ryan's thrusts, Zach fell into sync with Ryan's movements.

"Zach," Ryan panted, his voice thin and desperate. Zach quickened his movements, wanting Ryan to come down his throat. Instead, Ryan beckoned him closer. "Switch places with me. Want you up here, close."

Zach hadn't expected that, and his heart clenched in sudden happiness. Ryan moved over so Zach could lie back on the seat, one leg propped up near the window, the other sprawled on the floor. It wasn't the most comfortable position, but Ryan was naked and kneeling over him, and Zach couldn't care less about being comfortable.

Humming, Ryan undid Zach's belt and tugged down his jeans. Zach realized it was the *Jurassic Park* theme and burst out laughing before he could stop himself. Ryan's mouth quirked but he remained focused on his duty, slapping Zach's ass to get him to raise his hips, and Zach obliged with a groan. Grinning, Ryan yanked Zach's pants and underwear down. "Like being slapped, huh? We can explore that some other time."

He groaned at the thought. Doing anything with Ryan sounded fucking amazing.

Ryan closed his fingers around Zach's cock, and a shudder racked Zach's body. His hips lurched into Ryan's touch, his balls drawing up so swiftly Zach thought he'd come on the spot. He fisted Ryan's cock and worked him in tight, hard pulls that left Ryan whimpering. Ryan leaned down, their noses bumping and lips colliding. Craving more of his taste, Zach plundered Ryan's mouth and their tongues glided together, twisting and tangling.

Ryan grinned down at him, his eyes heavy-lidded and fangs sharp. "Fuck, Zach, you're making me come."

Zach urged Ryan's hand away from Zach's dick. He didn't want to finish until Ryan was good and satisfied. "Touch yourself for me," he said. He held his fingers to Ryan's mouth, enjoying the wet, hot suction of his lips around the digits. Ryan went to town, pumping his hand up and down his shaft. Massaging Ryan's balls, Zach stroked and tugged ever so gently, and then his other hand sought Ryan's tight hole. Ryan groaned, his hole clenching under Zach's damp fingers. "Zach, come on. Give it to me."

He pushed a finger past the tight ring of muscle, groaning when Ryan clenched around him. He was so hot, so tight. When Zach curled his finger, Ryan cried out, "Fuck, yes!" Biting his lip, Ryan jacked his cock so hard and fast it might have looked painful if not for the jubilation on Ryan's face.

Zach pegged his prostate again, stretching his fingers wide until Ryan whimpered and threw back his head. "Zach..." Ryan whined, his chest rising and falling quickly. "Fuck, I'm so close. Look what you've done." His cock was drenched in precum.

Ryan cried out Zach's name, shaking out another spurt of cum. Zach's balls drew up just watching Ryan cover him in spunk. Gathering his spunk between his fingers, Ryan wrapped them around Zach's cock and jerked him.

Stars burst behind Zach's eyelids. "Oh, fuck... Ryan!"

"Look so beautiful covered in my cum, baby," Ryan crooned, leaning down to kiss Zach's neck, fangs nipping at his skin and making him gasp. "How could you think I'd ever want anyone else when you're so fucking perfect?"

A choked sound escaped Zach.

"Answer me."

Closing his eyes tight so Ryan wouldn't see they were damp, Zach stammered, "D-don't know. It's stupid. I'm—"

"Don't you say you're stupid." Ryan snarled the words into Zach's ear while he stroked him. "I will never want anyone else but you. Nobody gets me harder than you. Nobody makes me cum like you."

"Why?" Zach gripped onto Ryan's arms, squeezing tight. "I'm a mess."

Ryan shook his head, pressing kisses into Zach's neck. "I love how beautiful you look when you stop trying to be in control all the time, when you let yourself feel all those complicated feelings and you trust me to talk you back from the edge. Nobody makes me feel needed like you do. You understand? Nobody. If you let me, I'll tell you how damn perfect you are every day until I finally get you to see yourself the way I do."

Tears dampened Zach's cheeks, even as he rocked into Ryan's fist. "Don't deserve you."

Ryan claimed his mouth in a breath-stealing kiss, twining his tongue around Zach's, sucking his lower lip. "You deserve everything," he growled against Zach's mouth. "Tell me, baby. Tell me you deserve everything."

"I…" Zach arched into Ryan's fist. "I deserve—" A strangled sob escaped him. Embarrassment burned him up from the inside out.

Ryan nipped his ear. "Say it."

"I deserve everything." The words broke on Zach's tongue, and he clutched at Ryan's shoulders, hauling him closer.

"Good, baby. So good." Stroking him faster, Ryan kissed Zach's trembling mouth. "Tell me you're worthy, tell me how perfect you are, and I'll let you come."

Riding Ryan's every stroke higher and higher, Zach choked out, "I-I'm worthy. I'm perfect. Fuck. Ryan. *Please.*"

Growling low in his chest, Ryan kissed his way down Zach's writhing body. Hot, hungry lips suckled on his nipples and sent bolts of electricity to Zach's aching cock. Pleas and gasps fell from his lips by the time Ryan had licked his way down Zach's abs. When the heat of Ryan's mouth wrapped around him, Zach was reduced to whimpers and shameless moans.

Ryan bobbed his head, gliding up and down every throbbing inch, and Zach was helpless but to thrust into his mouth. He tried to go slow so he didn't choke Ryan. That ended when Ryan kissed the head of his dick and said, "Choke me with this big beautiful cock, baby. Flood my mouth."

Unable to hold back, Zach grabbed his hair and thrust with abandon, chasing his release until, with a hoarse scream, he erupted down Ryan's throat. Ryan collapsed into his arms, and Zach held him tight and close. They shivered and panted together, two survivors in a raging storm. Zach pressed his lips to Ryan's cheek, then licked his ear, and his heart sang from the giggle he earned. Ryan's breath hit Zach's ear in warm, damp bursts, and he whispered something that was drowned out by a rumble of thunder.

Something that sounded heartachingly like "I love you," but Zach told himself he was only hearing what he wanted to hear.

Chapter 14

MAGIC

Grandma Rose was laid in her final resting place on an overcast Thursday. The funeral was very much in Rose's style, with wooden benches beneath an archway of emerald trees. Thankfully, the gray clouds didn't shower the congregation with rain. Never a religious woman, she had loved nature and cared for her garden like the plants were her children. A church wouldn't have suited her, not even one dedicated to the lunar deity Amaris, few as those were. Ryan smiled painfully, thinking she would have very much approved of being buried outside under an open sky.

The Kelly pack gathered to pay their respects, and Ryan had invited the LPA agents to attend. Today was the day he'd tell them about his magic and about the threat his gran believed was coming.

Would they even believe him? Would they still see him the same way or would they treat him differently?

"Okay?" Zach asked. He sat beside Ryan and had practically been glued to his side the whole time. Ryan didn't know if it was because Zach knew he needed comfort today or if Zach was making amends for bailing on him. Either way, he appreciated Zach's closeness.

Ryan tried to smile. "I think so."

Zach bumped their shoulders together. "Let me know if you need anything, okay?"

Heart full, Ryan leaned up and kissed Zach. "Thanks."

"Hey, boys." His father joined them on the bench. Ryan jumped away from Zach, his cheeks warm from almost being caught by his dad. His dad's mouth was in a thin line, and his hair was rumpled like he'd been twirling it the way he did when he was agitated. "Ry," his father began, speaking quietly, "I tried to text you."

Ryan knew that look. Something had happened.

"Hey, Mom," he said when his mom joined his dad.

She didn't even look at him.

His father nudged him gently and gave him a tense look.

When Ryan saw the confused look on his mom's face, his heart nearly shattered.

"Who died again, Dec?" his mother asked, her brows furrowed in confusion.

"My mother, Rose," he answered, trying to smile.

"Oh. I'm so sorry." She hugged his waist. "I wish I'd been able to meet her."

She realized Ryan was staring and looked in his direction, smiling politely. There was no recognition there, and from the agony that drove into his heart, Ryan felt as if his mother had died along with his gran. Goddess, his mother would be so crushed when she realized that she'd been forgetful during Gran's ceremony. That she'd missed her chance to say goodbye.

His throat felt tight. He had to master his magic. He had to, so he could give her the help she desperately deserved.

She asked Ryan, "Did you know Rose?"

"Yes. She was…" He hesitated. If he told the truth, she would become confused and panic. "A friend."

Her face crumpled. "I'm so sorry for your loss."

It was your loss too, he thought. *You should be here. You should be saying goodbye to her. You loved her. This isn't right. This isn't fair.* Tears spilled down his face before he could stop them. It was killing him, imagining how upset she'd be that she'd been here physically but not mentally. She would feel like she'd failed Rose.

His father gripped his arm and squeezed tight. "It's okay," he murmured, even though it wasn't.

She would come back, she always did, but every time she forgot him, it hurt as much as the first time.

Beside him Zach took Ryan's hand and leaned down to kiss his hair. The bond between them glowed warm and soothed Ryan's heartache. With Zach beside him, he held it together even if on the inside, he was falling apart.

After Rose's casket lay beneath freshly turned soil, the friends and family of the Kelly pack shared in the food on the banquet tables.

Gabe approached and yanked Ryan into a brief but warm hug. "Sorry, Ry."

Ryan thanked him, scuffing the ground with his toe. He'd never been good at the whole condolence thing.

Gabe raised a glass of wine and Ryan clinked their glasses together.

"My parents approved your request," Gabe said. "They sent you a book in the mail on sacred groves, so keep an eye out."

"Thanks, man. I appreciate it."

Gabe looked around at the sizeable crowd with wide eyes.

"The Kelly pack sure are breeders, huh?" Ryan said.

Gabe sputtered. "Was gonna say it another way, but yeah, you've got a big pack, man. Had no idea."

Ryan hummed, his eyes darting among the crowd. "That's one of my cousins, I think. My uncles are over there. My aunts and their parents. Got a lot of cousins on my mom's side."

He rarely attended when the whole Kelly pack gathered, but he was familiar enough with his family to recognize who was a Kelly and who wasn't.

"Same," Gabe said. "My family is spread out all over Mexico and Spain. Don't think we've ever all gathered in one place before. I'm not sure the world is ready for that much Reyes in one place, you know?" Amber eyes swiveled over the crowd. He waved. "Lobito! Over here."

Max's wide eyes lit up and he squeezed through the crowd to Gabe's side, looking squished and uncomfortable. He handed Gabe a plate of BBQ ribs Ryan recognized. It was probably from his uncle Frankie's Texas steakhouse. Max patted Ryan's shoulder. "Sorry for your loss," he said as he met Ryan's gaze with a sympathetic smile. Max gave him a tight, one-armed hug, and Ryan smiled at Gabe over Max's shoulder.

Ben pulled Ryan into a big bear hug. "How's your mom taking it? I talked to your dad."

"She doesn't remember Rose. Or me. She'll probably be out of it for a while." Ryan tried to keep his voice casual, but the hurt tightened around his heart like barbed wire. "It happens sometimes after a stressful situation." Zach put a hand on the small of his back.

Izzie hurried over and Ryan returned her tender embrace.

"How are you feeling?" she asked, rubbing his shoulders.

Ryan shrugged. "Fine, I guess." His eyes stung as if to contradict himself, and he wiped the tears away to no avail. "Fuck. Guess not."

"Hey, it's okay." Zach's low baritone made Ryan's stomach flip-flop. He looked up into warm brown eyes and his heart melted at the sight of Zach's sad little smile. Leaning over to hug him, Zach's big arms wrapped around Ryan's body.

Ryan found it in himself to smile. "I'm okay." He didn't sound too convincing and for a moment, he clung on tight to Zach's wide shoulders, needing the respite. Zach was tall enough that he draped over Ryan like a blanket, bundling him in protection and warmth. Kissing his cheek, Zach's big hand ran over Ryan's back.

"You two are so sweet," Izzie said, sounding choked up herself. "Are we allowed to talk about the fact that our friends are kind of sort of dating yet?"

Zach chuckled softly. "Not the place, Izzie."

She pouted. "Well, let me know when because I am *dying* for details."

They were all here, Ryan realized as Eddie and Vicenzo wandered over. He had to tell them now. And he wasn't ready or prepared. "I need to talk to you. All of you." He motioned for the pack to follow him up the trail away from the gathering.

"Serious Ryan makes me nervous," Gabe said, smiling as he sidled up beside him.

Ryan laughed humorlessly. *Wait until Gabe hears what I have to tell them...*

Eddie tapped his chin thoughtfully. "Let's take a guess at what you're going to say."

At that, Izzie's eyes lit up. "Did you finally realize that parting your hair makes you look like some uptight jerk who hates his office job?"

Ryan gasped, insulted.

Gabe wheezed.

Cocking his head, Zach asked, "You're moving?"

Max gasped. "Oh! You got a raise!"

Ben arched his brows. "What now?"

"You joined some motorcycle club and that's why you've got that weird tattoo on your neck?" Gabe said.

Ryan whipped around to glare at all of them. "What about any of those questions is so important I have to literally take you guys away from where anyone might overhear us?"

They blinked, considering. Izzie opened her mouth.

"And Izzie, my hair looks great, so shut up!"

Izzie hung her head. "If you're from the nineteen hundreds..."

Zach said unhelpfully, "Ryan's an old soul."

He considered dropping a tree on them but held out until he was sure the werewolves back at the reception wouldn't overhear them. The woods surrounded them, quiet and still. Ryan breathed in and listened to the wind whisper through the leaves in small green voices that soothed him.

"Ry?" Gabe cocked his head. "Everything good?"

Ryan exhaled and looked among them. These were his people. His pack. He could trust them with his life. And the magic in him thought so too. It reached out within him, toward the bonds that connected them.

"Actually, you weren't far off the mark, Gabe."

His brows disappeared into his hairline. Quirking his lips, he said, "Really? So what's with the tattoo?"

Ryan sat on a fallen tree. It creaked under his weight. The wind blew toward the pack, and dead leaves rustled over the ground toward them. The trees whispered, *Tell them. Tell them...*

So Ryan said, "I got this tattoo after my grandma died. It was the same as hers." He watched them. Izzie smiled, sweet and sad. Ben's brow furrowed, his mouth twisting in confusion beneath his beard. "She gave me this tattoo. She touched me, and I inherited it and our family's legacy."

Gabe squinted. "Ry, you're bein' real vague, buddy."

He closed his eyes tight. There was no simple way to say this. He opened them and looked up. "She was one of the last remaining druids in the world. And when she died, she gave me her magic."

No one reacted, at least not out loud, but their expressions shifted. Ben's frown got even more pronounced. Max's eyes were as big as the moon. Vicenzo's scowl had slipped off his face and Ryan could see the cogs working in Eddie's brain.

After a moment Zach opened his mouth. Nothing came out. He tried again. "But... Wait. That can't be. Druids were hunted to extinction. They—"

Ryan cut him off. "Not all of them. Some werewolves helped my family survive the genocide."

Frowning, Max said, "And you only recently learned this?"

Ryan clicked his tongue. "Yup. I'm about where you guys are right now in terms of confusion."

Izzie laughed, her back to a tree. "So this is why you've been all weird. I'm honestly relieved it's this and not something really bad."

Ben was the only one who'd stayed silent, his expression dour.

Ryan cleared his throat. "Ben? You okay?"

"You accepted her magic just like that?" Ben paced. "Can you even control it?"

"I can! Sort of. I will. Soon. I've been researching using all these tomes my gran kept and learning Gaelic so I can do spells and—it's a whole ordeal, but your light bulbs are safe, I promise!"

Ben backed away, wary. "Ry, what were you thinking? Just accepting a gift like that. There's a reason the druids were hunted. Magic can be dangerous."

Ryan's heart sank. Would Ben have a problem with this?

Zach stepped toward Ryan protectively. "Ben, this is Ryan we're talking about. He's not dangerous."

Ryan looked at Ben. "Druid magic might be dangerous, sure, in the wrong hands."

"Like Atticus," Ben said, voice dark. Ryan's heart sank even farther.

"But I'm not Atticus, Ben! Back in the old days, druids used magic to aid wolves! To help strengthen our ties to our humanity, repair fractured pack bonds, restore a feral wolf's sanity. I only accepted because I knew how helpful it could be to this pack! To my mom."

Ryan's heart cracked in his chest. He needed Ben to trust him.

Max looked from Ben to Ryan. "Ben," he said, touching his arm. "Ryan would never—"

Raising his hands, Ben said, "I know, I know." He deflated, his shoulders going slack. "This could be a great thing, Ry. But you need to learn how to control it. Promise me that."

Ryan met his gaze. "I will. My gran was going to make my dad her apprentice before she realized he couldn't inherit her magic, so he's been teaching me. Gran has notes in her grimoire about how she learned to control her magic. I need a focus for it, a special object that has significant meaning. Like how wolves need an anchor to their humanity. I'm trying. I have this leaf?" He plucked the gold-dipped leaf from his pocket and Zach smiled in recognition. "I mean, I don't know how helpful it's been, but it's something, right?"

Ben nodded, the tension leaving his face. Then he said, "Can I hire you for birthday parties?"

The pack laughed. Ryan grinned, though he felt he should be insulted. "You couldn't afford me if you tried. Anyone got something they wanna say?"

"Ryan Magic-Hands," Eddie said.

Ryan rolled his eyes.

Vicenzo said, "Tree hugger."

Max waggled his fingers. "Use the force, Luke!"

"Okay, I get it! Save it for the theater," Ryan snapped.

Eddie looked at him expectantly from beneath his leather hat. "Show us."

Ryan raised a brow. "Really?"

Clapping his hands together, Gabe said, "Come on! You can't just say 'I'm a druid' without proving it! So prove it, man! Light some shit on fire. Pull a rabbit out of your hat."

Max beamed. "I second that!"

Izzie twirled her hair. "Can you turn a pumpkin into a carriage, conjure me a dress out of thin air, and send me to a ball? Your girl needs a break!"

"I'm not a fairy godmother!" Ryan glowered at her.

Zach shrugged. "Seems about the same difference."

Ryan hated them. He loved them. By the She-Wolf, he loved them all with everything he had. Even Vicenzo and his scowling, grumpy ass.

Vicenzo said, "Do it. Or otherwise, I'm just gonna think of you as this sad hippie who lives in the woods, gets high, and humps trees. And that's not an image I want in my head. Ever."

Ryan looked around the woods, trying to think of what he could do to impress them. He grinned. "Okay. Hold on to your asses." He closed his eyes and felt the earth beneath his feet, the roots tangling and worms wriggling. The rocks deep within the soil. There was distant chatter from within the woods. A spark from an old campfire, burning bright. It tugged at him, so he pulled, curling his fingers.

The pack let out cries of amazement and Ryan opened his eyes. A flame danced in his palm, pleasantly warm. Ryan's mouth fell open. He'd never been able to control the elements until today. Maybe the gold-dipped leaf had worked as his focus after all. "I did it! I'm totally awesome!" But he got too excited. The flame roared, leaping up and scorching his hair. Ryan shrieked and patted the fire out, growling when the pack laughed once they were sure he was unhurt. Though he thought he'd heard Vicenzo laugh before he'd extinguished the flame. The dick.

"I'm still learning," he added, pinching out an ember in his hair.

"Evidently," Ben said, though not unkindly.

"Guys, there's more," Ryan said, clearing his throat. His somber tone made their smiles vanish. He blew out a breath and balled his hands into fists. "My gran sensed something was coming. Something only a druid can stop, and whatever it is, she believed it's happening soon."

Ben's jaw tightened. "That's awfully vague, Ryan."

"I know. I'm trying to gather as much information as I can."

Gabe's eyes widened. "Something connected to sacred groves?"

Nodding, Ryan said, "Whatever it is, it has to do with druid ritual sites. I don't know much yet, but I'm doing all I can. I need to be ready."

Zach gripped his shoulder. "Whatever it is, you won't face it alone. You know that, right?"

Ryan smiled and felt his worries dissipate. "Yeah, of course. Like you fuckers would let me have all the glory to myself."

Everyone laughed, and Ryan's heart lightened.

His pack had his back, and that meant more than he could say.

After the funeral concluded, the pack parted ways. Ryan was relieved the pack accepted him, but he found it hard to meet Zach's eyes for the rest of the day. Zach didn't smell agitated, but Ryan was worried he might be hurt he'd kept such a big secret from him.

His dad came up and hugged him. "See you for another lesson soon, okay?"

"Yeah, definitely."

"Gran would be proud of you, Ry." His dad cupped the back of Ryan's neck.

Ryan's heart clenched when his mother walked right by him. "Mo—" He snapped his mouth shut. She didn't remember him, and he knew better than to confront her. As much as her memory loss hurt him, she would only get freaked out if he insisted he was her son. The doctors had taught them that when she was forgetful, it was best to just humor her until she came out of her episodes. Usually, her forgetful spells only lasted minutes to hours. "Mrs. Kelly," he said, correcting himself. "Have a good day."

"You as well. I'm so sorry for your loss."

Ryan swallowed the lump in his throat. "Thank you."

"Dear, wait for me," his dad called after her as she walked away.

Ryan gripped his dad's arm before he could leave. "How long has she been like this?"

He sighed. "Since this morning. She'd forgotten today was the service and who it was for."

He thought back, trying to remember. "When was her last episode?"

"She..." His father bit his lip. "She's had a hard week. Maybe it was knowing that Rose was going to die that triggered it."

"Triggered what?"

His father dropped his gaze to the floor. "All week, she's been blanking. Losing her phone. Forgetting what day of the week it is, losing track of her appointments. Now this..."

Ryan's heart sank. "Dad, she's been forgetful all week?"

His father shook his head. "I think it's all just stress."

Or... or she was getting worse.

"She'll be okay, Ry. You're going to help her."

Goddess, he hoped so. He had to find his damn focus, and soon. "Call me when she's herself again, okay?" Ryan's voice trembled.

"I will. She'll be herself again in no time. You know how it is."

Ryan didn't know if he believed him. He sat on the cold stone bench and watched them leave. If he was a better druid, he could have helped her by now.

Zach's scent told Ryan of his approach before he saw him. He put his hands on Ryan's shoulders and squeezed, saying, "Hey, so I'm kind of tired. Do you mind if I stay over?"

"Sure." Ryan wouldn't say it, but he was grateful he'd asked.

They shared Ryan's bed that night, only this time neither was in wolf form. Zach, it turned out, was just as cuddly in his human form and migrated from his side of the bed to Ryan's, so Ryan's arms were full of his very tall, long-limbed friend. Zach yawned in his ear, and his big arms wound around Ryan and held him close. He fell asleep with Zach's heart beating a soothing lullaby in his ear, happy to have Zach so close.

In the morning, Ryan woke to the smell of bacon. He rolled out of bed and found Zach in the kitchen. The radio was playing some sappy pop song, of all damn things, and Zach was actually singing along under his breath, his hip cocked as he flipped the pancakes. He knew every word.

Putting his hand over his mouth to quiet a laugh, Ryan was content to just watch him, so comfortable in Ryan's space as he pulled a plate from the cabinet and grabbed some forks from the drawers. He knew Ryan's kitchen as well as if he lived there, and Ryan didn't know why that made him so happy.

Zach turned and smiled at the sight of Ryan. It was like sunshine, and the potted lavender plant on top of the microwave went from wilted to full bloom as Ryan's heart fluttered in his chest. "Hey, boyfriend," Zach said. Such a simple thing, but it made Ryan smile.

"Hey, beautiful boyfriend," he said back, grinning when Zach shyly averted his gaze.

Now this he could get used to. Nothing about calling Zach his boyfriend felt awkward. It felt right, like this was only a natural extension of their relationship.

They shared a kiss, and Ryan savored the coffee on Zach's lips, the way their bodies fit together, the sound of their breathing in the cozy quiet of the kitchen. Goddess, this felt so right.

"Want some coffee? I can make it Irish." Zach winked and Ryan's face warmed.

"Yeah, that sounds good after yesterday." He was astonished at the amount of food Zach had balanced on his arms: pancakes, a side of bacon, and eggs. Ryan ran to help him carry it to the table. "Damn, Zach. I should tip you. What's this all for?"

Zach doubled back to grab the coffee, splashing some Irish whiskey in each mug. He handed Ryan his coffee and they sat together. Zach took a sip and sighed, and Ryan copied him. It was fantastic. Zach said, "Just figured you could use a little TLC after the funeral. Damn, man. Your gran died *and* you inherited some magical abilities you didn't even know was a part of your family history?" He frowned. "I should have put more whiskey in these."

"You aren't mad at me for keeping such a big secret?"

Zach shook his head. "You had a lot on your plate. You'd have told me if you could."

Ryan squeezed the mug in his hands. It was as if Zach had no idea just what a grand gesture this was, how much it meant... The candlewick on the table burst suddenly to life. Ryan jumped and Zach chuckled. "Guess I'll need to get used to that."

Face hot, Ryan gulped his coffee.

"You looked like you were taking things in stride yesterday." Zach speared some eggs and a piece of bacon on his fork. "Are you okay? It's a lot to be handed that much responsibility."

Ryan chewed a bite of soft, fluffy eggs. "Dude, how did you cook these eggs? They're like a cloud!"

Zach stared, steam rising in tendrils from his mug.

Swallowing, the eggs hit Ryan's stomach in a hard ball. "I don't know how I'm feeling." It was a lie.

Zach scoffed. He must have heard the telltale trip of Ryan's heartbeat.

Ryan set down his fork. "It's like there's this weight on my shoulders that wasn't there before. Sure, I can do things like make candles light up, or make plants grow, or talk to trees—"

"What?" Zach squawked.

"—but druids are so much more than that. They were tasked with protecting werewolves, using their magic to aid the pack. Gran seemed to think I could even use my magic to help heal Mom's sickness!" Ryan scoffed, his breath rippling the steam from his coffee. "I couldn't even pull a rabbit outta my hat if I wanted to."

Zach frowned and set down his coffee. "You just started learning. There's gotta be somewhere you can find out more about magic."

"My gran left some tomes behind. Might as well have given me a book in another language before even teaching me the basics! Literally. All these spells are in Gaelic, and I'm rusty as hell. Magic needs a focus. Gran found hers in her mom's ring but I can't find mine." Ryan squeezed his fork tight. The candle burned brighter, flickering wildly as if in a breeze. "I don't know how to learn. I don't think I *can* learn, and if I can't learn, then—"

Then his mother would never get better. Soon her memories would fade for good. Every day would be like Gran's funeral, and she'd look at him like she didn't know who he was. He had to learn. He *had* to. The plants in the house rattled in their pots, ceramic shattering as Ryan's frustration peaked.

"Hey. Ry, come on. Give yourself some credit. You're the smartest guy I know. You aced all your history classes."

"I can't! I can't do this. Why did I accept this? She should have given it to someone who actually knew what the fuck they were doing!" Ryan lurched away from the table, trying to breathe, to calm the fuck down, but his senses were on overload. He could hear the water as it rushed through the pipes, feel the spark waiting to be ignited within the stove, and the electricity thrumming through the walls buzzed like insects in his ears.

"Ry? Calm down, okay? Talk to me." Zach's chair screeched as he stood.

"Can't. I don't know how to anchor it. Nothing's working!" He ripped the gold-dipped leaf from his pocket and smashed it beneath his boot. The fucking thing was as useless as he was. Maybe if he was a better druid, he would've been able to focus his magic through it.

Every light in the house went on. The lights hummed, surging brighter then dim, bright then dim. The windows rattled as green ivy obscured them.

"I mean, what did I think? That I would make a difference? That I could help? I can't even help myself!"

Then Zach's hands were on his shoulders, spinning him around. "Ryan!"

All the noise cut out. Everything stilled. The itching under his skin subsided. His tattoo stopped burning. It was like everything had been dialed down. All he heard was the steady thump, thump, thump of Zach's heart. All he felt was the warm touch of Zach's hands on his shoulders, anchoring him and keeping him from drifting away and being lost forever. The bond between them was like the sun, eclipsing everything else and burning with warmth. There was a lump in his throat when Ryan tried to breathe.

"What just happened?" Zach asked, his eyes studying Ryan's face.

"I... I don't know. You touched me and everything just stopped."

His magic wasn't a raging storm. It was calm. Focused. *He* was focused. More than ever before. And it was because of Zach.

"Pack bonds?" Zach guessed, his thumbs pressing into Ryan's skin, lightly massaging the tightness from his shoulders.

"No," he murmured, wetting his lips. "It wasn't like this around the others. I mean, my magic reached for them, sure, but this is more than that. I think it's you, Zach." Of course his magic would like Zach. Ryan gazed over his shoulder at the candle. It had burned out. He closed his eyes and focused on the bond between them, and the candle burst to life with no effort on his part. A grin spread across Ryan's face.

"Maybe Gran's focus was an object, but maybe a druid's focus is different for everyone..." Ryan whispered, understanding. "Maybe my focus didn't need to be something, but some*one*."

Zach's eyes were big and brown as he gazed at Ryan. "Your magic anchored itself to me?"

Ryan nodded, unable to tear his eyes away as the ivy died outside and let the sunshine in, lighting up Zach's face. "Yeah."

Zach's mouth trembled when he smiled and Ryan couldn't help it; he grabbed onto Zach and pulled him in, covering Zach's mouth with his. The sound of Zach's moan got the blood boiling in Ryan's veins. He didn't try anything with his tongue or grab Zach's ass, much as he wanted to. Instead, he cupped Zach's face in his hands, savoring the way their chests touched and their hearts raced as one.

Zach laughed breathlessly when they finally parted. "I knew you could do it."

Ryan bit his lip because if he didn't, he would have told Zach how much he loved him. He didn't know if they were ready for that since they'd only just started dating.

Zach frowned. "Shit. I gotta get back. Work's starting soon on my dad's final project, and my mom wants to meet." Ryan hated for him to go but forced himself to smile. Squeezing his shoulder, Zach said, "Look, Ry. You've totally got this magic stuff. And you'll help your mom. I know you will."

Ryan's heart stuttered. How had Zach guessed that was weighing on him the most? "Yeah, I... I know I will. Thanks, Zach. For everything."

Zach grabbed his hoodie off the back of the chair and smiled. "See you, Ry." With a wink that made Ryan roll his eyes, Zach hurried out the door.

The candle on the table fizzled out and died.

CHAPTER 15

ZACH KNOWS

Zach smiled during the drive to his mother's penthouse. He never would have imagined he'd become a focus for his best friend's magic. That he would matter to someone that much. And he wouldn't have it any other way. He was damn proud to be Ryan's focus, and he didn't want anyone else to have that honor. Whatever Ryan needed, Zach would be there to help him. Perhaps together they could help Ryan's mom.

Once he arrived at the penthouse, he followed his mother's scent to the drawing room.

It was his favorite room in the entire house. There were shelves and shelves of old books that smelled like yellowed pages and peeling leather, books on land development and architecture filling every shelf. The windows let in rays of golden sunlight that pooled on the carpet where his father had worn holes pacing up and down talking on the phone.

The room still smelled like his father, as if the world hadn't quite caught up to the realization that Josiah DeShawn was nothing but ashes. There hadn't been a funeral for him. He'd been cremated, his ashes in an urn in his mother's room, and that had been that. Zach felt like he didn't belong in this space, like he was an imposter as he sat at his father's drawing table and examined the blueprints of his father's final project. Unlike his rustic woodland resorts, this one was very modern.

Zach could appreciate his father's eye for detail, but there was a reason he'd never had a taste for land development work: his father built his resorts in places where people could come and appreciate nature, yet so many trees would be torn down to make space for the buildings and so many animals would be displaced from their homes or even killed as development began. It was hard for Zach not to see the irony in his father's plans, especially for a werewolf. He'd always thought it was their job to protect nature, not tear it down.

The door opened and his mother walked in, a mug of peppermint tea in her hand. "What took you so long?" she huffed.

"I told you, Mom, I was at Ryan's place. His gran's funeral was yesterday. He needed support."

She furrowed her perfectly plucked brows. "Doesn't he have others in his life to support him? This dependency on you borders on unhealthy."

Zach gritted his teeth. "You were going to give me more details about the project."

"Yes." She sat down opposite him. "The location is almost perfect. It's on Fire Island. It will be a wonderful beachfront location for tourists visiting the island."

"Why 'almost' perfect?" Zach asked.

She grimaced. "A few minor blemishes on an otherwise perfect canvas. For one, it's disturbingly close to one of those old druid ritual sites."

"A sacred grove?" Zach sat up straighter in his chair.

"More than that. This one is a druid burial ground. My workers have already begun unearthing the remains."

Zach tasted something sour in his throat. "Mom, that's wrong."

She waved a hand. "The druids have been dead for centuries, Zachariah."

There was a kernel of doubt growing in his stomach.

"There's another issue," she continued. "I don't know if this has anything to do with the site's proximity to the LPA headquarters, but a pack of wolves has taken up residence near the site. To say they've been protesting our presence is an understatement."

Zach tensed in his seat. "Wolves? Can they shift?"

"When the fancy strikes them. They're more animal than human. The beasts can barely string together a coherent sentence in human form." She sniffed disapprovingly. "The Council has territories specifically for wild wolves. Fire Island has no such territory. They've got to go."

Zach didn't like how disparagingly his mother spoke of these wolves, but they needed to be relocated for their own safety. They could be moved to a pack territory where they'd be among their own kind and away from nosy human tourists.

"Are they dangerous?"

"They scare off my workers but so far, they are avoiding conflict."

Zach gripped the arms of the chair, his nails biting into the leather armrests. "So, at worst they need to be moved. I can talk to Ben and we can find a solution that works."

"Is it as simple as tranquilizing the animals?"

Zach wrinkled his nose. "What? No. We only tranq and capture wolves if they're feral and pose a threat. You said these wolves can shift and speak, so there's no need for such extremes. We can't just go in and dart them. It's wrong."

She scoffed. "Then I'll have to get in touch with the Council, and it could be weeks before I hear from them. It will be a lengthy process. My alternative is quicker and easier."

Zach's mouth went dry. "And what *is* your alternative?"

She said, "Hunters."

Nausea churned in Zach's stomach. "You're going to *slaughter* them? Mom, you can't be serious! That isn't legal!"

She set her teacup down, the china clinking sharply. "Wolf hunting is frowned upon in our society, it's true, but not if the beasts present a danger to themselves or others."

"You just said they aren't dangerous."

She shrugged. "Nobody else needs to know that. If the Council throws a fit, I'll simply tell them the beasts were attacking my workers."

"Because you invaded their home! Mom, why can't you understand how wrong this is?" Zach lurched to his feet and paced. "There are ways we can settle this without bloodshed!"

She crossed her arms, her eyes like ice. "And I've told you, I'm not willing to waste time on any alternatives. If these animals wish to behave like beasts, then that is how they will be treated."

Zach couldn't believe her. "You're a werewolf! How can you be okay with murdering your own kind?"

Her painted lips thinned and she rose, staring him down through narrowed eyes. "How can you even compare wolves like us to creatures like them? They are no better than animals. A stain on all the progress we shifters have made. You have forgotten yourself, Zachariah. Forgotten your place. Those... *friends* of yours at the agency have turned you against me."

"No, you did!" Zach couldn't even stand to look at her.

Her nostrils flared. "All I have ever wanted, all your *father* wanted, was for you to honor our legacy!"

"If murder is your legacy, then I don't want any part of it!"

Not wanting to hear another word, he stormed to his room and hurled his clothes into his suitcase. He never should have come back. He was stupid for ever believing they could finally be a normal family.

His mother loomed in the doorway, a lit cigarette between her fingers. "I thought that for once you might finally be willing to contribute to this family. I thought you'd changed."

Zach slammed his suitcase shut. "That *I'd* changed? You mean giving up what I wanted to make you and Dad happy?"

She flung up her arms. "Because She-Wolf forbid we wanted you to have a sterling education! We handed you this business on a silver platter. I cannot believe how ungrateful you are!"

Guilt dug into him, trying to drag him down. Against his will, furious tears burned his eyes. "I tried, Mom. I dated all those girls, I got perfect grades, I suppressed who I was so I could be the son you and Dad wanted."

"Oh, for the goddess's sake! We never made you suppress anything!"

"No, just listen to me for once!" The roar erupted from him. His mother took a step back, eyes wide. His whole body trembled as years of pent-up fury surged through him. "I hated the person you and Dad wanted me to be, and I'm not changing who I am to make you happy. I'm happy, Mom; I'm proud of who I am and what I do with the LPA. If you can't accept that, then I can't be a part of this family anymore."

He forced the words out as they struggled to crawl back down his throat. Even after all these years, a part of him still felt guilty for not living up to her expectations. He was sick and tired of feeling that way.

His mother folded her arms over her chest. Wordlessly, she stepped aside. Zach clutched his suitcase and forced himself to walk past, each step heavy. Once she was behind him, he marched to the elevator.

The doors closed and Zach's knees wobbled as he exhaled, releasing all the air trapped in his chest. For a moment he felt sick to his stomach. He'd done it, he'd finally spoken his mind, and in some ways, he felt lighter for it. In others, guilt racked him for betraying his family.

They'd never had to tell him that what he wanted didn't matter. They'd shown him time and again and he'd started to believe that what he wanted came secondary, that it was wrong to want for more beyond the life they'd given him. And tonight he'd shattered the last of the shackles they'd thrown around him. He just wished he could feel happier about it.

Since he still had time off from the agency, Zach spent a few hours at the gym, then relaxed in the solitude of his apartment until dinnertime rolled around and he realized he'd neglected to go shopping. He'd been trying so hard to distract himself from his feelings of guilt that he'd neglected to eat. The idea of eating alone after the shitty day he'd had filled him with depression. He tried to call Ryan and invite him out for a bite, but he didn't answer. Ryan was probably training his magic. So, Zach called the next person he knew would answer.

"Amigo! How's it going, Mr. Businessman?" Gabe asked, sounding as jovial as always.

Zach laughed, the sound punched out of him. "I'm fine."

"What happened?" Clearly, Zach was bad at lying.

He didn't even know how to explain. "A lot. I won't waste your time with it." He really wanted to talk about it, but the last thing he wanted was to impose on his friends with his problems. "Do you and Max want to grab dinner?"

"Actually, we're almost done making dinner."

"Oh, sorry. Never mind, then."

"Whoa, hang on! How about you come over? It's Taco Tuesday."

Zach laughed. "It's not Tuesday."

"Yeah, I know, but who really cares? There's plenty to go around." Gabe chuckled. "I have to say, Tommy and Luna make mean tacos. They learned from the best, after all."

Zach smiled, very much liking the sound of an evening with his pack-mates. "You sure? I don't wanna intrude." With Gabe's vigorous assurances, Zach caved. "All right, but just because Luna's adorable."

"Riiight. See you."

The sun was setting by the time Zach arrived on Park Avenue. He still felt awkward crashing Gabe and Max's dinner but when Luna answered the door, she grinned brightly and cried, "Uncle Zach!"

"Hey, kiddo. How are you?" Zach knelt down to hug her tight. Maybe Luna wasn't his daughter, but he was more than happy to be Uncle Zach until he had his own kids someday.

"Hey, Uncle Z!" Tommy waved from the dining table, a smudge of sour cream on his mouth. "Tacos are hot and pretty damn good if I say so myself."

Max tousled his hair. "Language."

Zach joined Max, Gabe, and their kids at the table. Talking and laughing with them, surrounded by good food and even better company, Zach could never be ashamed of the choices he'd made. Not when they'd led him to his pack.

After dinner, Max did the dishes and Tommy and Luna went to their room. Zach offered to help clean up, but Max insisted he make himself comfortable.

"So, did something happen today? Gabe said you sounded pretty bummed out," Max said, scrubbing a plate.

He rolled his shoulders. "Oh, nothing, my mom just wants to murder an entire pack of wolves living on a druid burial ground where she wants to build my dad's resort."

Max dropped a plate with a clatter. "What? For real?"

"Yup."

Gabe grabbed a bottle from the kitchen cabinet. "Kids are down for the count! Who wants a drink?"

Max and Zach raised their hands.

Gabe poured some peanut butter whiskey into three glasses. "What's that about a pack of wolves?"

Zach sighed. "Apparently, on Fire Island there's a pack living on a burial ground where my dad wanted to develop his final project."

Confusion wrinkled Gabe's brow. "For real? How could we not know about this pack?"

"Because they're reclusive. They're not feral."

Max shrugged. "So if they're not feral, why can't she negotiate with them?"

"She says she tried that. Now my mom wants them gone. By force."

Horror left Max's eyes wide. "No!"

"So I let her have it. I'm done waiting for her to change."

Max grinned. "That's the spirit."

Gabe clapped him on the back. "All right! How'd that feel?"

He shrugged, trying not to smile. "It felt good, I think. But should I feel good for turning my back on my mom? Dad just died and I said I would help, but—"

"Hey. Cut it out." Gabe looked him square in the eye and Zach's breath caught. "You did the right thing. One hundred percent."

"Absolutely." Max sat down next to him and bumped him with his shoulder. "Zach, you don't owe them anything. Repeat it after me: you don't—"

"—owe them anything." Zach chewed on his lower lip, wishing he could let those words sink in and believe them. He exhaled and repeated the words again in his head.

Gabe sprawled out, an arm around Max's shoulders. "Hell, you gave her more than she deserved just by being there after your dad died. You're allowed to be happy with the choices you made, with who you are, even if your mom isn't."

Zach blinked hard, feeling his face get warm. It was one thing to think those words to himself but hearing them said aloud brought him such a rush of reassurance.

"Especially if she isn't," Max added. There was a darkness in his eyes. "I don't know what your parents told you, but you deserve happiness."

Speechless, Zach swallowed, trying to ease the tightness in his throat. "It's not what they said. It's everything they didn't. That I mattered. That—" He cut himself off, not wanting to unload all his baggage on them. He nodded, done speaking.

"I know." Gabe bumped his shoulder against Zach's. The lamplight turned his scars pale against his skin.

"Sometimes that's what hurts the most," Max murmured.

"But hey, you got us, for all that's worth. And we think you're great," Gabe said, sticking out his chest. "So, fuck 'em."

Zach laughed, "You're pretty great too."

"I'm great. My Lobito is great." Gabe smacked a kiss on Max's mouth. "We're all great!"

Max giggled. "Someone's tipsy."

Gabe took a swig of his whiskey, his cheeks flushed from the drink. "And hey, I know someone who thinks you're the greatest of the great. Ryan!

I mean, come on! That guy is so in love with you, it's crazy—" Gabe's eyes widened, and he froze, his drink halfway to his mouth. What? Of course Ryan loved Zach. They'd been friends for years. Zach loved him too. Confused, Zach looked from Gabe to Max and saw Gabe's horror mirrored in Max's face too.

At first, Zach didn't get it. What about what Gabe had said was so— Zach's heart thudded hard in his chest.

"What do you mean?" His voice was loud in the sudden quiet and Gabe jumped.

"Nothing." Gabe set down his whiskey.

Max put his face in his hands.

Ryan was in love with him? No. That couldn't be what he'd said. He must have misheard.

Max stood fast. "Huh? What was that? I think Luna called for me. Sorry, gotta go!" He tripped over the coffee table and practically fell into the kids' room. Tommy and Luna started laughing at him, their voices muffled by the door.

Gabe's shoulders rose and dropped, his throat bobbing as he swallowed hard. "So." His voice cracked. "You watched the latest Timberwolves game, right? How was it?"

Zach shook his head. "Gabe, what did you say?"

"Nothing!" Gabe lurched off the sofa like it was lava.

"Gabe, do you know something?"

"Everyone knows it, okay?" Gabe burst out, his face as red as Max's hair. "Everyone! Ben, Izzie, Max, me! That's right, I'm taking them down with me! Under the bus they go! And now you know, and Ryan is going to flay me!" Gabe caught his breath, his hands in his hair as he spiraled.

Short of breath, Zach doubled over. Ryan loved him. Had Zach seriously spent *years* thinking he couldn't have Ryan, beating himself up for loving his best friend, only for Ryan to have been in love with him this whole time?

Faintly, Gabe said, "Think I've said enough."

He sprang up before Gabe could leave and turned him around. "How long?" Zach's voice quavered.

Gabe slumped. "I... Zach, the guy's loved you since you were kids. He told me himself."

Since you were kids. Those four words flipped Zach's world onto its head.

It explained so much. The way he'd blushed when he was a kid whenever Zach had touched him. How Ryan seemed to know exactly what he needed without Zach having to say a word. It explained why Ryan had taken so long to warm up to Gabe. It explained so much of Ryan's behavior toward him recently, his attraction for Zach that had seemed to come out of nowhere. And oh Goddess, Zach's girlfriends... every guy Zach had ever dated... the way Ryan's lips had thinned whenever Zach talked about them, the way his smiles never quite reached his eyes when he said, "That's great, man. I'm happy for you..."

"He's in love with me." Zach's voice came out a whisper, realization sweeping over him. His knees buckled, and he sat back down on the couch. "He's been in love with me all this time?"

Gabe winced. "You okay, man?"

Zach slapped his hands to his head. How was he actually this stupid? "*What?*" His shrill voice rang through the room. "Oh Goddess. Oh my freaking—" Lurching to his feet, Zach paced the living room. "He blushed all the time around me, and he was so sad the day he moved to Cali 'cause he thought I'd forget about him! Oh my—" Zach turned away, the room a blur as he paced. "I made out with you in front of him!"

Gabe winced. "I know."

He wanted to kick something. "Oh Goddess. I dated other guys and told him all about them! Fuck, Gabe! I've been breaking his heart for years!"

Gabe flinched. "Probably..." he squeaked.

Zach wobbled, suddenly feeling dizzy. He collapsed into a dining room chair, at a loss for what to do with himself.

"How do you feel?" Gabe asked, eyeing him with concern. "No, seriously, man. Are you okay right now?"

Zach raised his hands and dropped them with a laugh. "Fuck, man. I don't know."

He was horrified. His best friend had been in love with him since they were kids, and Zach hadn't had the faintest clue. But... he was also happy. Because Ryan loved him. Ryan, who was kind and funny, who made Zach feel like it was all right to be insecure and a little messy because Ryan saw his core.

It all came rushing back to him—the times when he'd noticed just how handsome Ryan really was, the times when he'd reflected on just how simple life would be if they were together, how natural and right it would feel. When Zach was with Ryan, the world felt right and when they were parted, the world was a cruel and frightening place.

Gabe was watching him intently.

Struggling for words, Zach felt as if the world itself were tipping on its axis. "I think I..." He didn't have to think. He knew. He'd known since he was a teenager, or hell, maybe it had happened earlier. When they were younger, standing on the beach at sundown, their hearts breaking. When Ryan climbed into his arms and begged Zach not to forget him, and Zach's heart had split in two at the idea of being apart from him.

Zach knew. He always had, and he'd denied it for years.

No more.

"What are you going to do?" Gabe asked.

"I need to talk to him." Zach's heart rose from the pit of his stomach and fluttered in his chest. Zach loved Ryan, and Ryan loved him. This was the sign he'd needed all along. So much had come between them and yet, they'd never lost touch. All these years, through all of Zach's shitty mistakes, Ryan had loved him. And Zach's other relationships had never lasted. Now, he knew why. What more did Zach need to be convinced? Ryan had told Zach to trust him, to trust they were meant to be even if neither of them could sense it, and did he?

Zach did. At last, he had the proof he needed that he'd found his fated mate.

Are you sure? Whispered a little voice in his mind, clawing at him worriedly. *You thought the same way about Gabe when the seer told you that you'd be together.*

Zach shoved his worries down before they could drag him to the depths.

"You okay? You're grinning like a loon."

Zach hugged Gabe so tight, Gabe grunted. "Thank you for telling me."

"I—oh. Uh. Sure, man. You're really okay?"

Zach laughed, feeling lighter than he had in years. "Yeah. I'm great. I'm... I'm going to tell him I feel the same. This is everything I needed, a sign we were meant to be together. This is it!"

Gabe returned his smile. "That's the spirit!"

THE NEXT DAY, RYAN knocked on the door to his parents' upstate home.

His mother answered, and the smile fell off Ryan's face when confusion wrinkled her brow. "Hello," she intoned. "Can I help you?"

She was still trapped in her episode. Ryan's heart threatened to beat out of control. "H-hi, I'm Ryan. We met at Rose's funeral. I'm, uh... I'm here to see Declan."

"Oh! Come in, come in. Dec, your friend Ryan is here!"

Stepping through the front door, Ryan realized with a start that they had taken pictures off the wall. Pictures with him in them. It made sense. Since his mother didn't remember she had a son, she would panic if she thought she did. It still made Ryan's heart sink into his stomach. Like they had completely erased him from their lives.

Goddess. This couldn't be permanent. She had to come out of this.

When his father came downstairs, he led Ryan to the study where they usually trained.

"Why hasn't she come out of it?" Ryan whispered.

His father just shook his head. "I don't know. I've been on the phone with her doctor all morning."

"And?" They entered the study and Ryan immediately sought a chair to collapse into.

"They're... they're concerned. This is not usual for her."

Ryan's stomach churned. He hadn't seen his dad look so anxious before. There were bags like bruises under his eyes, and his hair was messy like he kept running his hands through it. "I want to be optimistic, Ry, but the windows between her episodes have been getting smaller and smaller. And now with this longer episode—"

No. Ryan wouldn't hear it. He wasn't ready. Rising from his chair, he focused on the scented candle on the desk.

"It's not too late, Dad," he said. "Look." He closed his eyes and thought of Zach, his big warm hands, his sweet smile, his deep laugh.

His father gasped. "Ry. Goddess, you did it."

Opening his eyes, he saw the candle was glowing with flickering light.

His father gripped his shoulder with a trembling hand, tears bright in his eyes. "How?"

"I found my focus." Ryan cleared the gravel from his throat, his eyes stinging. "All I need is the right spell. Dad, I could help her. She'll never forget us again."

His dad smiled, and the hope shaved years off his face. He wrestled Ryan into a hug and if they both cried a little, it was a secret between them.

"This is... this is wonderful, Ry. Here, let's take some of Gran's spell books out to the yard. Now, how about you and your old man open up some cold ones and enjoy the day?"

Ryan thought that sounded perfect and so, armed with handfuls of books, he went to sit in the yard. His father carried a case of beer from the house.

His mom came outside. "You gentlemen aren't going to invite me?"

Ryan grinned. "Sure."

She joined them, and Ryan and his dad drank cool, foamy IPAs. His mother wasn't allowed to drink since she was on antianxiety medication, but she had an iced tea. His parents talked about the renovations they wanted done on the house. Then his mother asked Ryan questions about himself she'd once known the answers to by heart, but it didn't sting like before. This wasn't permanent. Ryan was going to help her.

He checked his phone since he'd had it off during his training session.

Zach: Really wish you'd answer your phone. I didn't want to have to tell you this way. Ry, I know.

He hesitated, uncertainty tangling up his insides. Zach knew. He knew... what?

Ryan: I don't get it. Know what?

Pacing, he squeezed his phone in his hand. What was there to know? His phone vibrated.

Zach: About us. I know.

About him and Zach? There was nothing to know. Nothing except—

The bottom of Ryan's stomach fell out. All the breath fled his lungs and the blood in his body flowed to his face. Zach knew. "He knows. He *knows*. Oh fuck..." Ryan's hand trembled as it curled in his hair, his lips flapping wordlessly. He'd been so careful, had locked his feelings up tight, not wanting to complicate their fledgling relationship by confessing years of unrequited feelings. He'd been content to explore their newfound passion. And now... oh Goddess, Zach must be freaking the fuck out.

"Is something wrong?" his mother asked, looking frightened.

He clamped his hand over his mouth, realizing he'd been thinking out loud. "Sorry, just—" He jogged into the house, needing to get away before he unsettled her.

"Hey, everything okay?" his dad asked, following him inside.

"Zach knows! He knows! Oh crap! He knows!"

His father's jaw dropped. "About—"

"Yes!" Ryan shrieked, beside himself. He reread the messages several times. Zach knew, he knew, and he wasn't blowing Ryan off. His fingers trembled over the virtual keyboard. What did he say?

"Keep it casual," his dad said. "Definitely don't act like you're acting now."

So Ryan thought for a moment.

Ryan: Okay. Can we meet up and talk soon?

He kept it casual. Hopefully not so casual that he sounded indifferent or like a douche, though. He had to meet Zach, had to speak to him in person. He'd daydreamed, anticipated, dreaded this moment for what seemed like all his life—the day Zach finally realized how Ryan felt. This confrontation wasn't happening over the phone.

Zach: I have to meet Ben now but does tonight work? Under our oak?

Ryan: Yeah. That works.

He exhaled, feeling woozy.

It was time, time to bare his heart in ways he'd never done for anyone.

CHAPTER 16

IT WAS LIKE THE SUN

It was decided.

Zach would meet Ryan just after sundown in Central Park. At the thought his stomach churned and his heart wouldn't cease its relentless race. They should have had this talk at the beginning, after their first kiss. They'd put it off, compartmentalized things while exploring the sexual side of their relationship. But it was time to get real. His mind was in turmoil just trying to wrap around the fact that his best friend had been madly in love with him since they were kids, and he hadn't known.

A part of him worried Ryan must hate him. How couldn't he? Zach had unintentionally broken his heart for years and he hated himself for it. He didn't see how Ryan could feel any differently.

"You okay?" Ben had pizza sauce in his beard.

"Huh? Oh, yeah. I'm good." If the trip in his heart betrayed him, Ben didn't call him on it and took another bite of his pizza. This pizzeria near Ben's apartment in Brooklyn was out of Zach's way, but Zach had wanted to talk to Ben as soon as possible about the wolves on Fire Island, so they'd met up for a chat and a slice of greasy, cheesy pizza.

A yawn cracked Zach's jaw. He hadn't been able to sleep, his mind racing as he ruminated over every interaction he and Ryan had ever shared, seeing every little detail he'd missed. Goddess, how could he have been so blind? Giving his head a shake, Zach cleared his throat and focused. "So, Ben…"

Frowning, Ben swiped through his phone. His eyes widened and... was he *blushing?*

Propping an elbow on the table, Zach leaned in, grinning. "You're not reading something smutty, are you?"

Ben jumped and dropped his phone beneath the table.

Lunging, Zach snatched it up. "No way!" A picture of a shirtless hunky guy named Derek stared back at him. Before he could laugh, Zach covered his mouth. "Oh, twenty-five. I think that's a bit young for you."

Ben snatched the phone back, face so red it was hideous. "I know! This stupid app won't let me adjust the ages so it keeps showing me these twenty-somethings!"

They had important stuff to discuss but Zach was dying for more details since Ben had always been so tight-lipped about his love life. "I can't believe you're on Howlr. Find anyone you like yet?"

Grimacing, Ben shoved his phone in his pocket. "No. I don't get this online dating stuff. It takes the fun out of meeting in person. How do you know if they aren't axe-murderers? And what's with the obsession with all the shirtless gym pictures?" Balling up a dirty napkin, Ben chucked it in the trash can behind them. "Totally stupid."

"Why'd you decide to try it?" Zach took a bite of pizza.

Sighing, Ben rolled his shoulders. "I thought I could give dating a shot. Seeing Gabe and Max and you and Ry making goo-goo eyes at each other got me wanting something like that for myself. But... I don't know. Maybe online dating just isn't for me. I haven't clicked with any of the guys I've dated."

"That's fine. It works for some people. You could always try—"

But Ben shook his head. "Forget it. Maybe it's just me, or maybe..." Something devastatingly sad crossed his face, but it was gone swiftly and replaced by a grimace.

"Hey, you can tell me. What's going on?"

"Maybe I just can't get over him."

"Who?"

When Ben spoke, the words were barely louder than a whisper. "Isaac. My... mate."

Oh. Zach was so surprised he didn't speak for several seconds. He'd known Ben a long time and while he knew Ben had co-parented with his friend Heather, he'd never seen Ben with another guy or girl since he'd known him.

"What happened to him? If you don't mind."

"I don't know." Ben's eyes clouded over, like he was seeing right through Zach and into the past. "He left. Didn't say goodbye, or tell me where he was going." His face was hard as stone, but Zach couldn't miss the waver in his voice, the overwhelming scent of sadness that crashed over him.

"I'm sorry," Zach said, needing to say something. "That's awful, Ben. How long ago was this?"

Ben dropped his gaze down to the table. "Must have been over twenty years ago by now." His words walloped Zach in the heart. With a snort, Ben thumbed at his eyes and looked away from Zach. "I don't know why I can't let him go. Fucking hell, it's been two decades, and me and my wolf are still waiting for him to come back. Maybe it's not that I can't date other people. Maybe I just don't *want* to. Nobody else speaks to my wolf like that bastard did. It's like a damn curse."

Ice flooded Zach's insides. "Have you... I mean, there must have been *someone* you've liked since then?"

"A few people. Can count them on one hand. A couple times, I thought things would work out. I liked them. But... they weren't him."

For twenty years, Ben's fated mate had been gone and yet Ben couldn't move on.

If Zach's mate were out there, would Zach continue to love Ryan, or would their love only pale compared to what he could have with his mate?

Bile rose in his throat. Dismayed tears pricked his eyes. He struggled to hold on to the hope he'd felt when he discovered Ryan's feelings, the joy and certainty that had finally been within his reach, but the doubt and fear submerged him.

"Zach? Hey, what's going on?"

Zach realized he was panting, heart racing out of control in his chest. A thousand what-ifs thundered through his mind and consumed his confidence, his hope. He'd been wrong again. His relationship with Ryan was only going to end the same way as Gabe and Will or any other guy he'd broken up with.

He couldn't breathe. Everything was too loud, too close.

"Zach!" Ben's voice followed him out to the street. A hand grabbed at him, and Zach lurched out of reach.

"Don't touch me. Please. Just... I can't... Oh *fuck* I'm—" He leaned on a streetlamp and tried to breathe but his chest was too tight, heart racing too fast. Tears dampened his cheeks. He'd been so certain, so sure, so fucking happy.

"Zach, breathe with me. Follow my breaths."

Zach inhaled around a sob, hiding his face against the lamppost. A few breathes in, and Ben said, "That's good. Tell me five things you can see, touch, and smell."

Zach did, speaking through a thick, aching throat. Finally, his heart settled into a somewhat normal rhythm and his breathing slowed. He still felt like a sack of shit.

"What happened?" Ben asked, his voice a low, soothing rumble.

"I was wrong again," Zach croaked, wiping his streaming eyes.

"About what?"

"Ryan. Me. Everything."

"Wrong about... him being your fated mate?" Ben put the pieces together without Zach having to try. "Why do you think that?"

A shrug. He knew why, but everything felt too big to put into words. With a sigh, he tried anyway, needing to vent. "Ryan loves me. I love him. I... I thought that could be enough but then you started talking about Isaac and how you can't move on and—"

"Whoa, whoa, whoa. First, fuck everything I said. My situation differs completely from you and Ry. I haven't *tried* to move on. Not really. If

I really put in the effort, I could make myself settle for someone else. It wouldn't be as great as a bond with a fated mate, and maybe it might not last, but I could make it work. Is that the problem? You're scared you and Ry won't last?"

Zach nodded.

Ben snorted, though Zach couldn't see what was so funny. "If you love each other, then that's all that matters."

"That's never been enough!" Zach snapped, not meaning to, but desperate to make Ben understand his point of view. "I can love someone with everything I have, and it still falls apart and I—I can't lose him, Ben." His voice broke. "But I will. I'll lose him when I leave him, or he leaves me." So what was the point in pursuing anything with Ryan?

"You can't know that."

But Zach did, because it had happened repeatedly. If it was enough to just love the person he was with, none of his relationships would have fallen apart. He'd known this, but he'd let himself be stupid and optimistic and believe that this time, *this time,* things would be different if he just wished hard enough.

"Oh, Goddess..." he croaked, remembering he was meeting with Ryan tonight, that he'd been planning to return his feelings. "I can't do this with him."

"Zach, you need to calm down and think rationally. If you break up with Ryan, that will only hurt both of you. What you're obsessing over is a what-if scenario that might not even happen. It's anxiety, but it's not how you really feel. Why assume the worst?"

"Because it's the only way to stay safe!" It was the only way he could be in control and protect his heart, and save Ryan from the disaster of being in a relationship with him. Pushing off from the lamppost, Zach wiped his eyes and nose on his sleeve and walked around Ben.

Ben took his shoulder. "Don't do this. Don't let fear wreck the best thing that could happen to you."

Sucking in a shuddery breath, Zach walked away.

It wasn't until he was on the subway that he realized he'd never mentioned the wolf pack or his mother's plan.

THE SUN HAD SET when Zach parked his car and entered the park, his shaking legs carrying him through the winding road beneath the trees with familiar ease.

He had to end things with Ryan. The very thought brought a lump to his throat, but he swallowed it down.

How stupid could he have been to get swept up in his fantasies, to dream of a future with Ryan? His talk with Ben had only made his worst fears a reality: a wolf couldn't be with someone they weren't fated to. He'd suspected this all along but he'd still foolishly hoped for a happy ending. Eventually, Ryan would leave him, or Zach would leave Ryan. There was no point in waiting around to get their hearts broken.

A silhouette stood beneath their oak tree, framed by silver moonlight. Ryan strode toward him, his steps slow and hesitant, and Zach's stomach did flips as, step by step, they neared each other.

"Hey." Ryan's voice was friendly but uneven, his green eyes avoiding Zach's gaze with uncharacteristic shyness.

"Hey, Ry."

Crickets chirped, and traffic buzzed far away.

Ryan met his gaze, and a smile broke across his face, stealing Zach's breath. By Amaris, how had Zach never noticed that before? The way Ryan looked at him as if Zach held the moon herself in his hands. How had he ever been so blind? Zach was unsure where to begin, how to start, and for once, Ryan seemed to be at a loss for words as well. Running his hand over the bark of the ancient oak where he'd carved their initials, Ryan said, "So. You know."

Zach exhaled and nodded. "Yeah. I know."

Ryan smiled again and motioned Zach toward him. "Wanna walk?"

That sounded perfect. "Where to?"

Ryan shrugged his shoulders. "Wherever. Maybe around the duck pond."

The trees sheltered them as they walked, the moonlight glimmering on the pond. Ducks roosted on the rocks, their feathers gleaming as they cuddled close to their mates.

"So..." Ryan tilted his head, a playful smile on his face. "How'd you find out?"

Breaking eye contact, Zach felt a nervous fluttering in his stomach. He shrugged. "I just guessed."

Ryan snorted. "Right. Zach, you're a smart guy and all but we've known each other for too long. Come on. Spill. Who told you?"

Zach swallowed, suddenly terrified. "Gabe."

Tossing back his head, Ryan barked out a laugh. Zach smiled as he watched him. He was taking it better than Zach had. "Promise you won't kill him?"

"Oh, I will. Slowly. Painfully." Ryan sobered and he watched his feet as they walked. "It's fine. It was gonna happen eventually. I wanted to wait until you were ready to hear it." He sighed and kicked a stone out of the path, down the hill, and out of sight. "You must have freaked out, huh?"

Zach wet his lips and studied his own feet, his fingers curling in his pockets. He had and was still freaking out, but he didn't say so. He forced his hands to relax. "How long?"

Ryan hummed and for a few seconds, he said nothing. Zach glanced at him and Ryan turned his face to the stars as the moonlight cast off the shadows, softening his face. He smiled, sweet and vulnerable, and for a moment, Zach saw the lovesick boy he'd once been.

"Since before I knew what love was." He looked Zach's way, his face so open and unguarded that Zach lost his nerve. He looked away quickly, his heart pounding.

"Be more specific."

Ryan tilted his head to the sky with a soft laugh. His face scrunched up thoughtfully, turning toward the moon. For a moment, the sound of their shoes on gravel filled the quiet. "Okay," Ryan began, shooting Zach a nervous but excited look. He wet his lips. "I always knew I liked you."

Zach laughed. "Still too vague."

"I'm getting there! I always thought you were super cool because you were the older kid, right? So, to my little kid brain, that meant you were like, uber cool. Like, whoa, this kid can do all this awesome stuff. He probably has his own phone, and he can stay out as late as he wants. I wanted to be like you. Then..." Ryan veered to the right and Zach followed him, the road softening to dusty soil as they walked the lakefront. Ryan continued, sounding out of breath, "The first time I noticed you... really noticed you... I think it was after summer break. You'd been away in Cape Town. I was so excited to see you. I couldn't sleep."

Flowers were blooming, growing thick and wild under their feet.

Zach's heart clenched and he couldn't look away as Ryan bared his heart and soul to him. No one had ever talked about him the way Ryan was now. He'd had no idea the depth of his feelings.

"And I saw you standing there, tall as hell, and I noticed you. There was this... rush." At a loss for words, Ryan began using his hands to communicate. "I was so happy to see you, but it was magnified. And then you hugged me and... and I never wanted you to let go." Ryan exhaled and didn't look at Zach. Then he smiled. "And I popped the biggest boner ever."

Zach doubled over laughing, the last bit of Ryan's story so unexpected it threw him completely off.

Ryan laughed with him. "I did! Don't tell me you didn't feel it!"

Gasping for air, Zach patted his shoulder. Ryan chuckled, his cheeks bright red. "I think I remember that," Zach said, trying to think back to that day. "You ran for the hills all of a sudden. Don't tell me it was because—"

Ryan bowed his head graciously. "Yup."

Zach wanted to hit himself. "You were so shy the next time I saw you. I seriously thought I'd done something wrong. And then I told you I was dating someone." He cringed at the memory.

"Yeah." The bitterness in Ryan's voice made Zach want to cry. "That hurt a bit."

Zach stopped walking, the guilt churning in his stomach. "But you figured it out eventually. Why didn't you tell me?"

Ryan raised his arms and dropped them. "I was never gonna tell you. First, the timing was never right. I moved, you started dating and exploring your sexuality, then I started dating."

Zach winced. "Right. But we were both adults when you came back to NYC. We could have—no, because I started crushing on Gabe," Zach murmured, piecing things together with heartbreaking clarity.

Ryan's shoulders slumped. "Yeah. Gabe."

"You just let us be together. Ry..." Zach's throat closed, and he battled the tears scorching his eyes. "That must have fucking killed you."

Ryan shrugged, nudging a pebble. "It did. But you were happy. I was never gonna tell you, Zach. I was so scared we'd ruin our friendship. I just wanted to be with you, Zach. Even if you didn't feel the same, I was willing to take whatever you could give me. I know, that's pathetic."

Zach sniffed hard and dragged his fist across his eyes. "Fuck, Ry. No, it isn't. Not at all." Ryan had loved him for years, never expecting a thing in return. No one had ever been so unselfish toward him before. Ryan handed him a tissue before he sat beside him on the rock, and Zach dried his eyes and blew his nose. "I thought I'd lost you for good when Gabe came along. So I decided I'd have you in whatever way I could. As a friend, as... whatever we are now. I don't regret it, not a thing," Ryan whispered.

The pond lapped gently at the shore as frogs croaked, and the night was full of the sounds of crickets and the faraway buzz of traffic from beyond the stone walls of the park.

Zach asked, "What changed? The day you kissed me for the first time?"

"I got tired of watching you date the wrong guys. Honestly, I wasn't sure you'd even feel the same but I had to know." Ryan's eyes glimmered when he smiled, his face alight with joy. "Then I realized you were getting so jealous thinking I was talking about another guy." Zach's face warmed at the memory. Before his eyes, Ryan's face came alive with boyish excitement. "I thought you'd never look at me the way I looked at you. But for a few seconds, you did—and it changed everything, Zach." Practically vibrating with excitement, Ryan lurched to his feet and paced toward the lake with a bounce in his step. He spun around toward Zach, happier than he had ever seen him.

Roses bloomed in the moonlight, their petals opening before Zach's eyes. He couldn't speak. He couldn't breathe. It was like he'd been living in the dark all his life and now all the lights were turned on. And he saw Ryan as if for the first time. He saw what had been right in front of him all these years. The light in Ryan's eyes when he looked at Zach. The way his cheeks burst with color as their gazes locked. The way he smiled... Ah Goddess, the way he smiled. It was like the sun, and it was for Zach.

The grass shifted under Ryan's feet as he came closer. His smile faded and Zach had never seen him so vulnerable, as if his heart lay in Zach's hands. Knees trembling, Zach rose to meet him.

Ryan exhaled shakily. Trembling fingers clutched onto the sleeves of Zach's sweatshirt. Ryan's eyes burned with urgency as he held his gaze. Then he looked away, combing his fingers through his hair. "I didn't ask you how you felt. I've been flapping my gums and I haven't even asked. Do you..."

Silence filled the space between them, crackling with a kind of nervous energy Zach had never felt before. "Ryan, I..." Loving Ryan Kelly was as effortless as breathing. Zach's heart had belonged to him the moment they'd met. It was Ryan for him. It had always been Ryan.

Now, all he wanted was to tell Ryan how much he loved him. How he'd always loved him. And yet when he opened his mouth, the words wouldn't come. He closed his eyes, breathed in deep. Ryan smelled as he always did. Clean and sweet.

And yet...

"I can't do this." The words cracked as they fell from his throat. He forced himself to take a step back, away from Ryan's warmth.

Ryan's smile fell from his face, and he looked so small and uncertain.

"I'm sorry. I'm so sorry. I believe you, Ryan. Really, I thought I could do this. I thought my feelings would be enough. But I just don't know. I don't know how to convince myself that what we have will last."

Ryan took in a shuddery breath. "You mean, because one day you or I might find our fated mates. Because I can't scent you, and you can't scent me."

"And that really doesn't concern you? That you love me now but someday, you might find someone who speaks to you more, who you can't imagine being without?"

Ryan growled low in his chest, the sound so startling that Zach jumped. "I will *never* want anyone else the way I want you. I don't need some perfect mate, and I don't need your scent, Zach. I never have. All I know is that nobody knows me like you do. Nobody makes me as happy as you do. Nobody has been as constant in my life as you. That's all I need, and fuck everything else."

Shame left Zach doubled over. "Stop it. I don't deserve this. You. Any of it. Just let me go and find someone who isn't a fucking mess who can love you the way you deserve."

Ryan took a step back like Zach had struck him. "You are not a mess, baby. You're everything I deserve, and I don't know how to get that through your thick, beautiful head."

"You can't. I shouldn't be making you say any of this stuff." He was the one who was too broken for anyone to love in the long run.

"There's nothing I can say to get through to you, is there?"

Zach couldn't speak and just shook his head.

A low, shaky sigh filled the space between them. "Then go, Zach."

His dismissal knocked the wind from Zach's lungs. Eyes stinging, Zach turned away.

"But this isn't how our story ends. I won't ever accept that. Not after everything we've been through." Ryan's eyes were wet, but they blazed with faithful determination. "I've waited fifteen years for you, Zach De-Shawn." A wobbly smile tugged at his mouth even as a tear spilled down his cheek. "I can wait a little longer."

Chapter 17

DESERVING

On Sunday, it rained.

Zach hadn't moved from bed in hours. His restless mind wouldn't give him peace, and he revisited his and Ryan's conversation in the park until he thought he'd lose his sanity. He replayed everything he'd said, obsessed over everything he could have done differently, and regret and heartache consumed him.

At times, he wanted to pick up the phone, call Ryan, and grovel until he'd earned his forgiveness. But he knew he shouldn't, not when he couldn't promise Ryan that he wouldn't freak out again. He was too insecure, too messy, too damn broken to be worth anyone's time. Ryan deserved better than someone who was too scared and damaged to give him their heart.

As the hours dragged by, he watched movies until his eyes were bleary, and ate his way through a box of doughnuts, calories be damned. When his bladder felt full to bursting, he dragged himself out of bed and noticed his phone had turned on, notifying him of a few missed messages. He'd had his phone on silent to give himself some space.

Was it Ryan? Was he messaging to curse Zach out? Zach wouldn't blame him at all. Bracing himself, he gingerly lifted his phone like it was a bomb. He had a dozen missed calls and texts from Gabe and Izzie. The latest one from Izzie read:

That's it. This is an intervention. We're coming over.

Shit. Zach chucked the empty doughnut box in the trash, washed the sugary glaze off his fingers, and tried to look like he hadn't been wallowing on the sofa all day. The intercom buzzed before Zach was ready. The siblings stood outside his door, wearing running shoes and athletic wear.

"Hi." Zach tried to smile but it felt too heavy on his face.

Gabe whistled. "Sheesh."

A sympathetic smile lifted Izzie's lips. "Hanging in there?"

"I'm fine." He might be more convincing if he didn't sound seconds away from throwing himself out the window.

"Yeah, not buying that for a second, bud." Gabe clapped his hands together. "Come on, get some shoes on and follow us."

"You're going jogging!"

A groan of dismay nearly escaped him before he bit it off. "I can't, guys, I'm doing..." Nothing, really. "You should probably go spend time with Ryan. He's more fun than I am."

"Ben, Max, and Eddie are on it," Izzie said. "But somebody needs to stop you from eating another box of doughnuts."

He should have known they'd smell it on him. A sigh escaped him. "Fine. Just give me a second." Before he closed the door, he added, "I'm thinking we're all too codependent."

Gabe shrugged. "We're wolves. Comes with the territory."

After he'd pulled on a fresh t-shirt and running shorts, Zach met Gabe and Izzie outside. The rain stopped and the clouds were breaking, revealing slivers of blue sky. Together, they jogged from his apartment to the Hudson River Greenway. The views of New Jersey, peaceful rippling river water, and the cry of seagulls lifted Zach's mood by increments as he jogged.

"So," Gabe huffed, arms pumping as he ran, "What exactly happened with you and Ry? You were really excited to tell him how you felt."

"I don't know, I... I panicked, or something. Started second-guessing everything. Totally freaked out in front of Ben." Shame burned the back of his neck.

"What made you freak out, though?" Izzie asked, ponytail swinging side to side as she jogged.

"Ben told me about his mate and how he lost him and nobody else could do it for him, and... it was like all my worst fears were confirmed." Lungs burning, Zach stopped for air and leaned on the railing. "I thought just loving Ry could be enough. And it was. Until I lost my damn mind." Frustration had him gnashing his teeth. "I'm never certain of anything. Not really. My head's full of constant what-ifs and doubts all the damn time."

Frowning, Izzie leaned beside him. She took a gulp from her water bottle. "Really?"

"I know on the outside I've got my shit together but inside, I'm a total mess."

"About what, specifically? Just this mate stuff with Ry, or other things?" Gabe draped his elbows over the railing, reaching up to sweep his hair from his forehead.

Now that he was thinking about it, there were things he'd obsessed over during different stages of his life. As a little kid, he'd had this fear that he'd get sick. When he was a teen, it had been his grades. Now, he was obsessing over his relationships.

As he confessed these worries aloud, dismay overwhelmed him. "Fuck. What is *wrong* with me?" He hit his head against the railing.

"That, my friend, is called anxiety." The warmth of Izzie's hand ran over his back. "Have you ever talked to a therapist about your obsessions? It might help."

Shaking his head, Zach shoved off the railing. "I don't need therapy. I'm a wolf. Wolves aren't weak." It sounded like something his father might say.

Gabe frowned. "Having anxiety doesn't mean you're weak, Zach. It means you're human, like the rest of us."

A laugh escaped Zach. "I can't have anxiety!"

Izzie crossed her arms. "Why not?"

"Because! Anxiety's for people who were traumatized. Sexual assault survivors. War vets. Not privileged rich boys who had everything they could want."

The saddest look darkened Gabe's face. "You had material things, Zach. Your parents deprived you of love. For a kid, that's fucking traumatizing. Don't trivialize your suffering just because you think other people have it worse. It's not a competition."

No. No, that wasn't right. "That's... No. That's not what happened. They never even hit me."

Izzie spat, "Zach, Ryan told us that your mother locked you in your room. That your father cancelled a vacation he'd promised you because you shifted at school. Dangling love in front of someone like a bribe and taking it away when they don't meet unrealistic expectations is abusive, deplorable behavior. If our parents had treated us that way, you would call them out as abusive pieces of shit. So why can't you do the same for yourself?"

The truth in her words made Zach's knees weak. "It's... it's because I disappointed them. I was a mess. I—"

"Don't." Izzie's eyes blazed. "I swear to the goddess, Zach, don't justify their abuse. It wasn't your fault."

He tried to speak but the aching lump blocked the words in his throat. All his life, he'd made excuses for his parents' actions, blamed himself for not being a better son. It was his mother and father who'd failed him in every way a parent could fail their child. The need to be perfect all the time, fighting to earn their conditional love, never feeling good enough—it had messed up his brain.

Gabe cleared his throat, "Did we break you?"

Sighing, he scrubbed a hand down his face, feeling the scratch of his unshaven jaw. "I'm already broken. All the more reason not to be with Ryan. He doesn't deserve to be saddled with my mess." He could never have made Ryan happy, just like he'd failed to make his parents happy.

Maybe his obsession over whether they were fated had been nothing but an excuse he'd weaponized to avoid being with Ryan and ultimately disappointing him.

"You guys should be therapists," he scoffed, turning away.

"Zach, wait." The plea in Izzie's voice made it impossible to resist. Going to her, he let her fold him into her arms and rub her small hands up and down his back. "If I told you I had anxiety, would you tell me I wasn't deserving of love?"

He shook his head and held her tight. "Never."

"Then don't do it to yourself. Zach, you are so deserving of love."

Squeezing his eyes shut against the sting of tears, Zach wished he could believe her.

On Monday, Ryan went upstate to visit his parents. He hoped that his mother had come out of her episode until she gave him a curious stare, then went into their home gym without so much as a hello. It hurt. Ryan really needed one of her hugs right now.

In the study, he and his dad poured over tomes, searching for a spell that would help his mom.

A delivery truck pulled into the yard. His father excused himself to greet the delivery woman and returned with a small box. "Ry? You order something?"

Ryan leaped out of his seat. It had to be the book about sacred groves from the Council.

In the kitchen he carefully opened the box with a knife. Once he'd brought it to the study, he flipped through the pages.

"Is that book about the map of sacred groves grandma had?" his dad asked.

"Yeah. It's the exact location of every known site." Ryan flipped to the page detailing American sacred groves. There were quite a few, mostly in

NYC, including one in Central Park. Not exactly helpful considering there were thousands of oaks in Central Park. Ryan paused. "Hang on. This is cool. There was once a sacred grove site on Fire Island. That one was destroyed too."

His father leaned over his shoulder and tapped the page. "More than that. It's a burial ground."

"That's weird. None of the other sacred groves were burial grounds. Why do you think that is?"

His father rubbed his chin. "Let me think... So, historically, the druids conquered territory all over Europe and eventually landed in America. The last known battle against the druids took place on—"

Ryan snapped his fingers. "Fire Island! That's right!"

"Yes. So therefore, the bodies of the druids were laid to rest on the island."

"That's so cool! Why don't more people know that? It's part of our history."

His father frowned. "From what I hear, that site's considered an evil location. Causes bad luck, if you believe that. Makes sense, considering who is buried there."

"Who?" Ryan asked.

"The king of the druids himself."

Ryan's mouth fell open. "You're serious?"

His dad ran to the bookshelf and pulled down a book on druid history. "Oh yes. There are a few detailed accounts of that last battle. I'm sure they have muddled the details along the way, but..." He flipped the pages and stopped, setting the book down on the desk. "Atticus was a formidable foe. Here's an account of how he drove wolves feral."

Ryan leaned over the book to read for himself. In the story of the battle, the narrator revealed how Atticus could see and manipulate the bonds of a pack, severing the wolves' connections to one another in only seconds. The wolves turned on each other, killing friend and foe alike. The battle would have ended in the wolves' defeat if the druids who'd turned against Atticus hadn't used their magic to kill him.

Ryan shivered. "Sounds like a scary guy."

His father frowned. "Interesting…"

"What?"

"Well, it's just that this book was originally written in Gaelic. The original translation…" Instead of finishing his sentence, his dad pulled another book from the shelf and opened it. It was the same book but written all in Gaelic. Ryan's Gaelic had improved, so he could piece together most of it. "Hey, that last part is different. It says they used their magic to *imprison* him. Not kill him. Why is the wording so different?"

A prickle of unease went down his spine.

His father stroked his goatee thoughtfully, looking very much like the scholarly teacher he was. "Historians have debated whether Atticus could ever truly die. There have been accounts of him dying on the battlefield, only to rise again. In fact, many theorized that he had bound his life force to every oak tree he grew. So the surviving druids burned as many of the trees as they could. I've never believed that myself. It's been centuries since Atticus's defeat; if he could have returned, why wouldn't he have done so by now?"

Ryan's mouth was painfully dry. "Dad. Gran said in her grimoire that there was danger coming, and that I had to be ready. What if it's him? What if it's Atticus?"

His father scoffed. "No. Ryan, come on. Atticus? Really?"

"Dad, Gran's visions were never wrong! This is something we need to take seriously." Ryan opened Rose's grimoire. He still couldn't make sense of the connection to the trees. Somehow, she'd thought they were linked to this coming danger. To Atticus. Goddess, he hoped his suspicion was wrong. "Damn it. I really wish you were here to tell me what to do, Gran…"

Chapter 18

UNCONDITIONALLY

Seeing Ryan again at work later that Monday morning was like a punch to Zach's gut. All the oxygen seemed to be sucked out of the room as their eyes met across the cafeteria. Ryan had circles that looked like bruises under his red-rimmed eyes and he froze at the sight of Zach. The bond between them that had once burned like the sun pulsed like a feeble, dying heart.

Zach stood up, bumping into his tray and rattling it against the table. He tried to find his voice, to call out to Ryan even though he had no idea what he could say. Before he could figure that out, Ryan turned and bolted from the room. Honestly, the light bulbs bursting again would have been preferable. He'd take anything over this canyon that had come between them.

Zach hoped Ryan didn't expect him to have gotten his act together over the weekend. Zach's mental health was just as shitty as before. Shittier, actually, because he missed Ryan so damn much. Zach gazed into his bowl of soup and tried to figure out how to drown himself.

Izzie wrenched his head up. "Talk to him."

He dropped his spoon into his soup and gazed at the doorway. Ryan's scent lingered, one of misery so thick it almost choked Zach. "I need to give him space."

"But if he knows you're sorry—" Izzie began.

Zach said, "I can't just take it back. I hurt him. I seriously hurt him. *Sorry* isn't going to cut it. I can't talk to him about us until I've stopped being such an anxious mess. I've got to be someone he deserves not... me."

Gabe rolled his eyes. "I don't know, I think he likes Zach the anxious mess just fine."

"Besides, if you don't say anything, that will just make things worse," Izzie added.

Zach gritted his teeth. "And saying something, even the wrong thing, won't?"

Across the table, Max nudged his salad around in his bowl. "It took me a while to stop being angry at Gabe. But we found our way back to each other."

Zach wished his words could comfort him. "You and Gabe were fated mates. Ryan and I..." He didn't know what the hell they were, or if they could ever come back from this.

Izzie sipped her tea. "Maybe if you just talk it out..."

Leaning back in his chair, Zach closed his eyes tight. "Fuck... How do I fix this? What do I do? How can I make this right?"

Gabe said, "You can't, man." He stared down at his empty plate. "Ryan's gotta have his space. Don't worry, he'll find you when he's good and ready."

Zach swallowed hard, blinking up at the white ceiling. "What if—" He stopped himself because the thought that Ryan would never speak to him again nearly shattered him right there.

Izzie touched his knee. "You guys will work through this. I know it. You're Zach and Ryan. Seriously, you guys are inseparable."

"Yeah," Max chimed in. "Just give him time. He needs to process this. You can figure out what your feelings are."

"I know how I feel," Zach stated, but he felt his heart trip in his chest. "He's my friend. That's it, that's all he can be. No matter how much we loved each other, I would have disappointed him in the end anyway." Zach growled before he could stop himself. He felt like the walls of a cage were closing in around him. What little appetite he'd had was thoroughly gone.

"See you guys later." Zach picked up his tray and dumped his uneaten soup in the trash. He dragged his feet up to the second floor, avoiding the library where he knew Ryan was likely camping out.

Enough. He'd had the weekend to feel sorry for himself. Today was the day construction would begin on his father's final project. Hunters hired by his mother would kill the wolves who called that scared grove their home. Hopefully once Zach told Ben, they could help them.

When Zach caught Ryan's scent down the hall, he hesitated. It smelled like Ryan had gone into Ben's office and he really didn't want to bump into him right now. Seeing him had felt like a knife between the ribs. Blowing out a breath, Zach forced himself toward Ben's office. What he had to say was important, and he couldn't let his personal feelings get in the way.

Ryan's voice carried from beyond the door. "I'm telling you, Ben, it's Atticus! I think my gran had a vision where he returned."

Ben scoffed. "Ry, that guy died centuries ago."

"Not according to the surviving druids. They said he was *imprisoned*. Not dead. And somehow, there's all these oak trees involved! I don't know what it all means yet, but—"

Unsettled, Zach knocked.

"Ry, just a minute. Come in, Zach."

Zach entered, his heart sinking when Ryan snapped his gaze in the other direction. "Uh. Sorry to interrupt. It's important. Ben, did you know there's a pack of wolves on Fire Island?"

Ben's brow furrowed. "News to me. How'd you hear about it?"

"My mother told me. She's spearheading my father's final project, and the wolves are occupying land she wants to build on. The land's an old burial ground. Something called a sacred—"

"A sacred grove?" Ryan whirled in Zach's direction. All the awkwardness between them was briefly forgotten when Zach saw the panic widening Ryan's eyes.

"Yeah. Exactly." He didn't understand why Ryan looked so afraid. "Ben, she wants to slaughter those wolves. She's hired hunters."

Ben looked tense too, his fingers clasped tightly together on the desk. "Well, shit."

Zach grimaced. "She refused to contact the Council, and she's determined to settle this with bloodshed. Ben, we have to help them."

"We will, Zach. I promise."

He sighed, relieved.

Ryan shook his head. "This can't be happening. That sacred grove rests on the bones of druids from centuries ago. Atticus himself is buried there."

Zach gawked at him. "For real?"

"Yes! Maybe nothing bad will happen if they go digging around a druid burial ground, but I'm not willing to sit around and find out. My gran saw Atticus's return. Atticus, who, according to eyewitnesses, isn't dead but imprisoned in that burial ground. Ben—"

Ben stood. "I got it, Ry. I won't pretend I believe every word, but we're going to do all we can."

Ryan sighed and smiled gratefully. "I know."

Ben said, "I'll brief the pack on the situation. Get ready. We're leaving soon."

BEN SUMMONED EVERYONE INTO his office. Zach had always thought of it as spacious, but that was before eight werewolves crammed themselves into the space.

Once Ben had briefed everyone on the situation, including the druid threat, the room erupted into chaos as the pack made their preparations.

Max and Gabe made arrangements for their kids to stay with Max's mom, Kendra, and her husband, Ronaldo.

Izzie said into her phone, "Yes, Ma, I'll be careful! Yes, I'll keep Gabriel from running headlong into danger! Love you."

Ben asked Izzie, "Any chance of Council support?"

She shook her head. "Not on such short notice. She and Dad won't be back from their business trip until tomorrow, so we'll have to handle this ourselves."

Vicenzo scowled, because of course he did. "How far away is this magical hippie grove?"

Ben said, "We can take a car to the nearest parking lot and walk the rest of the way."

Vicenzo grimaced. "Great. Gotta be crammed into a car with all of you."

"You don't have to come," Eddie grumbled. "Car will be cramped enough with you and your negative attitude."

"Oh, I'm coming," Vicenzo said, making for the door. "If we're biting hunters' asses, you bet I'm there."

Ben slumped in his chair. "We're not going there to start a fight, but if Zach's mother has hired hunters and we have to protect the wolves, we'll do it. Ed, we may need tips on breaking through the hunters' defenses if it comes down to it."

Eddie nodded. "Got it."

Minutes later, the pack piled into an RV. Zach expected Ryan to sit next to him as usual, but he squeezed into the back with Gabe and Max. Zach tried to pretend that didn't hurt and focused on dressing himself in tactical armor that would protect him from the hunters' bullets. Around him, the pack did the same.

While they rocked side to side in the RV, Ben said, "Since we're dealing with hunters, try to avoid shifting. Our bodies are too exposed in wolf form, and the last thing we need is silver or wolfsbane weakening us. Stay in human form. If it comes to a fight, use your fangs, claws, whatever you have at your disposal."

"Also," Eddie said, "hunters like to use grenades full of powdered silver. If the silver gets in your nose or eyes, you'll be incapacitated. So put these on if it looks like we're going to fight." He walked down the aisle between the seats while he spoke.

Ryan said, "I've also learned a few warding spells that should act like shields to repel the bullets as some added protection. Just in case."

Zach slept for fifteen minutes and when he opened his eyes, they'd arrived in a parking lot near the trail that would take them to the wolves. Anxiety twisted in his gut. Zach hoped it wouldn't come to a fight. His bladder was full, so Zach stood up and went in search of the RV's bathroom. As he passed his packmates talking quietly while they prepared to leave, he didn't see Ryan among them.

The bathroom door opened, and Ryan walked out. Zach froze, and when Ryan met his gaze, the narrow space felt even tighter. Ryan seemed smaller than usual, his head hung low and his eyes dim and pinched as he looked away from Zach. Stepping away from the door, he left it open. "All yours."

Zach grabbed his arm before he could walk past. Ryan stiffened at his touch, his tongue rasping over dry, cracked lips. Though he loosened his grip, he couldn't bring himself to let go. He was afraid if he did, the canyon would widen and he would lose Ryan forever. Zach searched for his voice and when he found it, it came out small and gravelly.

"I'm sorry I hurt you."

Ryan's heart was loud in his ears, and it sounded like it was breaking.

"I'm so sorry, Ryan." Zach's eyes burned and he gripped on tightly to Ryan's arm. "I understand if you hate me. If... if it's too hard for you to even look at me right now, I get it. Hate me for as long as you need to. Just not forever. Please."

The muscles in Ryan's arm were tight, and he was shaking. "I don't."

Zach struggled to breathe. "What?"

"Hate you." Ryan's voice was low and bitter. "I could never do that. You're not sorry for anything else, though. You still mean what you said."

"I..." Zach wished he could say otherwise, but he couldn't lie to Ryan. "I do. I can't love you knowing someday it might blow up in our faces."

"Like what happened with Gabe and all your other boyfriends. I get that, okay? I get you're scared of being hurt again." Ryan tugged his arm away. "But I was willing to chance that. Why can't you?"

Zach's hand thumped to his side. He supposed Ryan was braver than he was.

Then Ryan said, "Do you love me, Zach?"

He was struck speechless. "I..."

Ryan turned, crowding Zach up against the wall

"I..."

"You said you didn't know if I was your mate." Ryan's eyes narrowed. "Not that you didn't love me."

Zach didn't push him away. He couldn't. He was drowning in the scent of him, in the warmth of his body. Swallowing hard, Zach looked away. Ryan didn't touch him, not with his mouth or his hands. For a moment they just breathed. Desire spiked Ryan's scent, a spicy smell that made Zach's blood burn hot.

"I need to know, Zach," Ryan rumbled. "If you don't love me, then you need to tell me. Or did you push me away because you're scared you'll disappoint me?"

Zach couldn't breathe. Yes, of course he loved Ryan Kelly. He'd always loved him. But he didn't deserve him.

Zach's voice came out a croak. "I don't want to give myself to you unless I can give you all of me."

"How many times do I gotta say it?" Anger ignited in Ryan's voice, though he kept it low so their pack nearby couldn't eavesdrop. "I'll have you any way I can. You don't need to be perfect, or have yourself all figured out. Zach, you're enough just as you are." Ryan slumped, his forehead to Zach's chest. "I thought a lot this weekend."

"Me, too," Zach sighed.

"I said we could go back to being friends if things didn't work out."

Fear tightened Zach's chest. Ryan was going to tell him he'd changed his mind. He'd promised Zach but after what a shitty person Zach was, he was going to take it back. Zach would deserve it.

"I still mean that," Ryan said, and Zach's heart damn near stopped.

"Why?" Zach asked. How could Ryan do that to himself? Hadn't he been hurt enough pining after Zach all these years?

Ryan squinted at him, like Zach was the confusing one. "Because I told myself a long time ago that I'd have you any way I could. Would I miss getting to kiss you whenever I want? Holding your hand? Waking up next to you? Yeah. I would. And maybe I'd need space for a bit until things cool off for me. But being your friend isn't a consolation prize, Zach. I didn't stick around all these years because I was waiting for you to notice me. I stayed because a life without you isn't one that I want."

Tears stung Zach's eyes. "Ryan," he began, but Ryan pressed on.

"I made you a promise. And unlike your shitty folks, I keep my promises." Bumping his fist gently into Zach's chest, Ryan walked away from him and toward the bus doors. He stopped and looked back.

"My love's never going to come with conditions, Zach."

And then he walked out the doors and left Zach struggling to breathe around the shattered shards of his heart in his chest.

Ryan was wonderful and patient and far too understanding. Hadn't Ryan been hurt enough? Maybe he was willing to settle. Maybe Ryan didn't see it as settling for something less than he deserved. But Zach wasn't okay with that. Not at all. He didn't deserve Ryan. Maybe he never would. But was he willing to be the man Ryan deserved?

Yes. Yes. *Yes.*

As soon as they had time, Zach wanted to talk. If Ryan was still willing to give him a chance, then this time, Zach would be dead in the ground before he made Ryan regret it.

Chapter 19

THE SACRED GROVE

THE LPA AGENTS DISEMBARKED from the RV and roamed among the island greenery.

Ryan feared the coming confrontation between the wolves and Zach's mother and her team. He feared for Zach, who would have to confront her over this, and he wasn't sure Zach's relationship with her would survive this. What was left of it.

As for his and Zach's relationship, Zach kept glancing at him, an air of urgency radiating from him. He clearly had more to say about their talk in the bus. Ryan hoped he'd reassured him. Not being his boyfriend would fucking hurt, but losing him as a friend would be a thousand times worse. As soon as they had time, Ryan wanted them to talk more.

"Look up there," Izzie said, pointing further up the trail.

Cranes towered into the sky over the palm trees. Zach growled softly. "My mother's developers."

Ben's silver eyes narrowed. "Remember, we aren't going there to fight. We negotiate, keep both sides from breathing fire. We need to convince Rebecca not to destroy the grove."

A scoff escaped Zach. "Good luck getting her to do anything she doesn't want to."

Vicenzo curled his lip, his body stiffening beside Ryan's. "And if the hunters decide they don't wanna talk?"

Ben said, "Then we stand with the wolves."

They walked the hill toward where the once-lush forest gave way to vast, empty space where the trees had been ripped up by their roots. Ryan's stomach churned at the sight. The forest was silent, and the birds had all fled. There were no branches for the wind to whisper sweet words into. The forest was dead, and Ryan's skin prickled with contempt for the people who had done this. The air smelled like fur, urine, and scat. Wolves had made their home within these dead trees. They'd hunted and thrived, fallen in love, and started families. Now they were going to lose everything.

The earth shook as machines tore into the ground.

Furious howls echoed throughout the woods.

Ben broke into a run and the pack followed. Ahead, a crowd of construction workers formed a line as frightened voices mingled with angry growls and snarls. A roar tore from Ben's throat and all sound abruptly cut out. Heads turned and the crowd parted as Ben approached, his pack at his side.

Standing before them was a pack of wolves, most completely shifted into snarling wolves while others were only in a half shift, naked except for their fur, and showing off their fangs and claws. A dead tree formed a barrier between the humans and the wolf pack, its roots sprawling across the ground like intestines.

Pressed close, a man and woman stood at the head of the pack. They had mating bites on their necks and the man had a braided beard. He wore nothing, as did his mate, and they bared their fangs and claws defiantly at the humans encroaching on their land.

"Told you," the bearded man said, the words more of a grunt than anything. "Stay away. Pack lands. Don't belong here!"

"We have permits to clear this area!" bellowed one human, a woman in a hard hat. "You mutts are slowing us down!"

The woman snapped her jaws, a waterfall of curls sprawling down to her waist. "Our home. Not yours! Leave or die!"

"You creatures truly shame our kind." Rebecca DeShawn made her way through the crowd, coming between Ben and the agents. "Are some trees really worth dying for when there are so many others you could mark?"

She motioned and twelve hunters came to her side, armed with silver and pistols.

Ryan's stomach turned over and Zach growled, "I can't believe she'd really do this."

Gabe rounded on Ben. "Give us the signal. We'll tear those assholes apart!"

The wolves snarled behind their parents. The patriarch of the pack spat, "You dare to bring hunters here?"

"You have a choice," Rebecca said, calm and cold. "Leave and let us work, or we will hunt you like the animals you insist on behaving as! If you haven't made your decision come morning, I will make it for you."

"You wolf," snapped the wolf-mother. "You kill your own kind?" There was disgust in her voice, and her fangs were bared.

Rebecca turned up her nose. "I am a wolf, but I'm not a beast. You have until dawn." She glowered at Ben. "Come to be the champions to the poor animals?"

"Yes," Ben said. "You can't drill here, Mrs. DeShawn. This site was once a sacred grove, and the remains of the druids buried here may be cursed."

Tossing back her head, Rebecca laughed. "Listen to yourself, dear! You sound as ridiculous as these wolves. No one is stopping me from completing my mate's final project."

Zach came toward her. "Mom! We're werewolves. We should protect nature, not destroy it to build luxury establishments for rich humans!"

She curled her lip. "When did you become so high-and-mighty? This business is part of who you are. You associate with lowly werewolves too long and suddenly, you're too good for this family."

"Too good? Too *good,* is that how we're playing this?" Zach balled his hands into fists. "You decided I wasn't good *enough* because I wouldn't roll over and do what you wanted."

"Now, you wait just one moment!"

He shook his head. "I'm supposed to be thankful to you and Dad? You took that life of wealth and luxury away from me when I wouldn't be the son you wanted. You're lucky I still kept your name."

Her nostrils flared. "How dare you!"

He held his head high. "Ben Stroud taught me more about family and loyalty than you or Dad ever did. He taught me what it means to be a werewolf. It means pack; it means being a voice for people who don't have one, protecting not just our own interests but the interests of others."

She sneered. "He taught you weakness. To disrespect your own name. To protect the rights of animals who shame pure-blooded werewolves like us. This organization is a disgrace!"

Zach laughed, a shaky sound. "I won't let you destroy the lives of these wolves."

Reaching out, Ryan gripped his arm, squeezing tight. He was damn proud of Zach.

Ben said, "Move. I'll speak to them."

Rebecca turned on her heel and marched away, the hunters following her. Vicenzo snarled at them as they passed. With Zach at his side, Ben went to speak to the disgruntled pack. Gabe and the others stood close, shooting the hunters wary looks.

Max watched Ben while he addressed the wolves. "If they don't leave, they'll die."

"And if Zach's mom digs up those remains, who knows what will happen?" Ryan sighed.

Gabe touched Max's shoulder. "Ben can talk some sense into them."

Max frowned, anxiety darkening his face. "Did we come out here to watch a massacre?"

Cracking his knuckles, Vicenzo said, "Hell no. Those humans try to touch those wolves, I'll tear their arms off."

Ryan looked around at the trees in the distance, lush and green. The forest was old—he could see it in the moss growing thick and untouched on the trunks of trees. He closed his eyes, and his magic sought the roots deep within the soil, stretching deeper and farther than he'd ever imagined. "This place is their home. They care for this forest. Protect it, and it protects them. I can't bear to watch it all get torn down."

Vicenzo arched a brow. "Damn, man. You're such a hippie now."

Zach rubbed thoughtfully at his jaw. "Well, they can't tear down the trees if the machinery is busted."

Ryan eyed the machinery scattered around the encampment. "Yeah, but how—"

Zach gripped his shoulder. "Use your magic. Cover it in vines or something."

He grinned. "Oh, I can do more than just that." Ryan knelt, knee to the soil. His magic burrowed deep and tangled with the roots within the earth, and they stirred to life at his touch. Ryan closed his eyes and curled his fingers into the soil. "I need help. All of you, come here." The pack gathered close.

"What do you need?" Gabe asked. "We gonna hold hands and sing 'Kumbaya'?"

Ryan said, "No. The magic I'm going to do is intensive. I need you guys to give me the strength to see it through."

Izzie said, "Sure thing, Ry." She touched his shoulder. The rest of the pack placed their hands on Ryan's back and shoulders. He didn't bother telling them they didn't need to touch him to do this, but their warm touch grounded him and kept him calm. Closing his eyes, he sought the bonds of the pack, golden and warm.

The green thread of his magic danced among the bonds of his pack and when Ryan opened his eyes, he gasped. He could see the bonds sprawling around him, threads that glowed and shimmered and connected them one to another. He could see his own thread trailing from his chest and tangling among theirs. Gathering the warm, delicate threads into his hands, he felt the pack shiver around him.

"Whoa," Gabe whispered. "Anyone else feel that?"

"Y-yeah," Max said, his eyes wide. "It's like a tingling down my spine."

Ryan frowned. "Is it uncomfortable?"

"No!" Izzie smiled. "It feels wonderful. Like the chill you get when you see something beautiful."

He closed his hand around the bonds tethering him to the others and the grass grew beneath him, rising to his thighs. The pack uttered gasps of delight and amazement. The trees swayed their branches as if they were dancing, and the ground rippled like waves as the roots churned below the soil. Then the machines turned green as ivy and vines crept up their iron bodies. Looking around wildly, the construction workers shouted in alarm.

The machines rocked side to side as roots coiled around their wheels. Ryan curled his fingers in the earth and the ground shook violently beneath them. The earth shuddered as a bulldozer overturned, roots crawling up inside its metal guts. As bugs scurried across the forest floor and crawled over Ryan's feet, Izzie shrieked in alarm. Nearby, a crane swayed and came crashing down on the rocks with a roar that rang in his ears.

"What is going on here?" Rebecca stomped over, flanked by her hunters. "What happened to all the machinery?"

"An earthquake!" one of the construction workers squawked.

Rebecca rolled her eyes skyward and ran to investigate the downed crane. "When was the last time anyone cleaned these machines? They're overgrown and filthy! All of you get to work. We need to get these machines up and running ASAP!"

The triumphant pack exchanged high fives.

Ben was smiling drolly. "An earthquake, huh? Imagine that."

Zach's eyes were wide, a smile on his face. "Knew you could do it."

Cheeks flushing, Ryan smiled.

Ben sighed and sat on the stump of a tree. "The pack doesn't want to move, but not all of them want to fight. The pack's divided. If enough of them leave, the few that remain will follow. Strength in numbers and all that."

Ryan folded his arms over his chest. "They shouldn't have to. This is their home."

"If those remains are cursed, leaving might be for the better in the long run." Ben rolled his shoulders, wincing. "I told them we'd try to convince the humans not to drill, but that they needed to have a pack meeting about who wants to risk their hide and who doesn't. If they come with us, we could work with the Council to help them settle down somewhere protected. Don't know how thrilled they were about that idea, but we'll see."

Izzie massaged his shoulders. "You're doing the best you can, Ben."

A gaggle of construction workers was making a fuss by the overturned crane, pointing and shouting. The patriarch of the pack lunged toward them. "Away!" he roared. "Get away from there!" The workers huddled together as the hunters drew their weapons.

Ben lurched to his feet and leaped between the hunters and the wolves. "Hold it! What's going on?"

The patriarch snarled, his arms wide to show off his hooked claws. "Cursed ground! Evil! Get away! Get away!"

The workers didn't need telling twice and ran from the crane. Ben marched toward the wolves, baring his teeth when they snarled at him. Ryan hurtled to Ben's side in seconds, the rest of their pack snarling behind him as they faced down the wolves looking for a fight with one of their own.

"What's wrong?" Ben asked.

The female opened her arms, keeping them away from the crane. "Stay back. Stay away. Dangerous. Evil. Cursed!"

Ben shoved her aside and knelt. When the crane had toppled, it had blown a hole in the rock and revealed the hollow cavern of a cave below. Ryan craned over Ben's shoulder as Ben fumbled for his phone and shone a light down into the opening. Darkness stared back at them, and the cavern breathed cold, stale air on Ryan's face.

A chill ran down his arms and a growl rose to his throat. Beside him, Ben curled his lip. "What is *that*?"

There was no obvious odor Ryan could describe wafting from the darkness below, but his skin crawled and the hair on his body stood up. He jumped as insects crawled over his hands, centipedes and potato bugs and worms, all fleeing the very ground around the cavern.

"I think we found the druid burial ground," Ryan said, his throat going dry.

So of course the workers wanted to investigate.

"No!" the matriarch of the pack snapped. "Stay back! Evil magic!"

"Listen to them!" Ben said, but the workers rolled their eyes and shoved past. They threw down some ropes and lowered themselves into the cavern.

"Bunch of idiots," Ryan grumbled. It seemed the humans were determined to ignore all warnings.

Though Ryan and the wolves gave the cavern a wide berth, it was like whatever evil energy within was creeping into the surrounding air. The air turned moist and cold, heavy and oppressive like mist. It felt like an incoming storm.

"Can we leave now?" Max asked, keeping close to Gabe, who held him tight.

"No," Ben said, though he was stiff and his eyes darted around uneasily. "We've gotta see this through."

Ryan shivered as the earth stirred beneath his feet. The roots themselves were creeping away from the unearthed cavern. "I think we've got a bigger issue than wolves and humans squabbling."

Eddie nudged Ryan's shoulder. "Any of your magic books say anything about creepy energy?"

He shook his head. "It feels old. As old as this forest, but it doesn't feel elemental. It feels... like sticking your hand into a cold, rotting tree stump."

Atticus had to have something to do with this.

Grimacing, Zach took a step forward, crowding in front of Ryan as if to protect him. Ryan's face warmed. "Zach, move. I don't need you to protect me from some cave farts."

Vicenzo groaned. "I hate you guys."

One by one, the humans climbed out of the cavern, chattering among themselves. Ben cocked an ear toward them. "They found human remains. And... shit." Ben's face drained of color.

"What?" Ryan asked.

Ben said, "A coffin."

And Ryan wished he hadn't asked at all.

CHAPTER 20

RISE OF THE DRUID KING

THE HUMANS STRUGGLED FOR over an hour, straining to get one of the smaller cranes upright while others ventured into the cavern to truss up the stone coffin. Even though the agency wolves urged them against it, the humans were determined to ignore them. Ryan watched them like characters in a horror movie, the kind you screamed at to not go into that creepy-ass house but who, of course, went in any way.

Rebecca had left for the night with orders to have everything cleaned up and ready for work come morning. Of course, the humans had said yes to her face but immediately decided they'd rather get the coffin out of the cavern. Her hunters remained, shifting from one foot to the other. The wolf pack lurked within the trees, their fangs flashing and eyes burning. Ryan had the feeling they would have attacked the humans by now if not for the hunters' presence. They'd been adamant about the humans avoiding the cavern.

"It's Atticus buried down there. Has to be." His skin was crawling and itching.

Ben threw a twig into the firepit they'd built. "There's nothing we can do." The hunters kept them from interfering in the humans' efforts, and no one was willing to start a fight that could result in a body count on both sides.

Vicenzo gnawed on some jerky. "Maybe Ryan's turning me into a hippie or something but whatever's down there, that shit's just radiating all kinds of evil energy."

Izzie tightened the drawstrings of her sweatshirt's hood around her head. "It definitely isn't you. I've never felt anything like what I'm feeling now."

Ryan sighed and pressed his forehead against his knee. "It's Atticus…"

"Whatever it is, it's dead," Ben said, as if that would put an end to it. "It can't hurt us, so everyone just chill out."

Max gnawed on his lower lip. "That's not the way ghosts work in paranormal movies…"

Izzie took his hand. "I'll kick the ass of any ghost who tries to drag you around by your ankle!"

Eddie sighed. "Great. Now I'm thinkin' 'bout *Paranormal Activity*. Thanks, Maxwell. I couldn't sleep for a week after I watched that shit."

Ben rolled his eyes. "You're all acting like children. If you're done eating, get some sleep. I'll stand watch and make sure no oogie boogies bother us."

The pack spread out and unfurled sleeping bags. Gabe, Izzie, and Max lay beside each other, and Izzie and Max held hands while Max rested his head on Gabe's shoulder. Vicenzo sat away from the others, his back against a tree. Kicking off his boots, Eddie lay down next to the dying fire, and Ryan spread his sleeping bag nearby. Zach hovered close, gazing at him. Heart racing, he patted the empty grass beside him. Zach set up his bag and bundled himself inside it with a gap between them Ryan could bridge if he only reached out his hand and touched Zach's face. He didn't.

With the pack huddled close and Ben's silhouette visible across the firelight, Ryan closed his eyes and slept.

When he opened his eyes, everyone was gone. He lay on the floor encased in darkness. The skeletal silhouettes of dying trees reached bony branches to the moon. Dark clouds hid it, and Ryan whimpered for her guiding light.

His skin was cold and clammy, and he was sweating despite the chill. His feet were bare and streaked with cold soil. Worms writhed cold, slimy bodies over his feet and between his fingers. Ryan waved his hands and kicked his feet, scattering them.

The wind blew the sweet smell of rotting wood to Ryan's nose. His gag reflex prickled, making his eyes water, and leaves crunched, the sound like bones. Ryan whirled around, his heart racing and breath short. His eyes couldn't pierce the veil of darkness that fogged the woods.

But he didn't have to see to know he was being watched as every hair on his body stood on end and cold sweat leaked from his pores. In creaky, dying voices, the trees groaned, *Run away, our king. Run away. He will catch you. He will kill you.*

Ryan's knees shook as he took a step back, the soil freezing between his toes. He told himself to run, but this was a nightmare and his body wouldn't obey.

From the woods, Ben Stroud stepped from the shadows as a silver wolf. His fur was matted with blood, glistening thickly. He panted, and blood trickled from his throat and puddled on the ground. Ryan wanted to scream but he couldn't. He couldn't even move.

Izzie dragged herself from the trees, leaves scraping beneath her broken back legs. She collapsed, her sides heaving between sharp whines of pain. Dragging a three-legged red wolf by the scruff, Gabe followed his sister. Max wasn't moving as Gabe crumpled, the black wolf draping himself over his mate's body.

Ryan wanted to find who had hurt his pack and break them into pieces with his magic and his fangs.

"I can see you, little wolf."

He would have screamed if he could, but the sound of that voice silenced him in sheer terror. The voice was male and Irish, low and gravelly, wet and slimy. That voice made him feel like he was sticking his hand in a cold, rotting tree stump. It was worms, writhing within the soil. It was rabbits, twitching in the snares around their necks. It was death and decay.

"Soon, false king, I will water the forest with your pack's blood. I will fill the trees with their dying howls. I will rip the magic from your chest. And I will take back what's mine."

The moon emerged from behind the clouds and revealed the blood, leaking like sap from the trees and dripping from the branches. The trees writhed, and they had red eyes and jagged, gaping mouths.

Paws splashed in blood. Ryan turned as a brown timber wolf limped from the trees. It was Zach, and he couldn't stop bleeding. He collapsed, blood pooling from cuts and burns that wouldn't heal. Ryan ran to him, gasping wordlessly as he touched his bloody fur, his hands coming away red.

A growl rumbled from Zach's throat, and around him the pack snarled as their bodies spasmed, broken bones healing and cuts closing. Ryan looked down to express his relief to Zach, and feral yellow eyes burned back at him. He crashed onto his back as Zach towered over him, his lip pulled back from his fangs, his eyes wild and crazed.

"Zach," Ryan whispered. "No, no. Don't do this. What's wrong with you? Oh fuck, what's wrong with you? Stop. Stop it! You're hurting me. You're killing me, Zach! Stop, *stop!*"

Ryan lurched upright, kicking and clawing, thrashing and screaming for Zach to stop, to please stop.

"Ry! Ryan, it's okay. Everything's okay! I've got you. I've got you." Arms flew around Ryan's shoulders, pulling him back toward the snarling wolf with blazing yellow eyes.

"Ry, wake up! It's a nightmare. Wake up!" Gabe shouted.

But Gabe was feral, wasn't he? They were all feral, they—

Ryan's eyes flew open to see a clearing dimly lit by a fire. Zach stood over him, human, his eyes a warm brown. The pack gathered around him, their faces pale and distressed.

"You're okay," Zach said, his voice shaking as he captured Ryan's face in his hands. "I know. It was scary. It was horrible, but it was a dream. A messed-up dream."

Ryan's heart slammed against his chest, and he couldn't stop shaking as he collapsed against Zach, clutching at his shirt as he gasped. He breathed in Zach's scent of ocean and warm sand and his breathing slowed, his shaking subsiding as Zach rubbed his back. Through the panic fogging his mind, a chilling detail made Ryan's guts spasm.

"You had the same dream?"

Zach nodded, lips dry and face ashen.

Gabe said, "I think we all did." His voice cracked.

Ryan pulled away from Zach, looking around in shared horror at the pack. "No. No, that's wrong. That doesn't make sense. You guys saw a dying forest?"

Max's lips trembled. "Yes," he croaked.

"You guys were hurt."

Zach gripped Ryan's arms. He nodded.

"Feral," Ben rasped, his voice hollow.

"You heard a voice too?"

They looked confused at that. Izzie said, "No. Just wolves, howling. Like they were dying. They were in so much pain…"

Ryan slumped, holding his head as if it would split apart. "But no voices, any of you? 'Cause I heard some creepy voice telling me I was a false king. That he was coming for us. That he was gonna take back what was his."

"Oh fuck." Eddie sounded faint as he leaned on a tree.

Vicenzo shook his head. "We need to leave. Now."

Ben nodded, sweat glistening on his forehead. "Yeah. I think you're right."

From within the trees, eyes winked at Ryan. They were the eyes of wolves but not feral wolves. The wolf pack watched from the shadows. Ryan stood, brushing off Zach's arms. He went to them and met them halfway as they loped from the trees.

"You mentioned evil," Ryan said. "You know who's buried here, don't you?"

A wolf shifted before his eyes into the pack's matriarch. Her eyes were huge, her face pale as bone in the dark. "Druid. Witch. Evil magic."

Ryan's stomach turned over, but it didn't surprise him, not after what he'd seen in his dream. "His name was Atticus. He died during the witch hunts."

"No," the woman said. "Not dead."

"Oh no." Eddie groaned. "Please not zombies... please not zombies..."

"How?" Ryan asked. "How is he still alive?"

"Magic," she said. "It keeps him alive."

Ryan's skin crawled with dread.

People cheered behind them. Ben whirled toward the humans. While they'd slept, the workers had used ropes to hoist the stone coffin from the darkness of the cavern. Ben ran, tearing toward them, and Ryan pelted after him.

Ben seized the nearest worker by the shirt and hurled him away from the coffin. One hunter took aim at Ben, and Gabe wrestled Ben back. "No one touch that! Would you fucking listen to us!" Ben roared, and the humans cowered from him. "That thing is dangerous!"

The hunter sneered. "What bullshit you hollering about, doggy? It's nothing but some old bones." He grinned. "Want a bone, good boy?" Ben snapped his teeth at him and the hunter leaped back.

Ryan approached the coffin. His fingers itched and tingled. Grass grew between his toes, and roots rippled like worms under his feet. Whatever evil magic was within there, it was causing a reaction in the environment. Bugs crawled over Ryan's feet and the humans hollered in disgust, kicking insects from their shoes. They withdrew from the coffin, their eyes wide in newfound fear.

As the coffin was carved from stone, the lid was heavy and likely impossible for him to lift by himself. The ancient celts had carved runes all over the surface. Since he'd been studying his gran's tomes, Ryan recognized them as runes of binding. "Okay. Makes sense. They imprisoned him within the coffin using magic." Faded Gaelic writing had been carved into the stone, but it was nearly illegible. He squinted, trying to recall his Gaelic. "I think I can read this. Hang on." He murmured the words to himself, piecing them together.

"You wolves are superstitious morons," the human said. "Get out of the way so we can loot this thing before DeShawn comes back!"

Ryan shushed her. "Oak. Something about an oak and immortality." Hadn't it been said that Atticus appeared to rise from the dead over and over? Perhaps that was why he'd been imprisoned rather than killed. Word by word, he pieced together the translation, excitement mounting as it all came together. "I did it!" His exclamation made the wolves jerk awake.

Groggily, the pack gathered around him, and Ryan read from his phone screen.

"Bound to the oak, he could not die. Imprisoned here, forever will he lie. Betrayer of wolves, tormenter of men. This world will fail, shall he ever rise again."

Bound to the oak. The words repeated in Ryan's mind. The scholars had theorized that Atticus's life force was bound to the oaks he'd grown himself, but all the sacred groves were gone. Yet his gran had sensed danger. Was it possible not all the sacred groves had been destroyed?

"What's written here is a warning." Ryan's hands shook. "No one can open this thing. It has to go back in the ground where it belongs." Using his magic, Ryan grew more vines to crawl around the coffin. "I'm putting this thing back."

"The hell you are!" the human shouted and lunged toward Ryan. Ben bolted after him, but the man got there first. The worker shoved Ryan and caused him to lose concentration of the spell. The vines snapped and the coffin fell, disappearing into the dark and shattering with the force of a meteor against the rock below.

Peering into the cavern, Ryan held his breath. The dawn sunlight illuminated the shattered chunks of stone and the yellowed bones and tattered cloth below. It didn't look like anything special, only bones and ash and scraps of cloth. For a moment, Ryan let himself believe the pack had gotten themselves worked up for nothing. That the druid was as dead as dead could be.

Then the earth shuddered and cracked. Zach's arms flew around his waist, and they tumbled back from the cavern as a cataclysm of magical energy erupted all around them. The blast bowled them over and sent them tumbling across the forest floor. Zach collapsed atop him, shielding him from the screaming wind and the debris that hurtled past. The humans screamed, and the wolves yelped as wind blew them off their paws, their claws scrambling for a foothold.

Closing his eyes, Ryan clutched onto Zach's arm until the wind died to a whisper. He looked up and gasped. The force of the explosion had bent some trees and toppled others, and their leaves littered the ground, leaving their branches bare. The ground was barren around the site of the explosion as if a comet had struck the area.

Ryan looked around and found the pack slowly finding their feet around him. They all looked unharmed, if a bit shaken up. Ben stumbled toward the cavern. Finding his feet, Ryan brushed away Zach's grabbing hands as he followed Ben. The cavern had been blown apart, nothing left but chunks of rock. Those rocks shifted, shaking the ground as they rolled toward each other and, though it seemed impossible, formed a staircase. Ben peered into the crater as Ryan held his breath.

Nothing had changed, the old yellowed bones and rags lying in the same place they'd fallen, completely untouched. Before Ryan's eyes, the bones suspended, flying together to form a skeleton. Flesh grew over the rattling bones and the skeletal figure doubled over, clutching onto a walking stick with a gnarled hand.

"Ben," Gabe squeaked. "I want to go home now."

Ryan did too, but he couldn't move, transfixed by what they'd unleashed.

A ghastly groan raised the hair on Ryan's arms as the man below shuddered and held on to his walking stick. A mane of long white hair burst from his skull and cascaded down his back. Starting at the roots, it slowly regained color, red chasing silver. A pair of sunken green eyes gazed up at Ryan.

The jaw cracked and creaked as the old man parted his lips, a hollow sound escaping his throat. "Wh... Wh... Where?"

Ryan realized it was a word spoken in a raspy Irish accent.

"Where. Are. They?" the old man groaned. His voice was familiar, the Irish accent a stark reminder of Ryan's dream. It made his skin crawl.

No one spoke. Ryan didn't think anyone could.

"Where. Are. My. People?" Those green eyes filled with fire.

Ben spoke first. "People? Who?"

"Druids," the old man said, seething. "Wretched. Beast. Where are my people?"

Ben said, a tremor to his voice, "I'm sorry, but the druids were hunted to extinction three-hundred years ago."

A long, heavy silence followed Ben's words.

"No. No, that can't be." The old man's eyes had gone wide, and his lips quivered. "How long have I been asleep? Where am I?"

"New York. Fire Island. Where you fought your last battle," Ryan answered, clearing his throat. "You were imprisoned, and your supporters were hunted and killed. They're gone."

"Gone?" He took a step back. "All of them?" His voice sounded younger, smaller. Full of gut-wrenching pain. His hair was rapidly turning red, his posture straightening with a quiet crack and a snap of bones.

This old man didn't look like the feared king of the druids who had almost conquered the entire world. He looked lost, like he was seconds away from falling back into pieces. Ryan felt for him.

"N-not all of them," Ryan said. He raised a hand. "I'm one of them."

The old man stepped back like someone had slapped him. "You. You are a *wolf.*" He spat the word with such poison, it surprised Ryan he didn't choke on it. "A wolf who stole the power of my people. Just like you stole this land. Stole our place in this world. You and the humans." He seethed through gritted yellowed teeth. His once-gnarled hands grasped the walking stick with surprising strength, and it quivered in his hands.

"The trees, they call you a king. They bow to you. But the true king has risen again." He stood straight and tall now, all the age gone from his face, which had gone from gaunt and sunken to hard and cold. He took a staggering step, then another, his movements growing faster as he ascended the stone stairs toward them. Backing up toward the pack, Ben urged them away. Wide-eyed, the humans were whispering, while the wolves snapped and snarled as the druid stood nude before them, his forest-green eyes ablaze in his face. Wind blew, whipping his long beard around his chest.

Green eyes flickered around the forest, narrowing at the sight of the barren woods. The hand gripping his walking stick trembled. "I see man hasn't changed in the time I've been asleep. Still you destroy everything you touch. You've hurt my forest. You've bent and broken this world to your whims for the last time." He raised his walking stick and slammed it to the ground. The roots churned the soil beneath Ryan's feet.

"A staff!" Ryan roared. "It's a—"

The workers screamed as roots burst from the soil, constricting their waists and hoisting them off their feet. Ryan tried to run to them and smashed headlong into an invisible wall of magic. The druid king extended a hand, magic crackling at his fingertips. The humans choked and gasped, struggling and screaming, but their screams cut out as the roots forced themselves down their gaping mouths and into their throats, blood burst as the roots pierced their eyes and popped them out of their skulls. Ryan closed his eyes, unable to watch, but their choked grunts and gurgles made his stomach churn. Blood spattered thickly to the ground, sounding like a heavy rainstorm.

The roots hurled their broken bodies into the trees, killing them on impact if they weren't dead already. Ben was shaking against Ryan, his face bloodless. Ryan had never seen Ben Stroud so scared before.

The druid came toward them, the shimmering barrier he'd erected dissipating like mist. Gabe growled, but it was a weak sound as the pack pressed close, readying themselves for an attack they had no hope of defending themselves against.

"Wait," Ben croaked. "We tried to stop the humans from destroying this place. We're on your side. *I* failed to negotiate with them. If you've got a problem with any of us, take it up with me. Okay? What's your name? Tell me your name. Let's talk." He was pleading, and Ryan's knees shook as his fingers clutched at the back of Ben's shirt.

"Ben," Izzie whispered, sounding as if she were crying. "Ben, don't."

Stopping, the druid cocked his head, and his fingers curled around his staff. Ryan tensed, reaching for Zach's hand. The druid said, "Atticus."

Ryan's heart tripped in his chest, though he'd known the answer.

"King of the Druids." Atticus's moss-green eyes flicked to Ryan. "I hear the tripping of a wolf heart. You know my name, beast."

"Y-yes," Ryan said, peering out from behind Ben's shoulder. "I read about you. My gran was from the Kelly Coven. Her ancestors fled when the druids and their wolf allies turned on your kind."

"Kelly... Kelly." Thin fingers rasped through a long beard, dislodging lice. "Yes, I remember your coven well. Good people, or so I believed." Fury burned in those green eyes. "Until they abandoned their king and fled with the traitorous wolves."

Ryan's heart sank. "But you're still alive! Sure, people betrayed you, but you're fine!"

"What do you want?" Ben rasped.

Atticus stopped walking, his mustache twitching as he smiled. "I want what should have always belonged to me. What the wolves stole, and the humans plundered." He opened his arms and the trees shuddered.

Ben snapped, "Then have it. Have the forest. Just let us leave."

Laughter crawled from Atticus's throat. "This forest? This puny thing? No. No, wolf. Amaris created us to serve your wretched kind, but we were always better, stronger. Aye, we were meant for more. I want the wolves, bent and broken at my feet like the slobbering servants you are. I want the humans to bow before my magic."

"Why?" Ryan croaked. "For what purpose? The druids are gone. I'm all that's left."

Something shuddered across Atticus's face. Something that looked suspiciously like fear. "No! I will never believe that. Some must still remember my legacy! They're only hiding away, keeping their magic a secret. It's no way to live. This isn't the world I promised my people. When they hear of my return, they will step out of the shadows and into the light. I will lead all druids into the future we deserve, and we will never have to hide our gifts!"

Fur grew on Ben's face and his fangs lengthened. "It sounds like you truly care for your people, Atticus. But I'm sorry. The druids are gone, and we won't allow you to harm wolves or humans. We won't let you leave this forest."

Ryan's heart thudded nonstop. They didn't stand a chance. "Guys, it has to be me." His gran's written words came back to him. Only a druid could stop Atticus for good. Goddess, he wasn't ready. He'd only just found his focus, and his relationship with said focus was strained. He couldn't do this alone, but he had to try his damnedest. "Get back. All of you. Let me—"

"No." Zach's fingers curled around Ryan's hand. He squeezed back, the roots roiling beneath his feet and the trees whispering to him. Zach held his gaze. "No, Ry. We do this together or not at all."

If this was how it ended, Ryan would die standing with the man he'd wanted so badly to call his mate, and with his pack.

Atticus laughed softly, his hands clasped on top of the staff. "To think, you truly believe you have any power over me at all. Little wolves, don't you see? It is I who has power over you. As your wretched kind betrayed me, I cursed the wolves. Silver, to weaken you."

Eddie made a choking sound.

Vicenzo said, "Hey. What are you doing?" His eyes widened in horror, and his voice grew shrill. "What the fuck are you doing to him?"

Eddie screamed, clutching at the silver around his neck as his flesh smoked and burned.

Baring his fangs, Vicenzo said, "Son of a bitch!" And he sprang before they could stop him. He began to choke and wheeze as purple flowers burst from the soil, smelling of poisonous death.

"Wolfsbane," Atticus said. "To poison you."

Ben seized Vicenzo and hurled him toward the pack. "Back!" he roared as the flowers bloomed, spewing toxic purple mist as more burst into existence before the pack's eyes. Ben snarled, "Nice trick, druid. But we're a pack. We're stronger than you'll ever be!"

Atticus sneered. "Pack. Pack! You think such a thing gives you strength, but it's your greatest weakness yet." He raised his hands and Ryan gasped as what felt like a hook lodged in his chest. Around him, the pack reacted with cries of shock and discomfort, gripping their chests.

The bonds. Oh Goddess, the bonds.

"No!" Ryan roared and, spitting out an incantation in rapid Gaelic, he erected a shimmering barrier around his pack. "I won't let you!"

Atticus howled with laughter. "You, little druid, are but a sapling. As if you could stop me from taking what I want!" He thrust out his hand and tendrils of golden magic ripped from his fingertips like missiles. Each magic missile hit the barrier, and each collision was like an explosion in Ryan's skull. A scream tore from his throat. His knees buckled as cracks formed in the barrier, but Ryan poured more of his magic into it to strengthen it.

Zach screamed for him, gripping Ryan's shoulders as he begged him to drop the barrier, to please stop hurting himself. Ryan wouldn't. If Atticus's magic got hold of them, it was the end for them all.

But he wasn't strong enough. He wasn't good enough. If he'd been a better druid, then he wouldn't have collapsed, clutching his aching skull in his hands. Atticus's magic wouldn't have shattered the barrier to pieces. His pack wouldn't have been knocked off their feet as Atticus's magic hooked into their chests again.

Gabe groaned, "What is that? Is that—"

In his hand, Atticus held the golden threads of the pack, each thread connecting and tangling from one pack member to another. Atticus said, "And I curse you here and now with feral madness."

Ben whispered, his eyes full of despair, "Don't. Don't!"

Atticus bared his teeth in a grin. He grasped the threads in his hands and pulled, and the strings frayed.

Dropping to all fours, Ben lunged toward Atticus as a wolf, his jaws agape. A root burst from the earth and slammed into the silver wolf's ribs. Gabe screamed as Ben hurtled into a tree, his back snapping on impact. The wolf's paws twitched, and he whined weakly.

Ryan roared his fury and dropped to all fours, his hands turning to paws as the pack charged toward Atticus. Roots bowled them off their feet. Ryan dug his claws into the earth and sent a column of dirt rolling toward Atticus. All Atticus had to do was swipe his hand, and it parted around him. The king only smiled before he grasped the pack bonds tight, the bonds that connected Ryan to Zach, Max to Gabe, and everyone to each other. He pulled them apart like they were paper.

Ryan collapsed with a scream as a lance of pain penetrated his heart. The pack howled and screamed, doubling over as the bonds connecting them to one another tore apart. When they fell, the wolf pack they'd come to save charged, stampeding past Ryan and leaping over him. They didn't make it to Atticus—not even close.

They screamed and yelped as a blast of wind lifted them into the air. Atticus chanted lowly in Gaelic and the wolves howled in terror, their bodies twitching and spasming as their bones broke.

"I have slept for far too long," Atticus said. "The world will once again know the wrath of the druid king!"

And the wolves' bodies ripped apart, their blood raining down on the soil. From their blood grew saplings and the saplings became trees, trees the size of men but taller, with gangly limbs and mouthless heads, their eyes burning in their blank wooden faces. They flocked to Atticus's side, their hands raised to the skies. With their palms open to the heavens, they blackened the skies with an impending storm, and lightning split the trees to their roots.

Ryan ran, grabbing his backpack beside his sleeping bag and whatever else he could carry, and screamed, "Run!" Gabe and Izzie hoisted Ben to his feet and ran, Ben's arms over their shoulders. The wind roared as a hurricane racked the hilltop, ripping trees from the ground and hurling rocks over the pack's heads.

"Run, little sapling!" Atticus roared. "I will find you and rip that magic from your unworthy body!"

Ryan ran with his pack, Zach's hand in his, and they didn't look back.

CHAPTER 21

FERAL MADNESS

ZACH RAN WITH RYAN'S hand in his, squeezing so tight he thought the bones would crumble to ash. The storm had knocked the RV off the road and overturned it. They had to run to town. Ben roared over the wind, "Keep running. Don't stop!" The surrounding woods thinned and they ran toward the winking lights of the town of Kismet. The Fire Island lighthouse loomed over the town, the beacon glowing bright in the gathering dark of the storm.

Zach slumped, his lungs aching. "What do we do? Holy shit, what do we do?"

"Give me a second!" Ben snapped. His fangs were sharp, his eyes blazing. They were yellow, then flickered back to silver. The sight made Zach's stomach churn.

Gabe panted, "We need to... get out of here. Go far away so he can't get to us. To Ryan."

Ryan wiped sweat from his brow. "Me?"

Slumping over, Max had his hands on his knees as he panted. "Didn't you hear the contempt in his voice? He hates your coven. He hates wolves, and you have magic in you. Magic he wants."

Izzie's eyes burned. "But he won't get it! Not while we're around. I'll kick his ass before he—" A sudden snarl tore from her throat. Her eyes flashed yellow.

Gabe's face went pale. "Izzie? You okay?"

She stumbled, her eyes flickering back to normal. "I... I don't know."

"No," Ben said bitterly. "She's not okay. None of us will be for long." He slumped against a tree. He was still nude from his shift, the rain racing down his bare skin. "That son of a bitch did something to us. To our bonds. He shredded them in his hands."

Gabe swallowed. "He could see them. Manipulate them. Touch them. Like what Ryan did when he caused that earthquake, but when he did it, it felt warm. Pleasant. When Atticus snapped the threads, it hurt like nothing else."

Zach closed his eyes, feeling for the pack. There was a blank space in his head and heart where his connection to the pack should have been.

Ben closed his eyes tight, looking pained. "You know what he did, don't you? All of you."

Atticus had shattered the bonds connecting them to each other. To that reminder of their humanity every werewolf needed to stave off the feral madness of the wolf.

Zach didn't want to believe it. "We can fix it, everything he broke. Ryan, can't you fix this? His magic is the same as yours."

Ryan shook his head. "No. It's the same type of magic, yeah. But it's nothing like mine. I use mine to help the pack. He's used it to shatter our bonds. To drive us feral."

A spasm of dread racked Zach's chest. No. No, this wasn't how their pack ended.

"But you can fix it." Zach gripped his shoulders. "Can't you?"

Ryan's chest rose and fell quickly as rainwater glimmered on his naked skin. "I... I don't know."

Zach sucked in a calming breath. The salty sea breeze covered Ryan in a comforting scent. He smelled like warm sand, even though their environment was anything but warm and comforting. His wolf, so close to the surface with the pack bonds shattered, rumbled approvingly in his chest.

"We need to get back to HQ," Ben said, His eyes kept closing and he swayed in the wind. "If we can't repair the bonds he shattered, we'll tear each other apart before we can even face Atticus."

Max's eyes were huge, his freckled face pale as rain lashed at his skin. "What if we can't? What if—"

Gabe put his arm around his shoulders. "Don't. We can fix this. We've faced worse."

Vicenzo hung his head with a low sigh. "Nothing like this."

Zach realized for the first time that Vicenzo's bond had been tied up with theirs too. He'd only realized now that it was gone since Vicenzo had never attempted to communicate with the pack through the bonds. He'd acted as if he weren't pack, but he had been, Zach realized, as Vicenzo's eyes flared with yellow light. Otherwise, he would have gone feral before now.

Ben tugged a change of clothes from his duffel bag, and Ryan caught the backpack Gabe tossed him and changed as well. Stepping into his pants, Ben said, "We need to get back to the agency before this gets worse. Once we're there, we can work out a plan, but we need to be somewhere familiar right now or we'll just lose our heads that much faster." He tugged a shirt on, buttoning it as he set off toward town.

Ryan wasn't moving, so Zach tugged his arm. "What is it?"

He said, "Atticus wants me. If I leave, he won't hurt you guys. If I—"

Zach snarled at the very idea and wrenched Ryan to his side. "If you so much as try to be self-sacrificing, I'll chain you to me. We're in this together, Ry. No one's running away. Got it?"

Ryan hung his head, looking miserable. Zach held his hand tight to make sure he didn't disappear, then walked the road into the town with his pack.

Ben said, "Anyone feeling murderous yet?"

Shrugging, Gabe said, "A little growly. No more than usual."

Ben motioned toward an oceanfront diner. "We can rest in there while I call a car service." Ben held the door as the pack headed inside. Zach squeezed Ryan's arm, holding him back. When Ben met his gaze, Zach jerked his head toward the door and Ben went on ahead.

"What's up?" Ryan asked, his brows furrowed.

Zach snorted at his casual tone, though his insides were quivering. "Do you feel okay?" He hadn't seen Ryan's eyes glow yellow yet, but the bond between them was gone and Zach felt lost without it, like he might drift away at any second and lose himself forever. The wolf growled low in his chest and Zach gritted his teeth against the sound.

Ryan shrugged. "I mean, it hurt like hell when he shattered our connections to each other. But I feel... okay, I guess? I don't wanna maul you to death or roast your flesh. But the magic's pulling at me again, like it was before I anchored it to you. Around you, I felt in control of my magic. Now... I just kinda wanna blow up that lamppost over there. Or lock myself in a room, somewhere quiet where my senses aren't on overdrive."

Ryan gritted his teeth, his eyes closing as sensations Zach couldn't feel clawed at him. Goddess. Helplessness tugged at Zach's chest. He needed to do something, needed to make it all better for Ryan, for all of them.

"Ry. Hey." Zach grabbed his shoulders and tried to reach across the thread connecting them to comfort, to reassure. Instead, all his thoughts flew into a black void, and there was an empty ache inside him, like a missing tooth. The loss of their bond had his fangs sharpening and carnal fury surging within him.

Give it back, the wolf snarled, louder than he'd ever been in Zach's life. *Give it back!*

"Zach, that hurts!" Ryan hissed.

To his horror, Zach realized his claws had dug into Ryan. "Shit. I... I'm so sorry."

Ryan rubbed his shoulder where droplets of blood were dampening his shirt. "It's fine. Not your fault."

Without the pack bonds connecting them, there was nothing to keep Ryan from going over the brink, nothing to hold Zach back from falling into feral madness. The realization drove a shudder through him. "We can fix this. We're going to fix this."

Ryan smiled. It looked forced. "I know. We'll try." Zach heard the way his heart tripped over itself. Ryan didn't believe that, and knowing Ryan was scared left Zach terrified.

Grabbing his hands, Zach said, "Listen to me. I'm not losing you. Not to this. Ry, you made me promise not to forget you, remember?"

Ryan closed his eyes tight, nodding. "Yeah. 'Course I do."

"I won't let you break that promise either. We're fixing this, then we're kicking Atticus's ass back into that coffin where he came from."

Ryan smiled but it was pinched. "Yeah. Okay, Zach."

He tightened his grip when Ryan tried to pull away, afraid of what might happen if he let go. Afraid Ryan might descend into feral madness and be lost to him, or that Zach might lose himself first. Loosening his grip, Ryan's hand fell from his. Ryan went into the diner and Zach followed, drunken laughter and loud chitchat overwhelming his ears. Heads turned as they entered, wary eyes taking in the pack's bedraggled appearance.

They found a table in the back away from most people. When the waiter came to take their order, Ben said they were waiting out the rain for a car and to just bring water. The waiter frowned but didn't argue. The surrounding seats were mostly empty, so Zach figured they weren't taking a table from anyone. Ben got on the phone with a car service and the pack sat around in silence.

Grimacing, Vicenzo sniffed the air. "What *is* that?"

Eddie winced and touched the burns on his neck. "Someone's wearing perfume." Eddie was in his human form, his wolf locked up tight by the silver collar around his neck. He would stay human while the rest of them lost that piece of themselves.

"Can we take that collar off so we can treat your wounds?" Izzie asked.

Eddie's eyes widened. "No. No, last thing I need is this collar comin' off. I haven't shifted in so long, I'd probably lose my head faster than all of y'all combined."

Vicenzo curled his lip, his fangs sharp. "Fuck, it stinks." His claws raked over the table.

Zach's stomach churned. Vicenzo was always hot-headed and with the pack bonds gone, those emotions would be fuel for the wolf within.

Eddie lunged, grabbing the back of Vicenzo's shirt. "Come here. You can't eat people." Vicenzo snapped his jaws but allowed Eddie to tug him out into the fresh air.

Zach bit back a sigh, curling his fingers tight around Ryan's. Once they were back at HQ, Ryan could fix this. He would use his magic to repair the bonds and if he couldn't, they could always use Humanity Restorative Treatment methods. *They could fix this.*

"Ry, druids used magic to serve their packs. There must be a spell to reverse this."

Ryan slowly shredded his napkin into strips. "My gran has a lot of spell books. I was making my way through all of them, trying to find the right one. I brought a few over to my bungalow."

Gabe's cheeks puffed out as he sighed. Max sat beside him, his eyes flickering around the room, and Izzie sat on his right, her head on Max's shoulder.

"Going to the bathroom," Ryan muttered and left.

Gabe watched him go, then turned to the others. "We need to talk about what we're going to do if he can't fix this."

Zach gritted his teeth. "He can."

Shaking his head, Gabe said, "We can't just assume he can. We need a backup plan so we don't hurt others or one another."

Zach said, "Humanity Restorative Treatment. We can use the treatment if the magic fails."

Gabe's brow furrowed. "I know that, Zach. And if that doesn't work? What then?"

Izzie folded her arms over her chest. "How about you tell us, Gabriel? Let's hear it."

Scowling at her frustrated voice, Gabe said, "What are you snapping at me for?"

"Do *you* know how to fix this, Gabriel? You have some big, heroic plan that will keep us from losing our minds?"

Max closed his eyes tight, hitting his head against the back of the booth. "Stop..."

Ben shot them a warning look, his phone cradled to his ear. "Hey, it's Ben Stroud. We have a situation here in New York..."

Gabe bristled. "I'm a berserker, Izzie. I'm the biggest threat there is. So if nothing works, someone needs to lock me up somewhere I don't have a chance of escaping."

Zach's stomach churned. Berserker wolves could transform into a bipedal beast that was a mixture of man and wolf. If he wanted to, he could kill them all with a single swipe.

Max said, "Stop it, Gabe." His voice was pleading.

With a sigh, he said, "I could kill all of you in seconds if I snapped. So if it comes down to it..." He swallowed hard. "If Ryan can't fix this, if we can't treat this like we normally would, I'm going to leave. And no one can stop me."

Anger roiled in Zach's gut. "That's stupid, Gabe. How will you leaving and running around wreaking havoc somewhere else help anyone?"

Gabe pressed himself against the booth, eyes blazing. "I don't fucking know. Do you have a better idea? Huh? Tell me, Zach. You gonna fix this?"

Zach's fingers curled into fists. "You're not leaving. Ryan's not leaving. Why is everyone in this pack such self-sacrificing fucking assholes?"

"Quiet, all of you!" Ben snapped. He lurched from the booth and paced away, his phone shaking in his hand. "I don't know. He's got a small force with him, so any help you can spare would be—"

Izzie said, "Because my big brother's a moron!"

Gabe rounded on her, and his eyes flashed yellow. Her face paled, and she inched toward the edge of the booth. Max sat between them, his face hidden, his claws digging into the table. Gabe panted, "I'm trying to protect all of you! Chains won't hold me. I've got to leave, I—"

And Max roared, "Shut up!"

Everyone fell silent. Max's eyes blazed, wet with furious tears, and he slammed his fists on the table. "Everyone, shut the hell up!" He shook, quivering with anger and fear. His lips trembled, his eyes wild with rage.

Zach tried to apologize but he was speechless.

Ben looked toward them, his phone hanging from his hand, in danger of falling.

Gabe blinked at his mate and the feral anger left his eyes. His lips quivered. "Max," he began, and his voice was so broken.

Max's claws bit deep into the wood. "You all are so stupid. This is what he fucking wants. Don't any of you get that? The angrier we get, the more we fight—it'll just make us lose our minds that much faster, so would all of you just—*stop.*" His face crumpled and tears fell fast down his face.

Gabe made a wounded noise in his chest. "Max. I'm so—

"Max, I didn't mean to—" Izzie said.

Zach bowed his head, ashamed. He never lost his cool; he didn't snap at his packmates, didn't upset them, or contribute to causing Max, who was always calm and soft-spoken, to have a breakdown. Groaning, Zach covered his face in his hands and winced—his claws had come out. "Sorry. I'm sorry, Max. All of you."

Max smacked away Gabe's hand when he reached for his mate, scrambled out of the booth, and marched outside. Tears glittering in her eyes, Izzie covered her mouth as Zach swallowed the lump in his throat. Gabe pulled his sister into his arms, murmuring in broken Spanish as his shoulders shook. Izzie gasped and nuzzled into his shoulder, holding her brother tight.

"Whoa," Ryan said. "The hell happened while I was gone?"

Zach's heart ached at the sight of him. How long before Ryan's eyes flashed yellow? How long before he was snarling and deranged, before he forgot Zach and everyone else they loved?

"Did I seriously just hear Max lose his shit?" Ryan asked.

He nodded grimly.

Exhaling, Ryan swept back his hair. "Shit..."

Zach wanted to lurch from the booth and throw his arms around Ryan. He wanted to hold him tight until he was pieced back together again.

Ben slumped, his phone in hand. "The Council is going to try to send help to New York. But with this storm like it is, they may ground flights. I hate to say it, but we might be on our own here."

Someone tapped on the window. Eddie stared in at them, his eyes wide and face pale.

"Shit," Ben growled and ran for the door, and the rest of them tore after him.

The wind slammed into Zach as he ran outside, bowling him into Ryan. Eddie, Vicenzo, and Max stood outside, their faces turned toward the road. Street signs rattled in the wind, and the sign over the diner creaked as it swung up and down.

"The hell is this storm?" Zach asked, shielding his eyes as dirt caught in his eyelashes.

Ryan said, "It's no storm. He's here."

Gabe snarled, the sound feral and furious. Zach's claws came out before he could stop them. He had no control as his fangs lengthened, a growl rumbling from his chest.

Atticus came toward them, his long hair and beard billowing in the wind. He still wore his rags, and a tattered cape billowed behind him.

Ben said, "We can't fight him. Not like this. The blood, the adrenaline, it'll drive us feral. We have to keep him at bay until the cars arrive."

A burst of lightning split the sky, illuminating Atticus, staff in hand, and the army of living trees at his back. There had to be twenty of them at least, their eyes burning in the dark and the rain coursing down their wooden bodies. Atticus looked around the streets in wonder, craning his neck to stare up at the buildings.

"It's amazing, isn't it?" Atticus said. "What humanity has become while I've slept. Once, these streets were villages. There were more trees than people. The air was pure." He wrinkled his nose as a car skirted past, belching fumes.

Ryan rolled his eyes. "And let me guess. 'Humans have ruined Mother Nature, and I'm angry about it. So angry, I'm gonna kill everyone! 'Cause it's been centuries, but I just can't get a fucking hobby and move on from past grudges! Please, please, why won't someone just think of the trees!'"

Zach covered his laugh with a cough.

Atticus bared yellowed teeth in a grin. "I was going to say it's quite a marvel. The things you and humans have created while I slept. Incredible. It would be a shame if it all were to simply… crumble. Wouldn't it?"

The ground trembled. The tremble became a quake, and Zach's feet slid out from beneath him. Every streetlight lining the road hummed, dimming and brightening. The wind howled and Ben latched onto a lamppost as it bent in the wind. "Hold on!" he roared.

All around the street, windows cracked and shattered, storefronts were blown in, and trees groaned as they were bent and bowed. Zach gasped as the streetlamps exploded around them, plunging the streets into total darkness. The lights inside the stores ruptured and went out.

Headlights lit up the road. The cars were coming to pick them up, fighting their way through the wind.

"Run!" Ben roared.

Zach helped Max to his feet and dragged Eddie upright. He turned to follow them and fell, catching himself on his hands and knees as roots exploded from the cracks in the concrete and wrapped around his ankles.

Ryan roared, his fangs bared, and the magic exploded from him. The concrete shattered, chunks of stone hurtling toward Atticus. Atticus's grin faded and he lunged, waving his staff and sending the rocks flying into buildings. Ryan slashed at the roots around Zach's legs and hurled him to his feet, his arms around Zach's shoulders as they rushed through the wind toward the cars.

Ryan shoved Zach toward a car. "Go!"

"Not without you!" Zach latched onto a streetlamp and reached for him.

Bowing his head, Ryan murmured in Gaelic to form a barrier around Atticus. Atticus levitated a chunk of concrete and hurled it toward him, and Zach lunged, wrapping Ryan in his arms to shield him, but the slab exploded against thin, shimmering air.

Ryan ran, holding tight to Zach's hand. "I put up a ward! He won't be able to follow us, not until he breaks through!"

Hands reached for them as Gabe and Max pulled them into the car. The wind slammed the door behind them, and the cars spun around and drove from town. Zach looked out the window, making sure Ben and the others were following in the car behind them.

Zach panted, "Will he be stuck there for long?"

Ryan shook his head. "No. But we've got a head start. That's what counts."

Zach got a look at Atticus silhouetted by the taillights. He was watching them leave, a flame crackling in his hand.

Then they rounded the corner, and Atticus was gone from sight.

THE PACK RETURNED TO the agency grounds.

Time was running out fast, and Zach found himself adrift, lost and unsure of his role in the chaos that followed. Usually, he would give orders and try to keep a level head during the storm. Now, his mind was fogged and focusing was difficult.

Ben snapped his fingers. "Zach, your things. Grab 'em."

"Right." He grabbed some of his favorite belongings from his bungalow bedroom—a signed Timberwolves' jersey, a photo of him and his parents in Cape Town, and a snow globe Ryan bought him in London.

"I know," Ben said, his boots crunching over the dirt road as they returned to HQ. "Focusing is hard for me too."

Zach squeezed the snow globe in his fist. "Think these will help?"

Ben shrugged hopelessly. "We've gotta try everything we know."

As Zach held the door open into the agency HQ, there came a crash from the dining room.

"Vico, stop!" It was Eddie, his voice shrill with panic.

Ben charged ahead of Zach, racing into the dining room. Eddie's arms were around the middle of a bristling black wolf with tattered clothes dangling from his fur. Vicenzo's jaws snapped, his teeth bared and eyes flashing yellow as he lunged toward one of the staff who was cowering in fear.

Ben threw himself on Vicenzo, trying to hold him. As Zach went to help, Ben roared, "He needs to be restrained! Hurry!"

His heart in his throat, Zach ran from the dining room and jumped the stairs until he was on the second floor, racing for the kennels. He threw open the door and grabbed a catch pole and a tranquilizer loaded with silver-tipped darts.

When he returned, Vicenzo had broken free from Ben. The black wolf rounded on Eddie, fangs bared.

Eddie raised both hands. "Vico, hey. It's me. Stop. You need to stop!"

Vicenzo lunged and Ben tackled him out of the air. Snarling, Ben shifted to a wolf and the pair became entangled. Hand shaking, Zach aimed for the black wolf, but Ben got in the way, his jaws around Vicenzo's throat as the enormous silver wolf pinned Vicenzo to the ground.

With a crack, Zach shot a dart into Vicenzo's leg. The wolf yelped but he was too far gone to shift back. He struggled weakly as Ben crunched down on his neck. "I got him," Zach said, lengthening the catch pole and approaching Vicenzo. "Ben, let go."

Ben didn't. His body vibrated with snarls as he shook Vicenzo around by the throat. His eyes were yellow. "Shit," Zach whispered. "Ben, let go!"

Eddie shouted, "You're gonna kill him, Ben! Let him go, now!" He looked to Zach, wide-eyed. "Stop him! Make him stop!"

He took aim at Ben. "Sorry, old man." Ben yelped as the dart lodged in his back leg. He stumbled off Vicenzo and collapsed to his side as his snarls died to a low rumble, his ribs heaving. Ben's paws turned to hands, the bones grinding as his fur receded and he lay before them as a man.

"Shit," Ben croaked, yanking out the dart. His face went pale as Eddie knelt beside Vicenzo.

"Vico? Hey, Vico?" Eddie felt around the bite in Vicenzo's throat, the black fur glistening with blood.

Ben moved toward Vicenzo, and Eddie rounded on him with a snarl. It was human, but he was as fierce as a wolf as he crouched over Vicenzo's weak form.

Ben stumbled into a table, his eyes heavy-lidded and dazed. "Did I... was that me?"

Zach said, "You didn't mean to. You were trying to stop him from hurting anyone else and—"

"I lost control..." Ben gazed at his hands, still clawed. His jaw tightened. "Is he okay?"

Eddie hoisted the limp wolf into his arms. "He will be, but the silver will negate his healing so Luke should patch him up. He needs to be locked up for his protection and ours."

Slumping against an overturned table, Ben said, "Take him to the basement."

Zach shivered. He'd been down there only once. It was where they kept werewolves who were too dangerous to be treated, whose humanity couldn't be restored. Wolves who went down there didn't return. How many of them would end up down there? Would they ever be able to leave?

"It's temporary," Ben said.

Zach wished he could believe him.

Eddie left, carrying Vicenzo.

Ben slumped further, his face in his hands. "Shit..."

If only he could find the words to console him.

"Go and meet the others," Ben said, wrapping a tablecloth around himself. "I'll be there shortly."

Zach turned wordlessly and left, following Eddie from the dining hall past the clinic and to a door made of silver at the end of the hall. Putting on a glove to keep from being burned, Zach opened the door and Eddie went down the stairs first with Vicenzo.

Zach hesitated. Hushed voices made him turn his head. Gabe and Max stood by the window, and Gabe had his arms around Max, his cheek on his red hair.

"So you're staying?"

Gabe kissed his hair. "Yeah. Yeah, of course."

"Good. I can't do this without you. I can't tell our parents everything that's going on by myself. I can't tell our kids…"

Gabe held him close, shoulders trembling. "I know. You won't do it alone. I swear."

Max nestled closer, his voice muffled as he said, "It feels like before. When I was locked in the pantry. There was this emptiness in my head and heart. I was so alone, and it feels like that all over again."

"I know." Gabe's voice was strangled, his head turned away to look out the window. "But you're not alone, Max. We're not alone."

Zach couldn't listen anymore. Blinking hard, he opened the basement door. The stink of silver blocked out all other smells.

Below, the pack had assembled, sitting on the floor of a long hallway lined with cells, the bars made of silver. Gabe and Max came down the stairs to join everyone else.

"Watch your step," Eddie grunted, walking over a line of powdered silver just before the stairs. Zach walked over it too, careful not to burn his toes.

For now, the cells were empty. The LPA rarely encountered a wolf so severely feral they couldn't treat them. Soon, though, they would be filled with his packmates. Eddie carried Vicenzo to a cell and Zach opened the door for him. Ignoring the concerned questions from his packmates, Eddie laid Vicenzo within, then locked the door and sat on the floor outside his cell, head bowed. Luke came downstairs, armed with a medical bag, and ducked into Vicenzo's cell to treat his wounds.

Ryan knelt before Izzie, holding her hands. He said, "I know a basic healing spell. Find the most powerful human memory you have. I'll use it to forge a bond from you to me."

Izzie closed her eyes, thinking.

Farther down the hall, their backs against the stone wall, Gabe and Max were FaceTiming someone. Zach ventured near to tell them Ben was coming, but he stopped when he smelled the salt of their tears. Gabe waved at the screen, wiping his eyes. "Hey, Tommy. Hey, Luna."

Luna's voice said, "Hi, Daddy! Hi, Papa! I miss you."

"Is everything okay?" Tommy asked. "I thought you guys were coming back tonight."

Gabe opened his mouth, but nothing came out.

Max smiled. "Everything's fine, guys. Dad and I will see you really soon. Can I talk to Grandma and Grandpa?"

Zach wished he could go to them and comfort them, but he felt cold and isolated. He turned back toward Ryan and Izzie. Their eyes were closed and they seemed Zen-like and peaceful as Ryan chanted softly in Gaelic, but then Ryan yanked his hands away as if she had burned him. Izzie doubled over, clutching her head. She panted, her claws lengthening.

"Shit! Izzie, you okay?" Ryan asked.

She lashed out at him, batting his hand away, and her eyes burned yellow. Zach ran, ready to hurl himself in front of Ryan if he needed to.

Izzie slumped, her eyes returning to their warm amber color. "What happened?" she asked. "I felt this stabbing pain in my head."

Ryan sighed. "I felt it. The bond forming."

"I did too. And then it just... snapped," Izzie said, her eyes wide and forlorn.

Ryan's lip curled in sudden savage anger. He propelled himself to his feet and roared, claws slashing across the stone wall. "Fuck!"

Ben stopped on the stairs, still buttoning his shirt. "Fuck, what?"

Ryan kicked over a metal chair. "I can't do it! The spell isn't strong enough!"

Raising his hands, Ben said, "Ry, you gotta keep your head. If you lose it—"

Ryan barked out a laugh, a hoarse and awful sound. "Or I'll lose my mind, isn't that right, Ben? What does that fucking matter when it's just gonna happen eventually? Might as well happen now!"

Ben leaped down the stairs and strode toward him. "We need your magic, Ry!"

Ryan balled his hands into fists. "My magic is fucking useless! Face it, Ben, we're screwed! Unless we can kill Atticus and end his hold over us, which isn't gonna happen because we'll lose our minds before he even gets here!"

"No," Ben growled as he paced, his clawed hand curving over his smooth scalp. "No. Like hell I'll ever accept that. Snap out of it, Ry. Didn't your gran leave you tomes, scrolls, whatever? There's gotta be something in those books that'll tell us how to break this curse he's put over us."

Ryan slumped, his fingers curling in his hair. "I don't know. I don't know. Maybe if I was a better druid—"

Ben grabbed his shoulders. "Go look. Now. And don't give up, you hear me?"

Ryan nodded, his eyes wide and glassy. "Yeah. Okay." He sighed, his shoulders slumping, and looked at Zach with so much heartbreak in his eyes. Zach took a step toward him to console him, to hold him before he lost the chance forever, but Ryan turned away and jumped up the stairs. The door concealed him from sight.

How much more time did they have?

A future with Ryan had always seemed so certain. No matter who came and went, Ryan had been a constant force in his life, always there when Zach needed him, sometimes without even having to ask. As sure as summer, Ryan would be there. Year after year, he would always be there.

Ben watched him and Zach's breath hitched. He knew what was coming. He knew what Ben wanted to say but he couldn't bear to hear it.

"You two have gotta resolve the shit hanging over you."

Zach closed his eyes, leaning his forehead against the cool stone wall. "Don't."

Ben folded his thick arms over his chest. "Someone's gotta be the one to tell you, Zach. 'Cause you're blocking your ears and burying your head in the sand."

"We'll be fine," Zach said through gritted teeth, his fingers curling into fists. "Ryan will be fine. I'll be fine. We're going to figure this out."

Ben sighed quietly, his nostrils flaring. "And if we can't? If tonight's the last night you have together? What then, Zach?"

"Stop it." His words clawed their way under Zach's skin and tore him to pieces. "What do you want, Ben? Huh? You want me to admit that I've spent decades of my life in denial? That I fucked up when I rejected Ryan? That we could have had so much more time if I hadn't been so fucking scared?" His claws scratched over the stone wall. In his despair, he wanted to scream, to rip himself apart with his fangs and claws.

All these years, he'd wasted so much time doubting his self-worth because his parents had shown him he came second, suppressing his feelings for Ryan because he was convinced he'd hurt or disappoint him. Like he'd disappointed his parents.

His father was dead, but he lived on, haunting Zach every time he tried to dream of a future with Ryan.

"I've let my father control me," Zach whispered. "My mom too. Ever since I was a kid, I let them control me and suppress my wolf."

Ben grabbed his shoulder. "You don't have to let him, either of them. You have a choice, Zach. You've always had a choice, and you chose us over whatever bullshit future your folks wanted for you. Time and time again. It's time to choose your own happiness."

Time.

It was running out, spilling between his fingers.

He tried to remember what his father looked like, his mother's smile. Their faces were blurry. It was happening, and it was happening fast. Feral madness was taking over, stealing the memories he held sacred, but he couldn't allow it to steal Ryan away from him.

Zach touched Ben's shoulder. "I'll be back later."

Ben nodded, squeezing his arm, and he turned away.

He was so sick of feeling this way. There was so much he needed to say if he wanted to be free. Zach passed by the basement bathroom, and Gabe walked out. At the misery surely present on Zach's face, Gabe asked, "What's wrong?" He snorted. "Aside from, you know... everything."

Zach chuckled, though his heart was in his throat. "I... I don't know if I ever told you this, but I'm happy for you. For you and Max, the life you built together." And he meant it, truly. He no longer envied Max's place by his side, and his heart didn't pang whenever he looked at Gabe.

Gabe ducked his head, his ears reddening. "Thank you, Zach. I'm sorry for being such a lousy boyfriend."

Zach laughed softly, but Gabe frowned. "I just hope you know that was all me, not you. I was lost, and I wanted you, someone, anyone, to save me." Gabe sighed. "I broke your heart, and I'll always be sorry I couldn't be the man you deserved. You thought we were mates, and I wanted to believe you. I—"

"I didn't," Zach admitted. He exhaled harshly, the truth bitter in his throat.

Gabe tilted his head. "No?"

"You were never my fated mate. I only believed we were fated because of the prophecy. I could just never bring myself to tell you that. I loved you. Of course I loved you, but the thing is, I've never found my fated mate. But I know who I want it to be."

Gabe smiled. "Ryan?"

Zach laughed. "Duh. I just want you to know I'd do anything for you and the pack." He clasped Gabe's shoulder and held tight. Long ago, he would have given this man anything, even if it meant receiving nothing but empty promises and crushed hopes in return. "Meeting you changed the course of my life. You're the one who inspired me to strike out against my parents." Zach laughed, pacing up and down as the words flowed from him "Without you, I wouldn't even be a part of the agency! I'd be stuck under my family's thumb, living a lie and wondering what I'd missed out on."

Zach clutched his shoulders again, needing Gabe to hear every word. He would never say any of this again. Not to anyone. "I loved you because you made me the man I wanted to be. And I won't apologize for loving you or beat myself up because we didn't make it. I love you, Gabe, and I'm happy we're still friends."

Gabe tugged Zach's head to his shoulder and held tight. "I wanted to be better for you, Zach. You made me want to be the guy you saw in me."

Zach shook his head. "I'm glad Max could do that for you."

When Gabe's arms fell away, Zach felt lighter than he had in a long time. It was time to start anew.

For however much time he and Ryan still had left.

HE LEFT HQ AND walked among the palm trees, following the dirt road to the bungalows. Ryan's bungalow was yellow, the one right next to Zach's house. The door was open, swinging in the breeze, and the moment he crossed the threshold, the breath flew out of him.

Ryan's house smelled of salty ocean waves and sun-drenched sand. A sweet aroma sent calm rolling through him and stirred memories of his youth to the surface. The memories frayed at the edges and blurry, but the madness hadn't touched them yet. He sat on a bench with Ryan, ice cream sticky between his fingers. He and Ryan ran together as wolves on a moonlit beach, the wind cool against his fur. Ryan emerged from the waves in a wet suit, sand in his hair, and Zach's world turned upside down.

At last, his wolf howled, *we've found him at last. He's here. We've finally found him. Mate. Mate. Mate.*

The joy that coursed through him would have brought him to his knees if he hadn't grabbed onto the staircase railing to steady himself. Tears stung his eyes and he sucked in gulp after gulp of ocean-scented air.

His mate. Oh Goddess, Ryan was his mate.

Zach doubled over, laughing as he wiped tears from his eyes. "Of course it's you. It was always you."

For so long, he'd ached to know if Ryan truly was the one destined for him. Now he would never have to guess. Never have to pray that this time, he wouldn't be heartbroken. Never have to fear losing him. Not ever again.

Now. Seriously? He had to find out now. Why, when he was about to lose it all, did he have to find the one thing he'd been looking for all his life?

It made sense, in a seriously fucked-up way, he supposed. All his life he'd kept his wolf locked up, but now his control was slipping and the wolf was taking over. His instincts were surging through him like never before, and so he could finally catch Ryan's scent.

The timing was all wrong, as it had always been between him and Ryan, and yet... and yet Zach wouldn't change a damn thing. If he had the choice between never knowing and only finding out now at the end, then so be it.

A crash came from upstairs, followed by a roar that vibrated through the walls. The wood groaned like bones before they snapped. Vines lashed at the windows and ivy crawled between the floorboards. The electricity in the walls hummed, the lights burning bright before shattering.

"Ryan?" Fear seized hold of Zach's insides. He jumped the stairs, slipping on the runner that stretched down the hallway as he hurtled to a door at the end of the corridor. He rammed his shoulder into it, falling onto his hands and knees as it gave way and skinning them on the carpet.

A beast stood in the middle of the bedroom, his claws slashing as he ripped out the yellowed pages of a tome and hurled them all around the room. Paper rained down on Zach, flying to all the corners of the room.

"Not good enough! Not good enough!" Ryan roared, his fangs flashing and fur thick on his face and arms as his eyes blazed yellow.

"Ry?" Zach's voice came out small and shaky.

Ryan ripped the spine in two and hurled both pieces of the book across the room. He howled, the fury of it bowling over Zach like a wave, submerging him in his own feral fury as his wolf tried to answer the feral song.

"Ryan," he said through gritted teeth, fighting through the waves of fury. His fangs pierced his lower lip, and his claws caught on threads in the carpet. He stood, knees shaking. Ryan's eyes burned, his face twisted in animalistic rage. His carefree smile, the light in his eyes—they were gone, and Zach could break at the idea of living even a day without him.

Chapter 22

BLOOMING ROSES

Zach reached out, hands trembling, because it wasn't too late. It wasn't. He wouldn't stand by and watch Ryan lose himself right in front of him. Not when Zach had finally figured out what he was to him. Not when they were supposed to have a lifetime together. Not when Ryan had made him promise not to forget him.

The ceiling shook, and dust rained down as vines tunneled through the slats in the ceiling, coiling around the burned-out ceiling lamp.

"Promised," Zach panted, but the memory of that day was blurry. He didn't remember where they'd been. How old they were. Why he'd promised. But he remembered Ryan in his arms as Zach made that promise. "I promised you, Ryan Kelly. 'I won't forget you.' Remember?"

The beast man snarled, his eyes yellow, his claws long, and his face full of white fur.

"You made me promise not to forget you, and I kept my word." Zach lunged, grabbing hold of Ryan's claws and trying to pull him close. The beast snarled and thrashed but Zach slammed him up against the wall. Hot breath scorched Zach's face as Ryan panted, his fangs glinting inches from him, but Ryan hadn't bitten him or hurt him yet. "Now it's your turn," Zach said. "Don't you forget me, Ryan Kelly. Don't you ever forget me."

Ryan stopped panting, his savage eyes wide and bright. The yellow in them flickered. "Zach," he panted. "Don't. Get out. I'll hurt you."

Zach wouldn't. He was done running from this, from them. "Promise me."

"Zach," Ryan croaked, voice broken. "I did this. It's my fault. Atticus took it. He took this from us." Ryan pressed his hand against Zach's chest, breaching the empty space between their hearts where a bond should be.

Zach's heart ached but he refused to believe this was the end. "No. He didn't take anything. Close your eyes. Breathe in. What do you smell?"

Sniffling, Ryan closed his eyes and took in a shuddery breath. Brows furrowing, he sniffed eagerly at the air. The sight was so amusing, Zach couldn't help but laugh when Ryan practically shoved his nose in Zach's face and sniffed him all over. "What? What is this? Why do you smell like that? Like—" His eyes flew open, breath hitching in his chest. "Zach. Oh, Goddess. You... you smell like..."

Tears stung Zach's eyes, and he squeezed Ryan's wrists. "Tell me. Ry, tell me."

A broken laugh spilled from Ryan's throat. "Like the ocean."

Clutching Ryan's face between his hands, Zach pulled him in and bumped their foreheads together. Closing his eyes, Zach breathed Ryan's incredible scent into his lungs. "So do you."

A big grin spread across Ryan's face. "You can *smell me?*" The joy in his voice had Zach fighting back tears.

"Yeah. Yeah, I can. You smell like the beach. Like the summers we spent together when we were kids."

"Damn it, Zach! Your timing seriously sucks!" Ryan laughed, or perhaps it was a sob. "I thought we'd have forever. Now..."

Zach turned his head, kissing the trembling hand splayed against his cheek. "Stop. Ry, stop. Atticus has taken enough from us, okay? Tonight's not about him. It's about us. If tonight's all we have, then let's not waste it."

Ryan's eyes went wide. "What are you saying?"

Zach swallowed, holding on tight to the words before they could run away from him. "Are you still angry at me?"

Ryan hesitated, then shook his head. "No. Not now."

Holding his breath, Zach willed his heart to ease its frantic race. "Do you still want me?"

Vines crawled up the wall behind Ryan's head and roses blossomed, crimson in the darkness.

Ryan laughed, tears wet on his cheeks. "Always."

He exhaled, his hands shaking as he framed Ryan's face. "Good." And he smiled.

There, in this quiet, dark bedroom overrun by ivy and blooming roses, Zach leaned down and kissed Ryan Kelly, let himself drown in the scent of the ocean and sun-warmed sand. The smell of his love. Of his mate.

Joy fluttered in his stomach as Ryan parted his lips, stepping into Zach's body so their chests touched. Ryan exhaled through his nose in a long, inaudible sigh, his fingers tingling like electricity over Zach's skin as he cupped his face. He sank his fingers into Zach's curls, and it was impossible to resist leaning into his touch.

Their bodies were aligned awkwardly. Zach had to lean down to kiss him, but Ryan stood on his toes, holding on tight to his neck and shoulders. Ryan poured his all into it, nipping and tugging on Zach's lips and swiping his tongue along the bottom one. Head spinning, Zach's breath grew short as Ryan's fangs scraped his teeth.

Zach ran his tongue over Ryan's bottom lip, then sucked, nipping lightly. Ryan groaned quietly, tugging on Zach's hair, and Zach's blood burned. He wanted Ryan. He needed him, here, tonight. In case tomorrow never came and he lost his chance. They broke apart for air, and Zach wanted to lunge right back in and kiss him some more, but Ryan's face captivated him. He leaned close, resting their foreheads together and trying to burn Ryan's face into his mind so he could never forget it.

Ryan's eyes were as dark as the ocean, his lips flushed and swollen from Zach's attention. He gazed at Zach as if studying his face, his breath puffing hot against Zach's damp lips. With a wild grin, eyes sparkling, Ryan threw himself into Zach's arms, raining kisses on his neck, his jaw, then finally his lips.

Zach moaned as Ryan licked hungrily into his mouth, his hands wandering low to grab his hips and steer Ryan close. He wanted so much more and could only hope Ryan felt the same. Zach lowered his hands, his fingers slipping into the back pockets of Ryan's jeans and squeezing. He was small but well built, and his buttocks fit Zach's hands perfectly. Ryan's hips arched and there was no question he wanted Zach as badly as Zach wanted him.

Closing his eyes, Zach took in another whiff of his mate's scent. His shoulders shook around a sob. "You smell so amazing," he whispered, his eyes stinging. Zach nuzzled into his neck and sniffed. He smelled the ocean, sea salt, and warm sand. It was Ryan's scent, he realized, bundled up in so many joyful feelings and memories of their childhood together. "I wondered so many times what you'd smell like if you were my mate. It's salty waves and warm sand and..."

"I know!" Ryan rubbed his face into Zachs neck. "Goddess, I could spend all night just basking in your scent."

Ryan lunged to meet his mouth in a desperate kiss, his lips hot as he kissed down Zach's neck. His lips parted, his fangs scraping Zach's skin. He breathed in deep, and Zach shivered at the gravelly undertone of a growl deep in his chest. Ryan's finger curled under his chin, compelling Zach's eyes toward him. Ryan's eyes were dark with longing, but every so often, they flashed yellow. His inner animal was there, just below the surface.

His mate's stubble prickled Zach's hand when he touched his face, his thumb running over the ridge of his high cheekbone. He'd spent so long denying himself the happiness he knew they could have had. No more. He nuzzled their foreheads together and Ryan choked out a gasp, clutching at Zach's arms. "I'm yours, Ryan Kelly. For however much time we have left together."

Nothing more needed to be said.

Ryan leaned in close, enveloping Zach in the scent of mate and mine, sealing their lips in a kiss that was gentle with love and rough with scraping fangs. "And you're mine, Zach DeShawn."

Zach dropped his hands to Ryan's thighs, squeezing tight as he hoisted him up and Ryan's legs went around his waist. He carried him like he'd done once when they were young and summer had seemed like an eternity.

Zach's knees bumped the bed frame and he lowered them both down gently into a sea of plush blankets. Leaves fluttered against Zach's ear as roses blossomed along the headboard.

"Romantic," Zach said. He plucked a rose and scattered the petals over Ryan.

He sputtered, spitting them out. "My magic's going nuts. I can't control it, not even around you."

Zach didn't mind. "Long as you don't cause an earthquake, I think we'll be fine."

Ryan's chest rose and fell quickly as Zach's mouth settled on the crook of his neck. The scent of his sweat here was especially sweet, and Zach's cock throbbed in anticipation. His wolf growled in his chest, the sound traveling up into his throat, and his claws lengthened, ripping into the sheets.

Taking in a breath, Zach found he was still in control. Maybe his inner animal wanted to ravage Ryan, but he was still human, and the human in him didn't want to rush this. He pulled back from Ryan's neck, taking in the emerald green of his eyes, the rose petals in his hair, and let himself revel in this. That he could have Ryan Kelly after all this time, after so many mistakes. That he hadn't blown his chance and could still have his best friend for his mate.

Ryan captured Zach's face in his hands, pulling him close. Their lips collided, and Zach tasted Ryan's lips, soft and warm against his. Their tongues tangled, licking and rubbing. Zach pulled away, panting, and dragged his lips along Ryan's neck, breathing that mouthwatering scent in. He dampened Ryan's skin with his tongue, his fangs hungering to bite him.

"Fuck, Zach." Ryan tilted his neck, voice strained and breathless. He arched his hips, rubbing his hardness against Zach's waist.

"I know," Zach assured him. He rocked against Ryan's hardness, thrilled by the breathless whimpers he earned. "I want you too. Wanna bite you. Claim you." The heat of Ryan's hands seeped through his shirt as he worked at each button.

"Damn. You always have to dress so impeccably, or is this for me?" Ryan's fingers trembled, slipping on a button.

Zach's face warmed but he said, "Rip it."

Ryan's eyes went wide, color dusting his cheeks. Fabric tore, and buttons scattered to all corners of the room. Zach chucked the ruined shirt somewhere behind him and his stomach did a flip when he turned back to Ryan. Dark eyes, glowing like fireflies, gazed at his bare skin, drinking in every detail as if Zach were a piece of art on display.

"Can I?" Ryan murmured, and Zach realized he was nervous too. His cock stirred against his jeans. If Ryan didn't touch him now, he'd lose his mind. He twined his fingers with Ryan's and guided them to his shoulders, over his chest, and down his abs. Ryan's breath came faster as he ran his fingers through the dark fuzz on Zach's chest.

"You're the most beautiful man, Zach…" Ryan uttered the words as if he were in a breathless reverie, and his hungry mouth attacked Zach's bare skin. Zach's eyes rolled back, his blood simmering as Ryan's hot mouth glided over his pulse, his fangs nipping at the hollow of his throat, his pectorals. Ryan's hands were steadier as they squeezed his chest, reveling in the hard muscle, and pinched his nipples until they were taut between Ryan's fingers.

Zach clasped the hem of Ryan's shirt and he wriggled out of it with a haste that made Zach laugh. He knew Ryan's body as well as his own, though it had changed over the years. His best friend had changed, they both had, and tonight Zach saw his beauty in a way he'd never allowed himself to see it before. His hands shook as they settled on Ryan's broad shoulders and worked down his firm arms to his chest, his fingers raking through the dark curls there.

As Zach unclasped Ryan's belt, tugging it free from his belt loops, Ryan's gaze never wavered from his. His briefs strained against the swell of his cock, and Zach squeezed the bulge, making Ryan arch off the mattress, a gasp escaping him. He pushed his hips into Zach's touch. Clasping him, Zach marveled at how hard he was. He squeezed the knot at the base of his cock and Ryan tipped his head back with a hoarse cry.

Zach grinned. "Shit. Ben's expecting me back. He's gonna figure out what we're doing."

Ryan's lips quirked against his neck. "Gonna leave me?"

Zach snorted. "Hell no. He can wait. The pack's never gonna let us live this down, though."

Sudden pain brightened Ryan's eyes. "Good thing we haven't got forever."

Zach struggled to hold on to his smile. His throat ached at the reminder of what was sure to come. He bowed his head, struggling to hold it together. For all he knew, this was the only night they'd have together. If he cried now, he'd ruin it. Ryan clasped the back of his neck and pulled him down, covering his lips with his.

"It's enough, Zach." Ryan's voice trembled but he smiled. "I'll take anything I can get. It's perfect."

Overwhelmed, Zach kissed him before he could break down, squeezing his eyes shut as tears stung and burned in them. He turned his sorrow to passion, raining kisses down on Ryan's chest. Wriggling Ryan's boxers down to his thighs, Zach kissed his way down his stomach, then licked up the length of his cock. The earthy taste of him made Zach moan. Ryan bit his lip, and breathing hard, raised his hips in encouragement.

Parting his lips around the tip, Zach swallowed Ryan's cock down. He bobbed his head, and Ryan squeezed and stroked his hair. Hoarse gasps fell from Ryan's lips and Zach reveled in every new sound he coaxed from him. He peered up through his lashes and something inside him quivered when

Ryan met his gaze. He always wanted to remember the way Ryan looked and sounded when his walls came down, his cheeks flushed and eyes dark and every sound so sweet and vulnerable.

If this was their last night together, then Zach wanted to be the best Ryan had ever had.

Suddenly, Zach found himself on his back. Ryan's eyes gleamed as he straddled Zach's waist. He waggled a finger. "Ah, ah. You don't get to be all selfless with me. Your turn." He tugged Zach's jeans down. Zach squeezed the sheets and had to bite his lip to stifle himself when the wet heat of Ryan's mouth wrapped around him. Ryan licked a long, wet stripe from Zach's hole to his tip, lighting every nerve ending in his body on fire. Everywhere he touched tingled and throbbed, and Zach growled, curling his fingers in damp hair.

Zach's eyes rolled back, and he let Ryan's mouth reduce him to wordless whimpers and moans. "Yeah. Fuck. So good, baby."

A drawer opened and Ryan waved a bottle of lube at him.

Zach rolled his hips, spilling Ryan off him. He opened the bottle and slicked up his fingers. Ryan's chest rose and fell faster as Zach's fingers caressed his entrance. "Do it," Ryan croaked, pulling his knees to his chest. "Please, Zach. Need you in me." He looked so lewd, his knees drawn up high, baring himself to Zach.

Zach pressed in slowly, his breath hitching at the tightness of his body, the heat that enveloped his finger. He curled it and Ryan squirmed, panting as Zach's finger sank in deeper. Zach watched, unable to tear his eyes away from Ryan's face. He curled his finger again, delighted when Ryan threw his head back, lips parted in a groan of bliss. Zach smiled when their eyes met, setting off another round of fireworks in his belly.

Raising his hips, Ryan rode Zach's finger. He liked this, Zach could tell, having his hole teased. He withdrew his finger and replaced it with his tongue, and Ryan cried out, clutching at Zach's shoulders as he licked him in one long stroke from his hole to his balls before sucking one of them into his mouth, then the other. Then he went back to Ryan's hole, pressing his tongue deep inside, his fingers working up and down Ryan's shaft.

"Now, Zach." Ryan's voice was hoarse and broken. "I need you now." Ryan pulled Zach to him, their lips colliding.

Zach patted the end of the bed. "Come here." Ryan shimmied to the edge. Zach's feet touched the floor, and he lined his hips up with the back of Ryan's thighs. He pressed in slowly, opening Ryan up as he squeezed the sheets, his mouth parted as Zach sank into him.

"Good?" Zach asked. He didn't want to hurt him.

"So good," Ryan said with a grunt, raising his hips.

Their bodies came together, and neither could stifle their gratified cries when they were finally one. Zach tried to be gentle and take it slow, but Ryan wouldn't let him, raising his hips to sheathe Zach deep inside. A gasp spilled from Zach's lips, and he let himself lie still and savor it, the way Ryan tightened around him, the heat of him.

When Ryan motioned for him to come close, Zach couldn't refuse, lunging down to kiss him. Zach gripped the backs of Ryan's thighs, hiking his legs up, and Ryan moaned against Zach's mouth when his pelvis slapped Ryan's buttocks.

Their lips collided, their tongues smoothing over any bruises or cuts. Zach drove into him, growling, and Ryan's claws bit into his back. Their bodies came together, hard and fast, and swept away any hesitance or fears. Zach hadn't realized he'd been worried, not until he realized just how naturally their bodies moved together, sliding into place like two puzzle pieces.

As he neared the end, Zach slowed, desperate to hold on to this time they had before it was stolen from them. His knot expanded with every slow roll of his hips, tying them together. Ryan gasped, his nails driving into Zach's back, Zach's name falling from his lips. Unable to pull out and teetering on the brink, Zach grasped Ryan's hips and pulled him onto him, gasping wordlessly as Ryan bucked up and met him halfway.

Maddeningly close, Zach's fangs came out, ready to bite, to claim. Ryan's eyes darkened, and his fangs gleamed. "Yours," he panted, his voice a growl as his eyes burned. "I'm yours, Zach! Fuck me, claim me. Now!"

Zach rode out his release, Ryan's name a growl on his lips before the wolf came out. His fangs sank into the crook of Ryan's neck, claiming his mate as he spilled deep inside him. Ryan was his, in body and in soul. He fumbled through a sea of blankets and grabbed Ryan's hand, squeezing so tight he felt their hearts race as one. Ryan finished with a hoarse cry, spilling hot and wet across Zach's stomach.

Though he gritted his teeth, he couldn't stifle his cry when Ryan's fangs drove into the crook of his neck. "Yes, Ryan! Yes. I'm yours. I'm yours..." The bite throbbed and bled but the pain quickly faded as the wound healed, pleasantly warm. Zach dropped into Ryan's arms and basked in the afterglow, every limb loose and tingly. Ryan clung to him, grabbing onto the curls at the nape of Zach's neck. Their chests touched, their bodies slick with sweat.

Ryan's nose nuzzled into Zach's neck and breathed in deep, scenting him. Shivering, Zach angled his neck so Ryan could kiss the bite mark there. "Zach..." Ryan's hands framed his face but when their eyes met, Zach found himself as speechless as his mate. He turned his head so his lips could touch Ryan's palm, his heart breaking into two when Ryan's trembling lips smiled.

There was so much Ryan wanted to say; his eyes burned with it.

Zach said, "I know. I love you too."

Ryan's breath caught and his eyes glistened with joyful tears. Leaning in, Ryan claimed Zach's lips, cradling his face in his hands as if he were something truly precious.

"I love you," Ryan whispered, and he said it again and again between kisses.

Zach crumpled into his neck, his arms around Ryan's shoulders. Joined, they fell asleep tangled up together, surrounded by roses.

CHAPTER 23

WHERE OUR BOND WAS BORN

SOMETIME LATER, RYAN OPENED his eyes. His mouth was dry. His muscles ached. A scent filled the room, salty as the ocean waves. Fumbling, his fingers curled in the bare space beside him. What was that scent? It was potent on the pillow next to his.

There was a buzzing in his brain as he sat up, a void in his chest that ached, instilling a restless sense of dread deep inside. His gums itched and his claws extended. He wanted to hunt and bite, rend bone and tear flesh.

He bent his head to the pillow and breathed in deep. The scent calmed the buzzing in his ears but only for a moment. It returned, louder than before. It made him want to growl.

Kicking off the blankets, he stood from the bed and realized he was naked and his shoulder burned. He touched the space between his neck and shoulder. It was slightly raised and rough with scar tissue. A bite mark.

"I'm yours, Ryan."

His head ached.

"Zach," he panted, remembering. "Zach." They were mates. How could he have forgotten?

"Ry?" Zach came in from the balcony doors, clad in his chinos and nothing else. His eyes flared yellow, then returned to their normal brown. "Are you okay?"

Ryan went to him, his arms flying around Zach's back. "Yeah. I'm fine for now."

285

Zach enveloped him in the warmth of his embrace. "Thank the goddess…"

Warmth bloomed in Ryan's chest and Zach gasped. "You felt that too?" Ryan asked hopefully. Within his chest was the thinnest thread that connected him to Zach. It was fragile, this thread, ready to tear. "Our mating. I think it bought us some time!"

But there was no time to lose.

Ryan untangled himself from Zach's arms and bounded to where he'd thrown his book bag. He overturned it, and spell books toppled to the floor.

"Can I help?" Zach asked.

"Can you read Gaelic?"

"Nope."

Ryan pulled on a robe and sat pretzel-legged on the floor. "Then just your company will do."

Zach sat behind him, his legs spread to make room for Ryan. He propped his chin on Ryan's shoulder, his breath warm against his neck. "So, since our mating weakened Atticus's magic, by that logic, we should just keep having sex."

Ryan snorted. "I wish. Can you pass me the grimoire?"

"The what?"

"The one with the leather cover. It's my gran's."

Zach handed him the grimoire, and Ryan's heart sank. "No. No, what happened?" He had ripped the pages out. "Shit!" On his hands and knees, he gathered up the ripped-out yellowed pages. "Did I do this?" He collapsed back against Zach.

"You were feral. It wasn't you."

Tears stung Ryan's eyes. What if he'd destroyed the very page he needed?

"Hey, it's okay. I'll help you find it. What am I looking for?"

Ryan shook his head. "No. No, you can't help. It'll be some Celtic symbol, and it'll all be in Gaelic."

"Well, let's just find all the pages and go from there."

Together, they searched the bedroom, even looking under furniture. Ryan found incantations for healing cuts and wounds and curing common illnesses, but he'd already tried one of those spells on Izzie and it hadn't been strong enough.

Zach cried, "Ry, I found another page!" He reached under the bed and waved the page at him. Ryan took it, running his fingers over the Celtic symbol for *Ailm,* a strong braided cross. His gran had annotated the entry. *The most important spell a druid can wield. This spell can bring healing and inner peace, and strengthen the bonds of a pack.*

Ryan blew out a shuddery breath. "This is it. Holy shit, I think this is the spell."

Zach's eyes widened. "Really? How do you know?"

"Only one way to find out."

Ryan motioned for Zach to sit opposite him. Murmuring the written incantation under his breath until he had it memorized, Ryan took Zach's hand. He chanted the incantation and with each word, Zach's thread materialized, twisting from his chest and connecting to Ryan's. Their bonds were black and frayed, ready to snap.

As Ryan chanted, his and Zach's bonds glowed. The frayed strings knitted themselves back together. Zach leaned in, his hand warm and strong when he cupped Ryan's neck. Their foreheads touched, and Ryan let the scent of sand and sea anchor him. The warmth of pack and love and mate and mine flooded his chest as the bond between them burst to vibrant life.

"Ryan." Zach's voice filled his head and heart. *"Ryan. My mate. My love. You did it. Goddess, you did it."*

Tears of joy burned Ryan's eyes. He gripped Zach's face between his hands and kissed him with everything he had. There were no scraping fangs to roughen the kiss, no coarse fur beneath his fingers, and when Zach gazed into his eyes, they never flickered. Their wolves were at peace.

"Wait," Ryan croaked, his joy faltering. "Do I... do I still smell like the ocean?" They were mates, even if Zach couldn't smell him, but Zach had been so happy to catch his scent, he would hate to have taken that away from him. Being feral had forced Zach's wolf out after years of careful restraint, and Ryan had locked it back up again.

Zach leaned in, rubbing his nose against Ryan's neck. He breathed in deep and made a happy little sound. "Yeah. You do."

Relief threatened to dampen Ryan's face with tears. He quickly wiped them away. "The spell worked. It really worked! We've gotta go help the others."

Hand in hand, they ran back to HQ. The basement door crashed open, and they thundered down the stairs. Eddie slumped in his seat at the bottom of the stairs, snoring. He jolted awake when Ryan tore past, shouting, "Ed! I did it! I found a way to help them!"

Ryan leaped over the line of silver at the foot of the stairs. Vicenzo paced his cage, fangs bared. Izzie rocked back and forth, whispering, "Tommy, Luna, Gabe, Max... Ver... Veronica? Veronica. Goddess, how could I forget her name?" In their cell, Gabe and Max held hands. A growl vibrated Gabe's body, fur thick on his arms and face. In another cage, Ben slept, his claws raking over the stone floor.

Ryan murmured the incantation, and the bonds revealed themselves to him, writhing like sickly black snakes. He could see where they'd been severed, ripped clean in half. The pack must have felt the effect of the incantation because they became more aware of him. Max shook Gabe, making him look up. With a gasp, Izzie raised her tear-stained face from her trembling hands. Growling, Ben jerked awake, eyes bright and yellow. Ryan clasped the severed threads, holding them up high. The threads lengthened, reaching out to one another until they were whole. Golden light bloomed where the threads met, chasing away the darkness.

Vicenzo broke from his shift, gasping as his fur fell away like ash from his bare skin. The feral light left Ben's eyes. Gabe's snarling died to whimpers as Max threw his arms around him. When Eddie let Izzie out, she threw her arms around Ryan as Eddie ran around unlocking the doors.

The breath went out of Ryan when the pack enveloped him in their arms. The bonds that had been severed glowed bright and warm in Ryan's head and heart, connecting him to each of his packmates.

"You did it," Gabe choked out, squeezing Ryan tight. "You saved our freaking asses, Ry!"

"It's not over yet." Ryan swallowed, doubt threatening to swallow him whole. "We've still got Atticus to deal with. I've still got to stop him."

"Hey." Zach brushed the hair from Ryan's forehead. "You won't do this alone, never. You'll have me, the pack..."

Ryan exhaled, pressing his forehead to Zach's. "I know."

Zach leaned in, his lips pressing against Ryan's. "We'll do this together."

Vicenzo ran a hand over his short, prickly buzz cut. "What happened while I was out to lunch? Did I eat anyone?"

Eddie chuckled. "Almost."

Vicenzo's jaw popped as he rotated it. "Hope it was Ryan."

Feigning irritation, Ryan said, "Hey!"

Vicenzo grinned, his eyes lazy. He snapped his teeth.

Zach glowered. "You hitting on my mate?"

Izzie's eyes lit up and she failed to catch the robe Ben chucked at her from a basket in the corner. "Mate? You two mated?"

Tilting his head, Ryan showed off Zach's bite. The pack erupted into cheers and there were hugs and slaps across the back.

"You two finally got your shit together!" Gabe exclaimed as he tugged Zach into a hug.

"I'm so happy for you two!" Izzie said, squeezing Ryan tight.

Vicenzo scoffed. "It only took a werewolf apocalypse and a crazy druid to make it happen."

"Hey, don't discredit us!" Ryan boxed Vico on the shoulder. "Speaking of which, you and Eddie ever gonna—" He made a lewd gesture that made the pack squawk at him.

Vicenzo's eyelid twitched and Eddie's face reddened. "Maybe we should have given this joker to Atticus," Vicenzo said.

Zach growled.

Ben said, "All right, that's enough celebration for now. Zach, Ry, congratulations. Once we burn Atticus to a crisp, we can hold a formal celebration. We haven't got a lot of time to sit around. Everyone, meet me in the office."

For the first time in hours, Ryan had hope that everything would be okay. Atticus would regret fucking with their pack.

A LITTLE LATER, RYAN and Zach found Ben and the others crammed into Ben's office. The light of dawn spilled through the slats in the blinds. Ben slumped, digging his fingers into his eyes. He shook away the drowsiness and faced the pack. "How the hell do we stop this guy?"

"The ancient druids asked the same question," Ryan said, setting several items onto the desk: the map of trees his gran had sketched, the book on the druid war, and the book detailing sacred grove locations.

"Did they ever find an answer?" Max asked.

Ryan said, "They didn't think that Atticus could die. There are accounts of him rising from the dead on the battlefield."

"Just great..." Vicenzo sighed.

Ryan opened the book on sacred groves. "Lighten up. They figured out his secret. He bound his life force to specific oaks he grew. Now, my gran kept track of the oaks that were destroyed, and almost all of them were burned. Except one. One oak in NYC."

"Great," Ben said, looking as if it were the opposite. "Your gran happen to mention where this oak tree is, considering there are millions of oaks in New York?"

Ryan grinned. "You're a grump before you've had coffee. But yeah, actually. There's one oak in Central Park. But there's also, like, thousands of oaks in Central Park. So I guess I'll have to go around toasting them all until I find the right one."

Zach's eyes widened. "Ryan. It's our tree."

Ryan squinted at him. "How do you know?"

A grin burst across Zach's face, and Ryan wanted to kiss it off his mouth. "Remember? You were the only one who could touch it! I spent forever trying to mark that tree, but you showed up and just did it. It must have reacted to you because it sensed your druid heritage."

Ryan elbowed him. "Or I'm just way stronger than you—ow!" Zach stepped on his toe. "Dude, you're brilliant! I didn't even think of that!"

Zach forced a smile. "Ry, I love you so much, but if you call me dude again, we're not gonna be cool."

"Right. So, what should I call you?"

Izzie cut in. "You guys have a tree? That's so cute."

Ryan said, "Zach and I met under an old oak tree in Central Park. It's special 'cause it's planted around only elm trees, so we'd meet there and hang out and—oh no! Zach, I'm gonna have to destroy our tree!"

Zach sighed. "Yeah, that's a bummer."

Ben cleared his throat. "I sure hope you two can bring yourself to destroy the tree, 'cause we have trouble." He held out his phone. Ryan took it and his heart sank. The news was broadcasting a sudden severe storm that had come out of nowhere and left hundreds throughout the five boroughs without power.

An alarm on all their phones went off. The government was broadcasting an emergency alert, warning all residents to evacuate due to a Paranormal State of Emergency.

"Atticus," Ryan growled. "He must have broken through my ward."

Ben stood, his chair rocking back and crashing to the ground. "We need to get to the park. Now!"

THE PACK PILED INTO agency boats and rode as fast as they could back to Manhattan. The wind howled, rattling the windows, and the skies were the most menacing shade of gray Ryan had ever seen. Forks of lightning flashed over the Manhattan skyline.

"Holy shit," Gabe shouted over the wind, holding out his phone to Ryan.

He took it, his stomach clenching as a news outlet broadcast what appeared to be an army of people marching through the streets of New York. The "people" were carved from wood, their hands raised to the skies as they carried the storm throughout the city. At the front of the army, Atticus spoke, his voice magnified by magic. "To any and all druids in this wretched city, your king has returned. Never again will you have to hide your magic or live in fear. Wolves will break before our might. Humans will cower in our wake. Come to me at the sacred oak. I shall lead our people out of the darkness and into the light of a new world!"

The camera stopped rolling as a blast of wind hit the person filming. There was a scream and the footage cut away.

Ryan glowered. "You know, if he wasn't a prick, I might feel bad for him. Can you imagine, being the last of your kind? Everyone just... forgetting you like that. That's rough. But he deserves it."

Izzie was scrolling through her phone. "Thanks to the storm, flights are halted." She sighed. "Guess we'll have to do this without the Council's help."

Ryan reached for Zach's fingers, intertwining his with Zach's and squeezing tight.

After a rocky boat ride, they arrived in the city and piled into separate taxis that sped them toward the park. As they drove, the windshield wipers struggled to beat away the rain that sluiced down the windows. Lightning cut across the sky and thunder boomed. The trees of Central Park rocked in the wind. The pack burst from the cars and ran, following the road through the park.

Ryan ran with Zach, their hands locked tight together as the rain cascaded down and the wind slammed into them, threatening to knock their feet out from under them. Elm trees formed an archway of green leaves over their heads. The two of them ran toward the fence and jumped over, their feet splashing in mud that sucked at their shoes. Rain fell harder as the pack remained behind the fence, standing guard.

A lone oak tree stood among the elms like it always had, like he remembered from when they were kids. There were old chainsaw marks near the base of the tree, but no one had cut it down, so it had stayed, its branches spiraling up and out, the trunk thick and scarred. Ryan placed his hand where he'd carved their initials, then jerked his hand back. Now that his magic was activated, he could sense the poison flowing through this oak, but he wouldn't be deterred. This was their tree, their pack territory, not Atticus's.

Zach squeezed his shoulders. "Do you know what to do?"

Ryan nodded. He'd spent the trip here hunched over one of his gran's spell books. "Yeah, I know a cleansing spell but... he's poisoned this tree, Zach. It's dark, evil magic. He's so much more powerful than me."

Zach gripped his shoulders tight. "None of that matters. You can do this. Use me if you need to. Use our bond, use it to anchor your magic."

Ryan took in a deep breath, blinking rain from his eyes. The branches spread wide over their heads, shielding them from most of the rainfall. Touching the bark, Ryan closed his eyes as he spoke to the tree in Gaelic. He told the tree he was sorry he'd scratched it when he was a kid. Tears in his eyes, he thanked the tree for holding such a special place in his memory all these years, for being their special place.

The roots stirred beneath the soil, a low rumble of churning earth and life. Ryan found the bonds he and Zach shared, coiling tight around his heart. When he opened his eyes, golden threads swayed in the wind, tangling with one another as they connected him and Zach. Ryan clasped the golden threads in his hand and chanted in Gaelic.

"You've got this, Ryan." Zach pressed close to him, his chest touching Ryan's back, his hands warm and firm on Ryan's shoulders. "This is our tree. This is the place where we met. Where our bond was born. Atticus has no power here. This is ours. Ours, and he can't take that from us."

Ryan reached out, one hand upon the tree, the other moving to clasp the hand on his shoulder and squeeze tight. The rainfall around them ceased as the sun shone through a break in the clouds. It rained everywhere else but not on their tree. Because this was their place, his and Zach's, and it was sacred to them. The spell binding Atticus to this tree was warped and dark, hateful and full of a vengeance that left the tree's roots gnarled.

But if there was one force in this world that could rival hate, it was love, and it was love that Ryan called on from the bonds that connected him to Zach. This was where they'd met. This was where their bond had been formed, a bond that transcended time and distance and anyone who would come between them. He poured all that love into the spell, and he could feel Atticus's dark magic pushing back as the light broke through.

The tree shuddered, coursing with golden light that traveled up the roots and into the leaves. The wilted, withered leaves cascaded from the branches as Atticus's dark grasp over the tree crumbled.

Ryan was breaking through, peeling away layers of hatred and rage to the sickly core of the tree. The sickness at the core shriveled and died as Ryan's healing magic cleansed it. It was time.

"Ry, Zach!" Eddie called. "We've got company!"

Figures made of wood marched toward them, tall and gangly with burning red eyes. In the lead was a man, shorter than the rest, his cloak billowing around him. Rain dripped from Atticus's beard and from the tip of his nose. The trees shuddered at his passing.

The old druid halted, his green eyes darting around. "Where are they?" he growled.

Ryan shrugged. "Told you, man. The druids are gone."

Fury made Atticus flare his nostrils. "No. You lie. They will come and stand with their king. They have *not* forgotten me."

"Enough talking." Ryan opened his palm, warm from the flame that flickered there. Though the rain fell hard, nothing could extinguish the fire in his hand. "Your connection to this tree is done for."

Atticus sneered. "So. You learned my secret."

"Hope you enjoyed your little jaunt outside your tomb while you could."

With a curl of his lip, Atticus spat, "As always, you wolves betray. Amaris created me from such an oak and gave me life, only to expect me to be a servant to wolves. When I dared to believe in the superiority of magic over beasts and men, I was punished. The cowardice and treachery of your kind should not still surprise me."

Ryan raised a hand toward the tree and touched an invisible wall as one of the living trees lunged forward, arms raised. The barrier exploded at Ryan's touch, and he and Zach flew off their feet and tumbled over in the mud. Roots exploded from the soil and bound Ryan's hands into the dirt as a living tree advanced on him, arms out and eyes burning.

Zach snarled, fangs bared and claws long as he lunged, slicing at the roots binding Ryan's hands. The earth exploded beneath Zach, bowling him off his feet. The roots tied him down and Zach struggled but couldn't break free.

In Ryan's hands, the flame surged, burning through the roots and spraying a blast of flame into the tree's wooden face. The flame ate up the tree's body and Ryan hurled himself to his feet, leaping over the cracks Atticus's magic had split into the ground. Ryan hurled the flame at the roots binding Zach, and the brown wolf tore free and lunged, his fangs snapping around the throat of the tree keeping the barrier up by the oak. The barrier shattered.

Howls and snarls split the air as the pack attacked, hurling themselves upon the trees and shattering their wooden bodies. The agency wolves came at the living trees from all sides, fangs snapping wooden arms and splintering slender necks. The trees summoned lightning to strike the wolves, and it forked from one to another as the wolves' bodies spasmed and their fur smoked.

Atticus roared as he leaped in front of the oak, conjuring a wall of thorns that sprang up around the tree. Ryan sprayed the thorns with a gout of fire, and the flames burned away the thorns and vines, only for them to grow back thicker. "Zach! I need you!" Ryan called and Zach was by his side in seconds, his tail curled around Ryan's waist as he offered his strength.

"Keep them off us!" Ryan roared as a bolt of lightning scorched the ground just inches from them, igniting the grass.

Gabe roared and grew rapidly, standing up on his back legs and towering over the pack as a berserker. With a single swipe, he bowled the trees off their wooden legs and shattered their bodies into twigs and sticks with his fist. Izzie pounced, jaws crunching around wood as she yanked a tree to the ground. Eddie stomped on a wooden skull, caving it in, and shot a bolt into the face of another. Max dashed in, his fur bright as a ball of fire, and knocked a tree off its stick legs.

The flames sprouting from Ryan's hands flared up, leaping up the wall of thorns. The magical barrier beneath the thorns cracked, and Atticus roared his fury. Zach snarled at Ryan's side, his brown fur bristling. The bond between them burned like fire and Ryan fastened onto it, onto the threads connecting him to his pack, and roared back. A wall of fire crashed through Atticus's barrier, shattering it like glass and setting the ancient oak ablaze.

Then the fighting stopped, the wolves panting as the living trees suddenly crumbled to nothing but sticks and twigs. Atticus writhed, clutching at his burned, blackened body as he screamed in agony and fury. "Where are they? Why aren't they here when I need them? Why have my people abandoned me?"

Atticus howled his rage and anguish to the lightning-streaked sky. The disgraced druid collapsed to his knees as his legs turned to ash, one hand disappearing into soot that was blown away in the wind. Panting, he snarled from a lipless mouth that exposed his teeth to the gums. His face was black and disfigured, the flesh so badly burned Ryan could see the red muscle and white glint of his cheekbones.

Atticus laughed. "The arrogance of wolves!" He howled, laughing like a madman to the night sky.

Ryan curled his hands into fists, burning hot from the flames he held there. They'd won. What in the hell was so funny?

Atticus's eyes blazed, bulging and lidless. "For hundreds of years I've slept, only to die when I've finally tasted freedom! Tell me, foolish dogs, did you really think I came unprepared? Did you truly think I did not anticipate this? You beasts betrayed me once. Never again!"

And the ground around them erupted in chunks of rock and soil. Ryan flew off his feet and into the mud, crushing Zach beneath him. A wall of rock shot up from the earth, cutting them off from the pack. Zach hurled himself to his paws and lunged for Atticus. Roots erupted from the ground and ensnared Zach's waist, hurling him away from Atticus. Ryan cried out in horror as Zach smashed against the rocks, bones breaking on impact.

He stood, his fingers curling into fists, a fire blazing in his gut. "Shouldn't have fucking done that..." He charged, his clothes ripping as his shift burst free, his jaws open wide.

Roots burst from the soil, wrapping around Atticus and raising him high off the ground. Atticus's bony fingers wrapped around Ryan's throat and his shift melted away as he choked and struggled, suspended by the neck. Atticus sneered at him. "False king. You were given a gift that does not belong to you."

Ryan would have screamed if he could as insects writhed in the holes burned into Atticus's face. The druid grinned, laughter crawling from his throat along with the centipedes and worms that wriggled from his lipless mouth and crawled up his decaying arm toward Ryan.

"I'll make good use of that gift. It's powerful magic you've got within you. Your wolf's blood has defiled it for long enough!"

Ryan choked as the insects crawled into his mouth. As Atticus's body crumbled into slimy black insects that poured down Ryan's throat, crawling over his eyes and turning his vision black, Atticus laughed.

Zach howled for him, a song of heartache and fear, before everything he was faded away.

CHAPTER 24

THE MOON OVER THE OAK

ZACH SCREAMED FOR RYAN as his mate collapsed face down in the mud. Atticus was gone, turned to thousands of insects that were corrupting Ryan's body from the inside. Zach tried to move but pain racked his spine as the bones, discs, and joints slowly mended. Ryan was motionless. Trying to focus, Zach strained to hear his heartbeat, but it was slow and quiet. The bond that tied them together was no longer bright and warm. It was black and twisted, like poison in Zach's head and heart.

"Ryan?" Zach choked. "Ryan, answer me!"

He didn't speak, his eyes wide open and glassy. His lips were a pale, frightening blue.

Zach dug his fingers into the mud and crawled toward him. He had to do something, anything. He couldn't lose Ryan; he couldn't lose his mate.

Ryan's fingers twitched, curling in the mud. His eyelids fluttered rapidly as his eyes flickered from emerald to a moldy green. He sucked in a great gasp of air, color returning to his lips and cheeks. As he hoisted himself up, his arms trembled and mud dripped down his bare body.

Zach tried to speak, but his voice died in his throat as a cold, callous fury twisted Ryan's familiar face until it was unrecognizable. Ryan spread his arms out and turned them, his green eyes sweeping up and down his own body. "Not bad," Ryan said. "Strong. Young. A wolf," he spat with distaste. "But it's better than nothing."

"R-Ryan?" Zach's voice wobbled. Something was off. Ryan sounded like himself. Looked like himself. Smelled like... no. The scent of salty waves and warm sand was gone, overpowered by the reek of dark magic, pungent as rotting wood. Zach clutched his chest. Their bond burned like acid, corroded but still there. A wave of noxious dread crashed over him.

"Looking for your mate, wolf?" Ryan sneered. "He's mine now."

Zach struggled to speak around the lump of fear tightening his throat. "What... What did you do to him? Give him back. Give him back to me, or I swear I'll—"

Ryan laughed. "You'll what, exactly?" He scowled, feeling the bite mark on his own neck. "It's said mating bonds are some of the strongest forms of magic a wolf can experience." A laugh escaped him. "I'd like to meet the fool who told such a lie so I can show them what true power really looks like. As for you, little wolf, I'm afraid you and your pack don't stand a chance. I will make this world bend to my magic once again."

Zach's arms shook as he pushed himself up, biting back a grunt as his discs popped back into place and his spine mended. "Fuck you. I'll—"

Ryan tilted his head, a cruel smile playing about his lips. "You'll what, pray tell? Kill me? When I look like your dear, beloved mate? I'm afraid that's not an option, considering if I die, Ryan dies too."

Zach's breath hitched. "He's still—"

"Alive? Yes. My body died, so I... borrowed Ryan's. I can hear his thoughts. He's furious and scared. In time, he may come to see me as a friend. After all, we're both druids, even if he's half beast. Unfortunately, if you kill me, hurt me, he'll feel every ounce of pain I do, and he'll die along with me. So, you see, you're stuck."

Zach's heart ached at the sight of that familiar face, Ryan's face, smiling at him with such contempt.

"So, little wolf. What will you do?"

Zach didn't know. His arms trembled and his heart sank. "Ryan," he croaked. "Ryan! Can you hear me?"

Ryan's grin disappeared from his face. His head snapped to the side, his face elongating and his fangs sharp as the wolf surged to the surface. Ryan shook his head and the white fur receded. "Oh dear. Seems I have to teach the unruly beast what his place is."

Ryan was still in there. He was fighting to get back to Zach and his pack. "Ryan!" Zach shouted. "Ryan, I'm here, I'm—"

A blast of wind sent Zach flying backward to crash into the wall of rock as Ryan advanced toward him, his arm extended and teeth bared in a grin. "You have no power over me, dog!" he roared, and a force of magical energy bowled into Zach with the impact of a truck. The wall of rock crumbled around him as Zach smashed through it, tumbling over into the mud.

The wolves yelped and snarled in alarm as Atticus strode toward them in Ryan's body.

"Ryan?" Gabe gasped, black fur framing his face and covering his body. "Ryan, what the fuck are you—" A blast of wind hurtled Gabe into the air and slammed him into a tree. He screamed as his bones shattered.

Max cried out in horror. "Ryan, stop! What are you doing? What is *wrong* with you?"

Zach pushed himself up, slipping in mud. "It's not him! It's Atticus! Ryan! Stop, can you hear me? Fight him off!" The ground exploded beneath Zach's feet and sent him crashing into Ben, knocking the silver wolf off his paws.

At Atticus's command, saplings grew into living trees, their eyes burning.

Ben shifted to a man covered in silver fur. He roared, "We can't fight him! Retreat!"

The wolves turned and fled, and Zach ran with his pack.

IT WAS DARK WHEREVER Ryan was. The silence buzzed in his ears, unbreakable. He stretched his hands into the darkness, feeling the emptiness around him, searching for someone, anyone.

"You're alone, wolf." From the darkness, a man came. He had long red hair and an unkempt beard, his green eyes like moldy growth—Atticus, but something was wrong. His teeth were long and sharp like a wolf's, and white fur grew thick on his arms.

"Where am I?" Ryan asked, his eyes struggling to pierce the darkness, to see beyond.

"Somewhere no one can ever find you."

Ryan shook his head, squeezing his kneecaps until his fingertips ached. "You're wrong. My friends will find me, they'll—"

Atticus laughed. "Your friends. Oh, they forgot all about you."

Ryan's stomach clenched. "What? No. They wouldn't."

He closed his eyes and searched for the threads connecting him to his—

"What?" The word shuddered from his lips.

The bonds were gone. He couldn't feel them. Even Zach's had disappeared.

"This is a lie. You're hiding them from me!" Ryan stood, swaying in the black void around him.

"Is it really? I don't think you understand just how easy you are to forget, Ryan Kelly. After all, your own mother can't remember you."

Ryan lurched back, the words like a fist to his gut. "What did you say? How do you—how could you possibly know about that?"

Atticus ran a hand thoughtfully through his beard. "She forgets you all the time, doesn't she? In fact, she's forgotten you for good. She's stuck in one of her episodes, and she can't come out."

Ryan trembled, curling his hands into fists until his blunt fingernails dug into his skin. "Get out. Get the fuck out of my head, you son of a bitch!"

"Why, Ryan? Why would your own mother forget about you? If you were a better son, if she really loved you—"

"She... she doesn't mean to. She's sick. It doesn't mean anything!"

Atticus arched a brow. "Then how come you're alone, Ryan?"

Wetting his lips, Ryan said, "My pack is coming for me. I know it. They are. They wouldn't just leave me!"

"Then where are they?"

Ryan's mouth moved but no sounds came out. He didn't know. He had never felt so far away from them, so alone.

"They forgot all about you. They left you alone."

The darkness pressed in on Ryan, never-ending and suffocating. It was easy to believe everything Atticus had told him.

"Because you weren't a good enough friend. You weren't a good enough mate. You weren't a good enough son. They forgot. If you'd only been better—a better wolf. A better druid. Now you'll never help your mother."

Ryan couldn't breathe. It wasn't true. It wasn't, it—

"Stop," he gasped. "Please. Stop." His face was wet. His eyes burned.

Atticus knelt before him. "You have nothing left to lose. There's no reason for you to fight the power I have over you. Surrender to me, and the pain will be over. You'll forget. You'll never be hurt or left behind again."

It was tempting, so tempting.

Why not just give in? Why not allow the pain to end?

Ryan would never be forgotten again. Never again would he have to feel the ache of never being important enough to remember when his mother forgot.

Shaking, Ryan closed his eyes as tears ran hot down his face.

BELVEDERE CASTLE WAS AN ancient structure recently remodeled. It wasn't much of a castle, boasting only a single stone tower overlooking the lake. However, from the top of the tower, Zach had a view of the surrounding trees. They would see Atticus—*Ryan*—coming from miles away with his druids. Zach wiped rain from his stinging eyes, blinking hard. If he was crying, he couldn't tell, but if he wasn't, then he was on the brink.

"Breathe, my friend," Izzie said, rubbing his shoulders.

Zach tried, but his throat was so tight he could only manage a pinch of cold, wet air.

"You really think we'll be able to stop Atticus?" Zach couldn't see a way out of this. "Without killing Ryan?" His voice broke.

"We need to try." Izzie looked lost, on the brink of drowning.

Zach wasn't sure if they could succeed or if they would be enough to save Ryan, but he would die trying to bring him back.

Going through life without Ryan Kelly wasn't an option.

"Zach," Izzie said. "If anyone can bring Ryan back, it's you. Whatever magic Atticus is using, it's nothing compared to the bond you two share."

Zach exhaled, trying to believe her. "He's still in there," Zach said, squeezing his fists tight as he held on to what he'd seen. "Ryan heard me call out to him and tried to come back to me."

"Exactly!" Izzie said.

He paced, his feet splashing in the rainwater. "I'm not a druid; I can't just cast a spell and cure this!"

"Like that matters," Izzie scoffed, pushing her wet hair back from her face. "All Atticus knows is hate and fury. He doesn't know a thing about love, about the bond between you two, or the power of a wolf's mating bond. We'll bring Ryan back, and then we're going to beat the crap out of him for worrying us like that, and then we're gonna go clubbing with him and drink the city dry."

Izzie led the way down the narrow spiral steps. Zach hesitated, taking in a deep breath and letting it out. He knew what he had to do. If he had doubts, it didn't matter. He would give his all to bring Ryan back.

At the bottom of the stone stairs, Gabe stood beside Ben. Max, Eddie, and Vicenzo were spread out, and Vicenzo was glaring out the window. Eddie sat with his head against the wall, eyes closed, and Max was standing close to Gabe, clutching his arm.

Zach swallowed hard, trying to find his voice as doubt and fear waged war within him. "Ryan is still in there. I called out to him, and his wolf tried to come out. Atticus is controlling his mind, but Ryan and I are mates." He closed his eyes, feeling the blackened, twisted thread that still connected him to Ryan. "Atticus isn't breaking that connection. He's a werewolf now and he knows without it, he'll lose control. A part of Ryan is still tied to me through that bond, and I think... I can use it to bring him back."

Max's eyes brightened. "You think so?"

Zach didn't know. He wasn't sure he was enough to bring Ryan back from the hell Atticus had trapped him in. "I'm going to give it everything I have, but I need to get him alone. I need those creepy trees kept at bay."

Eddie stood, slapping his crossbow against his hand. "You got it. We'll divide and conquer. Split them up as best we can so you can get Atticus alone."

Vicenzo growled. "Those walking trees are awful fun to chew on... I'll gladly kick their asses."

Ben said, "Gabe, Max, you two go with Zach. Have Zach's back while he tries to reason with Ry." Gabe and Max nodded, their faces set in determination. Ben motioned for his pack to follow him. "Come on, all of you. Atticus is almost here. We need to be ready to move."

The wind howled around the castle as they watched Atticus stride toward them in Ryan's body. Living trees flanked Atticus on all sides, their eyes burning red fire in their blank wooden faces. He'd grown far more than the twenty he'd had before. They were outnumbered.

Ben's voice filled Zach's mind. *"Remember the plan. Divide and conquer."*

Zach thought, *"Separate into groups, make them pursue you. Pick them off. Leave Atticus to me."*

As Atticus stopped before them, an ugly smile twisted Ryan's face. Zach's heart tore in two to see Ryan used in such a way, but he swore it would be over soon.

"Still, you wolves persist. Your stubbornness in the face of your own doom would be commendable. It terrifies you animals, doesn't it? The idea of being treated as the druids were. Hunted. Hated. Erased."

Ben curled his lip. "You caused your own downfall, idiot. The eradication of your kind resulted from your own actions."

The wolves pressed in slowly, their bodies low as they prepared to pounce, their pelts heavy and glistening with rainfall.

"Because of the wolves' betrayal, the druids were forgotten!" Atticus's—*Ryan's*—fists tightened, and his lips pulled back as he snarled. "All I ever wanted was for my people to be free from servitude to wolves, to be masters of our own fate!"

Ben hung his head with a low sigh. "Werewolves aren't the masters of anyone. Conquering others by force isn't the way to achieve peace. Change doesn't happen overnight and with you around, you'll only set our progress back thousands of years. You did this to yourself."

"Ryan!" Zach shouted.

Atticus suddenly doubled over, clutching his head. His jaws snapped, his face elongating. Ryan's jaws opened impossibly wide, and a wolf snout protruded from his gaping mouth before it was pulled back down. Atticus gasped, his face twisted in rage. "Kill them!" he roared, and his trees charged.

The wolves spread out into groups of two: Eddie with Vicenzo, Izzie with Ben, and Gabe and Max watching Zach's back. The trees scattered, some with their wooden palms raised and shimmering with balls of fire while others raised their wooden arms to the skies and conjured lightning bolts to strike the earth.

Gabe shifted to his berserker form, towering over Zach. Black fur rippled over his body as he stood tall on his back legs, his massive arms open wide to show off his claws as he threw back his snout and roared to the skies. He lifted a heavy boulder and hurled it as if it were a tennis ball. Atticus levitated an enormous rock from the ground and hurled it toward Gabe, and the boulders shattered against each other.

Atticus whirled toward them, eyes blazing. They'd caught his attention. "You," he snarled at Zach. "I grow weary of the hold you have over this wolf's mind."

As a red wolf, Max nipped at Zach's arm. *"Come on! Let's lead Atticus further away!"*

They ran toward the stone castle and Gabe threw himself against the doors. An explosion of stone hurled Gabe off his claws and into the wall, cracking it. Max growled and stood protectively in front of Gabe, but Atticus only had eyes for Zach. Storming into the tower, Atticus's eyes were wide and feral as he set his sights on him.

"Gonna kill me?" Zach growled around his fangs. "You know what happens to you if you do. You're a wolf now. If you kill me, you'll lose control and become the mindless beast you've sworn to destroy."

Atticus panted, looking more wolf than man as his eyes flashed yellow and his fangs elongated. The fetid bond between them was falling apart, drawing him closer to feral madness. "No. You lie, like all wolves. I'm stronger. Better. I don't need a pack. I don't need allies! Once, I burned this world, and I'll do it again!"

The stone walls of the castle cracked and the ground shook as a chunk of stone fell from the ceiling, crashing down behind Zach.

"Fine. Maybe druids don't need a pack. But wolves do. And Ryan is a wolf." Zach looked his dearest friend in the eyes. "Ryan? Can you hear me?"

"Shut up." Atticus's clawed hands slammed over his pointed ears.

Zach's heart soared as his eyes flickered from yellow to Ryan's pure green, then back to yellow. Yes, Ryan could hear him.

"Ryan, it's Zach. I'm here. I love you, and I'm not forgetting you. Remember what we promised? When we were kids?" Zach inched toward him, hand outstretched.

"Shut up!" Atticus roared, and the stone walls exploded around them. Chunks of castle rock soared over Zach's head as he flew outside, tumbling over until he was dangerously close to a steep drop into the lake below. Max yelped as he was knocked off his feet and Gabe pounced, shielding Max's body with his as blocks of stone hurtled out over the lake.

Atticus panted, his face pale and slick with sweat. "I am in control, beast! I am Atticus, King of the Druids, and I am in—" He doubled over with a retching sound. A single black centipede crawled from his throat as his eyes flashed from yellow to green, then yellow again.

Zach took a step back as Atticus advanced, his back arching as bones ground together, his head snapping to the left as his face elongated and his fangs lengthened.

"Tell me what I promised you. I know you can remember! I know you can hear me, Ryan! He has your body, but he doesn't have your heart, you hear me? I do! You're mine, Ryan Kelly!"

"Promise me that you won't..."

A howl tore from Atticus's throat as he dropped to his knees. He thrust out his hands, fire blazing in his palms, but they curled into fists and slammed into the ground, extinguishing the flames. Harsh pants spilled from Atticus's throat.

"That you won't forget me."

Atticus looked up, and his eyes were green. "Don't..." His voice was a hoarse snarl, caught somewhere between man, wolf, and druid. But he was there, Zach realized, heart galloping with joy as the fetid bond between them came alive. Ryan was there. "Don't you forget about me."

Zach swallowed hard. "And did I?"

Ryan choked out, "No. Not ever."

"So, you have to make me that same promise." Zach took one step then another. "Don't forget about me, Ryan. Fight him, do you hear me? Fight it!" Then, he got an idea.

"Ryan! Tell me our password."

Ryan's eyes flew open and tried again to pierce the veil of darkness around him. That was Zach's voice. He could have sworn it was...

"No," Atticus snarled, and he slammed his hand against Ryan's head. "They forgot about you. They left you behind! Give in!"

"Ryan! We had a password!"

A password. A password... Memories, faded at the corners, raced before Ryan's eyes, the faces of those he loved blurring until they were unrecognizable. But one stuck out. A day on the beach. A terrible day, because his mother had forgotten him, but then Zach had said they were best friends. Ryan had said that since they were best friends, they needed a password. And the password was...

"The moon over the oak!"

This wasn't real. This void. The horrible words Atticus was spewing. It was all a trick.

Ryan lunged, crushing Atticus's bony wrist in his grasp. That was Zach's voice. He would know it anywhere. "Where is he?" Ryan snarled. "Where is Zach? What the hell did you do with him?"

Atticus gritted his teeth, his fangs long and sharp. "He is gone! Your precious mate forgot about you and left you behind!"

"Tell me what I promised you. I know you can remember! I know you can hear me, Ryan! He has your body, but he doesn't have your heart, you hear me? I do! You're mine, Ryan Kelly!"

That day on the beach. Was it a beach? The scenery was blurry, overexposed. His arms were around a tall boy's neck, his legs around his waist. Tears were hot and wet on his face. The boy's arms held him tight and close, hoisting him off the ground. "Promise me that you won't," he croaked. "That you won't forget me..." The promise surged from his lips. "Don't... don't you forget about me."

And Zach never had, not once. Distance had come between them. Lovers had come and gone. Their paths had forked, and though they'd taken different roads, they'd always found their way back to each other. Zach would never forget about him. His pack would never leave him behind. And Ryan would be damned before he let anything come between him and Zach again.

"And did I?"

"No. Not ever," Ryan choked out.

"So, you have to make me that same promise. Don't forget about me, Ryan. Fight him, do you hear me? Fight it!"

And Atticus screamed as his hand burned in Ryan's grasp.

Ryan stood, tugging Atticus close as he whimpered and writhed, the flesh of his arm melting, the bones crumbling to ash. "Fuck you," Ryan said, seething as the pitiful man before him howled and dropped to his knees. "You're the one the world forgot about. You're the one who was left alone! Even after all the terrible things you did, all the power you wielded, you have no one! What was it all for if you have nothing to show for it?"

Atticus's eyes were huge, full of pain and fear. "I was hated. I was feared. All the world knew my name!" His voice shook as his arms burned away up to his shoulders, as his knees crumbled to ash. "My druids are gone. All gone..."

Ryan almost pitied him. "Don't worry. I'll make sure druid magic isn't forgotten, but I'll use it to help and heal and strengthen my pack. No one will remember you or what you almost succeeded in doing. All you'll be remembered as is the man who tried to divide us and failed."

Atticus's torso was gone to ash. "Don't go," he rasped, his eyes huge and glassy as he stared up at Ryan. "Please. Don't leave me like the others did. Stay here, and we can bring this world to its knees. The last two druids, Ryan. You'll be the last of our kind. You'll be lonely. No one will understand you. You'll be feared and hated for the magic in your veins, but I can help. I can make you untouchable!"

"Like everyone feared you? Like everyone hated you?" And Ryan felt for him, he did. This pitiful, hateful man who'd nearly brought the world to its knees once and who in the end was utterly alone. He thought maybe there'd been a reason Atticus had sought him out and not just for the insult of being a wolf with druid magic. The druid king hadn't wanted to be alone or forgotten.

"See, maybe you should have thought about all that before you decided to be an enormous dick." Ryan flipped his middle finger at the king of the druids as he turned to ash.

From far away, there came a howl that ignited the bonds glowing deep and warm within his chest. It was a song of *love, mate,* and *mine.* Shards of light pierced the void around him. Ryan threw back his head and did the only thing he could.

He answered his mate's song, and the darkness shattered like glass around him.

ZACH GASPED AS THE fetid bond within his chest burned bright and warm. Ryan shifted, and a white wolf bounded toward Zach as insects flew free from his coat and crumbled to ash in the wind. With a laugh, Zach raised both hands but landed flat on his back as the white wolf pounced on him. He sputtered as the wolf rained kisses on his face, his tail wagging so hard the wolf's bottom shook.

The fighting had stopped in the woods, and they could hear only celebratory howls. Upon Atticus's death, all the living trees had shattered to splinters.

"We did it!" Izzie cried, pouncing on Gabe and Max.

"Hell yeah, we did!" Max wrapped his arms around Gabe's neck and kissed his cheek.

Eddie huffed, lowering his crossbow. "Hey, Vico. Go fetch!" He threw a tree's severed arm into the woods, and the black wolf that was Vicenzo glared disapprovingly.

Zach snorted, dropping his head to the stony ground and closing his eyes. There came a shift of muscle and bone above him. Warm lips touched his, revitalizing Zach as he wound his arms around Ryan's shoulders and held tight. When he opened his eyes, Ryan was grinning at him, his smile warm as sunshine and so tender it cracked Zach's heart clean in two.

"Hey."

Zach laughed. "Hi. You scared me for a minute there. I wasn't sure I could bring you back."

Ryan scoffed, pressing his forehead to Zach's. "*I* wasn't scared. Okay, maybe a little."

"Yeah?" Zach brushed strands of hair from his face.

Ryan smiled without hesitation. "I knew if anyone could bring me back, it was you. You're just that awesome."

Face hot, Zach pulled him close to kiss him again.

When he opened his eyes, Ben stood over them. He looked away. "Guess I'm gonna have to get used to seeing that around HQ, huh?"

Zach accepted the hand Ben extended. "We'll keep it professional, I promise."

Ryan picked up the glasses he'd dropped when he shifted. "By that, you mean we'll have quickies in the broom closet, right?"

"Yup."

Ben sighed but a reluctant smile brightened his face. "If I catch either of you slacking, I'm docking your pay."

Zach took Ryan's hand and bent over to whisper in his ear. "We'll just have to be very sneaky."

Laughing, Ryan hid his smile behind his hand as Ben shot them a look. Hands clasped, Ryan and Zach followed their pack toward the skyscrapers of the city. Toward home.

EPILOGUE

"It won't hurt, will it?"

Ryan smiled at his mother's wide, worried eyes.

"I promise, Mrs. Kelly."

His mother glanced worriedly to Ryan's father, who was holding her hand on the couch seat beside him. He smiled encouragingly. "You can trust him. He's a... a good friend."

She sighed, biting her lip. "I know. But still, this magic is so new to us."

Ryan knelt on the carpet in front of her. "You won't regret this, I promise. Tons of werewolves have benefited from my magic."

"Even ones with my condition?"

"Yes." Now that he knew the spell, it would be easy to create a thread that connected him and his father to his mother. He'd done it yesterday for the pack before their fight with Atticus, and was confident in his abilities, but his nerves still fluttered in the pit of his stomach.

He looked over his shoulder at Zach, who was leaning in the doorway. His mate offered Ryan a smile, and the tightness in Ryan's chest eased a little.

"Mr. Kelly?" His mother blinked at him. There was no recognition in her eyes, and she'd laughed when she'd found out they shared the same name. "What a coincidence," she had said, squeezing her mate's arm. "Our name is Kelly too!"

Ryan never wanted her to look at him like a stranger again. "I'm ready when you are."

Squeezing his father's hand, she nodded bravely.

Ryan clasped her other hand in his and chanted in Gaelic. A quiet gasp fell from her lips.

"You look familiar..." she whispered, gazing at him in wonder. "Why do you look so familiar? We haven't met before, have we?"

Ryan's heart quickened.

His mother's voice trembled. "I feel like I... I know you. I..."

Golden threads knit themselves together, connecting him to his mother, then through her to his father.

"I know you," his mother whispered. "I—" His mother's eyes rolled back, and she pitched forward.

Ryan lunged to catch her in his arms, pushing her back against the sofa. "Mom? You okay?"

Zach was by his side in seconds, putting a hand on Ryan's shoulder.

His father looked from Ryan to Zach. "What happened? What's wrong?"

Before Ryan could speak, his mother's eyes fluttered open.

"Mom? Are you okay?" Ryan asked, holding her hand tight.

"Oh Amaris," his father whispered. There were tears in his eyes. "I can feel it. I can feel her. Ry, do you feel that?"

Ryan blinked fast, his eyes burning. His mother's bond glowed warm in his chest, but it wasn't enough. "Mom." She blinked at him, dazed as her hand fluttered over her chest, as if she could feel the warm threads connecting them. "Say it. Say my name. Please?"

She reached for him. Her hands trembled as she grasped his face, a tear spilling down her cheek. "Ryan." His name was a tearful whisper on her lips. "Ryan. *Ryan*. I remember. Oh Goddess. I remember you, of course I remember you."

Ryan launched himself into her arms and cried like he had the day he'd thought she would forget him forever. His father held them both in his arms and cried with them while Zach watched, a smile bright on his face.

Following Atticus's defeat, life among the LPA returned to normal but not without some bumps along the way.

Not all the bumps were bad. The mayor honored the LPA with an award for their service during the Druid Invasion, as he called it.

For weeks, reporters demanding to know all the details behind the return of the druids and the paranormal battle that had destroyed parts of Central Park surrounded the agency's gates. Everyone wanted to meet the LPA's new druid. Ryan received emails from scholars around the world, asking to interview him or for his insights for their newest books on the druids. Ryan was tempted but didn't want to shirk his duties at the LPA. Ben advised everyone to keep their heads down and in time things quieted down as they always did.

Left in place of the chaos was the joy and surety Zach felt the day he and Ryan moved in together. He was excited for their future. They had all the time in the world to make up for the time they'd wasted denying themselves the happiness they deserved.

Zach smiled when Ryan leaned into his body, angling his head so Zach could kiss the bite mark on his neck. He was achy and sore from unpacking and more than ready to relax in the respite he found in Ryan's body. Summer sun pooled golden on the floorboards, offering a beautiful view of Central Park below. It was the perfect spot, close to the park so they could join Gabe and Max for midnight runs through the woods and so Ryan could practice his magic.

"Right," Ben said with a grunt, setting down a heavy box full of Ryan's books like it held nothing but pillows. "That's the last one."

Ryan fist-bumped him. "Thanks, Ben." He ducked into the bathroom.

Ben cracked his back, his hands on his hips as he surveyed the apartment. "Real nice place you boys got here. Invite me over sometime, huh?" He turned to leave and something fell onto the floor. Zach realized it was his old leather wallet. "Ben, wait." He scooped it up and noticed something nestled among his credit cards.

It was a photograph, faded and curling around the edges. In it was an unmistakably familiar face, although much younger: Ben, with a full head of hair worthy of a Viking warrior and a scruffy beard. Despite the beard, he looked years younger. He bared his teeth in a radiant grin, and without the hard lines of age and grumpiness, Zach was sure he'd never seen him so happy. He had both arms around a man with a handsome, scruffy face. The man had one hand resting tenderly on Ben's wrist and his cheeks were pink with happy embarrassment. With smiles like that, they could only have been—

Ben cleared his throat and held out a hand. His face was like stone.

"That's Isaac, isn't it?" Zach handed over the wallet.

Ben shrugged.

Isaac. Ben's mate. The one he was still hung up on.

"What happened to him?" Zach asked. "If you don't mind."

"Hell if I know." Ben's silver eyes were cold, his face carefully guarded. His hand lingered over the shape of the wallet in his pocket, his fingers moving gently.

"You mean you don't know what—"

Ben raised a big hand, his mustache quirking when he smiled tartly. "Gonna hit the bar down the street. Call me when you guys are all moved in. We can piss off the neighbors."

Zach wished he hadn't said anything. "Ben…" He pursued him into the hall. "Sorry. I shouldn't have asked."

Ben offered a hollow smile. "It's fine. I've moved on."

Had he really? While he and Heather were amicable, Zach hadn't seen him dating anyone since. He supposed Ben was too busy with the agency and his own teenaged sons.

"Zach." Ben squeezed the back of Zach's neck. "I've got everything I need. The LPA, my boys, and you agents—anything else would be overkill."

Zach smiled. "Thanks for the help, Ben."

Turning away, he raised a hand. "Anytime, kid."

Zach walked back to the apartment as the elevator descended. He was glad he hadn't upset Ben, but he hoped that someday his friend would find someone who could melt his grumpy exterior and warm the big heart he guarded.

As Zach returned to the living room, Ryan walked to the window and sighed, his arms opening to embrace the sunlight on his skin. "Summer's almost over. Huh. Remember when we were kids and the end of summer felt like the end of the world? Man, school sucked."

Zach chuckled and draped himself over Ryan's smaller form. "I know. Summer break always meant we could hang out and go to your family's beach house."

"And now"—Ryan touched Zach's forearms and leaned into his body—"I'm stoked for summer to end. I wanna see what the rest of our lives has in store for us."

Zach squeezed him tight, too happy for words. He felt the same way. "First, let's start with organizing this beast. I can just see it," Zach mused, propping his chin on Ryan's shoulder. "We'll have the dining room there, arrange some nice sofas by the balcony door... And we can put all your comics and figurines in the closet."

"Hey! They're collectibles!"

"They're lame."

Ryan slumped, his head collapsing against Zach's shoulder. As Ryan went limp, Zach grunted as he crumpled to the floor with him, and then Ryan rolled onto Zach's chest. "No more unboxing. No furnishing. Not today! We're relaxing now."

Zach chuckled, adjusting Ryan's glasses, which had gotten crooked. "Fine." He sniffed and made a face. He'd worked up a sweat lugging boxes, and he smelled like it. They'd have to bathe. "Come on." He grabbed Ryan's smaller hands in his and helped him up. "Let's christen the shower."

His eyes lighting up, Ryan practically ran to the bathroom. They left their clothes in a pile, their bare feet slapping over marble-tiled floors. Zach plucked Ryan's glasses from his nose and leaned down, capturing his lips and being careful to drop his glasses gently on top of the clothes pile. The bathroom warmed as steam misted the air and water spattered over the glistening tile. Hoisting Ryan easily into his arms, Zach grinned when he giggled at the water raining down on his face as Zach carried him beneath the showerhead.

Their lips met, hot and damp beneath the spray. Ryan's arms went around Zach's shoulders, his legs clamping tight around his waist. A hand fisted in Zach's hair, and his fangs nipped at his lips. Zach parted his lips, sighing as their tongues tangled. A shiver ran through him as butterflies took flight in his stomach. Kissing Ryan Kelly still felt like the first time. When he stopped and really thought about it—that they were finally together, mated for life—it all felt like one amazing dream.

He clasped a taut buttock, squeezing it tight and grinning at the moan he received. Grabbing lube from the shelf in the shower, Zach slicked his fingers and coaxed them inside Ryans tight heat. A soft moan escaped Ryan, and Zach swallowed down his whimpers with eager kisses while he prepped him. He flicked his tongue over Ryan's plump lower lip. Nope, definitely not a dream. Ryan was here in his arms and all his.

"Can't believe it," Ryan panted, his breath hot on Zach's wet mouth.

"What?"

Ryan held his gaze, his hands capturing Zach's face and his fingers running over his lips to his jawline and his cheekbones. "That you're here. With me. I'll never get over this." He smiled, the sight squeezing tight around Zach's heart. "Fuck. Zach, whenever we kiss, it's like my heart's gonna burst." Cheeks flushed, he gave Zach's lips a peck. "You're the most magical thing in my life."

Zach looked away, flustered and impossibly happy. "That's coming from a guy who can make flowers grow at his touch."

"I know. So you better believe me."

Zach met him halfway, their lips colliding with such eagerness and passion it made sparks erupt deep in his belly. Ryan's cock pressed hard between them, and Zach's own body ached with need. Grabbing onto Ryan's hips, he turned him around so his chest was flush with the shower wall. Ryan arched his hips as water ran between his cheeks.

Ryan shouted in complete satisfaction as Zach sheathed himself inside in one stroke, his voice magnified as it bounced off the tile. Their bodies moved together in perfect unity, Ryan's hips arching back to strike Zach's pelvis. Zach grabbed harder onto his hips, deepening their union as he drove himself home again and again. If he cried out when he finished, he couldn't tell, his ears ringing as Ryan tightened around him, sucking him in deep as if he never wanted him to leave.

Zach's arms wrapped around Ryan, drawing his back flush to his chest as he caught his breath, biting down on Ryan's shoulder to anchor himself. Panting, Ryan turned his head, his lips parting, and Zach obliged, his arms squeezing his mate tight.

Ryan grinned when they parted, his face beautifully flushed, his eyes heavy-lidded and warm. "Welcome home."

Zach parted his lips against the bite mark on Ryan's neck. "Welcome home."

LATER THAT EVENING, ZACH and Ryan met with the pack. They crowded into Gabe and Max's apartment and Max grilled up elk burgers while Gabe poured everyone drinks. Ryan recounted how he'd helped his mother, and the pack was delighted for him.

Zach's phone rang in his pocket. He sighed. It was his mother, calling for the second time in a week. Stepping into the bathroom for some quiet, he answered the call. "Mom? What's up?" He had a feeling he knew.

"You really aren't going to take responsibility, are you?"

"For what?" Zach sighed, rubbing his fingers against his tired eyes.

"For refusing to help with your father's final project!" She'd gone ahead with construction but clearly, that wasn't enough. She'd only be happy if she could control him and dictate his every decision.

Zach rolled his eyes toward the ceiling. "And how do you propose I do that, Mother? Move back in and help salvage the company?"

"It's what a responsible son would do, instead of sniffing trees and hunting with those animals you call your friends!"

Zach gritted his teeth. He was done with this shit. "You need to stop calling me. Those 'animals' have been more like a family to me than you or Dad ever were."

"How dare you!"

"No, how dare you!" Zach's voice bounced off the tile. "The LPA is my family. They gave me a home and acceptance. You want my help, my support? Maybe you should have been there for me when I needed you. I owe you nothing." He exhaled, uncurling his trembling fingers. In the stunned silence, Zach realized how quiet everything was beyond the bathroom door. "I love my life. I love who I am. And I found someone who loves me for me, unconditionally. I don't need a damn thing from you." He hung up before she could guilt trip him and blocked her number.

He waited until his heart had settled, then opened the door. Izzie and Gabe stopped cracking jokes to look his way. Max turned and shot Zach a worried frown, and Ben glanced in his direction and cracked his knuckles. Ryan brushed past Eddie and hurried up to Zach.

"You okay?" Ryan asked.

Looking around at his pack, Zach smiled. "Yeah. Yeah, I'm good." Ryan swung an arm around Zach's shoulders as Izzie splashed drinks into shot glasses. Zach rolled his eyes and took a shot, grinning when the pack cheered.

Where the hell would he be without these rowdy wolves?

"You were amazing with your mom today," Ryan said as he walked the pavement with Zach, their hands clasped. The sun was going down as they walked to Central Park. Ryan smiled to the night sky above, squeezing Zach's hand tight. "I'm proud of you, babe. She had that coming."

Squeezing his hand, Zach said, "Yeah, I know." The guilt that had been there before had faded. "You, Ben, and the others—you're my true family."

Ryan's cheeks colored. "We're a hell of a lot more fun, aren't we?"

Zach bumped his shoulder against Ryan's body. "You sure are."

Fireflies winked in and out of the darkness and the buzz of traffic faded to the soothing whisper of the wind through the trees. Zach had his mate and his pack, a life full of adventure—there was nothing more he could possibly need.

"Hey, mind telling me where we're going?"

Ryan grinned. "Be patient. It's a surprise."

Zach sighed exaggeratedly and Ryan laughed and tugged him onward.

They walked beneath the elms of the Literary Walk toward Bethesda Terrace. The air was sweet with the smell of leaves and grass. Ryan climbed over the fence and tripped, and then Zach hiked his legs up high and walked over the fence with ease.

Bristling, Ryan said, "Yeah, yeah, I get it. You're tall."

Zach tousled his hair and followed Ryan among the elm trees. When they were a little farther in, Ryan stopped and Zach walked into him. Zach slumped, saddened by the singed patch of grass where their oak tree used to stand. "Man, I miss that tree."

Ryan knelt, touching his hand to the soil. "Honestly, knowing Atticus corrupted it kinda ruined it for me. I'd rather have our own, without his crummy influence over it."

Zach gasped as the soil churned and a sapling curled up through the earth. Ryan stepped back, bumping into Zach's chest as the tree grew before their eyes from a sapling to a young elm tree, its branches spreading wide beneath the indigo sky.

Growing one claw out long, Ryan carved his initials into the tree.

Zach swallowed, overcome by the memory of the day they'd met in this exact spot. They'd both been so lost and uncertain, but meeting Ryan had turned everything around. Ever since that day, he'd brightened Zach's life.

Ryan said, "It's our tree. Not Atticus's. Go on. Write something."

Zach touched the bark as he once had. He dug his claw into it, and the tree didn't fight back. Touching the bark filled Zach with a sense of calm. He carved his initials next to Ryan's and encircled them with a heart.

Ryan chuckled. "Sappy."

Nudging him, Zach said, "Says the dork who just grew a whole-ass tree for me."

Ryan tugged him down into the grass, the trunk of their tree against their backs. He propped his cheek against Zach's shoulder, and Zach leaned his head on Ryan's hair. Happiness swirled within Zach as the fireflies danced around them, filling the darkness with sudden bursts of light.

"Thank you," Zach said, kissing Ryan's shoulder.

Smiling, Ryan cocked his head. "For?"

A lump rose in Zach's throat. "Loving me. All of me. The anxious me. The put-together me. When it was too hard to love myself. Thank you for your patience. For waiting all these years. Just... I love you, Ryan."

Lifting Zach's hand to his lips, Ryan brushed a kiss over his knuckles. "You were worth the wait. Love you, too, baby."

"Promise me something," Zach said.

"Anything."

"Promise me you'll never let me forget tonight. Here. With you."

Ryan kissed his cheek, and Zach's heart was so full. "That's a promise."

What's next for the Agency wolves? Discover what really happened between Ben and his fated mate, Isaac. Will Ben finally get his Happily-Ever-After? And why did Isaac disappear all those years ago? Find out in

The Lycanthrope Protection Agency #5 – Redemption Under The Moon.

322

THANK YOU!

Thank you for reading! If you enjoyed, please consider leaving a review on your preferred platform of choice. Indie authors like me depend on word of mouth reviews like yours. Additionally, please consider recommending this series if you enjoyed it! Thank you again!

Sign up to my newsletter to receive a free prequel to The Lycanthrope Protection Agency series, Before Moonrise. This novella features forbidden love, friends to lovers, possessive werewolves who adore their mates, and sexy times on a beach, in a barn, and a broom closet just to name a few locations. Additionally, you'll receive bonus content, cover reveals, and news about new releases. What are you waiting for?
Sign up now at www.CJRavenna.com!

ABOUT CJ

CJ Ravenna loves to tell stories where the ordinary meets the extraordinary. Her books often feature an explosion or two, possessive and protective werewolves who adore their mates, steamy and swoony romance, and of course a happy ending. Connect with me on:

My website: cjravenna.com

My Facebook group: Ravenna's Ravens

Instagram: @cjravenna

TikTok: @cjravenna

Goodreads: goodreads.com/cjravenna

Bookbub: bookbub.com/authors/cj-ravenna

ALSO BY CJ RAVENNA

The Lycanthrope Protection Agency Series
Before Moonrise (Jin & Marcus. Newsletter exclusive)
To Hunt A Moonborn Beast (Gabe & Max)
Child Of The Moon (Gabe & Max)
The Moon Aways Rises (Gabe & Max)
The Moon Over The Oak (Zach & Ryan)
Redemption Under The Moon (Ben & Isaac)
Fire and Moonlight (Eddie & Vicenzo)